SUSIE IN SERVITUDE

Pressed up against the oak door, Susie shuddered as hot lust coursed through the veins of her kneeling body. Inside the room, Madame's strong hand remained on the trembling Finnish girl's bare left buttock. The girl gasped out joyfully in her torment and rose up to offer herself in submissive surrender to the fierce pleasure. Susie couldn't help herself; the scene was so arousing that she had to rub herself through her soaking, white cotton panties.

D1550244

By the same author:

THE ACADEMY
CONDUCT UNBECOMING
CANDY IN CAPTIVITY
THE MISTRESS OF STERNWOOD GRANGE
TAKING PAINS TO PLEASE
BROUGHT TO HEEL
INTIMATE INSTRUCTION

A NEXUS CLASSIC

SUSIE IN SERVITUDE

Arabella Knight

This book is a work of fiction.
In real life, make sure you practise safe, sane and
consensual sex.

First published in 1997 by
Nexus
Thames Wharf Studios
Rainville Road
London W6 9HA

This Nexus Classic edition 2003

www.nexus-books.co.uk

ISBN 0 352 33846 6

Typeset by TW Typesetting, Plymouth, Devon
Printed and bound by
Mackays of Chatham Ltd, Chatham, Kent

One

The tip of the index finger tapped the outer curve of the bare bottom twice.

'And this is a perfect example of a pear-shaped bottom. Please note the narrow waist. Trim, to be accurate, but not tapered. This is an important point for you all to remember.'

The inquisitive fingertip traced the velvety cheeks before pausing to hover over the tempting cleft between them.

'And here we see rounded hips. These frame the full buttocks perfectly. Note how generously fleshed the buttocks are.'

The dominant fingertip tapped the shapely thigh.

'And do not overlook the contours of the outer thigh. Yes, girls. A perfect specimen of the pear-shaped bottom. Note these points down. Good. Now who can tell me what is the overall effect? What, as we say, is the keynote?'

'Mellow?' volunteered the petite brunette in tones of eager anxiety.

'Mellow,' confirmed Madame Seraphim Savage.

Susie dutifully noted it all down on the already crowded page of her jotter. She had known the answer, of course. Bottoms were her special study: her project folder was bursting with sketches and photographs of the female buttocks. She had known that the keynote of a pear-shaped bottom, when naked and utterly unadorned in its feminine splendour, was mellow. She had known the answer but her tongue was growing thick and swollen in her dry mouth. It was always like this, when the stern madame gave the lecture, especially a lecture on the female bottom.

1

The tip of madame's index finger was now imperiously tapping the creamy flesh of another naked bottom.

'And this is what we call the hour-glass. Please observe the distinguishing features. The shapely rump with buttocks somewhat firm yet slightly heavy. And you will not fail to miss the strict differentiation between the waist, the hips and the thighs. The hour-glass outline, girls. And the dominant keynote is?'

'Shapely,' Susie murmured to herself. Again, the brunette sitting beside her gushed out the answer aloud at which Madame Seraphim Savage nodded her approval.

'Jolly good. Now, girls. Where we discover a slim waist,' she continued effortlessly, 'with minimum tapering and slightly flattened cheeks, we term it boyish. Please note the hint of a firm muscle tone.'

Her busy fingertip tapped the third bare bottom firmly.

'This is a boyish bottom, frequently found on a younger woman who has yet to ripen and mature. And what is the dominant keynote of the boyish bottom?'

Trim. This time, the question was correctly supplied with an answer by several voices.

'Trim. Very good. Note it down, all of you. Bottom number four.'

The overhead projector clicked once more. A huge bare bottom loomed up on the screen, filling the white with delicious flesh tones.

Susie swallowed with difficulty. She was finding it increasingly hard to hold her pen between her trembling fingers which were aching to touch and soothe her stiffening nipples. She gazed, almost mesmerised, up at Madame Seraphim Savage. At the full Venus figure of the 39-year-old woman. At the lipstick-free mouth, pursed and resolute, the slender hands, the swell of the heavy breasts tamed within the tight silk bondage of the high-collared blouse. Susie shivered with pleasure and switched her gaze away from the capable hands back to the bottom on the screen. For a fleeting moment the idea of madame's hands coming down to ease and soothe her aching nipples sent Susie's brain into a delicious spin. She held her breath as she imagined the slender, strong hands cupping her breasts from behind, then palming and massaging her prinked nipples.

She exhaled slowly, causing the brunette beside her to steal a sideways glance of surprise. Blushing, Susie bit her lower lip in an effort to concentrate, and grasping her pen firmly, gazed upon the shimmering globes of the latest bare bottom. The rich, stern voice of madame informed the spellbound class that this bottom, being smooth, trim and sporting well-defined contours, was termed the athletic type. Susie closed her eyes for a brief moment, savouring the words that described so perfectly the delightful image up on the screen.

'Velvet-muscled with a resulting rubbery softness to the touch, girls. The dominant keynote being?'

'Sleek,' murmured Susie, as if in a dream. Sleek.

Down the King's Road, the sudden sound of two clamouring sirens bruised the April afternoon. Would they fade as the red engines charged across Battersea Bridge, Susie wondered, or would they grow more urgent in the dash towards Sloane Square? Susie closed her eyes and listened. The sirens, their braying synchronised now into one harsh blare, approached as the tenders sliced through the thick traffic snarled up between Peter Jones and the Royal Court. Seconds later, they had faded, the gleaming engines no doubt already within sight of teeming Knightsbridge. Susie opened her eyes and drank in the vision of the bare bottom before them, her nipples tightening sharply in response to the seductive sweep of naked flesh. Unable to endure the delicious torment a second longer, Susie deliberately dropped her pen, crushing her bosom into the desk top for relief as she scrabbled to retrieve it. Resuming her position, she found herself subject to madame's keen scrutiny. Susie's face flushed, betraying immediately her guilt and shame.

'Slender,' the imperturbable voice of Madame Seraphim Savage intoned, equal to any intrusive sirens. Her inquisitive fingertip traced the outline of the naked buttocks on the screen with a delicacy not utterly devoid of dominance.

3

'Narrow hips and slender thighs. Note the neat little waist, girls, and the nicely rounded pair of cheeks. Normally, the flesh of the bottom is satin smooth. And so who can tell me what the dominant keynote is, hmm?'

No voice broke the ensuing silence to supply the expected answer.

'Come along, come along. The dominant keynote of the slender bottom is?'

The eager brunette avoided the gaze of the impatient questioner, as the rest of the class squirmed in their seats. Susie lowered her eyes to her jotter.

'Supple,' snapped madame. 'Supple. Be sure to make a note of that, girls. I shall be testing you all very soon, and shall be vigorous when doing so. Most vigorous.'

Susie flickered her large eyes up. A deeper shade of indigo darkened their customary cornflower blue as she focused on the image of the naked buttocks. Beside her, the pert brunette rasped a pencil noisily in her yellow teddy-bear sharpener. Susie turned slightly to watch the curls of shaven wood tumble silently to the floor. Next to the pencil-sharpening brunette sat Svetlana, the new Russian girl. Svetlana had joined the class three weeks ago. Russian money was flowing freely into London these days, and already the pretty assistants in Bond Street were learning to say 'da'. Susie, who had been accepted by madame's private school of fashion, La Bella Figura, just before Christmas, had not yet spoken with Svetlana. She had just shivered deliciously as her eyes had met the ash blonde Russian's pale grey gaze.

Svetlana. Susie's bosom grew heavy as she pictured herself swimming with Svetlana, their svelte bodies tightly sheathed within the second skins of stretchy swimsuits. Susie's a red one, Svetlana's black. Susie trembled as she imagined Svetlana easing herself up the steps out of the lapping water. She pictured the Russian girl's bottom swaying sinuously, sensually. A bottom ripely rounded with its tight curves, the cheeks glistening as they dripped water. Behind her closed eyes, Susie saw it swaying with insolent pertness as if welcoming a spanking hand. Her throat tightened at the idea and her pulse quickened as she

4

continued to imagine the ash blonde gracefully mounting the water-logged steps after a swim. And what would Svetlana see from such a vantage point if their positions were reversed, Susie wondered. Ruthlessly, she ran through a quick self-appraisal. Her petite figure was slim and alluring. Looking upward, Svetlana would see Susie's jet-black hair spilling down over her milky white shoulders, narrow waistline swelling gently into rounded hips and supple thighs, and of course her pride and glory: her beautiful peach-cheeked bottom. Yes, Susie smiled contentedly. Svetlana would see all of these attributes in such an intimate perusal. But would Svetlana like what she saw? And would Svetlana want what she saw? Dismayed by the possibility of rejection, Susie switched her focus back to the Russian girl. What type of bottom, Susie wondered, what type of bottom, according to madame's classification, would Svetlana have? Susie opened her eyes and stole a furtive glance, but it was very hard to tell under the loose denim of Svetlana's designer jeans.

'Peach-shaped,' intoned Madame Seraphim Savage. 'A pert, rounded bottom. With slightly fleshy hips, hence the strongly defined contours. But a bottom with definite curves, within which one finds heavily pronounced buttocks. They are so very shapely and so very, very feminine. The flesh of the cheeks, you will find upon acquaintance, is singularly pliant to the touch. A small point to note, girls. The peach-shaped buttocks are often termed Eve's fruit, their dominant keynote being of course, ripe.'

Susie groaned silently at the sound of the word. Svetlana would be blessed, she did not doubt it for an instant, with just such a soft, velvety ripeness: a pair of swollen peaches worthy indeed of being termed Eve's fruit. So ripe, so full and heavy with promise: would Susie ever harvest and enjoy their bounty? Susie whimpered softly as a sudden thought clouded her brain: would Svetlana's bottom, like Eve's original fruit, remain forbidden to her lips? Comforting herself, Susie dropped her hand down to absently scratch at her upper, inner thighflesh. When the tickling itch had been eased, Susie's fingers remained, only to inch

5

furtively toward her lap. Beneath the desk, moments later, she luxuriated in the sensation as her thumb slowly stroked the firm warmth of her pubic mound.

'And finally,' continued the seemingly indefatigable madame, 'I want you all to observe this specimen. It is a beautiful bottom. My favourite.'

Susie glanced up immediately, her interest keen and sharp.

'Apple-shaped: affectionately referred to as a pippin.'

As the apple-shaped specimen filled the screen, Susie's heart skipped a beat. Studying the contoured, fleshy weight and the sheer beauty of the bottom before her she recognised her own buttocks. 'Apple-shaped,' she purred contentedly to herself. If she owned the most desirable bottom, then surely Svetlana would be tempted and succumb, she reasoned wildly.

With an increasing frankness, Susie's mounting desire for Svetlana grew more urgent. With her eyes tightly shut, she conjured up the image of the Russian girl emerging from the swimming pool once more: the vision seemed to haunt her. Now, diamonds of water droplets spangled the lissome thighs and legs. Then, she swallowed thickly, she saw the soft towel dabbing gently at the bare bottom, now fully revealed after the stretchy black swimsuit had been peeled away. A riot of confused thoughts crowded Susie's brain. She shivered with delight at the sheer audacity of her lustful imaginings. Beneath the desk, her labia grew warm and sticky under her exploring thumb. In her brain, chaos reigned as she tumbled into the servitude of the overwhelming urge to slowly kiss and softly bite Svetlana's naked buttocks.

The pert brunette coughed pointedly, dragging Susie back into the present moment. Opening her eyes slowly, she saw her fellow student staring down at where her thumb was so busy. Blushing furiously, Susie withdrew her hand and placed it on the desk. Shrugging off her temptations, she focused down intently on to her notes. After a minute or two of hasty scribbling, Susie peeped across at the brunette, and discovered the younger girl gazing at her with intense interest.

'Apple-shaped bottoms are invariably tight-buttocked, girls,' madame gushed, warming to her task. 'The cheeks are firmer than those of any other specimen. It is the perfect bottom. Pay attention, girls. Note the distinctively curved cheeks which give the dominant keynote?'

'Rounded,' replied Susie in a tone of barely contained excitement. Meeting madame's vigilant gaze, Susie bowed her head down and briefly doodled a sketch of two luscious globes next to her hastily written notes.

'That will suffice for this afternoon, girls. We have been taking a very close look at the types of bottom shapes which will stretch your skills as corsetières. And remember, the successful corsetière must become intimately familiar with all those features. Before any discussion of material takes place or patterns are cut, you must both recognise and fully appreciate your client's bottom. Know the qualities and contours of the flesh you are about to tame within the strict embrace of silk, satin, leather or indeed rubber. The corsette,' madame was in full flow now, 'be it a full basque or a simple suspender, will only fit perfectly if the corsetière uses her eyes, her judgement and her hands. Fingertip touch is essential, girls. Mere measurement is not enough. When appraising a bare bottom, use your hands, and use your fingertips. Cup the full cheeks within your palms to sense the weight of the flesh. Cup and hold the buttocks until you truly know their nature. And never overlook the pliancy of the skin. A little squeeze will tell you all you need to know. A successful corsetière is one who loves her bottoms.'

The spellbound girls nodded their understanding and agreement. Several licked their lips involuntarily.

'Jolly good. That will be all, girls. Enjoy your half-term break. We will commence our next series of lectures with a careful consideration of the bosom. Miss Pelham-Heys.'

Susie, startled to hear her name announced so formally, looked up.

'Wait outside my office door, if you please. Class dismissed.'

* * *

Sitting in the corridor outside the oak-panelled door, as instructed, Susie squirmed uncomfortably. The low, wooden chair was hard and her plump bottom was soft, and she was beginning to feel the discomfort of pressing her cheeks into the polished wood as the long minutes dragged by. Gently easing the weight of her buttocks from one cheek to the other, Susie glanced briefly at the firmly shut door. It gleamed with the dull patina of years of cursory polishing. LA BELLA FIGURA was emblazoned in ornate gold lettering. Below, in neat black capitals, Susie read for the seventh time: PRINCIPAL, MME. S. SAVAGE. Madame's claim to academic success was spelt at considerable length immediately after her name.

Sighing softly, Susie turned as she heard the light-hearted laughter and giggled whispers of the other girls attending the private college of fashion as they scampered down the Adam staircase and out into the bright evening sunset. They would be heading off towards Fulham in an armada of taxis. Style was ebbing westward in London, pausing for the time being at the river. Susie even knew a viscount who kept a tart in splendour off the North End Road. The girls, eager to start their half-term, would not have long to wait. The taxis always came to collect the students from the exclusive Sloane Square school promptly, as the cabbies seemed to have a sixth sense for single girls with four-figure allowances.

Susie, who never seemed to have a problem getting a cab across to her Holland Park pad, frowned as she heard the taxis arriving to collect the girls out in the street. It was half-term, and she had some vague plans about spending some time with Svetlana. As the last of the taxis departed, Susie sat with her chin in her hand. She enjoyed studying at La Bella Figura, which was very expensive and even more exclusive. It had a great reputation in the smartest of circles: several dukes simultaneously equipped their daughters and their mistresses with La Bella Figura satin scanties. No bosom or bottom captured by *Society Spy*, as it monitored the antics of Belgravia babes, had escaped the intimate touch of a corsetière from the successful school.

Cadogan cadettes flocked to it, for no satin basque unzipped after the Benbridge Ball, or suspender enticingly snapped at the Cowes week squadron bash was considered quite right if it did not bear the La Bella Figura logo: a tiny, naked Eve bruising her bosom with an apple. And the quality of teaching was simply excellent, Susie realised, as was the networking with the glamorous world of fashion.

Susie had decided to make underwear her speciality. She was already becoming familiar with the sensual, silken secrets of brassières, panties, balconette bustiers, basques and suspenders. That hectic February weekend in Milan had convinced her that both her choice of school and subject specialism had been inspired. Milan had been a privileged glimpse behind the scenes allowing Susie to witness at close quarters the scurrying, near-naked models. She recaptured her delight at the sight of the proud beauties being sharply admonished by brusque matrons. Severe, competent matrons who had orchestrated the backstage chaos with sharp words and sharper spanks.

Susie had seen, and had relished, the sight of internationally celebrated models being scolded and disciplined as they struggled into underwired bras and out of shining, seamed stockings. Especially, she remembered with a smile, that delicious French minx: the one spotted twice by the tabloids, crouching down in the mud-spattered Range Rover of a minor royal buck. Susie had seen her wrestling, tearful and red-bottomed after a severe spanking, into a daringly cut chemisette before diving through the velvet curtains to take the cat-walk and explosion of camera flashes in her sure and certain stilettoed stride. Susie had stumbled upon the unexpected delights of the fashion world and had found them to be both exotic and exciting, and success here at La Bella Figura, under the strict tutelage of madame, would secure her a passport into its spangled mystique.

Susie squirmed in her chair and sighed impatiently once more. It was getting late. The fading sunlight on the patterned carpet at her feet reminded her of Milan. Susie drifted back into her reverie of that memorable weekend.

She had been a 'runner', helping out backstage just as a call-boy does in a theatre, and mixing with the hubbub allowed her to see the beautiful girls being scolded and spanked. Watching the models hastily dress and undress had been exhilarating: those voluptuous bosoms squeezing into tight bustiers, the pert bottoms wriggling within the confines of satin and leather. But what did madame wish to see Susie for now? Why, she wondered, had she been so peremptorily summoned to sit outside the polished oak door? Had Madame Seraphim Savage already spotted Susie's talent and flair? Was there to be another trip abroad? Next week, during half-term? Munich was next week, she remembered. Munich, where there was always a whiff of decadence. Or could it be Paris? Oh, yes, please let it be Paris, pleasure pen of the pampered.

Susie, born into wealth and bred into privilege, was constitutionally optimistic in all things and on all matters. But beneath her blithe optimism, something stirred uneasily. She sensed an uncertain shadow lurking beneath her radiant expectations. The faint flicker of some memory seemed to trouble her. The memory congealed into an image like a negative. But what was it? Susie shivered slightly as she suddenly understood. Of course, it was Wyevenhoe Hall.

Wyevenhoe Hall, her boarding school: the negative of memory developed into a film whose images now flickered into a fluent stream of recollection. She suddenly recalled sitting on a similarly hard chair outside some other polished oak door, and those identical anxious moments of waiting. There had been a dread suspense then, the kind which always attended the possibility of punishment. Susie gulped, savouring once again the delicious dread of punishment, then closed her eyes and shivered as her thoughts revisited Wyevenhoe Hall, where misdemeanours and minor transgressions were quickly and painfully dealt with by the dorm senior.

It would always be after supper, in the silence of the spellbound dorm, when all the girls would gather around the penitent's bed to hear the dorm senior solemnly reading out aloud from the punishment book the nature of the offence. Borrowing – it was never called stealing – was considered very bad form. A captain of the squad of prefects would always be in attendance listening in grave silence to the dorm senior. After the sentence had been pronounced it was entered into the punishment book below the miscreant's name. The captain of prefects would peruse the entry and slowly, maddeningly slowly, ask for a fountain pen with which she would sign her name. A spanking – the usual punishment most frequently dispensed – was always calculated in the number of minutes it would take rather than the actual number of smacks to be administered. Such spankings were invariably barebottomed affairs, with the guilty girl pinned down across the dorm senior's lap, her naked cheeks upturned and vulnerable: so thrilling.

Swearing, Susie recollected, merited the harsh bite of a wooden backed hairbrush: so searching. Slacking (doing badly in prep) and slutting (leaving the dorm untidy) both earned the scorching strokes of a leather-soled slipper: so scalding. How red the bare bottoms blazed after the administration of severe chastisement. The assembled girls, quiet and wide-eyed, adored these punishments where ritual was strictly observed and dark delights enjoyed by all. Susie smiled and wriggled in her chair as she enumerated the Wyevenhoe Hall code of conduct. She savoured the memory of the huddle of excited girls, clad briefly in vests and panties, assembling around the bed of the accused. All eyes focused on the guilty girl as she sat on her bed, fiddling with her white vest or tugging nervously at the elastic of her navy blue serge knickers – or for those expecting to be very severely spanked, hands folded and head bowed down in shame. Soon the dorm senior would intone the sentence of punishment with a crisp severity in her voice. This was always greeted with a stifled gasp of murmured pleasure by the watching girls. In strict accordance to ritual the punishment was written into the book, a task which deliberately took several agonising minutes – then, at last, the moment arrived. A strange

11

silence would settle on the dorm as most of the lights were extinguished, leaving the anxious girl on her bed of shame singled out by a single light bulb above.

Susie remembered the intense hush; the loud silence broken only by the soft rustle of navy knickers being peeled down to reveal swollen, creamy cheeks. Short gasps of suppressed delight would greet the bottom as it was bared and prepared for punishment. Next, the penitent girl would be bent over the awaiting thighs of the dorm senior. Pinned firmly by the nape of her neck, the bare-bottomed girl would wait in silence for her impending pain.

Then (Susie swallowed as she squeezed the burning memories from her brain) the staccato spank, spank, spank as the rain of ravishing smacks came down across the exposed buttocks. A sightly curved palm, or biting hair-brush, or a wickedly supple slipper, would cause the naked hillocks of creamy flesh to slowly turn pink, and then an angrier red. All the time the collective gaze of sparkling, avid eyes missed nothing from the drama of the discipline: the slender hand pinning down the punished girl; the clamped thighs of the punisher trapping the futile writhings of the victim. The dorm resounded to the haunting echoes of the spanking hand, or the sharp crack of the cruel hairbrush. Susie particularly enjoyed the cutting swish of the swiping slipper across the upturned globes. After a particularly severe slippering, Susie yearned to hold the punished bottom close to her face, then bend down and kiss the ravished cheeks.

Or, on more memorable nights, usually in the late spring when the mischievous girls were more prone to wanton naughtiness, there would be the hiss and sharp kiss of a wooden ruler. Yes. Susie tossed her dark hair as she remembered the harsh gleam of the shining, varnished wood coming down across blushing, defenceless buttocks. On reflection, Susie liked the softer swish-swipe of the leather-soled slipper as it blazed against the curved peaches of the punished girl. Susie had once retrieved the still-warm slipper after lights out and secretively kissed the springy hide.

Punishments in the dorm at Wyevenhoe Hall: how those

bare-bottomed girls wriggled and squirmed in their hot torment. Under the gentle savagery of discipline some squealed, some yelped and often silver tears were shed. But for the very, very naughty – those caught using lipstick or wearing nylon stockings down in the village on their half-day – punishments were administered by the captain of prefects herself. Bent across her superb, supple thighs, the punished girls would remain passive and tamed after the first flurry of spanks. Those wearing lipstick would have it firmly wiped away with a large white hanky; those sneaking out to the village in nylons were spanked in their seamed stockings – worn with nothing else during the punishment – with the captain of prefects pausing to gently finger the darker bronze stocking top in between the spanks.

Whatever the offence, soft bottoms suffered as stern discipline was dispensed by the cool goddess of the upper sixth. Those girls, and there were many, Susie suspected, who nurtured a 'pash' for the captain of the prefects, were deliberately naughty – and deliberately caught. All so they could surrender to the sweet touch of her slender hand resting against their naked cheeks. Possibly, Susie smiled in recollection, remembering the upturned bottoms, just possibly beause the spanker had the unswerving habit of gently palming their rounded rumps for several bewitching moments before the grimmer business in hand commenced.

Susie, who had a delicious bottom, was frequently taken to task by the dorm senior. Susie's pert buttocks were bared and prepared for punishing spanks as often as the dorm senior could contrive to do so. Wyevenhoe Hall hosted a great many hot, sweet chastisements which were enjoyed by all. Especially later, in the darkness of the dorm, under the crisp, cool sheets, when the girls' furtive fingers scrabbled down within their fluffy pubic hair to conjure up and trigger further bouts of hot, wet joy.

Outside, Sloane Square throbbed with the rush hour traffic it was not built to cope with. Tempers and engines began to overheat. Susie blinked away her reverie, startled by a sudden noise. The polished oak door opened briskly and the stern face of Madame Seraphim Savage emerged.

'Ah, the Pelham-Heys girl. Most distressing,' she said with concern. 'I will be ready for you presently.'

The door closed firmly. Susie's heart skipped several beats.

Another vivid recollection from her days at Wyevenhoe Hall flashed across her brain. Another polished oak door, opening and closing. Miserably anxious minutes stretching out into an age of uncertainty. And those very words – 'I will be ready for you presently' – spoken in the same sharp tone of admonishment by her former headmistress. Susie had skipped her French prep and had consequently been tempted to cheat during the Saturday morning test. Tempted, she had succumbed, only to be caught in the act of surreptitiously peeping at the pluperfect of an irregular verb penned into her soft, pink palm. The grave offence, considered an enormity, was reported directly to the headmistress. After a desultory lunch of haddock and boiled potatoes, for which Susie had no appetite, and when the rest of the girls were out in a baying pack on the windswept hockey field, Susie had been instructed to wait outside the forbidding oak door.

Out in the grey afternoon, squealing and shouting as they charged up and down the immaculately manicured pitch, the gleeful girls tripped and fouled one another monstrously. Bosoms bouncing and knickers peeping shyly from beneath the scant modesty of swirling pleated navy blue skirts, the breathless girls waged battle royal as Susie, sitting in the gloom where the faint odour of haddock lingered, could only squirm.

The door had opened. 'I will be ready for you presently.' Those were exactly the words the headmistress had used. The door had then closed shut. Then, ten or twelve aching minutes later, during which Susie had suffered unimaginable torments, the door had yawned wide and Susie had been curtly instructed to enter.

Inside the study of the headmistress of Wyevenhoe Hall, a log fire flickered sleepily in a wide hearth. The hearth was surrounded by original blue and white Dutch tiles which were veined with age and the heat of the fire. The Dutch tiles, depicting a variety of rural pleasures and pastimes, framed the flickering flames which danced up from the glowing logs. Susie's eyes turned to the imposing desk, and widened at the sight of a yellow bamboo cane at rest, lengthways, across the dull leather surface. Her eyes never left the supine length of menacingly supple wood – wood grown and gathered for only one possible purpose: the punishment of bare female bottoms.

It lay, passive, yet potent, eloquently silent in its promise of pain. The very sight of it had sent tiny spiders of alarm scurrying down her soft neck and furrowed spine. Harsh words began to break into her almost hypnotic state while Susie stood to attention and listened meekly. The headmistress of Wyevenhoe Hall had remained seated throughout the ensuing sermon and Susie had begun to shuffle uncomfortably as she stood with her head bowed down and her hands clasped nervously behind her. Despite her proud nature, she managed to achieve what she hoped was the very picture of remorse and penitence. Unmoved by this artful display of contrition, the headmistress had continued her tongue-lashing unabated, causing Susie to squirm and blush in her mounting misery. In the fireplace, an apple log settled softly, sending up a swirl of orange sparks. The terse lecture came to a pointed conclusion peppered with stinging rebukes.

Cringing under the onslaught, Susie had blushed a fierce pink. Looking down at the leather-topped desk, she shivered as she saw the headmistress lean forward and stroke the length of the bamboo cane with the quivering tip of her index finger. The gesture was lingeringly repeated several times, in response to which Susie clenched her buttocks anxiously. After those biting words, would there be scalding stripes? Again, the firm finger stroked the length of the cruel wood in an almost affectionate manner. The sinister gesture made Susie's pulse quicken to a gallop.

A ragged cheer rose from the distant playing fields. The headmistress stood up, smiled thinly and strode across to her mullioned window. Peering out into the fine drizzle now gently whipping the wisteria adorning the façade of

Wyevenhoe Hall, she narrowed her eyes and studied the hockey match.

'We have the makings of a decent team this year. There may be a medal for us at county level by Candlemas. A cup, perhaps. Who can tell, hmm? Bend over, girl.'

Memorable words, at which Susie, uncertain and confused, faltered. As she timidly bent down, her dark hair cascaded in a curtain across her eyes. She tossed her head: a gesture mistakenly intercepted by the headmistress as one of defiance.

'At once,' she thundered.

Susie stooped, her dry lips almost kissing the dull leather of the desk top.

'Hands apart. Wider. No, girl, spread them further apart. Feet together, for the moment.'

Susie's splayed fingertips gripped the carved edge of the desk, only an inch from the square green blotter.

'I am going to punish you quite severely, my girl. Your offence being of some considerable enormity the chastisement must be, accordingly, commensurate with the crime. I propose to cane you. Bare-bottomed. Nine strokes.'

Susie, bending over the desk as instructed, automatically fluttered her fingers out behind her. They fumbled awkwardly in their attempt to raise the hem of her short, pleated gym slip.

'Hands on the desk, girl. I will see to your skirt and knickers all in good time,' the headmistress purred in a tone of velvety menace as she paced back from the window towards the desk to scoop up the two-foot length of pliant, yellow bamboo.

Susie's inner thigh suddenly itched maddeningly. She risked a furtive scratch.

'Hands on the desk, girl. I will not tell you again. Leave those knickers alone,' the headmistress rasped, tapping the leather-topped desk imperiously with the quivering tip of the cane. 'I will attend to the necessary preparations for your punishment.'

Slowly – tantalisingly slowly – the stern headmistress had unfastened and then removed the pleated gym slip. Susie felt the fingers at her waist, hips and outer thighs. Released, the gym slip slithered down in silence to curl up

16

in surrender around Susie's white ankle-socks. Feeling its presence, she buried her toes into its encircling softness.

Slowly – insufferably slowly – the intrusive fingers dealt briskly with her tight knickers, prising the elastic waist-band away from the spot where it bit into her warmth. Susie's heart had pounded in her ears as the clinging fabric was fingered from her swollen cheeks, her fullsome curves rounded all the more by her bending posture, and peeled down to rest against her trembling knees. Trapped and pinioned by the tight elastic, her legs and thighs remained immobile rendering her naked, rounded rump poised and positioned perfectly for the impending cane.

Swish – the cane sliced through the air. Susie had clenched her eyes and buttocks fearfully but the headmistress was only flexing the supple wood to test its whippiness. Far away, on the hockey pitch, a whoop of delight broke the afternoon calm, just in time to applaud the practice stroke. Susie glanced down through her curtain of hair at the desk top. On it she saw a catalogue from an antiquarian bookseller which was open at page eleven. Reading the upside down lists, she noticed that the headmistress had marked two items with a neat blue pencil tick in the wide, left hand margin.

The cane swished again and the first stroke seared across her upturned bottom with a fierce tongue-kiss of flame. Blinking away the scorching surprise, Susie read:

Item 18. 'The arraignement and just punishment by whipping of certain Lewde womankinde' by Tom-Teltruth 1688
      (Pub. at Ye sign of Ye Cock hard by Paul's Yard)

The second stroke of the slicing cane stung her bare cheeks with stinging accuracy. Biting her lower lip, Susie bowed her head and read the other ticked item:

Item 26. 'A treatise on sorrow, being an Essay on Disciplining wilful Virgins who have Erred most Sinfully'
      (Pub. Sienna 1506 from the Weemes trans.)

The third stroke was a withering cut which made Susie hiss with suffering. Swish, swipe. Swish, swipe. Again and yet again, the thin whippy wood sliced down across her poised peaches, each time leaving a faint pink stripe that rapidly deepened to a darker shade of red.

Legs astride, with her polished brogues planted into the richly woven carpet, the headmistress had plied the cruel bamboo crisply, ruthlessly and with an unerring exactitude nine times that sorrowful afternoon. That sorrowful afternoon, in the study, behind the firmly closed polished oak door.

How Susie's beautiful buttocks had suffered, and how becomingly they had blushed in the sweet pain. Just the one silver teardrop had splashed down on to the leather-topped desk. Afterwards, Susie remembered, the cool touch of the caner's hands on the bare, hot bottom of the caned. A cool touch which had almost caused Susie to swoon. Yes. Wyevenhoe Hall had been quite an educaton for the pert eighteen-year-old girl. Especially that very private tuition, a lesson never to be forgotten, meted out behind the polished oak door.

The clamour of the impatient traffic choking Sloane Square dragged Susie back from her riot of memories. Sighing, she tidied her long dark hair with her hand. The oak door swung open abruptly. Susie, startled, blushed as she looked up, instantly tossing her hair into its customary untidiness.

'Miss Pelham-Heys.'

Susie swallowed.

'Come inside at once.'

The interview with Madame Seraphim Savage was brief. Scandal, Susie was informed by the frowning madame, loomed large over La Bella Figura. The source of this scandal was Susie, and the interview ended with her being sent away into a spell of exile.

'We will go at once, tonight.'

How fortunate, Susie was grimly reminded, that it was approaching half-term.

In the short time Susie was given to pack a few things, she recalled the words that had crashed through the ceiling of her carefree existence.

'They will be in all the papers tomorrow, that is why we must leave tonight. At once, in fact. Holland Park, isn't it, girl? I'll drop you there. Pack a bag but be quick about it.'

Stuffing her bag with a spare bra and some fresh panties, Susie recalled the final moments of the interview with madame, and how she had learned of their destination – in deepest Devon – with alarm and dismay. She had protested.

'Nude snapshots. How disgusting,' madame had clucked, silencing Susie.

Very, very revealing photos of Susie, captured naked in the fitting rooms of the exclusive fashion college, had somehow found their way into the hands of the tabloid press. The story threatened to break the following day, and even *Society Spy* had, madame groaned, acquired several of the juiciest snaps. The Sloane Square academy would, Susie was informed, be under siege for several days. Shame, its principal snapped angrily, and scandal loomed large.

'It was only a joke,' Susie had explained, lamely.

'A joke, as you misname it, in very poor taste, girl,' madame had retorted crisply, cutting off any line of retreat for the luckless girl.

Susie cursed her bad luck. After all, it had been such a silly prank, just a girlish frolic that had got slightly out of hand. A bevy of naked girls had been measuring each other's bosoms and bottoms as aspiring corsetières are bound to do, but the workshop had degenerated into robust horseplay. Bare, bending buttocks had been flicked at with measuring tapes, and soon mayhem ensued. Amid the squeals, a camera had been produced. Susie, a spirited and vain young thing, had vamped provocatively before the avid lens in a frenzy of frank and utter narcissism.

'A terrible business, girl,' madame had fumed. 'The scandal; the good name of my school.'

At these words, Susie had been forced to suppress a

19

sudden desire to giggle. For a brief moment, she had imagined herself back in Wyevenhoe Hall, back in the study of her grim headmistress, behind the polished oak door. Surely madame was not about to spank or cane her bottom?

'You will remain out of sight until all of this has blown over. A little work experience in my corsetière establishment in Devon will do you no harm at all.'

The matter had been decided. As her exile away from London had been pronounced, Susie scowled. She would miss Sloane Square, her Holland Park pad and the emerging possibilities of the enigmatic Svetlana.

'Don't scowl, girl. I should of course expel you.'

'Oh, no, please. I will do as you say. Anything,' Susie pleaded. She was clearly prepared to bargain away everything for the chance to stay within the fashion circle she had come to adore. 'Anything.'

'I am so pleased to hear it,' murmured madame. 'You have been a very wicked young lady. I am most displeased with you, girl. Most displeased. Come along.'

The neon blaze of Bristol glowed ahead. The digital clock on the dashboard winked seven fifty-five. Nearly eight, Susie mused. Another two hours and they would be there. Susie stirred and stretched, her mind dulled into sleepiness by the M4 through Wiltshire. Devon, she decided, was going to be very grim, and her destination in deepest Devon even grimmer. Madame's place was called The Rookery, but little was said as she gunned her battleship-grey Bentley westward.

In the oppressive silence, Susie did some reasoning: it was a remote setting (such a big saving on business rates) where, no doubt, patterns were cut and fine broderie anglaise was stitched (such a saving on low unit costs) for retail in the more select Bond Street and Knightsbridge outlets (at such very high mark-up prices). Susie, having worked it all out to her own satisfaction, congratulated herself on her growing acumen as a budding entrepreneur.

'Work experience will be very salutory for a giddy young

thing like you,' madame observed, stamping down on the accelerator to leave a Fiesta driver pale and gasping in her wake. 'You will learn much, I can assure you, my girl. Pick up many new and useful skills.'

Just as the gleaming figures on the dashboard showed four minutes to ten, the Bentley swept off the narrow country lane and scrunched along a cinder track. In the swathe of yellow light punched out by the strong quartz beams, Susie caught a fleeting glimpse of jewel-eyed rabbits scampering for safety. The rutted track was narrow, causing the fat tyres of the Bentley to bruise the sedge verge twice. Ahead, up on a dark ridge, Susie saw the gaunt silhouette of The Rookery. They slowed down and stopped where the track was barred by a low, wooden hurdle gate. As instructed, Susie climbed out.

'Here, take this. It's padlocked,' grunted madame, twisting to unpocket a small key.

The Rookery was in total darkness as they approached. How strange, Susie reflected, expecting some sort of reception – especially as Madame Seraphim Savage had barked long and loud instructions into her mobile phone. A former rectory, built in the gloomy, grandiloquent style of two centuries ago, it breathed all the charm of a granite fortress. Stark elms huddled closely around the bleak pile. Susie shivered as she closed the heavy door of the Bentley.

The bell-push at the front entrance appeared to be out of order, for it summoned no response. They trudged in the gloom around to the rear of the building and found a bright yellow window marking the kitchen. The back door, frequently used and regularly oiled, opened with a silent yawn.

Stepping into the bright light, Susie entered a vast kitchen with a low ceiling. A kettle was singing lustily on top of a long, black range. Gleaming saucepans winked from shelving around three of the white-washed walls. The only other sound, apart from a large fridge humming tunelessly to itself, was the tinny buzz of a personal stereo worn by an enraptured young girl of Susie's age who was down on her knees against a throbbing washing-machine.

Head tossed back, eyes closed tightly, her arms waving and her fingers snapping, the lithe beauty was thrusting her pelvis up against the clear, convex door, gyrating her hips and pounding her pubis into the hot perspex. Had Susie looked more carefully, she would have noticed that the ecstatic girl's left hand was sinuously dipping down to unzip her tight jeans; but Susie was not looking that closely. She was sniffing inquisitively at the supper which was spoiling in the belly of the Aga.

Swish, swipe: a soft gasp of sweet suffering immediately followed the unmistakable sound of a cane-stroke. Susie froze, though the pulse at her throat quickened and raced. Swish, swipe: again, the sound of chastisement eliciting a moan from the chastised. Somewhere, somewhere very close at hand, a bare bottom was being crisply and competently caned. Swish, swipe: Susie flinched slightly as another whipping cut from the Judas wood caused a gasp to escape the parted lips of the unseen sufferer.

Blinking, Susie clenched her hands in an automatic reflex. The rounded cheeks of her buttocks tightened, along with the muscles in her tummy, as her body recognised and responded to the sounds of punishment. Recognised, Susie became aware as her nipples tingled, and responded with a delicious sense of dread. Low, stern words now reached her straining ears. Susie frowned as she tried but failed to catch their meaning. Madame Seraphim Savage, the caner, was rebuking the domestic who had let their supper spoil. Susie wondered if the bare, striped bottom of the bending girl was being menacingly tapped with the tip of the supple bamboo to emphasise the points being made by the chastiser. The words remained indistinguishable, but the tone was unmistakable. A silence ensued as the angry words ceased. The slight pause unsettled Susie. She strained up on tiptoe to listen, gently thrusting her nipples into the lace-trimmed cups of her brassière. The tiny, firm peaks, already thickening like her tongue, rasped against the fabric of their nest and burgeoned. But all Susie heard was the thumping of her heart as the tension dragged its nails down her soft spine until she almost squealed. Then the stern voice spoke briefly. The tone was brisk – asking a question, perhaps.

Swish, swipe: Susie heard the gasp that followed. Swish, swipe: eliciting another muffled sob. Susie sighed aloud, her delight drowning the softer moans of the suffering girl being caned. The softer, sweeter moans of the unseen whipped one.

Swish, swipe: Susie heard a higher, plaintive voice – that of a punished nude having her cheeks searchingly striped – respond to the slicing strokes. Urgent words tumbled forth. They were unstoppable, like all penitents' promises secured under the shadow of a hovering cane. An ominous silence returned. Susie, her labial fleshfolds now sticky and hot, sat down at a scrubbed pinewood table, her moistened palms pressing down into it as she tried to steady herself. Her head swam after such a heady cocktail of fascination and fear. Her nipples ached longingly, her swollen breasts weighed heavily as they strained within their strict silken bondage. Out in the darkness, beyond the warmth and yellow light of the kitchen, a wooden chair squeaked harshly as its legs scraped across flagstones. Susie's imagination hungrily devoured the sound. Had the punisher, shouldering her cane, instructed the bare-bottomed domestic to bend over once more and grasp the back of the chair? Or approach it, head bowed, to place her forehead down on to the seat thus presenting her already faintly striped buttocks up for more intimacy with the whippy wood? Or perhaps the whipped one had been commanded to ease her nakedness belly-down across the seat of the chair.

In her fevered imaginings Susie saw the tip of the yellow cane imperiously tap-tapping the appointed spot in stern invitation. Or had the punished supper-spoiler been ordered to kneel on the hard chair, utterly exposing her naked cheeks to the threat of further hot cane-kisses? The images of dominance and submission, punishment and exquisite torment, burned behind Susie's eyes: the naked, kneeling, bare-bottomed girl; the quivering length of cruel bamboo brandished aloft by the indomitable chastiser.

Four more strokes thrummed in swift succession. Susie, squeezing her thighs together, glanced at the dried up chicken casserole which was to have been her supper. In the congealed sherry sauce, she could just make out the remains of charred mushrooms.

A movement in the far doorway startled her. Turning, she saw madame buttoning the sleeve of her blouse. It was the sleeve of her right arm – the arm, Susie knew, which had just administered the caning.

'Chicken's ruined.' Madame nodded at the blackened casserole dish. 'That lazy girl won't be letting many more suppers spoil.'

The curt comment, which neither confirmed nor denied the whipping which had just occurred, made Susie shudder.

'We'll have to make do with a salad. Cheese all right?'

'Yes,' whispered Susie – who hated cheese – her eyes never leaving madame's bosom as it rose and fell, disturbed by the recent exertions. 'A cheese salad would be fine.'

Susie watched in awe as the austere madame busied herself across at the sink, washing and then expertly tossing leaves of rocket and cos in a tea towel. Almost twice Susie's age, the dominant woman exuded absolute authority and agile grace.

'Bad mistake, that business with the camera, wasn't it, my girl?' she said over her shoulder laconically as she cut a generous wedge out of a truckle of farmhouse cheddar.

Susie, blushing pinkly, gazed down at the bone-handled breadknife placed across the wooden bread-board.

'I will not tolerate any of that nonsense here. Plenty to be done.'

'Lots of orders to process?' Susie rejoined, eager to appear bright and businesslike.

Ignoring the interjection, the stern women continued to grate the cheese then deftly dressed the salad with a drizzle of virgin olive oil. She approached the table.

'Eat up. After supper, a quick bath, then bed. And hurry up,' she chided Susie who dallied with her cheese, 'I've had a busy day and an even busier evening.'

Madame made short work of her supper which she

forked down wolfishly. Susie, acutely conscious of the slicing strokes madame had meted out, looked down at her plate hastily trying to avoid the shrewd, appraising gaze of her stern host.

'We'll speak at length in my office tomorrow morning directly after breakfast. But be warned,' she added ominously, her tone growing harsh. 'I will expect diligence and obedience. And I mean complete obedience. Or else.'

The potent menace of her concluding words hung heavily across the late-night supper table. Susie swallowed awkwardly.

'In my office tomorrow morning. Be prompt. Goodnight, Miss Pelham-Heys.'

Before Susie could reply, madame had swept majestically out of the kitchen. Susie crumbled her bread between anxious fingers, her face clouded by a deepening frown. She recalled the ominous words: diligence, obedience. Or else. The words made her shiver, adding a delicious sense of dread to her increasing unease and dismay. A pang of fearful doubt stabbed at her heart: would she herself be subjected to the crisp hot kiss of madame's cane? Become, bare-bottomed and bending, acquainted with the striping strokes of the thrumming bamboo? Be soundly whipped if she failed to show the prescribed degree of diligence and complete obedience? Susie shuddered as a terrible truth revealed itself to her: she was in exile, far away from her familiar stamping ground. In exile, here at The Rookery, in deepest Devon. It was so isolated here, and she had no friends. Consigned to the strict supervision and stern tutelage of madame, who she had already grossly displeased, Susie realised that she would have to curb her wanton wilfulness and be prepared to submit to the strictures of diligence and obedience. Or else.

Stripped down to her bra and silk panties, feet planted slightly apart, Susie bent down and gasped aloud as the cold water she splashed up into her face with cupped hands sparkled on the quivering curves of her bosom. After dabbing herself dry with a towel, she turned, switched off the light and closed the bathroom door behind her. It clicked but swung silently open again as Susie retreated down along the cool corridor towards her bedroom.

Inside her quarters, Susie pulled a face of disappointment. The room was small, spartan and sparsely furnished. How different these privations seemed from her sumptuous Holland Park pad. A graceful motion of her hand behind her back rendered Susie braless. With her lovely breasts now loose and gently bobbing, she sat down before a small mirror. In the poor light from the naked bulb above, her reflection in the mottled glass was no better than a shadow. Sighing, she lowered the polished pearwood back of her hairbrush into her upturned palm. Twenty strokes. Every night she dutifully punished her rebellious locks of dark hair with twenty brisk strokes. She had learned that to fully master her wilful hair she had to be very firm with it. And as mistress to her mane, Susie was very firm indeed. Sighing once more, she rose up and retraced her steps back towards the bathroom. The light was much better there.

The bathroom light was on. And the troublesome door had, once more, defied the latch and partly opened. Ajar, it allowed Susie a glimpse from the corridor of a naked young woman at the sink. As Susie paused, her pulse quickening, she gazed from her surrounding darkness into the blaze of light which sharply illuminated the naked girl at her intimate toilette. She was bending down, as Susie had been some minutes before, to splash her face with cupped handfuls of water. It was not the sight of the tumbling breasts or the sweep of silken thighs that caused Susie's eyes to widen with wonder. It was not the splayed, shapely legs, or indeed the pubic fringe peeping shyly at their shadowed juncture, that caused Susie's throat to tighten. It was the bare bottom. The superb bottom offered up in almost meek submission for Susie's full and frank appraisal. It was a gorgeous bottom, the flesh-globes luscious yet firm. A peach of a bottom, so delightfully curved. Susie judged the bending buttocks to be bewitching, and she yearned to finger the sleek surface of the rounded cheeks, then cup and weigh in her own open palms their warm flesh.

26

It was a bottom which had been recently whipped. Susie's eyes narrowed as she counted three, five, seven or more faint pink stripes across the bunched cheeks. Spellbound, she swallowed silently and re-counted, slowly, the tell-tale marks of the cane. Of course, it was the naughty domestic who had ruined their chicken casserole. This, Susie realised, must be the bottom she had heard being caned by madame. And those, Susie mused, must be the stripes – pain made visible – that were the fruit of the unseen, but overheard, punishment.

Absently pressing her hairbrush inward against her left breast, Susie drank in every detail of the recently whipped buttocks. Slowly, silently, she dragged the prickling bristles down across her peaking nipple. Crushing the pink stub of tingling flesh down, Susie carefully re-counted the pink stripes.

Suddenly the shape of the naked bottom changed as the nude girl stood up straight, her eyes tightly shut as her wet hands pawed the air around her for the towel. Susie tiptoed silently away.

The Rookery was a bleak house. A bleak house in a remote setting. Gazing out through her tiny window, Susie could not see any sign of neighbourhood farms or nearby dwellings. She drew her single curtain across, blotting out the gaunt elms in the garden whose branches clawed at the inky night around them. Snuggling down into her fresh linen sheets, she explored her bed with scrunched up toes. They rejoiced at finding a rubbery hot water bottle in a far corner of her bed. Susie hauled it up towards her thighs and cradled it there, hugging it as much for comfort as for warmth. Soon the spartan room, her narrow bed and the heat from the rubber bottle conjured up vivid memories of her school days – and nights. Days at Wyevenhoe Hall which came to an evening close with punishments in the spellbound dorm.

Susie shut her eyes and let her thoughts linger on remembered spankings. Spankings and the slightly more severe slipperings. Cuddling and clamping the hot water bottle between the softness of her inner thighs, more recent, and more potent, images blossomed with the spreading warmth. With the hot rubber squashed against her wet slit, Susie recalled the sounds of madame caning the domestic. Then came the naked girl in the bathroom: the vision of the whipped girl bending at her ablutions, fully exhibiting her striped bottom.

The urgent heat against Susie's pubis was delicious and she squeezed her thighs tighter, making her butterfly-labia spread its delicate flesh-wings further apart. Fully opened, they submissively kissed the dimpled hot rubber bottle, causing Susie to squirm and groan. More sweet moans escaped her dry lips as the heat blazed against her ultra-sensitive wet flesh. Susie's mind was also blazing with images which she hugged to herself as fiercely as she hugged the hot torment at the base of her belly. In a sudden shiver of delicious pleasure she recalled the desk across which, as a naughty sixth former, she had been so searchingly and searingly caned. As sleep approached, however, the images blurred. A bare bottom, striped, being offered up for more. Whose bare bottom? Her own? Or that of the naked domestic glimpsed through the bathroom door?

Dreamily, the images melted into a confused mosaic as Susie hovered above the abyss of sleep. Tugging at the hot water bottle, she loosened it from her clamped thighs and dragged its warm weight up across her belly, bouncing it twice against her bosom before easing it up over her shoulder and dropping it down by her bedside. In the darkness, she caught the tang of her wet excitement glistening on the hot rubber.

Swish, swipe. Swish, stripe. Susie's fingers stole down to where the hot rubber had warmed her innermost flesh. Once there, her fingertips slowly strummed her weeping wound. Swish, swipe: the sweet pain of her own caning merged into the sounds she had heard from the kitchen. Swish, swipe: sleepily, all Susie understood was that a bottom was being caned. She turned over in the bed on to her tummy, squashing her breasts down firmly beneath her.

Her fingertips remained at her splayed labia, stroking and rubbing, plucking and teasing rhythmically. Her soft buttocks wobbled as she shivered with renewed pleasure. Swish, swipe. How she had suffered across the desk in the study; how much more that domestic must have sweetly suffered under madame's cane as it rose and fell insistently.

Madame Seraphim Savage: Susie smiled dreamily into her white pillow as she pictured the beautiful, stern woman – her gorgeous bosom heaving, her supple hips swaying – dispensing the discipline. Inching her buttocks up, Susie imagined herself to be the recipient of the strokes. As the pliant cane fell across her upturned cheeks she imagined the biting burn of the cruel cane-kiss against her ravished rump. Strumming herself with eager excitement, Susie buried her hot face into the cool pillow. The cool linen wiped the images away, leaving Susie suddenly aghast at her feelings and the fantasy they fuelled. Her hand froze suddenly as she recoiled from these unsuspected yearnings. She thought it utterly impossible that she desired to taste madame's displeasure. It was utterly impossible, wasn't it?

Sleep and lust were confusing Susie's usually sharp mind. Blinking, she struggled to concentrate. She was down here at The Rookery for a brief spell of work experience. Madame Seraphim Savage would never – could never – discipline and punish her. Never. The rational thought calmed Susie's tired brain but as she settled down to sleep darker feelings bubbled up from the depths of her subconscious. These feelings entwined her dull mind, startling and amazing the naked, sleepy girl.

Susie yawned and snuggled into her sheets. Slowly, almost involuntarily, her hand at the base of her belly began to finger her hot wetness as delicious images seeped back behind her closed eyes. They were images of herself, bare-bottomed and bending, receiving madame's strict chastisement. Swish, stripe: each measured, accurate stroke slicing across her naked cheeks. No, not that. Never. Her heart now thudding wildly, Susie propped herself up on her elbows, her face ablaze with shame and fury. Once more, her conscious brain battled to reject the fantasy of submission to, and domination by, the principal of La Bella Figura but her resolve crumbled before the implacable desires.

Nestling back in the warmth of her bed, and once more on the brink of sleep, Susie arched her supple hips up so that her bottom rose as if to meet and greet madame's cane. Swish, swipe: Susie fingered her hot slit with increasing intensity. Capitulating completely, Susie surrendered to the potent image as she succumbed to her innermost desire: a desire she now recognised and acknowledged. She keenly sought to be given a bare-bottomed caning; a slow, strict caning, by Madame Seraphim Savage.

Grunting her bewildered yet satisfied groans into the pillow, Susie moaned as her wet warmth quickly turned her scrabbling fingertips sticky. Seconds later, her thumb slid up towards her clitoris and slowly stroked the tiny thorn of tingling flesh until Susie felt the walls of her belly collapse as the first of four orgasms welled up within her.

Two

'Corsets accentuate the breasts and make the wearer feel as feminine, as voluptuous, as a champagne bucket brimming with roses.'

Susie nodded her understanding.

'The effect is achieved, of course, by the balcony which thrustingly uplifts the bosom. Best demonstrated by the basque. Corsets,' Madame Seraphim Savage continued sonorously, 'should enhance the svelte silhouette. They are certainly not about cinching and puckering, but grace the female form to smooth and shape, mould and flatter, contour and bewitch.'

As the teacher launched into the historical development of the corset, the student unclenched her buttocks and relaxed a little. Susie had breakfasted on coffee, toast and prunes without much enthusiasm and had then approached madame's office, as ordered, with mounting fearful expectation. Mindful of the whipping meted out to the careless maid, Susie perceived her host in a totally new light. Twenty-four hours ago, she had regarded the principal of La Bella Figura with admiration and respect. An eventful twenty-four hours later, she viewed her with delicious dread. But the tutorial progressed swiftly, drawing Susie deep into the world of the corsetière.

Madame Seraphim Savage was an eloquent and knowledgeable speaker, and Susie gradually set aside her fears of the cane, almost dismissing them entirely. What a ridiculous idea, she chided herself. She was simply down here for a brief spell of work experience. It was an excellent opportunity, really; the other girls would be so jealous if they knew. Satisfied with her fortunes, Susie listened to madame attentively, all the time struggling to banish from her mind the lingering memory of those final moments before sleep overcame her last night. Those final moments in which her naked buttocks, upturned cheeks squeezed together and aquiver, had actually inched up willingly to receive the imagined strokes of madame's cane.

'Which brings us to the Spirella, the classic white number from the fifties, from which we can draw an evolutionary line to Le Petite Basque by Berlei.'

The words grabbed Susie's attention and she resumed her avid note taking.

'Ushering in those ultra-feminine appurtenances: the satin pencil-skirt, seamed nylons, suspender girdles and the clinging bustier.'

More followed as madame effortlessly listed the retail outlets: Rigby and Peller for the establishment, with Agent Provocateur of Soho and Boisvert of Neal Street for the more adventurous adventuress. Haute couture's involvement was acknowledged, with reference to Lagerfeld's waspy satins; Gaultier's black leather; Gianni Versace's tightly bodiced creations, and Dolce and Gabbana's flesh-toned foundations often worn beneath see-through outer-wear for that extra frisson.

'And now, as the nineties draw to a close, fashion historians will come to regard this as the decade of the voluptuous. A decline into decadence, perhaps. But let the sociologists debate over the arrival of the corset in time to witness tight fiscal controls, squeezed profit margins and restrictive base rates.'

Susie smiled, eager for more. She drank in the reference to the introduction of black and grey velvet, white lace, red satin and pink silk. The corset, she learned, was designed to enhance and to ensnare, to bind and bewitch. Women who wore them, Susie scribbled in the margin of her jotter, were certainly bound to please.

The office was spacious, with a swathe of expensive Berber carpet covering the limewood floor. The walls were painted light beige, a neutral tone intended to enhance the eighteenth-century prints that adorned them. A splendid desk – Italianate quattrocento littered with modern electronic office equipment – basked in the sunlight streaming through a large bay window. Large, four-drawer filing cabinets lined one wall. Above them, the beige wall was covered with corsets, splayed and mounted like the pelts in a hunter's trophy room. From time to time, madame illustrated her lecture by pointing to a satin waspie or fingering a frilly suspender belt. Susie sat in a hard wooden chair behind a squeaking school desk. She found both chair and desk humiliating and irksome, and wriggled with gathering resentment. Already her calf muscles ached as she disciplined her body to remain upright and still in case any movement caused the desk to squeak and groan. Previous creaking had raised madame's eyebrows querulously, kindling a flicker of fear in Susie's belly. Rendered rigid within the controlling stricture of the school desk and chair, Susie smouldered in sullen silence.

Through the window, beyond the ornate desk, Susie glimpsed a kestrel hovering against the clear April sky. The trembling wings which looked so stiff were, she knew, in reality supple and flexible. Just like a quivering cane – pliant and potent. The kestrel shimmered in the morning sunshine, as if savouring the intensity of the moment before swooping down upon its quarry below. Susie blinked as the image of a whippy cane stole into her imagination. A length of yellow bamboo, hovering above its quarry of helpless, upturned buttocks: like the kestrel the cane remained aloft, soon to swoop and strike.

'A high-waisted cut is strongly recommended for the more pronounced hips,' intoned madame.

Susie swallowed silently. The kestrel had just swooped down. Through the window, she scanned the blue sky and green fields. Her throat tightened as she saw it soaring and wheeling upward. Moving slightly to ease the intolerable tension within her rigid body, she made the desk groan as her bosom brushed against it. The teacher glared; the squirming student blushed. Launching into the secrets of latex gussets, madame resumed her lecture. Susie, dutifully taking notes, speculated as to where exactly in Devon she might be. The rolling landscape, denuded of trees by generations of sheep, stretched out towards the far horizon. The nearest village might be sheltering just behind that distant tor, she mused. Or twenty-six bleak miles beyond.

'And pay particular attention to the profile of the buttocks,' madame concluded, looking briefly at her watch. 'With the bottom, we aim to achieve pertness, not a protuberance.'

Susie closed her jotter and placed her pen silently down on the desk.

'I'm expecting a client this morning. I alone will attend to her needs. You will remain in here, girl. Your knowledge of Victorian corsetry is sadly deficient. This book should remedy that,' she remarked, handing Susie a slim, well-thumbed volume bound in black leather. 'What you seek will be found there. I will examine you after lunch.' She paused, turning to the window at the sound of an approaching car. 'My client is punctual.'

Glimpsing out, Susie just caught the kingfisher-blue flash of a speeding Rover 100 Kensington. The nippy little car scrunched to a halt out of her line of vision.

'Maritta. A Finnish nurse who was employed to look after a local dowager. The dowager died, sadly, but the nurse stayed on. Maritta married into the family. Farmers. A country family who occupy the magistrate's bench and run most of the committees hereabouts. Poor Maritta. Bit of a fish out of water down here. Husband's past his prime and by all accounts can just about manage to cock his twelve-bore from the back of a Land Rover at a rough shoot. Ah, there she is.'

Susie caught sight of a trim, young strawberry blonde striding past the window. The clothes were good: tight-fitting and expensive. Susie noted the pale, lemon leather gloves.

'Remain in here and do not disturb us. I do not feel that you are quite prepared enough to deal with our clients just yet.'

Alone in the office, Susie leafed through the required reading. As she turned the pages, she found that bulging bosoms seemed to feature largely in the text. And what, she suddenly wondered, would breakfasters up and down the land think of La Bella Figura this morning? How strange, Susie thought, that the principal had made absolutely no mention of the wretched business. What words – worse still, what lubricious images – would greet the nation's readers over their eggs, coffee and unopened junk-mail? Fuelled by both vanity and anxiety, Susie's curiosity grew intense. Her breasts were good, her bottom better. How had they come out in print?

Despite elaborate accounts on the methods used to encase the bosoms of Victorian maidens within the fierce strictures of boned calico, accounts Susie knew she must become familiar with by lunchtime, she could not concentrate. Her head swam with so many unanswered questions. Had she been identified in the tabloids' revelations? Had they used her name? Had they spelled it correctly? She remembered that she had been quite naked in some of the snapshots: had one of those little black bars been discreetly placed over her? Not across the nipples but across the eyes? Unable to contain her anxiety anymore, she approached the Italianate desk and picked up the phone. Seconds later, Susie was chattering with a contact who worked in the picture library of a trade fashion magazine. A minute later, she had learned that no mention of La Bella Figura had been made in any of that morning's press.

'And no pictures? You are sure?'

'Nope. No pics. I've read every paper for cuttings. Nothing about your place in any of 'em. Why the interest? Place gone broke?'

'No,' Susie said with a laugh, 'I'll tell you later. You know a girl who helps on the diary page of *Society Spy*, don't you?'

'Should hope so. She's my flatmate. Why?'

'Oh, yes, of course. Are they doing a piece on La Bella Figura?'

'Shouldn't think so. She's an old girl, remember? Went

there two years ago. Doesn't do to dish the dirt on the alma mater. What dirt, anyway? Do tell.'

'Later, perhaps,' Susie said. Thanking her friend, she replaced the phone. Turning back to her desk, she froze. Madame Seraphim Savage was standing in the doorway. How long had she been there? What had she heard? Susie flushed a guilty shade of pink. Something in madame's stern gaze quelled Susie's rush to break the news. Later, she told herself. She would tell madame later, and prepare for her return to London.

'Files,' the dominant woman murmured in a neutral tone. 'I forgot Maritta's files. We open up files for every client,' she added, unlocking a cabinet.

Suddenly resenting madame's cool authority, Susie blurted out her news in an increasingly defiant tone. Completely unperturbed, the principal tapped the files she had drawn and explained, in a patient voice as if to a child, that an up-to-date filing system was the key to any successful business venture.

'Helps keep track of their various tastes and preferences.'

'But, madame, the papers. There is no scandal,' Susie repeated.

'Finished your reading task so soon?' said madame suavely. 'Surely not.'

Susie reddened and fell silent, completely crushed.

'I thought I told you that I would be testing you at lunch. And test, my girl, I most assuredly will.' Slamming home the cabinet drawer with her supple thigh, and pocketing the key with which she briskly locked it, madame turned on her polished brogue and abruptly left the office.

Wild thoughts tumbled through Susie's brain. Had it all been a hoax? Had she been tricked? Had madame used bullying threats and outright deception to spirit her away down here for a fortnight's unpaid work? Burning at the enormity of the ruse and at her own gullibility, Susie flashed a resentful look at the closed door. Damn. Never mind, she consoled herself. After the client had been measured and fitted, Susie would calmly confront the principal. Better not lose her temper, though; it was best to remain calm. Treat it all as a bit of a jape and maintain a light-hearted note. A taxi would get her to the nearest station. Why, she'd be in Paddington then back to her Holland Park pad by dusk.

Closing the book on Victorian corsetry after carefully noting its title for future reference – Susie was a serious student with ambition – she wandered over to the filing cabinets. Tugging at them absently, she remembered that they were locked. Returning to the computer on madame's desk, she fingered the mouse. The screen came to life, glowing a pale sepia. Little orange ciphers swam across the screen in a meaningless stream. Susie stemmed the flow, using the mouse to delve into the memory. A logo flashed up in the top left-hand corner: the little figure of a naked Eve pressing an apple to her bare bosom. Susie smiled, happily familiar with the provocative motif. Scores of files flickered before her eyes as the data-base emptied itself. Business must be brisk, she mused, judging by the volume of records.

She double-clicked the mouse, and immediately summoned up another logo on to the screen. It was, she saw, the tiny naked Eve, this time sporting shiny black stockings and pressing the tip of a riding crop into the upturned palm of her small, pink hand. Susie gazed down at the little figure fixed behind the tinted screen of the monitor. Puzzled, she clicked the mouse to scan the files but was thwarted by a flashing demand for a password. Susie shrugged as the screen informed her that access was denied. Frustrated, she clicked again and brought back the logo. What could it mean? Gazing at the crop, she suddenly grinned. Of course, after the pleasure came the pain. They would be financial accounts, detailing all the clients' bills. After the indulgence of silk and satin, the sting.

Despite her initial fascination, Susie's thoughts strayed to Maritta. As she was leaving The Rookery after lunch, why not peep in on Madame Seraphim Savage working with her client? Although strictly forbidden to do so, Susie

37

decided to ignore the command. It could prove to be a very valuable experience, watching a skilled corsetière at close quarters. Watching an expert at work.

Exploring the silent gloom of The Rookery on tiptoe, Susie at last approached a pair of oak doors. Instinctively, she bent down and placed her ear to the brass keyhole. She heard the low tones of madame. Good, she thought. She had found them.

Kneeling quietly against the closed doors, Susie squirmed to peer through the keyhole. Through it, she saw the lithe figure of a partially naked strawberry blonde. Susie saw Maritta's gloved hands pawing at her hair as if containing her ecstasy. The young Finn was standing, her lissome legs parted slightly, facing the doors. Susie's eye raked the length of the supple nude, widening a fraction as the gloved hands dropped down to cup and squeeze the heavy breasts, the pale lemon leather clasping the imprisoned flesh with cruel affection.

Susie, despite the full frontal appraisal, could not tell if the naked beauty was a natural strawberry blonde for the pubis was clean and closely shaven. Susie swallowed, her mouth felt thick and dry. The keyhole framed the pert blonde perfectly. Into the picture strode Madame Seraphim Savage. Susie gasped. The principal was wearing a black leather basque. Her pale skin shone, accentuating the athletic menace of her smooth-limbed body. In her strong, slender fingers rested a coiled up measuring tape, the last inch of which was made of a dull gold metal.

Positioning herself directly behind the slightly trembling Finn, madame slipped the tape around the blonde's belly, drawing the nude's buttocks into her basque as she tightened it. Maritta shuddered and Susie knew full well why: the blonde's bare bottom had kissed the black leather basque as her soft cheeks had been crushed in against the firm body of the dominant corsetière standing behind her. Maritta dropped her leather-gloved hands, revealing her proud breasts splendid in their ripe nakedness, quivering as she shivered in delicious expectation. Susie yearned to reach out, stretch out her hands and palm the heavy breasts, then slowly weigh their rounded warmth. The desire grew more intense as she gazed longingly at the Finn's superb bosom, the desire to still the breasts with her cupped hands and then firmly squeeze the soft orbs.

Susie felt the pulse at her throat quicken as the measuring tape deftly encircled the naked breasts, ensnaring the dark pink nipples. She watched as the tape tightened once again, making the soft flesh slowly bulge. Susie smothered a groan as a deep, inviting cleavage appeared between the swollen globes, and stifled a second groan of desire as the urge to tongue the breasts gripped her. Yes. To tongue the breasts; to trace the tip of her quivering wet tongue around the burgeoning contours of the trapped breasts, then slip it down into the cleavage and bury it deep within the secret soft warmth.

Tormented by her slit-tingling desires, Susie pressed her tongue against the bitter varnish of the wooden door, squashing it firmly into the hard oak. Her fingers flew up to seek and find her own nipples now stiff and erect beneath her white silk blouse. They hardened with pleasure as she nipped and squeezed their sensitive peaks.

The tape measure slithered silently to the floor, but madame continued to hold her captive in an intimate embrace, weighing the Finn's loose and lovely breasts within her hands. Susie watched, enthralled, at the display of tender but absolute dominance. Maritta's gloved hands flew up to her open mouth, the leathered fingers peeling down the thickly fleshed, sensual lower lip in a slow salute to ecstasy. Susie echoed the gesture, fingering her own dry flesh. The pert nude, utterly delicious in her submissive repose, nestled back against the shining black leather of madame's severely cut basque. Susie's white cotton panties grew damp as her sticky labia unfurled, the pink, wet lips opening to kiss the sheath of tight fabric.

Madame Seraphim Savage, totally in control, brought her strong face down, lips slightly parted in a carnal snarl, to her captive's bare shoulder. Susie gasped as she saw the red lips glisten and the small white teeth enclose the Finn's exposed flesh. The stern face distorted somewhat as the biter sucked deeply into the flesh of the bitten. Maritta moaned softly, her gloved fingers dabbling at her arched throat. Copying this gesture, Susie fluttered her fingertips down her pulsing neck.

The two women beyond the closed door were now, it seemed to Susie as she gazed hungrily through the keyhole, fused together. The younger woman's buttocks thrusting back into the lower belly and thighs of her sweet tormentress: the tamer and the tamed. The image burned in Susie's brain, along with new, strangely disturbing yearnings. She shivered as she felt the scalding splash of her sticky response soak into the stretched cotton of her panties: panties now quite soaked with her wet delight.

Madame smoothed her capable palms downward and cradled the Finn's soft belly. Maritta's gloved fingertips flew up to her neglected breasts, squeezing and gently punishing their bobbing, swollen warmth. Susie's hands followed the gesture, clasping and cupping her own bosom as it strained against the silken bondage of blouse and bra. Through the thin fabric, she felt her aching nipples peak as she palmed them with renewed savage tenderness. Through the keyhole she saw Maritta inching her lithe legs wider apart. The sparkling flesh of the Finn's peeled fig glittered, making Susie's lips quiver as her desire found its focus. She burned to bend down towards the oozing fruit as it dripped its honey-juice openly. Susie ached for a splash of the nectar on her outstretched tongue, and ached more keenly to use her tongue to probe the sweet flesh.

Her own hot slit was now juicing her inner thighs freely and Susie burned with pleasure-shame as she squeezed her thighs to stem the seeping delight. Never before had she felt such urgent pangs, such intensity of desire. Never before had she experienced such wanton lust. Through the narrow keyhole, her eye devoured the scene inside the room, feeding the flames of her hot yearnings. Voyeur to Maritta's sweet suffering, Susie gazed intently on that which she burned to possess.

A deeper desire, one which voyeurism alone could not quench, gripped Susie as she knelt and peeped through the

40

keyhole. What, she wondered, was the true nature of the carnal ache within her? Suddenly, Susie knew: the absolute knowledge imploded in her whirling brain. She desired to be in Maritta's place. To be naked, utterly naked and passive, within the thrall of the leather-basqued Madame Seraphim Savage. To feel the sheer skin of the black leather against her trapped buttocks. To feel the white teeth of the dominatrix nipping at her soft flesh. To feel the slender hands – so cruel, so capable – imprisoning her swollen bosom.

Pressed up against the oak door, Susie shuddered as hot lust coursed through the veins of her kneeling body. Inside the room, madame had stepped back a single pace, her strong hand remaining on the trembling blonde's bare left buttock. Madame's fingers taloned, painfully squeezing the captive cheek. The Finn gasped out joyfully in her torment. Madame brought her free hand down to the right buttock and began to cup and punishingly spread the soft cheeks wide apart. Maritta rose up on her tiny white toes, offering herself up in submissive surrender to the fierce pleasure. Her gloved fingers now pawing frantically at her belly and thighs, the naked strawberry blonde thrust her bottom back for further, fiercer delights.

Susie closed her eyes and pressed her hot face against the cool oak door, imagining her own buttocks to be in madame's controlling hands, almost swooning as she arched them up. She was now Maritta, and all the delicious agony, all the sweet surrender, was not Maritta's but hers. Susie's fingertips sought out her labial fleshfolds. Her hot slit pulsed with an almost hypnotic throb. Through her soaking cotton panties she pressed and probed, rubbed and stroked, soon approaching the point of no return. Yes, she was almost there. She rubbed harder. Suddenly a sharp cry from within the room froze Susie's scrabbling fingertips. Glimpsing through the keyhole, she saw the svelte nude down on all fours.

Susie heard a snapping and saw the principal of La Bella Figura straddling the crouching Finn. With one arched foot resting lightly but firmly across the dipped nape of

Maritta's neck, madame whipped the upturned buttocks with the measuring tape. Snap, snap, snap: the tape, doubled up within madame's sure grasp, cracked down again and again. Maritta's naked bottom, the superb cheeks heavy and rounded, rose up to meet Susie's wide eye. The tape flickered down, swiping the proffered cheeks with brutal affection. Susie, her breasts squashed into the unyielding oak, drank in every detail of the discipline: the supple grace of the punisher; the jerking response of the bottom as the tape whipped down. It was a thrilling sight to see madame, her breasts swelling up in the basque as her punishing arm straightened above the bare bottom below after each withering slice. Snap, snap, snap: a triple echo as the lash came down with searing accuracy. Susie saw the faint pink stripes across the curved cheeks deepen beneath the fresh onslaught.

'Down,' commanded madame curtly as Maritta strained beneath the dominant foot of her mistress.

Obediently, the Finn lay spreadeagled face down on the carpet. The dominatrix paused in her administration of the discipline and knelt down alongside the whipped blonde. Susie saw that madame clasped the tape measure within a clenched fist. Was there to be more? More of the delicious discipline? Was Maritta's bare bottom to be whipped at such close quarters? Were those passive cheeks about to be more searchingly, more intimately lashed? Susie's heart hammered and her wet pussy throbbed. Reeling slightly, as if tipsy with lust, she supported her kneeling body against the door.

Holding the tape tightly, madame's hand hovered eleven inches above Maritta's buttocks which visibly quivered with fearful expectation. A trickle of sweat momentarily blinded Susie's vision. She wiped her brow with a brief dab of her forearm. Glancing down at her silk sleeve, she saw the wet stain.

Through the keyhole, she watched in awe as madame rotated her wrist slightly and loosened her taloned fingers. Inch by inch, the dominant woman fed the tape down until the yellow metal tip skimmed the curved surface of the freshly punished rump. Maritta squealed, thrusting her hips up eagerly to greet this tantalising torment. Susie's belly imploded as she watched the metal tip of the tape teasingly drag across the striped flesh-mounds.

Now, thought Susie. Now. Stripe her. Lash her bottom. Now. But madame did not crack the tape down. Instead, her firm fingers grasped the metal tip and guided it into the dark cleft between the whipped buttocks. Susie watched wide-eyed as it slipped down into the warmth to stroke the velvety ribbon of flesh buried deep inside. Shrieking obscenities, Maritta pummelled the floor, her clenched fist drumming the fury of her imminent orgasm into the peacock-blue carpet as madame's restraining hand pinned her firmly down. Tamed and helpless, Maritta lay still though her hips and thighs twisted and writhed in their sweet anguish.

Bending down over the nude, the corsetière began to intimately measure the passive flesh, murmuring soothingly as she did so. Face down on the carpet, Maritta mewed like a kitten as she surrendered to the strict calibrations of the cold tape against her soft warmth. Between the shoulders, around the waist and plumper hips, madame plied the tape. To Susie's delight, she saw the final measurements being taken from the nape of the pale neck to the swell of the rump, along the furrowed spine. The watching girl, frantic with pent up longings, unbuttoned her blouse and quickly unburdened her bosom from the tight bra restraining it. Tumbling forth in their newfound freedom, her soft breasts ached; the nipples now sheer peaks of exquisite pain. Pinching each nipple, she coaxed back her welling climax. Between her clamped inner thighs, Susie's slit was seething.

Suddenly the tape cracked again; madame had pinned Maritta firmly down and, wielding the last nine inches of tape expertly, struck each rounded cheek methodically. This time, Susie shivered as she gazed, madame whipped down the metal tip across the upturned buttocks. Susie spasmed in her belly and dropped down on all fours: she had started to come. Behind the closed doors, she pictured the naked Finn squirming beneath the fierce onslaught. Susie's fingers flew to her clitoris and massaged in time to the renewed sound of the staccato discipline. Unable to resist missing the sight of the strawberry blonde being whipped, Susie scrambled back upon her knees with her eye to the keyhole and her fingers at her clitoris.

Maritta wriggled free from her oppressor and stumbled drunkenly towards a full-length mirror. Turning her back to it, she bent down and, peering over her shoulder, studied her ravished rump in the glass. The tips of the pale leather-gloved fingers appeared at the cusp of each reddened cheek. Slowly, the splayed fingers dragged the hot buttocks apart as the punished intimately examined her punishment.

Susie sank back briefly, her soft buttocks pressing on to her heels. The plucking pulse at the base of her belly surged downward and she thrust her hands, palms pressed together, between her clamped thighs and dragged them against her wet labia. The violence of her orgasm caused her to shudder and jerk, squashing her splayed buttocks into her heels so hard the torment made her grunt thickly. Panting heavily, she slumped back against the door desperately trying to steady her eye at the keyhole despite the climax that rocketed within her kneeling body.

Madame Seraphim Savage – who had momentarily stepped out of the frame provided by the narrow aperture of the voyeur's keyhole – returned. Bearing a snow-white underwired brassière, she lingeringly addressed the Finn's bosom, from behind, easing each soft breast into an awaiting cup. As the strict disciplinarian became the attentive corsetière once more, Maritta's gloved fingertips fluttered down to her closely shaven pubis. Susie moaned as she watched the leather-sheathed thumbs tease apart the Finn's glistening labia, revealing the pink wetness within which slowly stained the lemon hide.

Crack: Susie saw the cruel tape flicker in from beyond her field of vision and lash the plump, rounded cheeks. Maritta, bending as she perused the previous punishment, jerked upward with a squeal. Madame pounced, briskly dragging the lemon-gloved hands behind the struggling Finn's back. Susie gasped softly as she saw the pinioned hands being firmly bound together at the wrists with the measuring tape.

'Kneel,' thundered madame.

Maritta submitted to the stern order. Dominatrix once more, the woman in the black leather basque gathered up a handful of the kneeling nude's strawberry blonde hair. It was a supreme display of absolute dominance which caused Susie's orgasm to renew itself with a fresh intensity. Stooping, madame gathered up the tape measure and drew it up between the Finn's wet labia. It bit deeply into the dark cleft as it arrowed down from Maritta's bound hands, sliced between her thighs and streaked up to madame's controlling hand. Planting her legs astride as she faced the kneeling victim, madame tugged at the tape: Maritta moaned uncontrollably.

Susie, shivering in her powerful climax, almost swooned as she clamped her thighs to contain and prolong the sweet suffering of her ravishment. She narrowed her eyes and avidly watched the tape tugging at the bound wrists, then sinking into the cleft between the splayed, fleshy buttocks. She could almost feel the bite of the tape between the Finn's tormented slit. Madame twitched the tape once more, dragging it slightly this time from right to left, spreading her captive's wet labia wider apart.

Susie crumpled to the floor, utterly lost for the moment in a spinning vortex of sheer delight. In the eerie silence of her orgasm, despite the pounding of blood as it rushed through her head, Susie heard the shrill cries from the Finn beyond the door. Further squeals of frenzied pleasure brought Susie, lust-drunk and barely able to focus, back to the keyhole. Spellbound, she gazed intently at the bound, leather-gloved hands of the kneeling Finn. Another thin squeal escaped Maritta's lips as the tape tugged, jerking the pinioned hands behind her. Susie was barely able to suppress the animal grunt of satisfaction that came in response to the sight of the leather-sheathed fingers splaying out in an anguished reflex. Susie sank back down, certain in her knowledge that the subjugated strawberry blonde had just that moment climaxed.

Despite its venerable age, The Rookery boasted the benefits of modern plumbing. In her shower, Susie offered up her nakedness to the welcome sluicing of hot water. Buttocks thrust back against the slippery white tiles, Susie stood with her legs apart as the drumming stream raked her upturned face. She shivered deliciously at the thrill of the cascade as it stung her breasts. Feeling for the tablet of soap with groping fingers, and finding it despite the swirling steam, she slowly soaped her shoulders then gently crushed her bosom and belly with her flattened palm. The creamy suds slithered down the valley between her shining breasts. Straining slightly, she thrust upward on tiptoe to receive the warm deluge as she rinsed the suds away, twisting and turning to vanquish the glistening bubbles gathering in the cleft of her soft bottom.

The foam shimmered at her feet, draining away slowly along with her exhaustion after the rigours of several intense orgasms. With her body aching sweetly and her mind a little calmer, Susie stretched out and turned off the water. Gathering a large white towel around her nakedness, Susie scampered back along the corridor, leaving a trail of footprints behind her. Invigorated, she towelled herself roughly in the intimacy of her bedroom.

Normally, Susie would have taken time and pleasure in this process of tenderly dabbing at her bosom with the towel, then lingering down at her pubis. But not this morning, which was almost reaching noon. She was resolute in her determination to confront madame. Diplomatically, of course. Susie harboured a fearful respect for the indomitable principal of La Bella Figura. After the events she had just witnessed, her feelings were now tinged with delicious apprehension. But despite these qualms, Susie would brave madame, pack and return to London. On that specific course of action she was determined. The Rookery was not the place for her. Susie suddenly had to ignore the image of the kneeling Finn. No, not the place for her at all, she decided.

46

Her towel-filled fingers strayed at her pubic fringe. Strayed then settled on her warm, pouting labia. She shivered. Again, the memory of Maritta returned to haunt her. Shaking the vivid image of the punishment away, she stiffened her resolve. As she powdered her bottom and thighs, her thoughts turned to madame. What would she tell her? Then, there was the packing to do and she would have to organise a taxi.

Busying herself with plans and preparations for her departure, she did not immediately become aware of the dormant urges, now awoken, stirring luxuriously deep within her. Battle as she might to deny the delights she had witnessed and relished, Susie could not quite extinguish that fierce flame now flickering inside: a flame which cast strange, dancing shadows not unlike the silhouette of the strawberry blonde presenting herself for domination.

Tucking away her wet panties into her holdall, Susie retrieved a fresh pair and, prinking her foot, stepped into them. Pulling them up swiftly, she relished the kiss of crisp cotton against the swell of her taut buttocks and smiled as she thumbed her cleft to ease the tightness of the cotton between her heavy cheeks. Still slightly hot and troubled, she shirked the strictures of a brassière and slipped straight into a fresh silk blouse. Her breasts greeted the cool fabric with twin frissons of joy. Her nipples nuzzled the sheen of silk eagerly as she buttoned down her blouse firmly. On the bed, her orange holdall yawned open, waiting to be packed.

'Miss Pelham-Heys.'

Susie froze guiltily as she heard madame's voice floating up. Blushing slightly at the prospect of the impending interview – Susie hoped that there would not be a scene – she strode through the bedroom dcoor and into the corridor.

'Could you pop along and get Maritta's purse. She has left it behind. Bring it out to the car, would you?' the unseen speaker asked sweetly.

'OK,' Susie called down.

Damn. She slipped up badly there, she chided herself.

How on earth was she supposed to know where the purse was?

'Where – where will I find it?' Susie added quickly, in a tone of polite enquiry.

'Just get it, girl,' came the stern response.

Susie blazed pinkly as she scurried down the staircase. Somehow, she realised, her witnessing of Maritta's discipline and domination session had itself been witnessed. Susie shivered despite her mounting shame, as she returned to the oak doors at which she had knelt not an hour before. Beyond them, all was calm and still. The Finn's purse lay forgotten on a small, mahogany occasional table. Susie picked it up. Padding back across the richly woven carpet, she spotted a small, dark stain. Drawn to it, as though hypnotised, Susie stretched out and dipped her fingertip into the damp spot. Raising the wetness up to her nose, she sniffed and shuddered violently at the tang of another's arousal, and again at the memory of the kneeling, whipped blonde. Susie rubbed her fingertip against her thigh, pausing as it struck her that Maritta had climaxed in bondage formed by the very tape with which she had been so expertly lashed.

The Rookery had a massive front door and Susie had to struggle slightly with its stubborn weight. Out in the sunshine, she shivered as she realised that she was still briefly dressed in her scant panties and thin blouse. Maritta's car was parked a few yards away on the driveway of loose chippings. Susie tested the gravel timorously with her foot. Her naked legs atremble, she skipped back on to the large stone doorstep. The engine purred, pulsed effortlessly and in seconds, the trim little car had scrunched to a stop mere inches away. Susie, smiling shyly, bent down and offered the purse to its owner. Colourless eyes scrutinised Susie closely as they gazed up at her through the tinted glass. The window slid down. The watching eyes widened and a slow smile spread across the Finn's generous mouth.

'Thank you,' she murmured, stretching out a gloved hand.

Susie's fingers brushed against the damp, leather-gloved palm as she deposited the purse. Maritta's stained fingers enfolded the purse, grasping it tightly. The glimpse of leather punishing leather made Susie swallow thickly, her mouth hot and dry. She was acutely aware of the leather-sheathed fingers and remembered how they had stretched apart the ravished buttocks so that the whipped one could intimately examine and peruse her own whipping.

'Thank you,' repeated Maritta, dropping the purse into her lap, and reaching out her empty hand once more she patted Susie's affectionately.

Susie gulped and smiled awkwardly, shivering slightly as the brief touch of the moist leather against her flesh detonated memories once more in her brain. Turning back into the house, she suddenly paused in the doorway and glimpsed over her right shoulder. Maritta's colourless eyes had narrowed into fierce slits, and seemed to be devouring the full cheeks of Susie's retreating pantied bottom. A single fingertip teased the Finn's thick, lower lip. Susie felt as though some unseen hand had cracked an egg inside her belly; she felt the yolk slip-slither down along her inner-most flesh. She must get away back to London. At once. Even before the damp lemon glove had guided the key into the ignition, Susie had dashed upstairs to her bedroom. She must pack, speak with madame, and go.

'Packing?' the voice enquired from the doorway.

Susie spun around, startled by the sudden appearance of Madame Seraphim Savage. Angered by the intrusion, Susie frowned. Really, this woman was impossible. Didn't she even observe the common courtesy of privacy.

'I see you found the purse,' madame observed drily, cutting across Susie's resentment and, in those few, crisp words, affirming her dominance by reducing Susie to a sullen blush.

'I –' Susie began hesitantly, 'I was thinking of going. Back –' she gestured to the packing in progress on her bed '– to London.'

Madame remained impassive in the doorway.

'I'm going back to London,' Susie declared. 'It seems,' she continued hastily, trying to avoid madame's stern gaze, 'that there'll be no scandal and La Bella Figura won't be in *Society Spy* or any of the tabloids.'

'Silence, girl,' intervened madame curtly.

'But madame,' Susie wailed in mounting protest. 'There's no need for me to stay. I want to go.'

'A rope of pearls, did you say?' madame asked, turning her head into the corridor and ignoring Susie completely.

'That is correct,' replied the voice of Maritta.

Susie, burning under madame's dismissive gesture, stamped her foot and turned towards her bed.

'The girl was packing. Actually packing. I believe we've caught her red-handed,' madame continued, talking over her shoulder to the unseen Finn.

More stripes for that poor little domestic, I shouldn't wonder, Susie thought to herself as she zipped up her holdall. A rope of pearls, her brain computed, and she had been caught red-handed. What a silly girl. Heavens, how she would be punished. Thank goodness I'm getting out of here.

'I'll check the bag,' madame declared.

That's it, Susie shrugged. The domestic's fate was sealed.

'Better come on in. I may need you as a witness.'

'I'm coming,' Maritta murmured.

A chill finger of fear traced the full length of Susie's dimpled spine. Her pulse quickened as her brain decoded the events unfolding around her. They were both coming into her bedroom. Not the domestic's. Hers. Turning, her face pale, she saw Maritta who was just entering the bedroom. The Finn paused and placed a stained fingertip against the door frame. Susie stepped back in alarm.

'Packing. Our little bird was just about to fly. A sure sign of guilt. In here, I think,' madame grunted, pulling Susie's holdall up from the bed and unzipping it briskly.

'No. I didn't –' Susie cried.

'Silence,' thundered madame.

Susie watched in fascinated horror as a closed fist was inserted into her holdall only to emerge, open-palmed, bearing a small rope of pearls.

'That's not fair,' Susie shouted hotly, tossing her mane of dark hair defiantly. 'I didn't touch them.'

'I told you to be silent, wretched girl. Kneel. Down on your knees this instant.'

Stunned by the majesty of the command, Susie sank down on to her trembling knees before the dominant woman.

'Twelve months, would you say, hm?' madame asked Maritta.

'Oh, yes, at least,' Maritta said. 'The bench in these parts deals very severely with theft.'

'I'm so very glad to hear it,' madame muttered with a nod.

'Very severely,' echoed the Finn.

Susie's head swam. It was a shameful ruse. The net was tightening around her; she sensed the knots of her doom beginning to bite. The victim – and convenient witness to this supposed crime – had married, Susie remembered, into the county set. It would go hard for her in court. Very hard.

'We could, if we chose so to do, settle this matter here and now. Just between the three of us. Justice must be done, and felt to have been done,' Madame Seraphim Savage observed in a cool tone. 'Are you agreeable, Maritta?'

'Perfectly, provided the punishment is harsh.'

Punishment: the word exploded softly inside Susie's brain. Burning under the enormity of the monstrous injustice, she had been blind to this impending possibility. The possibility of punishment, here and now. A punishment the Finn would find agreeable, provided it was harsh. Harsh: Susie's buttocks clenched anxiously. Surely not. They wouldn't dare, would they?

'So be it. And of course the girl will stay on here at The Rookery for a spell. She will, I believe, benefit from the experience.'

Susie, hating being spoken of in the third person as if she were a child, flashed the principal of La Bella Figura a sullen glance.

'Stay on?' asked Maritta doubtfully. 'Does she –' the Finn paused. 'Does she meet the requirements, do you think?'

51

'Oh, yes. Miss Pelham-Heys understands very well what our little enterprise here is all about,' madame replied, quickly fishing out Susie's damp panties from the bottom of the holdall and spreading her strong fingers wide within them. 'And not only does she know, but she approves. Look,' she continued, holding the wet knickers aloft. 'She was spying on us this morning.'

'I see.' Maritta nodded with the ghost of a smile. 'So we will punish her and then put her to work.'

'Exactly. Girl,' madame barked harshly, sitting down on the edge of the bed, 'come here. Across my knee at once.'

'But I didn't –' Susie wailed, reluctantly rising from her knees.

Despite her outrage at the ruse, the promise of chastisement kindled an ambiguous flame within her. As she approached madame, who sat poised on the bed, the flame flickered and tongued the inner walls of her belly.

'Bend over.'

Obedient to the curt instruction, Susie eased herself down over the warm, waiting thighs. The principal had drawn up her skirt, revealing shapely legs which were bewitchingly sheathed in honey-bronzed nylon stockings, the dark tops of which were dragged by the bite of white suspenders. Susie's bloused bosom brushed the sheer nylons fleetingly as she draped herself across the lap of her stern chastiser. Her bosom squashed into the warm flesh below as madame's controlling hand grasped the nape of her neck, pinning her down firmly.

'Take her panties down, will you. I believe that this should be a bare-bottomed spanking.'

Maritta obliged. Susie, blushing and squirming, shivered as she felt the damp gloves peeling down the soft cotton, leaving it in a restricting band where the sweep of her supine thighs melted into the swell of her buttocks.

'Hold her. Hold her fast. We must make this, our first punishment, a memorable one.'

First? Was there to be more? Susie squeezed her legs and thighs together, offering up her bare cheeks. Her anger became a fearful dread as she felt Maritta encircling her clamped thighs with a surprisingly firm arm. But that dread was blushed with both curiosity and expectation as she felt the kneeling Finn press her face close against her quivering flesh.

'She is prepared,' whispered the strawberry blonde in a tone of husky excitement.

'Not quite,' murmured madame, her control over her voice as supreme as her control over Susie's naked bottom across her knee. Sweeping her palm up across Susie's poised cheeks, she removed the flap of the blouse, revealing each tremulous buttock to her stern gaze. 'I have something to say to this young lady before I spank her bottom hard.'

The palm hovered above the bare cheeks for a moment then settled down across them. Susie hissed as the cupping hand squeezed the outer buttock. Returning her hand, palm down, across the swell of the ripe rump, madame smoothed the flesh with rhythmical circles. Susie twisted slightly across the stockinged thighs of her punisher but the hand at her exposed nape tightened, as did Maritta's controlling grip. She was trapped, bare-bottomed and pinioned. Spread helplessly across madame's lap, Susie realised that she was prepared and positioned for her imminent punishment.

'It was the contents of your note-books and of course your choice of subject specialism back at La Bella Figura that betrayed your secret desires, Susie. Both clearly indicated your intense interest in the female bottom. The buttocks.' The principal was almost whispering her words. 'And you were never more attentive than when gazing at naked cheeks. The swell of their flesh exercised a strong fascination. Am I not right?'

Susie remained silent.

'Am I not right?' The hand that cupped the flesh now squeezed it harshly. 'Mm?'

'Yes,' mumbled Susie, hating yet loving having her innermost thoughts being forced out this way.

'There is a dormant desire in you, girl, that I recognised. Having spotted it, I decided to act. It is, shall we say, a sleeping sensuality that I propose to stir. Your spell of servitude here at The Rookery will provide you with the best apprenticeship a girl such as you could possibly wish for. Submit to me, absolutely, and I will teach you much, show you plenty. You will,' madame said, palming Susie's bare bottom more urgently now, 'have much to contribute. But before you can demonstrate your skills, you must be prepared to learn. We will consider this to be your first lesson.'

Smack, smack. Susie's bottom bounced beneath the firm spanking hand. Squealing softly, she closed her eyes. Wriggle as she did, there was no escape. Spank: the measured crack of flattened palm across rounded cheeks echoed sharply. The strong hand swept down again and again, scalding the wobbling globes. Susie drummed her feet in protest but Maritta's grip was sure. A deep blush spread across the rubbery flesh of her upturned buttocks. Ablaze under the strict discipline, they were glowing hot and red. Spank: Susie clenched her cheeks, squeezing them tightly together.

'Relax your cheeks,' instructed madame. 'Do not clench them.'

Susie whimpered softly but obeyed. The punisher felt the body across her thighs slacken as the punished relaxed the tension in her hot buttocks.

'That is much better,' madame whispered, imperiously tapping the cheeks as they softened.

'Please, madame –' Susie moaned.

Spank, spank, spank. The severe triple onslaught silenced Susie, who buried her face into madame's glistening nylons.

'The female bottom is such a beautiful artefact of nature, Susie,' madame sighed, a thickening note treacling into her voice. 'A most beautiful thing. It is so soft, so ripe, so splendidly curved. The hand that cups and weighs its heaviness –' madame matched her words with appropriate actions '– finds such delight. Thus. My hand on your bottom, Susie. Feel how my cupped palm fits your rounded cheeks. And fits so perfectly. It is quite clear to me that bottoms were fashioned for pleasure,' madame sighed. Spank, spank: her hand flew down sharply, twice. 'And pain.'

Susie could feel the firm palm rubbing dominantly across the swell of her punished cheeks. The tense rigour of her arched body eased slightly as she slumped down across her strict chastiser's thighs. Once more, Susie secretly delighted in nestling her tummy down into the hot nylon stockings. She sighed deeply as the dark desire within her boldly asserted itself: this was what she truly wanted. It was what she had wanted from her first days at La Bella Figura all those months ago. This was what she had wanted but had dared not name. To be pinned down and punished by the stern principal. To be given a bare-bottomed spanking as she lay pinned and helpless across the honey-bronzed stockings. Yes. At long last, her desire was being fulfilled.

'You will come to see and understand,' madame encouraged. 'I am always right.'

'Yes. Madame is always right,' echoed Maritta, mumbling the words dreamily into Susie's thigh, her warm lips pressed firmly into the captive flesh.

The principal smiled slowly. Clearly her student was already learning. Suffering a little, but learning a lot. Her smile widened as once again she felt Susie ease her hips upward, inching her spanked bottom up for more.

Once again the harsh rain of pain drummed down across the upthrust cheeks – cheeks so deliciously curved, so delightfully reddened.

'In a little while, Maritta will inspect your punished bottom to ensure that sufficient discipline has been dispensed. She has a certain expertise in these matters,' madame said, exploring the warmth of the cleft between Susie's hot cheeks. Her inquisitive thumb paused at the anal whorl.

A bead of sticky pleasure glistened on madame's nylon stockings as Susie's labia unfurled. They kissed the nylons submissively as the intimate threat of Maritta's damp, gloved fingertips prising apart her reddened cheeks approached. The thumb in her cleft probed searchingly, dominantly. Susie swallowed silently and accepted madame's utter ownership of her bottom.

'You make a willing pupil, Susie. I am so glad my judgement is still sound.'

Later, Maritta would examine Susie's bottom intimately. The damp gloves would be busy at her passive buttocks. Later, Susie trembled apprehensively, would come the moment of her utter surrender to the Finn.

Susie moaned softly. Now, in the eternal moment, there was only the dreadful pleasure of her delicious pain. Madame Seraphim Savage's hovering hand swept down again and again and again.

Three

In madame's office, Susie sat and squirmed in the hard chair of her school desk. Dressed in a white vest and tight-fitting shorts, she felt next to naked. The uniform had been prescribed by madame after the spanking Susie had suffered, and Susie connected it with her ignominy and shame. The cotton vest stretched across the proud thrust of her braless breasts to reveal rather than conceal their heavy splendour. The tight shorts were cut high at her thighs, and she considered them little more than panties.

'We will continue with that lesson you seemed to enjoy so much at La Bella Figura, my girl. Bottoms.'

Susie looked up. Her training for work in madame's establishment was about to begin in earnest.

'I will name the bottom type, and you will tell me both the description and the most suitable form of punishment it requires. Cane, strap or spanking hand.'

Susie nodded and took a deep breath. She hoped she could remember her earlier lesson. Svetlana had been such a distraction, and so much had happened since that fateful Friday afternoon.

'Pear-shaped,' madame murmured.

'Mellow,' replied Susie immediately, 'with a narrow waist and a rounded bottom. The full buttocks are very generously fleshed.'

'And for punishment?' madame continued.

'Spanking. And the paddle,' Susie answered.

'Well done, girl. Hour-glass?'

Susie promptly defined the hour-glass type as being shapely, with trim, slightly heavy cheeks. She commended the cane.

'Boyish?'

'Trim,' responded Susie without hesitation, vividly remembering the slides on the huge wide screen. Relaxing a little, her confidence grew as she warmed to her task. 'Slightly flattened cheeks with subtle contours. And with minimum tapering at the waist. Hairbrush and slipper.'

'Good. I am so glad you are taking your studies so seriously. I am reluctant but not unwilling to resort to certain measures with the lazy and the dull.'

Susie gripped the edge of her desk at these words, imagining full well exactly what those certain measures would mean for her bare bottom. She had answered three questions so far. Not bad, so far, but too soon to celebrate. Susie knew that she was not even half way through her rigorous grilling: there was still time for her to slip up and pay the painful price.

'Athletic?'

'Sleek. A sleek bottom which is softly muscular with a rubbery, fleshy feel to the cheeks.'

'And?'

'And well-defined contours,' Susie added. Quickly remembering the punishment, Susie said that she would use both the strap and the paddle.

'Would you?' madame replied, smiling indulgently at the eager tone of her student.

Susie blushed.

'Very well, girl. Let us continue. Supple?'

Supple? Susie frowned. She recognised the word, but it did not fit into the catechism. Of course: madame had cunningly switched track. Supple was the keynote, not the term.

'Supple is the keynote of the bottom-type known as slender,' Susie said slowly, anxious not to appear too confident. 'The features are a slim waist, narrow hips and slender thighs. Best punished,' Susie said, reflecting judiciously for a moment on the matter, 'with either the cane or the crop.'

'Excellent. You are going to give great satisfaction to my clients once you have been fully trained, my girl. Peach?'

The peach bottom-type, Susie's favourite, could best be dealt with by the spanking hand. Susie spoke at some length when giving her answer, dwelling in detail on the ripeness of the cheeks, and on their pert, slightly swollen quality. She did not overlook the fleshy hips or the fully contoured thighs. An utterly feminine bottom-type, and spanking, Susie repeated gravely, was the most fitting pleasure and punishment for such penitent peaches.

'And finally,' madame almost whispered as she approached Susie's desk.

Susie swallowed.

'Stand up, girl. Come here.'

Susie meekly obeyed.

'Turn around. No, right around.'

Susie turned, presenting her bottom to madame.

'Look. Over your shoulder into the mirror.'

The principal thumbed down Susie's white shorts. They slid over the swell of her rump, offering little resistance. Holding a small looking-glass close to the exposed bottom, she ordered her pupil to study the naked flesh which filled the glass with its reflection. Peering over her shoulder, Susie gazed down at her rounded buttocks, still pink from her earlier spanking.

'Apple-shaped,' intoned madame.

'Apple-shaped,' echoed Susie, her voice thickening. 'The keynote is rounded and they are firmly fleshed. Much tighter than –'

'The peach. They are perfect specimens of female pulchritude, having the allure of distinctively seductive cheeks,' madame intervened in a husky tone. 'For the peach-buttocked female's discipline and delight, I recommend spanking, and the cane. Do you agree, girl?'

'Yes,' murmured Susie, clenching her bottom.

'Speak up,' madame said crisply.

'Yes,' Susie replied clearly.

'Are your buttocks apple-shaped, girl?'

Gazing down at her reflection in the mirror, Susie nodded.

'Then your punishment must be –?'

'A spanking and then the cane.'

'I'm so glad you agree,' madame said softly, tapping Susie's bare bottom with the cold glass of the hand-held mirror. 'So glad.'

After coffee the following morning, just as a small clock in a walnut casement struck eleven in Cambridge chimes, Susie received her first client. Susie immediately dubbed the petite brunette the Sultan's Favourite as she watched the dark-eyed beauty in her late twenties slink towards her. They were not in the large room where madame had whipped the Finn, but in a smaller, more intimate fitting room lined on three walls with full-length mirrors. As her client undressed slowly – every graceful movement of the approach to her ultimate nakedness being sinuous and seductive – Susie inspected her closely. She was not exactly tall, but had lithe, supple legs, a gorgeous bottom and brooding, almond eyes. Yes, Susie thought, she was indeed the Sultan's Favourite. Her body held the secrets of both giving and receiving many dark pleasures, many fierce delights. When her client demanded to examine some stockings, Susie's mouth dried and her tongue thickened. As she slid her fingers along the cool nylons and teased them out of their tissue wrapping, Susie felt her nipples stiffen. Presenting an array of seamed, glistening nylons to the waiting nude, Susie was surprised at the curt command which greeted her attentiveness.

'Dress me, girl.'

Susie bent down, blushing slightly at the rudeness of this petulant beauty. The sharp order from the sulky, wide mouth had come as a shock: Susie had expected meekness and compliance, a certain submissiveness. After all, Susie reasoned, soon I will be caning this young woman's bare bottom.

'Hurry up,' snapped the nude, stamping her foot impatiently.

Bending to her task, Susie eased the rolled up seamed stocking over her client's prinked foot and gently palmed it up the length of the smooth, shapely leg. Fingering the band of darker nylon into place at the top of the naked thigh, Susie looked up.

'Now the other one,' was all the almond-eyed woman said.

Susie obeyed, quickly sheathing the flesh of the second leg in the whispering rustle of nylon.

'Are the seams straight?' the crisply stockinged nude rasped ungraciously, swivelling her bare bottom.

'Yes,' whispered Susie, spellbound. 'These are self-support. Suspenders are optional.' As she spoke, Susie checked the straightness of both seams, absently running her fingertip up along the back of each leg from the ankle to just below the swell of the buttocks above.

'I know, I'm not completely stupid. I'll try those black mesh ones next.'

Gently peeling down the stockings, Susie's eyes devoured the bare bottom before her. How she was going to thoroughly enjoy striping this rude bitch's bare buttocks. The Sultan's Favourite. Susie smiled darkly. There'd been a rebellion in the seraglio and little Miss Almond-eyes here was about to pay the full penalty. It would be a slow caning, Susie suddenly decided. A slow, measured, deliberate administration of bamboo punishment.

'Hurry up, girl. Don't daydream.'

The curt admonishment broke into Susie's reflections, spurring her on. She quickly and deftly replaced the seamed, honey-hued nylons with a pair of black mesh stockings. Their seams were ribbed and thicker, giving a tarty look to the superb legs before her.

'These require suspenders,' Susie explained.

'Just hold them up in place while I look,' the brunette snapped.

Susie inserted a thumb under each black stocking top and cupped the naked cheeks above with her hands in order to hold the stockings up. Her client studied the effect in all three of the full-length mirrors.

'Hmm,' came her non-committal reply.

'We have some new opaque tights in from Italy,' Susie suggested. 'Red?'

'Blue,' replied the near-naked woman.

Susie offered the blue tights and stood back as her client abandoned the black mesh pair and stepped into the blue, her breasts bulging as she stooped. The sheer tights were high-waisted, the band of darker blue coming to rest well above the plump swell of the hips. As the brunette turned on tiptoe to examine herself, Susie's eyes drank in the heavy buttocks tightly sheathed in the opaque blue. Her heart fluttered and her pulse raced as she studied the effect of the light above glistening across the swell of the cheeks.

'I'll take four pairs of these. Panties – I only wear silk. Let me see what you have in ivory.'

Fitting on the panties was an act of utter intimacy, bringing Susie's breasts into repeated contact with the brunette's warm nakedness as she eased the panties into place. Susie paused to consider the fit, judged it perfect and fingered the fabric to prevent it from biting too severely into the deep cleft.

'A bit too tight,' snapped the ungracious woman.

Suppressing an impatient sigh, Susie tugged at the silk, gently dragging the stretchy panties over the heavy bottom. Pretending to select another pair, but actually using the same panties, Susie resheathed the bare bottom in silk.

'I thought so. Much better.'

Susie, emboldened by the thought that very soon she would have this bitch bending, bare-buttocked, before her cane, casually thumbed the pubis behind the taut silk, then tidied away a wisp of stray pubic hair.

'Much better,' muttered her client. 'Six pairs; put them on my account.'

Susie nodded and jotted the order down. Returning to her client, she cupped the pantied buttocks firmly, sensing the contours of the hips and thighs. The Sultan's Favourite was, Susie decided, shapely. The buttocks were hour-glass, which meant the cane. Susie recalled madame's vigorous nod of assent when Susie had suggested that the most fitting instrument for administering pleasure-punishment was the cane.

Susie moistened her lips before speaking. 'Do you need a bra?' she enquired.

Her client's brunette curls tossed as the impatient young woman studied her naked bosom in the glass before her. Susie, standing behind, appraised the proud breasts in all three mirrors. Moments later, her labia itched and scalded and then her panties grew damp.

'Not today. I've finished buying. I'll just have the other services now.'

The words caused the wet patch in Susie's panties to spread. The other services. The moment was rapidly approaching when power would change hands. Any minute now, Susie would have this almond-eyed nude at her complete mercy. And after the rudeness she had experienced, Susie was not feeling the least bit merciful. The caning, she decided firmly, was going to be severely administered.

'Ah, finished your purchasing?' madame asked as she entered, fingering the length of the long, yellow cane she carried.

Susie flushed violently with excited anticipation and wiped her moist palms against the taut cotton of her pantied bottom. Her fingers itched to grasp and ply the sliver of wood.

'You are in very capable hands,' madame said in a velvet voice as she placed the cane against the glass of a full-length mirror.

Susie beamed with pride. A compliment from madame was a compliment indeed. Would madame stay to watch her dispense the stokes, Susie wondered. It would be so thrilling to cane her first client – cane her crisply across her bare bottom – with the principal of La Bella Figura in attendance. Susie's fingers stole down to ease the wet cotton clinging to her excited pussy.

'Bend over, girl,' ordered madame briskly, a sterner note in her voice. 'Twelve strokes.'

Girl? Susie grinned briefly. The Sultan's Favourite, despite her seductive beauty and bewitching allure, was in her early prime perhaps but was by no means a girl. Susie's grin froze then disappeared as alarm clouded her mind. Her client was picking up the cane: picking it up and thrumming it as if to test its whippiness. Judging it to be satisfactory, she slid the tip of her index finger along its wicked yellow length, turning the gaze from her almond eyes from the wood to Susie.

'Bend over, girl,' she echoed.

'Twelve strokes, we agreed. I'll enter it into your account, my dear,' madame said as she turned to depart.

Susie's head swam as the terrible truth became fully apparent. The fitting and purchasing session was over. It was now time for the client's special services: a caning. But unlike Maritta, the strawberry blonde Finn, this client had a taste for giving, not receiving, punishment.

'Hurry up,' prompted the brunette.

Susie tugged at the hem of her vest.

'Leave your panties alone until I tell you otherwise. Now bend over. Right over. Touch your toes. Give me your bottom, girl. I want it up. Now.'

Adopting the punishment position in fearful expectation, Susie presented her beautiful bottom, now bulging within the thin protection afforded by her cotton panties, up for the cane.

'Twelve strokes,' the brunette whispered. 'There is a reason for that precise number of strokes,' she continued, tracing the tip of the quivering bamboo along the swell of the upturned buttocks. 'I have just completed a little poem. It is a poem I am quite pleased with. I would value your opinion, so please pay close attention. It is written, you may be interested to know, in rhyming couplets. Panties down to your knees, girl.'

Slightly bewildered by her client's unexpected references to poetry, Susie's confusion sobered up instantly at the closing words of instruction. She dragged her panties down obediently, leaving the elastic waistband to bind her knees tightly together. The effect was to render her bare cheeks rounder – a more tempting target for the slicing cane strokes to come.

Swish, thrum. Susie flinched, but the brunette was merely testing the wood once more for suppleness. The eerie song of the bamboo made Susie shiver with delicious dread.

'I'm thinking of calling it "Ode to Obedience". Feet together, girl. No, closer. And keep touching your toes.'

Susie strove to fulfill these pre-punishment requirements. The triple tap of the cane's tip on her left buttock served to remind her of her subjugated role and of the powerful dominance of the beautiful brunette who was about to whip her naked bottom. Despite the promise of impending pain, the probability of pleasure excited Susie: her nipples stiffened and peaked; she ached to crush them within her palms.

'Head down.'

Susie meekly lowered her head, adopting the supreme posture of submission.

'The crop, the belt, the whippy cane –'

Swish: the first stroke stung sharply. The caning had commenced.

'Across bare cheeks spell out sweet pain –'

Swish: the second lashed Susie's bottom lovingly.

'Above pale trembling orbs they reign –'

Swish: again, the cruel wood sang.

'To slice and stripe, again, again –'

Swish: the fourth stroke bit deeply into her flesh, the kiss of the cane leaving a fourth pink line of fire. Susie's fingers splayed out at her toes, then taloned in an anguished spasm. Around her knees, the restricting panties bound her trembling legs together, leaving her utterly passive and immobile. Out of the corner of her eye, she saw her tormentress approach a full-length wall-mirror. Stepping up to it, the brunette thrust her breasts, belly and thighs into their own reflection. Susie's eyes widened with wonder as she saw the bottom of her stern chastiser sway and shudder as the pubis in front was ground against the cold glass. Moments later, returning to Susie, the caner tapped the proffered buttocks with the tip of the hovering cane.

'Kneel for the next four strokes. Head down, bottom up.'

Susie sank down to her knees, then pressed her forehead down into the carpet. As she thrust her striped rump upward, she felt the cane tracing the swell of her stinging flesh.

'With tight white panties peeled and stripped,
Bare bottom up and belly dipped,
Velvet peaches are keenly whipped
'Til nectar sweet is slowly dripped.'

The brunette intoned the second verse of her 'Ode to Obedience', whipping the cane down across Susie's up-turned cheeks as each line approached its ending rhyme. The bamboo whistled down across the suffering buttocks to punctuate viciously the Sapphic poem, leaving the kneeling girl's naked flesh on fire. Once more, Susie eyed the feet of her punisher pace towards the full-length mirror. Once more, she saw the feet arch up onto tiptoe as her tormentress pressed her pubis against the glass. Gyrating her hips slowly and moaning softly, her warm breath clouded the glass at her lips.

Susie shivered with delight. Although her bare cheeks stung it was a sweet pain. And she ached to finger herself, so hot and sticky had she become. Squeezing her thighs together, she half-dreaded, half-longed for her concluding stripes. The cane with which she was being punished was of a light, springy quality: probably Indonesian bamboo she thought, not Malayan. It was ideal for the task of striping female flesh. She made a vow to secure such a cane for herself. It was so supple, so responsive. It loved the bottom it lashed, adoring the buttocks it blistered.

'Face down, girl. I want you stretched out full length on the carpet.'

Susie gulped as she complied instantly with her stern chastiser's command. Wriggling and squirming, she both loved and loathed the panties that still bound her legs together tightly at her knees. She sensed rather than saw the cane-bearing brunette approaching from behind. Suddenly she felt the length of cool bamboo easing down along her cleft. A little pressure from the hand that controlled the cane forced the wood down between Susie's hot cheeks. Her punisher knelt directly behind her and Susie scrunched her toes up as they fleetingly touched the knees of the Sultan's Favourite. Pressing the cane down firmly into the punished girl's cleft, the punisher tamed and utterly

66

dominated her trembling victim. Susie rocked gently from hip to hip, inching her cheeks apart to accept the tormenting presence of the length of bamboo, surreptitiously pleasuring her pubis against the rough carpet. Her labial lips and inner thighs glistened with oozing lust-juice. Gripping the carpet with her fingers, Susie tried to drag her tiny, erect clitoris against the carpet but the brunette denied her this ultimate delight by raising the cane aloft.

'Bottom up, girl.'

Reluctantly, Susie obeyed, peeling her breasts, belly and below away from their secret pleasures. The caner knelt down at right angles to the bare bottom she was about to resume striping.

'Then down on bended knee to praise,
The tearful whipped one homage pays
Her mistress from the bamboo maze:
Stern one who makes soft buttocks blaze.'

As with the second verse, so with the third: Susie received a crisp cut of the cane across her naked bottom with each of the concluding four lines which brought the 'Ode to Obedience' to a close. Dropping the cane, the Sultan's Favourite leapt up and fell upon the mirror, dragging her belly and upper thighs across it several times before pounding her pubis into the glass. Susie, fingering her scalded cheeks with delight, pressed her face down into the carpet, then stole a glance up at her punisher just as the brunette grunted and came. Susie moaned softly and sought the same pleasure: her scrabbling fingers worried the hot sticky flesh below her belly, and a flash of raw delight signalled their success.

'What do you think of my little poem? My "Ode to Obedience"?'

Susie paused in the act of self-pleasurement and twisted her face around. Looking up, she saw the brunette leaning with her legs apart, her bottom squashed up against the mirror.

'Well?'

'It is a very beautiful poem,' Susie murmured.

'Do you like the last verse?'

'Yes. Yes, I do. It is so – truthful,' Susie whispered softly.

'Then come here and prove it,' challenged the brunette, tossing her curls back in a cascade into the glass behind her.

Susie rose to her knees then shuffled across the carpet towards the splayed thighs of her punisher and the wet pubic curls between them. Closing in on her dominatrix, Susie encircled the brunette's buttocks with her arms and buried her face into the wet, tempting pussy.

'Then down on bended knee in praise,
The tearful whipped one homage pays –'

The Sultan's Favourite moaned, her voice trembling slightly as she felt Susie's lips upon her labia.

'Her mistress from the bamboo maze –' hissed the caner as she felt the caned girl's tongue probe her hot slit.

'Stern one who makes soft buttocks blaze.'

The brunette repeated the verse, then clasped Susie's hair fiercely and held the kneeling girl against her splayed thighs. Susie was instructed to repeat the third verse, which she managed to do from memory, mouthing each word into the sweet flesh of the poet's pussy. The brunette gasped and inched herself further onto Susie: Susie's sweet lips sucked hard on the sweeter lips between her chastiser's soft thighs. The Sultan's Favourite whispered the words of the first verse intensely, but stifled by her surging climax, her voice faded and died, drowned out by the fierce lapping down below.

'Ooh, that's a sore bottom.'

Susie peered over her shoulder into the cheval-mirror. In the glass she saw her rounded cheeks bearing the stripes of her recent twelve strokes. Kneeling at her thigh was Annette, the domestic who had let supper spoil on the night of Susie's arrival at The Rookery.

'Never mind about the uniform now. Come.'

Susie felt Annette's hand slip into her own. The domestic, who was also completely naked, led Susie to the bed.

'Face down. I'll soothe your stripes,' she said softly.

68

Susie obeyed, luxuriating in the cool silk eiderdown into which she pressed her breasts and thighs. Seconds later, she felt the other girl's tongue flicker across the hot flesh of her punished bottom. Grasping the eiderdown, Susie dipped her tummy and eased her buttocks up for more of the healing treatment. Annette's wet tongue-tip lapped at the reddening cheeks, then slowly and deliberately traced each of the horizontal cane stripes that burned on the creamy hillocks. Susie squealed with sheer delight as each of her twelve stripes was soothed. Squirming with pleasure, Susie immediately felt the firm, steadying hands of her comforter frame and still her bottom. First Susie felt Annette's warm breath on her rump, then came the gentle brush of parted lips. Soft kisses followed, at which Susie moaned sweetly into the eiderdown, submitting and surrendering her bottom to the aftercare completely.

'Did you have the poet?'

'Mm,' Susie replied.

'I've had to service her twice,' Annette continued, mumbling her words into Susie's bottom. 'She gave me "Kiss the Rod" and all six bloody verses of "Disciples of Discipline".'

Susie giggled.

'But she's one of madame's best clients. No, stay still. I'll get the cold cream.'

Susie waited expectantly on the bed as Annette scampered across to a small dressing table and returned with a porcelain pot. Moments later, the domestic's fingertips, glistening with blobs of cold cream, were caressing Susie's left buttock. The caned girl sighed with delight as the fierce heat of her stripes was cooled beneath the circular sweeps of the healing touch. The right buttock, which had been nearer to the caner and so had suffered more, was dealt with differently.

'Roll over onto you side, Susie,' Annette whispered. 'Right knee up to your tummy.'

Susie did as she was told, offering up her rounded right buttock to Annette. The domestic daubed the cheek with a smear of cold cream and, cupping her hand slightly, applied her palm to the punished flesh. Susie gasped as she felt the tender touch of another's skin in such intimate contact with her own. As she lay in blissful repose, she listened to Annette's account of how she had been lured to The Rookery. Susie heard that Annette's family had caught a financial cold recently. A cheque for her fees at La Bella Figura had subsequently bounced. To avoid the inevitable shame, madame had suggested that Annette should come down to The Rookery and enter her employ. Susie smiled to herself at the cunning of the principal and recounted to Annette how she too had been duped. Annette's palming of the punished flesh slowed imperceptibly; Susie squirmed on the bed and eased her cheek back into the cupped hand, signalling her desire for more. Annette sensed the gesture and obliged.

'I – I hated it at first,' Annette confessed huskily. 'But now –'

'Now?'

'I'd hate to leave,' she said frankly.

Susie closed her eyes and thought hard. Did she hate it down here at The Rookery? Or would she too hate to have to leave?

'Better?' murmured Annette, pausing in her act of aftercare.

'Lovely,' sighed Susie, rolling over onto her tummy and unselfconsciously parting her legs a little.

'Good.'

Annette's index finger gently alighted down into the top of Susie's cleft at the base of her spine and traced the velvety flesh between the passive cheeks. A spasm of pure pleasure tightened the flesh-domes as Susie responded with a soft squeal. Encouraged and emboldened by the response, the probing finger repeated its intimate journey down between the cheeks of Susie's upturned bottom three more times, the pressure of its touch growing firmer with each deft stroke. On the fourth occasion, Susie held her breath as she felt the fingertip pause over her anal whorl, then gently begin to worry the sensitive flesh of her sphincter.

'The Rookery has taught me so much,' Annette purred as she eased herself alongside Susie's outstretched nakedness. 'So much.'

Susie opened her cheeks to accept the finger, almost hypnotised by its tantalising touch. Prone and passive, she eagerly welcomed it and desired its deeper presence within her.

A shrill bell from a telephone extension on the upstairs landing broke the spell. Annette sighed and eased her finger slowly out. Susie whimpered her disappointment and clenched her cheeks to trap and retain it.

'Later. Tonight, perhaps,' Annette soothed. 'We'd better get on with the fitting or madame will –'

'Punish you both very severely,' barked the principal from the doorway. 'Wicked girls. I sent Susie to you for a fitting, girl. You are both to offer full maid service to my clients later on this afternoon.'

Susie, blushing with shame, scrambled up from her bed of pleasure. How long had madame been standing there, watching and listening? What had she seen? What had she heard? Susie desperately tried to recall what had been said, then reddened as she remembered what had been done.

'Annette, you must teach Susie her duties. These are very special clients, girls. I expect you both to be on your best behaviour. Make sure that your maid's uniform fits perfectly, Susie. Never forget that at all times you are demonstrating the accomplishments of La Bella Figura.'

When madame had swept out of the room, Susie giggled and turned to briefly embrace Annette. They kissed slowly, and the embrace lingered. Annette's hands cupped Susie's rounded cheeks and slowly spread the captive buttocks apart. In response, Susie rose up on tiptoe and squashed her breasts into Annette's firm bosom.

'Later, Susie,' Annette whispered as she peeled herself away from Susie's naked warmth. 'You heard what madame said. We'd better get you ready for your maid service.'

Susie sat on the bed and watched as Annette stepped into a snow-white pair of cotton panties and then eased her heavy breasts into an underwired, half-cupped bra. When

71

Annette stretched to adjust the catch of the bra at her back, Susie's nipples prickled as she saw the swell of the captive bosom bulge. A skimpy suspender belt was soon hugging Annette's waist tightly, then the dark-haired girl was bending to guide her foot into a sheer black stocking. When her second shapely leg was similarly sheathed, Annette's slender fingers snapped the suspenders into the darker bands of both stocking tops, dragging the black nylon up into the milky flesh of her thigh. Pausing, the brunette smoothed the cotton against the sweep of her buttocks with her palms, then fingered her cleft to ease the tightness of the clinging cotton.

These simple, slow gestures triggered a heightened response in Susie. Sitting on the cool eiderdown, her plump cheeks squashed down into its sensual satin, she felt her labia prise apart and caught the sharp whiff of her arousal as it rose up to her nostrils. Her eyes sparkled as she gazed longingly, lovingly at the semi-naked domestic, now bending forward to rummage in a chest of drawers for a blouse. Susie slipped her hand down between her thighs and furtively rubbed at her pussy. Before her, Annette seemed to linger at her task remaining at the chest of drawers, her black-stockinged legs pressed together, her tightly pantied bottom offered up submissively to Susie's unwavering gaze. Susie fingered her wet slit more vigorously as she took in the full splendour of the long legs, the shapely thighs and the pert buttocks, enjoying her secret pleasure all the more because it was furtive and stolen. Then her hand froze as she glimpsed Annette's smiling face gazing back at her from a small mirror on top of the chest of drawers. Who had been controlling and exploiting whom? Susie suddenly felt the thrill of being discovered by Annette, and realised that the balance of erotic power between them was far from being resolved.

'You'll have to wait.' Annette grinned.

'Can't we –' Susie blurted, instantly regretting her display of eagerness.

'You heard what madame said,' Annette replied sternly, enjoying taking the upper hand in matters. Susie squirmed, and looked away. 'Do you want another taste of her discipline so soon?' Annette teased.

'No.'

'Or would you prefer a taste of mine?' taunted Annette.

'Don't know,' Susie said sulkily.

'You mustn't sulk, Susie. You know what happens to young ladies who sulk, don't you? They get spanked on their bare bottoms. Spanked very hard.'

Despite herself, Susie looked up eagerly.

'You'll have to wait for that too,' Annette said gently as she fingered the cup of her bra. 'Come along, let's get you dressed.'

The domestic assisted her newfound friend in the intimate stages of acquiring a second skin of underwear. Annette, two years Susie's senior but with the confidence of both experience and self-knowledge, managed the younger girl deftly and competently. A touch of dominance, which Susie adored, came with the weaving of the suspender belt around Susie's waist. Then, the palms that smoothed the black stockings up towards Susie's trembling thighs felt a little firmer than when soothing her hot bottom earlier.

'Panties not too tight?'

'No,' Susie whispered softly.

Despite her answer, Annette fingered the edge of the panties where they bit into the swell of Susie's proud buttocks, establishing beyond doubt exactly who was in control.

'We are required to wear a silk blouse. Very décolleté and long-sleeved, with four buttons at each cuff.'

The crisp blouses were, as Annette had promised, very low cut. Susie secretly thrilled at her cleavage and paused before the looking-glass. An adventurous shopper who dressed both to tease and to please, she had never managed to achieve an effect quite like this: the pert maid's black skirt and tiny apron rendered her a demure tart. Annette was equally gorgeous in her uniform, and Susie's labia grew sticky and hot as she stole furtive glances at the brunette in her figure-revealing, sensually severe outfit.

'Ready?'

'I'd rather stay here with you,' Susie confessed frankly, 'than go serving tea and cake to some old biddies. Boring.'

Annette, who was checking her stocking seams in a full-length mirror, did not reply immediately. After patting her dark hair beneath the little lace cap which crowned it, she looked back at Susie.

'Oh, I don't think you'll be bored this evening. Don't forget madame's motto down here at The Rookery: the client always comes first.'

High tea was served at the customary time in accordance with the traditions of large country houses. Susie followed Annette into the large drawing room set in the east wing of The Rookery to discover four of madame's clients already seated at the table. Expecting to find powdered and rouged dowagers, afternoon tea not being a vice of the younger set, Susie perked up at the sight of four vivacious women, all in their early thirties and all in sharp, chic attire. One in particular caught Susie's eye: a green-eyed, slightly cat-like brunette with a cruel, red mouth. Susie fleetingly hoped never to play the mouse to this feline specimen.

Following Annette to a serving table and standing smartly to attention in her trim maid's uniform, Susie absently twiddled with her apron until a disapproving glare from the ever-vigilant madame stilled her fingers. Though pleased by the youthful elegance of the clients waiting to be served with high tea, Susie still smarted at this unwelcome task: how much better it would be if she were to attend to the needs of a single customer, preferably one with the needs and desires of Maritta. Maritta, always gloved in leather the same colour as the pale lemon sunlight which played upon the mahogany furniture in the drawing room.

The table was vast and already prepared with sparkling china and silverware. A sudden April shower rattled against the window panes and darkened the room. Madame nodded to Annette who stepped across to the bay windows and drew the heavy curtains just as madame

74

fingered a brass switch and flooded the drawing room with soft light. It was almost as if she was giving the signal for some impending drama to unfold, Susie thought. How like the theatre, only in reverse: for there the lights were dimmed and heavy curtains drawn apart. No drama here, she mused, glancing at the beautiful young women seated decorously at the table. Just high tea and vapid gossip for these bored, pampered creatures.

'You may commence serving our guests with tea,' madame ordered.

Following Annette's example closely, Susie set about the task of presenting the four clients with a choice of delicious savoury treats to eat: scotch woodcock; angels on horseback; egg and cress rolls; finely cut cucumber sandwiches; fingers of golden toast spread with dark relish and buttered muffins bursting with warm crabmeat. She was kept very busy and had to concentrate hard to avoid displeasing the continuous demands of the clients, but busy as she was, Susie could not quite suppress a growing sense of indignation. She was courteous and attentive to every whim but they merely rewarded her efforts with disdain and silence. Between greedy mouthfuls, the foursome gossiped noisily about money, the servant problem, scandal and local intrigue. Pointedly ignoring both Susie and Annette, they discussed the merits of sex toys and the foolishness of modern young girls. Susie was kept on her toes and grew silently furious with their rudeness.

Beside her, Annette appeared to be calm and unflustered as she removed the savoury dishes and brought the first of several delicious cakes to the table. Susie grew hot and cross as she watched the manicured fingers daintily dab at perfectly lipsticked mouths and toss away the soiled napkins which it was her task to retrieve and replace. She was bored and angry, and had to fight the impish impulse to spill hot tea over her obnoxious clients or comment pointedly on their banal chatter.

'I will continue with a reading from the diary of the French ambassador's sister which you all seemed to find so diverting last time,' madame announced to her soirée.

A lull descended upon the tea-table and their idle babbling ceased. Susie placed a rich chocolate cake and a plate of gingerbread fingers down upon the white lawn table-cloth and withdrew to join Annette at the serving table.

'Shall I begin?' madame asked.

Her clients nodded eagerly.

'We left our heroine in the clutches of some very uncivilised pirates, did we not?' madame continued as she approached a desk. She sat down behind it, unlocked a drawer and produced a small volume. Opening up the book, madame began to read sonorously from the yellowing pages within the small, calfskin-bound volume. Susie listened attentively and quickly picked up the thread of the narrative. Madame Lollette, the French ambassador's sister, had been travelling incognito in 1742 when her boat had been captured by Turkish pirates as it passed through the treacherous Bosphorus. Smuggled to the Levant, Madame Lollette was about to be sold into slavery.

'At last I learned what my fate was to be. Fatima, the slave-dealer's daughter, came to me with two handmaidens as dawn broke. After a breakfast of bread, honey, dates and goat's milk, I was taken in fetters to the Pool of Roses in the bordello and there they stripped me quite naked. Foolish giggles greeted my pale skin, the whiteness of my breasts and thighs. They admired the comely shape of my occidental form, the European female buttocks being more slender than their plumper, pomegranate posteriors. Soon, Fatima and her helpers were naked, pressing their soft flanks against me and squealing with pleasure as their dark flesh touched mine. It was not unlike the honey upon which I had breakfasted at dawn contrasting with the goat's milk. I remarked upon this and they liked my conceit well.'

As madame read from the eighteenth-century diary Susie studied the four clients closely. She saw their expensively jewelled fingers, with nails polished scarlet and crimson, grasping the silver cake forks. She saw the rich cake swallowed greedily and the moist, red lips stain the white cups as tea was sipped silently. A tense silence

76

gripped the table as madame continued to read, narrating to her guests how the captive suffered intimate outrages in the Pool of Roses at the impudent hands of Fatima and her handmaidens.

'I was washed so carefully in places I seldom touched myself. Upon a showing of modest resistance, they became stern with me, punishing my hair and breasts until I allowed them utter sovereignty over my helpless nakedness.'

A cake fork slipped from one of the client's hands and bounced on the carpet at her feet. Annette nudged Susie, who was enraptured by madame's reading. Susie glanced at Annette and quickly understood her companion's mimed instruction. She approached the client, bent down and retrieved the errant cake fork. Returning to replace it with a clean one, she caught a glimpse of the client's lap: her skirt was drawn up over her thighs and her panties dragged down to her knees. Excited by the reading, the guest was fingering herself openly and wantonly at the tea-table.

'They took me from the Pool of Roses into a marble-walled antechamber which was windowless but lit by blazing torches and there they dried my wet body with towelling of soft Egyptian cotton. The swansdown touch against my more feminine parts was not, I must confess, entirely displeasing. I waited for them to dress me, hoping at least to be richly attired when facing whatever fate was to befall me but to my annoyance they left me naked and brought me to a couch, or sofa, of gilded cedar and crimson satin. It was, dear reader, what the Abbe of Rheims most surely meant when he wrote of a certain Bed of Sin. Forced down into the crimson satin, I surrendered to the handmaidens who oiled me most methodically and completely in my private and secret parts.'

As madame continued to read – quickly coming to a passage in which the diarist gave a vivid account of how her naked buttocks were whipped with a harsh leather scourge when she tried to resist the intention of oiling her sphincter with essence of attar – the tension at the tea-table was almost tangible. Cake and tea were ignored as the clients sat in the thrall of madame's sibilant tongue. Susie saw the shoeless, stockinged foot of the green-eyed, cat-like brunette stretch out under the table to seek out and find the parted thighs of the woman sitting directly opposite. The nylon-clad toes scratched at the nest of pubic curls before them, then pushed firmly into the wet flesh within. Her mouth dry and her throat tightening, Susie trembled as her own mounting excitement rose hotly at the base of her belly. She surreptitiously inched her hand towards Annette's and found a steadying comfort in the other girl's reassuring grasp.

'Neither my sobs, nor imprecations, nor even the promise of gold would make my cruel tormentors desist. The crack of the harsh whip filled my mind and brought me an unknown pain, which was not entirely without a harsh sweetness, to my naked buttocks. Soon their busy fingers were all about my naked person, touching parts I dare not give name to in these pages, and as if I were some sweetmeat served up at a banquet for a parley of Princes, their mouths – their very tongues – did taste me.'

Grunts broke the brief silence. Susie saw the cat-like brunette glide under the table and place her mouth where her stockinged foot had been moments before. The other couple were locked in a tight embrace, hungrily French kissing. Suddenly, Susie felt Annette's hand cupping her left buttock. Their eyes met and Annette's hand squeezed the firm cheek lingeringly.

'It was not as I thought it would be. The slave-owner showed his captives like the goldsmith shows his much prized wares to merchants from Persia. It was a private viewing, and the buyers were brought to me upon the hour throughout the hot day. I was displayed in my nakedness upon the couch of crimson, with only a chain of filigree silver that bound my wrists together. The slave-owner encouraged the prospective purchasers of flesh to examine me closely and they did so as if inspecting an Arab steed, counting my teeth and stroking my hair and judging each and every attribute of my naked femininity. Fatima was in attendance, though heavily veiled, and was quick to ply her rod of bullaca, the name given hereabouts to the plum-tree, with which she striped my buttocks most freely when I refused the buyers access to my person. Rough hands grasped my bosoms and gross fingers probed my mouth and more secret orifices. I burned with shame but, dear reader, being bound and naked before these hawk-nosed infidels did cause a certain thrill to stir within me and those weepings from below which betray a woman's pleasure did stain the satin couch beneath where I lay.'

The reading continued for a further twelve minutes, giving details of a Mammaluk who purchased the use of the diarist for two hours and who was, as it was recorded, of insatiable vigour when abed. Susie listened enraptured as madame went on to recount how the captive French-woman was finally bought and then soundly bedded by a succession of merchant princes and cruel moguls, all blessed with manhoods as thick as Genoan candles and appetites as keen as they were curious. As the reading drew to a close, the four guests resumed their appointed places at the table and called for a fresh pot of tea. The green-eyed brunette repaired the damage done to her red lips with a lipstick in a phial of pure gold.

'Strawberries,' madame announced as she closed the diary, locked it securely away and rose up from her desk. 'A little early for April perhaps but this is a special treat. With cream?'

The table gave its warm assent to this suggestion.

'Annette,' madame murmured, nodding to the table.

To Susie's utter amazement, Annette started to strip naked.

'Clear the table, Susie,' madame instructed. 'No, we will not require dessert spoons.'

As Susie collected the plates, she caught the sharp tang of female arousal as it mixed with the smell of the ginger-bread and the clients' perfume. Almost dizzy with delight, she returned in silence to the serving table and watched as Annette, now utterly naked, mounted the white cloth.

'Swiss. I have them flown in,' madame remarked

conversationally as she sprinkled at least three dozen of the scarlet berries over Annette's supine body. Several fell down into the deep valley between her proud breasts, others scattered across her firm belly, the rest tumbled down into her pubic nest. Madame held a silver cream jug high above the passive, fruit-strewn nakedness of Annette.

'Shall I pour?' she asked in an arch tone.

'Mmm,' came the collective response.

Madame dribbled the thick cream across the swell and into the cleavage of the breasts below, then trailed the slick of cream down across the belly and, lowering the jug until it was a mere inch away from the flesh below, carefully annointed the strawberries buried between Annette's splayed thighs. Taking a large strawberry up in a pincer of finger and thumb, madame dragged it across the cream on Annette's left breast and placed the glistening fruit between the naked girl's parted lips.

'Strawberries are served.'

They fell upon her like – what was that phrase from her poetry book in Wyevenhoe Hall? They came down like the wolf on the fold. Yes, that was it. Like wolves encircling a tethered lamb, Susie thought as she shivered. The green-eyed brunette took the strawberry from Annette's mouth with her teeth and after bisecting it precisely, swallowed both parts slowly. Lowering her cream smudged lips down upon Annette's, her tongue flickered out to tame and control that of her passive prey. Other mouths closed in on Annette's naked flesh, to guzzle the sweet fruits from her breasts, belly and from between her thighs. A large-breasted blonde was paying particular attention to a strawberry which madame had playfully popped in between the naked girl's labia. Susie gasped silently as she saw the blonde tongue the fruit up into Annette, then apply her mouth to the cream-smeared slit, sucking fiercely to retrieve the sweet berry. Annette moaned and writhed, but madame stepped smartly to the head of the table and grasped the wriggling nude by her wrists, dragging them back over Annette's head and pinioning her firmly. A flutter of concern clouded Susie's eyes as she saw her friend rendered helpless but the anxious, cornflower-blue eyes darkened with jealousy as she realised that Annette was relishing her impromptu bondage as the heavily breasted blonde's mouth worked busily at her splayed thighs.

Susie wiped her sweating palms against the curve of her buttocks as she drank in the scene before her. The fruit and then the last vestiges of the cream disappeared beneath the lapping tongues and sucking lips, but the sounds of feasting continued as the hungry mouths remained pressed into Annette's spreadeagled nakedness. Soon the shrill cry of ecstacy from the nude's lips signalled her orgasm, and the four young women withdrew slowly, satisfied with their banqueting. Napkins were distributed and used freely; Susie saw the large-breasted blonde wipe between her legs and toss the napkin aside. At a signal from madame, Susie stooped to pick it up. She shuddered as her fingers touched the wetness of the blonde's excitement, knowing that Annette had caused it and that later on, in the darkness of the Devon night, Susie herself would have much cause to be wet.

Soft music emanated from the corner of the room. It was a piece from Vivaldi which grew louder and more lively as madame adjusted the volume control.

'Annette, you may retire and take a shower. My guests are about to play a little game.'

Susie paled slightly as she saw Annette leave the drawing room. She felt vulnerable and alone. With the older, more experienced girl beside her, Susie had felt equal to the occasion: now she was merely a chicken among vixens. Whatever the little game madame had referred to was, she sensed she would have a vital part to play in it. Musical chairs? The four young women were arranging their chairs in a neat row along the carpet, positioning them so that there was a space of about three feet between them.

'You are familiar with the rules of Pass the Parcel, I trust?' madame asked.

Good, Susie thought with a mounting sense of relief. She was safe enough for the moment. The prize would probably be a small item of jewellery or an exotic sex toy.

'Susie, you are to be the parcel. Take your places everybody.'

The music was turned up to full volume as Susie stumbled across to the first chair. Seated upon it was the green-eyed brunette dressed in the chic Chanel outfit. She pulled Susie towards her and quickly tore off the tiny white apron using not her nimble fingers but her teeth. Susie shuddered as she felt the cat-like woman's hot, wet mouth biting at the buttons of her blouse. Before the music stopped abruptly, Susie's breasts were exposed. Pushed along to the next chair, a second hungry mouth hovered over her kneeling body. The music snapped into life and so did the teeth, immediately tearing into the flapping blouse, then the brassière beneath. After the music stopped and then restarted, the third client worked on the zip of her short black skirt. Soon Susie was left in panties, suspender and stockings alone. These proved more difficult to remove, and Susie – her near nakedness shining with the clients' saliva – had been passed between them twice before finally ending up, shivering in her cotton panties, before the cruel brunette. Standing before her as instructed, Susie presented her bottom to the green-eyed woman's teeth. She felt them nip at her soft left cheek, then slowly drag the crisp cotton that swathed her buttocks down over their double domes.

'I win,' cried the brunette, her voice thickened by the panties between her teeth.

'No you don't,' objected the heavily breasted blonde who sat in the next chair. 'You can't claim her yet. The panties are not completely down.'

'We will call it a draw,' madame interposed. 'You can both spank her.'

Susie, stepping out of the panties which had slithered down to her feet, shivered with delicious dread. Pass the Parcel had conjured up innocent pleasures on Boxing Day when excited children would scrabble frantically at a tightly wrapped Mars bar. The prize in this more adult version was to be her bottom and it was already bare.

With exquisite politeness which Susie found maddening

the heavily breasted blonde offered Susie's bottom to the brunette. The offer was refused and with generosity of spirit the brunette took Susie and spread her slowly across her short skirt and offered the naked bottom across her warm lap to the blonde.

Spank. Spank. The kneeling blonde brought her flattened palm harshly down against Susie's naked cheeks. She wriggled and squealed softly in response but the brunette pinned her down firmly, grasping her by the neck and lower thighs.

Spank. Spank. Spank. The unerring hand swept down eagerly across the bottom leaving crimson palm-prints on the defenceless flesh. Susie thrashed her tiny feet in protest but the capable brunette trapped and tamed them with her own strong left foot. Already, the creamy skin of the punished buttocks was blushing darkly. Her hot cheeks then suffered yet more stinging smacks which sought out every inch of their superbly curved surface. The spanking was expertly delivered with an economy and accuracy of style that left Susie writhing. She bit her lip, but as the intimate onslaught progressed she could not deny the delightful sensations of burning joy both at her tingling buttocks and at her hot, sticky slit. The taut skirt across which she was spread rubbed against her pubis and as the final flurry of spanks set her buttocks ablaze, Susie crushed her parted labia into its tightly stretched fabric. The blonde crowned the buttocks she had just punished by crushing her heavy breasts down into the hot flesh which rocketed Susie, who almost swooned under their soft weight, into fresh jerking paroxysms across the brunette's lap. The blonde withdrew, leaving Susie spread face down, reddening buttocks upturned, across the brunette's lap. She squirmed with sheer pleasure at the sensation of being utterly vulnerable and helpless before the collective gaze of the clients, and thrilled to the dominant touch which pinioned her so firmly in her position of surrender and submission. But above all, it was the green-eyed brunette's cool indifference to her sweet suffering which caused Susie's labia to weep. The sensation of utter helplessness across the lap of the brunette both as the blonde had spanked her so severely and now, as the brunette slowly thumbed Susie's hot cheeks, caused Susie to involuntarily spill her hot juices freely. The cat-like woman snarled softly and roughly pushed Susie into the arms of the blonde.

'Take her and hold her down. She has stained my beautiful Chanel skirt. Hold her down hard. I am going to punish her properly.'

Susie's heart hammered at these words. Properly? Was she to have her poor, hot bottom caned? Or would her scalded cheeks suffer the fiercer bite of the leather belt which the brunette wore around her trim waist? Stretched across the soft warmth of the blonde who had just spanked her so searchingly, Susie flinched as she felt the blonde lean across and encircle her lower thighs with her right arm. This not only trapped Susie completely but caused her bare bottom to grow rounder and more inviting.

'Anyone still peckish?' madame murmured as she approached, nibbling at a slice of gingerbread.

'It has been a spendid tea, madame. Quite splendid,' the brunette replied. 'I think, though, that I could just manage one more bite.'

The blonde tightened her grip on Susie's squirming buttocks as the brunette lowered her face down towards them. Susie felt the warm breath then the light brush of the brunette's parted lips, then the nip of cruel teeth on her recently spanked flesh.

Four

The cool linen of her sheet was a balm to her bottom. Susie stretched out luxuriously in her bed and sighed contentedly. It had been an eventful evening and her body ached with sweet memories. Turning over on to her tummy, she stretched out her arms to cup and squeeze her soft buttocks. Images from the tea party flooded her brain. She closed her eyes and saw Annette, pinioned by madame, yielding to the probing tongue of the blonde. Palming the swell of her splayed cheeks, Susie lingered over the delicious memory of the spanking the blonde had administered, followed by the more fierce attentions of the brunette's teeth and tongue. An owl hooted out in the darkness of the surrounding night. Annette was late. Susie knew that her friend was still busy downstairs in the kitchen under madame's eagle eye. Later, when her domestic duties were completed, Annette would tiptoe into Susie's bedroom and steal silently between the sheets, bringing her nakedness close against Susie's eager warmth.

A beam of light from an approaching car danced across the far end of the bedroom. Startled, Susie scrambled up from her bed and dashed across to the window. Peering into the inky darkness that drowned The Rookery, she saw the twin beams of the car and the little red light on the roof. It was a taxi. Who could it possibly be? A nocturnal lover for madame? Was this visitor expected and was Annette delayed in the kitchen below preparing for the late night arrival?

The taxi scrunched to a halt at the front entrance to The Rookery and a car door opened then clunked shut. Susie peered down but could see little behind the blaze of headlights. The taxi drew away, leaving the unseen visitor in darkness on the steps. Susie heard the bell-push tinkle and strained to catch a glimpse. She gasped when the gravel was flooded with yellow light as the front door opened and Svetlana was revealed. Svetlana, her ash blonde hair shining in the sudden light, stepped inside The Rookery and disappeared. The door closed returning the grounds to their gloom.

Svetlana. Susie jumped on to her bed, belly down, and snuggled into her pillow. Her yearning for Svetlana's svelte body had been buried beneath recent events but not extinguished. The fantasy Susie had openly enjoyed that fateful afternoon back at La Bella Figura returned to her, as fresh and as crisp as the original. Her hands found her breasts and squeezed slowly as Susie's mind flew back to the imagined swimming baths, where Svetlana slowly rose up out of the steaming waters, offering her beautiful bottom up for Susie's frank appraisal. With a finger and thumb at each firm nipple, Susie's imagination followed Svetlana into the changing room and relished the vision of the Russian girl peeling off her wet, stretchy swimsuit and bending for her towel. Susie's left hand slipped down below her belly to find and frantically finger her stiff little clitoris. With a hot urgency that swept aside the usual preliminaries of rubbing her labia and teasing the wet opening to her slit, Susie tweaked and nipped herself until her welling climax boiled over into a violent orgasm. Slightly shocked yet secretly thrilled with the ferocity of her response, Susie squeezed her thighs and buttocks together as the rippling spasms raked her nakedness. Again and again, the savage pulsing from the very base of her belly tightened the muscles between her clamped thighs and caused pure delight to possess her innermost part. With Svetlana's name smothered by the pillow into which Susie crushed her hot face, the girl in the grip of another masturbatory climax came violently again. Out in the void of the night, the lone owl heard her cry and echoed the sweet moan eerily.

A little later, Susie's curiosity got the better of her fatigue. She wondered what had brought Svetlana down from London to The Rookery. How long would she be staying? Had she been tricked down here? Perhaps. Or had madame, ever able to read Susie's mind shrewdly, brought the Russian girl down to be Susie's playmate? Her inquisitive mind ignored her aching body and Susie, robed in a thigh-high kimono of black and scarlet silk, tiptoed down to the kitchen where she knew Svetlana would be enjoying her supper. The mouth-watering aroma of fried bacon and eggs greeted her as she inched along the darkened passageway towards the kitchen door which was slightly ajar. Peering carefully through the narrow gap into the strong yellow light of the kitchen Susie saw two perfectly formed bare feet, toes pressed firmly into the floor, and the naked flesh of two legs up to the hollows behind the knees. Try as she might to stretch and strain for a better view, the narrow gap allowed her no more than a glimpse of the naked feet and legs. It must be Svetlana, Susie realised excitedly, because the flesh tones were pale, almost silvery. Annette's skin was darker, with an almost olive tint. It was Svetlana and from the position of her feet the Russian girl was already tasting madame's unique hospitality, poised as she was for a bare-bottomed spanking. Susie drew the broad sash of her black and scarlet silk kimono tightly around her belly in a vain attempt to quell the fluttering within.

'Absolutely disgraceful. To think of the shame and scandal you might cause to La Bella Figura. It is monstrous.'

Susie grinned as she recognised madame's pretence at alarm and outrage. Poor Svetlana was certainly getting the full Seraphim Savage treatment, and soon, Susie surmised, the chastisement would commence with the harsh sound of flesh punishing flesh as the impending spanking began.

'But madame,' Svetlana protested indignantly. 'I am sure my work papers are in order –'

'Silence, girl. I have only repeated what I learned, to my horror, from a well-placed friend. Your papers appear to be suspect.'

Susie quickly deduced that Svetlana had been summoned to The Rookery and instructed to keep a low profile until madame had ironed out any difficulties with the authorities over the work permit. Such a smoothing operation would take time, madame told Svetlana crossly. And to a busy woman like Seraphim Savage, time was money. The Russian would have to make amends.

'You will remain here, of course. I will train you and put you to work. You will learn much. The opportunities are much more interesting at The Rookery than at La Bella Figura. Our clients here have very special needs,' madame continued, words at which Susie grinned broadly. 'But you have caused me not inconsiderable distress, Svetlana. You must and will be punished.'

The Russian wailed. Susie's nipples grew erect beneath the silk kimono at madame's concluding words. 'You must and will be punished.' Susie stroked her straining nipples firmly with her thumbtips and swallowed silently. The naked feet, drawn tightly together, toes pressed into the floor, signalled that the Russian girl was already spread across madame's lap. Susie knew that, tantalisingly just out of sight, Svetlana's upturned bottom was already bared and positioned for the punishment madame was about to dispense. Already, perhaps, madame's left hand would be palming the exposed cheeks, flattening the superb naked buttocks with circular sweeps of her spanking hand.

Susie's fingers left her nipples to stray down and pluck apart the tightly bound sash at her waist. She stifled a gasp of raw pleasure as the kimono slipped apart, its cool silk dragging across her nipples then exposing them to the chill of the night. Immediately, her right hand swept down across her pale belly to alight, fingertips splayed, upon her nest of pubic curls. The tip of her index finger circled, then teasingly probed, the flesh beneath seeking to prise out the pink thorn of her clitoris. As soon as the spanking, unseen but understood through sound, commenced, she would pleasure herself in time to the punishment. Bending closer to the door, but cautiously avoiding contact with it, Susie held her breath.

Crack. Harsher and deeper than the expected ringing spank of palm across bare cheeks, the first stroke was administered. Svetlana's feet thrashed in response as the Russian girl squealed her anguished surprise. Crack. Too solid a sound for a supple belt. What was it? Susie thrummed her clitoris with her thumb, spreading her legs slightly and planting her feet apart. Crack. Was it a paddle? Hungry imagination formed pictures from the delicious sounds: Susie saw, as if for real, the punished cheeks growing slowly scarlet as they suffered madame's sweeping strokes. Svetlana moaned but Susie's ear caught the bass note of pleasure in the bitter-sweet response. The Russian girl was clearly enjoying her bare-bottomed chastisement, and was finding her distress unaccountably delicious. How red those blazing cheeks must be.

Susie peeped: Svetlana's legs trembled slightly as her toes stretched; the Russian was inching up her naked rump for more. Susie's thumb flew into a frenzy at the sight of Svetlana willing her bottom up to greet the fierce lash. Susie closed her eyes. She was wielding the instrument of sweet torment and in her hot imaginings, the Russian girl's suffering buttocks were hers. She opened her eyes. To her horror, the door had yawned open revealing the full view of the kitchen to Susie's gaze, and a full view of the masturbating Susie to madame's amusement. Svetlana was not spread across madame's lap as Susie had supposed but was arranged for her punishment over a three-legged stool. After a silent smile, and a nod of understanding, madame strode back towards the naked, upturned bottom. She raised her arm up to shoulder height and brought it down vigorously. Crack. Susie saw the naked cheeks flatten under the swift stroke. It was a large butter pat, and madame, standing serenely over the hot rump, weighed the thin blade fashioned out of pearwood in her left hand. Across her stool, the bare-bottomed girl tensed. Once more, madame swept the wooden butter pat sharply down across the defenceless, curved cheeks. A crimson blotch attested to the cruel accuracy of the stroke. Svetlana, thighs pressed together, squealed and squeezed her cheeks together tightly. Possibly to contain the pain, Susie thought, but probably to sustain the fierce delight.

Madame Seraphim Savage gazed knowingly at Susie over the butter pat which she was now pressing against her lips. In her gaze, Susie gleaned consent as if the punisher was silently giving permission to the voyeur to enjoy and gain full pleasure from the chastisement. Susie, hypnotised by the hot bottom of the naked Russian girl, trembled on the brink of orgasm. Quivering with ungovernable pleasure, she closed her eyes and tossed her unruly dark hair from her face. Crack. Crack. Madame's punishing hand was busy once more, making the pearwood sing as it stung the naked flesh beneath it. The punishing hand that wielded the butter pat was busy, but not as busy as Susie's hand that had become a mere blur at the base of her belly.

The whipping school was scheduled for two o'clock the following afternoon. Classes were extremely popular, madame explained to Susie as they approached the tutorial room. They entered the former billiards room which had a good view of the kitchen garden at the rear of The Rookery. Through the window, Susie caught a glimpse of redcurrant bushes in neat rows, and felt a pang of excitement at the shivering forest of bamboo canes sprouting from the dense foliage.

'I am expecting five students this afternoon, all desirous of punishment and discipline. They are new girls,' madame continued as she flexed a thirty-two-inch length of bamboo and examined it closely, 'and so we will have to put these beginners through the induction and assessment stages of their learning programme.'

Susie stole a shy glance at Madame Seraphim and saw that she was a principal once more, though of a very different school to that in Sloane Square. Here in Devon, students came to study suffering and sorrow.

'Induction and assessment,' madame repeated, 'to determine their precise needs and, of course, the best methods of meeting such needs.'

Spanking, strap or cane, Susie decoded. The five new

90

students would indeed be thoroughly and intimately assessed before their education began.

'Ah, here they are. I do appreciate promptness and always reward laxity with the lash.'

Susie shivered at madame's words, making a mental note of the warning. The ground rules at The Rookery were spartan and severe: Susie had infringed them unwittingly and had paid the painful price. She was keen to learn how to both please and obey the stern mistress of The Rookery.

'Strip off, girl,' madame instructed, already unbuttoning her own silk blouse.

The former billiards room was generously furnished with full-length mirror panelling. As Susie eased herself out of her pleated leather mini-skirt, cashmere jumper and then her lace-cupped bra and cotton panties, she peeped at the reflection of madame who was now quite naked.

'Warm work, punishment,' madame remarked as she admired the outline of her ripe, Venus figure in the mirror. 'We will take them all together, as a group. It helps to overcome any initial shyness or last minute reluctance. Besides,' madame observed as she smoothed her hips with her open palms, 'I find that group punishments are so much more exciting for the beginners. Bring them in.'

Susie, suddenly conscious of her total nudity, stepped into the small waiting room and stood at the open door. The intense whispering ceased abruptly and four faces looked up. Susie felt the four pairs of burning eyes devouring her nakedness. Tossing her head back she suddenly felt proud and in command. In a clear voice that denied her mounting excitement she ordered the four young women into the tutorial room. They rose up from their hard wooden chairs and followed the sway of her naked bottom into the next room where madame was waiting, cane in hand. A scampering of feet broke the solemn silence and a fifth young woman, blushing and slightly flustered, brought up the rear.

'Sorry I'm late,' she panted, shaking her blonde curls.

'Your apology is noted,' madame replied softly, tapping her open palm with the cane. 'I will, however, take certain measures to ensure that you are punctual for all future appointments.'

The blonde bowed her head in shame.

'Stand in a straight line, all of you. At once.'

The five young women, trembling with fearful pleasure, obeyed instantly and shuffled into a row ready for inspection.

'Are you all wearing what I prescribed?' madame asked.

Four of the girls nodded in unison. The blonde, Susie observed, looked away and blushed once more.

'Show me,' madame ordered crisply.

Five pairs of hands flew down to the hems of five pleated mini-skirts. The brief skirts rose up as one to reveal five pairs of panties and five shapely pairs of legs swathed in self-support, seamed nylon stockings.

'Excellent. Undress and fold your clothes up tidily. You may place them on the chairs behind you.'

Susie's thumb gently stroked the tuft of pubic fuzz at her delta as she perused the five beautiful young women silently undressing. Her thumb quickened when she saw their breasts bulge, as the women stretched behind to unclasp their restrictive brassières, then bounce in freedom as the bras were removed.

'Keep your panties and stockings on. I will remove them when the moment is ripe,' madame instructed.

When the moment is ripe. Susie shivered as she anticipated what the afternoon would involve. The baring of the five beautiful bottoms followed by intimate inspection of the naked cheeks. The careful weighing of each peach-cheek in the palm of her trembling hand and the gentle fingering of each dark, warm cleft. Then, in consultation with madame, categorising the types of buttocks and prescribing methods of punishment accordingly. Susie sighed softly and wiped her sweaty palms against her rounded hips. Finally, she reflected, the administration of the punishments: when the moment was ripe.

'Step forward and position yourselves against the rail.'

Madame pointed to a wooden rail attached to the mirrored wall just as in a ballet school. The five young women took a few steps forward and bent down, arms outstretched, to grasp the rail before them.

'Heads down. Right down,' madame ordered, pressing the golden curls of the blonde who had been late arriving down with the tip of her quivering cane. Susie felt her labial lips tremble at the display of dominance.

'Stand perfectly still. Do not be alarmed,' madame advised her bending class as she approached the wall, reached up and pulled at a small lever. With a soft squeak, the rail came away from the mirrored wall on extending struts and at the same time five wooden halters swung down from where they had been suspended from the ceiling. Susie gasped softly as madame quickly approached each semi-naked young woman from behind and, forcing them firmly by the napes of their necks, imprisoned them in the lightweight stocks. Trapped and subjugated within their wooden yokes the captives squirmed in their bondage. One girl in particular wriggled vigorously. Madame drew the tip of her cane down along the seam of the writhing girl's self-support stocking. The lithe leg ceased its quivering. Madame tapped the girl's pantied bottom and at the imperious touch of the cane, the girl froze obediently.

'Primitive but very effective, these stocks,' madame remarked to Susie as she tested each wooden halter to ensure that there was absolutely no escape for those held within. 'Excellent. Let the first lesson begin.'

Susie stepped up alongside madame to join her for the inspection of the first bottom. As she did so, their thighs grazed and Susie thrilled to the touch of the stern dominatrix's firm flesh. Her eyes narrowed and focused intently as madame cupped the passive cheeks of the first willing victim. The stockinged legs trembled as madame's expert fingers peeled down the tight cotton panties, leaving them stretched just below the swell of the exposed cheeks.

'Well?'

'Pear-shaped,' whispered Susie, brushing the generously curved buttocks with an upward sweep of her knuckled left hand. Sweeping her knuckles down more firmly into the silky flesh-mounds, she paused and cupped the cheeks to weigh them carefully. The imprisoned flesh quivered within her grasp. 'Pear-shaped. To be spanked and paddled.'

'Well done, my little one. You have learned well.'

The next bottom in line was an exquisite example of the sleek, athletic type. Susie showed no hesitation, after tracing the contours of the passive cheeks with her fingertips, in pronouncing the verdict. She added that discipline should be dispensed with both strap and paddle. Again, madame murmured her agreement as she lingeringly palmed the exposed buttocks. Susie's breasts grew heavy with pleasure, the nipples now painfully erect. Her voice was low with excitement and her inner thigh glistened with the wetness seeping from her slit. Never before had she experienced the delights of control, of sovereignty, over such beautiful bared bottoms waiting for pain. Beside her, madame remained outwardly unperturbed.

Serenely poised, she moved along the line of imprisoned, bending young women, her heavy bosom gently bobbing as she leaned forward to ease down their panties. Only the slightest tremble at her fingertips betrayed her evident pleasure, but in both her tone of voice and patient progress she successfully disguised her delight. Madame's self-discipline added to Susie's excitement, and the cool, unruffled calm of the older, more experienced dominatrix increased the delicious tension of the moment. They approached the third bottom, placing their hands down across the naked cheeks together. As their fingertips accidently touched across the cleft, Susie's slit pulsed, sending a hot spasm up into her belly. Together, they dragged the panties down, exposing an hour-glass bottom in all its shapely splendour.

'Firm, slightly heavy buttocks,' Susie whispered hoarsely. 'For punishment, I advocate the cane.'

Madame, who was absently running her straightened index finger up and down between the cheeks, silently nodded. Susie ached for the moment when the disciplining of these young women would begin. The slow process of their induction and assessment was proving to be too much of a tantalising agony for her own, untrained desires. With an intuitive understanding, madame paused, turned to her naked assistant and tenderly brushed the untidy wisps of stray dark hair away from the face beneath.

'Patience, my girl. Punishment has a very special pace and rhythm. To rush the process is to spoil the experience. We must remain in total control so that we can, like the conductor leading the orchestra, produce disciplined delights.'

Yes. Susie understood. Madame was right. Pace, tempo and rhythm. To own the right to produce sweet music one must exercise restraint and judgement. Nodding, Susie's eyes sparkled as she smiled in response. Madame, cane in hand, was about to conduct and achieve the sweetest notes from those under her rule. In every stage of punishment, the tempo must be strict and the rhythm tightly disciplined: the punisher, not the punished, must determine the beat.

'What is the meaning of this?'

Madame's stern question broke into Susie's thoughts. She glanced down and saw madame's capable hands tugging at a pair of pale blue panties. They sheathed the pert bottom of the blonde who had already incurred madame's displeasure by arriving late for her tutoring.

'I didn't have a pair of white –' mumbled the blonde.

'Silence. I specifically instructed you all to attend your induction and assessment class in white cotton panties. You seem to have deliberately ignored that request, for which you will suffer. And,' madame continued severely, 'I seem to recall that you arrived late. For these gross transgressions and breaches of the strict regulations you will suffer extra punishment. Do you understand?'

The disobedient blonde trod the carpet beneath her stockinged feet, the soft whisper of her nylons broke the silence as her legs brushed against one another.

'I said,' madame repeated, bending down to grasp each cheek and spread the passive flesh-mounds apart painfully, 'do you understand?'

'Yes,' whimpered the blonde.

Susie's eyes grew wide as she saw the dark cleft yawn wide between the spreading cheeks. Her throat tightened and the pulse at her neck fluttered as she watched madame ruthlessly thumb the moist, pink sphincter.

'Double punishment for this one. Please make a careful note of my decision.'

'Yes, madame,' Susie replied in a voice she barely recognised.

'Her bottom type?' madame enquired crisply.

'Boyish,' Susie responded smartly.

'Boyish?' queried madame, her tone rising half an octave.

'Yes, madame. The keynote is trim. The waist is slim, the cheeks slightly flattened at the cusp. It is a boyish type.'

'And for punishment?'

'Hairbrush. Hairbrush and slipper,' Susie gushed.

'Quite right, my girl. Well done. Go over to that drawer and get me a hairbrush and a slipper.'

Susie padded obediently across to a walnut chest and opened the top drawer. It slid out silently and from its dark recess she withdrew a supple, leather-soled slipper and a large, cherrywood hairbrush. Returning to madame, she handed her the hairbrush. Madame inverted the brush, bristles facing into the flesh, and roughly forced it down into the panties of the quivering blonde. Susie closed her eyes and almost swooned. The blonde, she realised, would feel the prickling bristles against the ultra-sensitive flesh of her inner cleft, and understood all too painfully that soon the hard, smooth cherrywood of the obverse side would be fiercely kissing her naked cheeks. Susie, sensing the bending blonde's torment, had to stiffen her left leg as a violent tremor of raw pleasure coursed down through its muscles. She ground her toes into the carpet to calm her rebellious flesh, just as madame strode around to the front of the line of imprisoned girls and held out the slipper to the blonde.

'Look. See the leather with which I propose to punish you shortly.'

The blonde flickered her eyes up to the hide.

'Taste. Taste,' madame instructed, 'with your tongue, the leather which will lash your naked bottom.'

Timorously, the blonde's pink tongue lapped at the slipper's sole.

'Now take the slipper between your teeth. When I have

used the hairbrush to my complete and utter satisfaction I will take this from you and complete your chastisement.'

The blonde grunted as she bit into the slipper and held it, as instructed.

'And if you let it drop, you will have cause to regret it. Bitter cause,' madame warned.

On close inspection, the fifth girl's panties were already soaking wet with excitement. Fully exposed, her buttocks were ripe.

'Peaches,' whispered Susie. 'To be spanked.'

'We will spank this one first,' madame said quietly in response, drawing Susie away. 'She has obviously got a very low boiling point which has already been reached. Quite a challenge, though, to discipline.'

Susie framed her unspoken question with a frown.

'Training that one could be very hard work. A cross word in a firm tone is enough to make her come, never mind a sound bare-bottomed spanking.'

'I think I understand,' Susie murmured.

'In fact,' madame continued conspiratorially, 'I think I'll leave her 'til the end. Just let her enjoy the other girls getting theirs. Here, take this strap and pay careful attention as I instruct you in the next stage of preparation.'

The two naked punishers resumed their positions behind the line of bending girls willingly waiting for their imminent pleasure-pain.

'For you,' madame said, stroking the cheeks of the first girl, 'a spanking and a taste of my little wooden paddle.'

Susie watched as the stockinged legs inched together in fearful response. Madame forced the paddle between the darker bronze bands of the self-support stockings just below the line of the stretched panties above.

'Legs a little more apart, girl.'

The stockinged legs obeyed, inching apart silently to reveal stray wisps of pubic fuzz within the shadowed thighs. Madame inserted the paddle down into the panties and adjusted it so that the surface of the flat wood pressed lightly in against the swell of the girl's exposed cheeks. The gesture drew a sweet sigh from the happy victim.

'For you,' madame said to the second girl, 'the strap and then the paddle.' She aligned the blade of the paddle against the bare buttocks and deftly held it in place using the strap as an impromptu belt. The girl wriggled her shapely rump but madame tightened the length of leather, securing the paddle against the satin cheeks within the taut band of hide. How exquisite, Susie thought enviously, to have the tangible presence of the punishment to come welded so closely against the flesh that was to suffer.

'It will be the cane for you, girl,' madame decided, standing back from the bare bottom of the third girl. She dragged the tip of her bamboo cane down the cleft between the heavy cheeks. The girl whimpered as madame probed the anal whorl with the tip of the cane. Dropping the end of the wood down a fraction she slid it in between the sticky labia, then withdrew the cane and held it aloft to examine it closely. It sparkled with the girl's wet excitement. Smiling and nodding her satisfaction, madame shouldered her bamboo and approached the bottom of the fourth girl – the disobedient blonde.

'I will deal with you, and deal with you most severely, all in good time, girl,' madame whispered fiercely, adjusting the inverted hairbrush wedged below the girl's buttocks so that the cruel bristles snuggled even more deeply into the squirming blonde's labia. The squeal of delight which met this gesture was rewarded with a further twist to the cherrywood brush. This time the blonde rose up on her tiptoes in an ecstasy of anguish and squealed again, dropping the leather slipper from her full, red lips.

'Goodness gracious me, you really are misbehaving today, aren't you? I really am going to have to be so very, very, firm with you,' madame said in a tone of sugared venom, as she walked around to the front of the wooden halter and stooped to retrieve the slipper from the floor. Susie clamped her thighs together with sheer excitement as she watched the leather-soled slipper being forced between the stubborn blonde's teeth.

'Mmmnnngh,' was all the unruly blonde could impenitently manage.

As the leather muffled the protests, Susie struggled to contain the hot wetness oozing from her fiery slit. Memories from her turbulent schooldays at Wyevenhoe Hall flooded back. Somehow, she realised, she simply must touch that slipper; she had to touch, fondle and caress the supple leather before, but preferably after, madame had scorched the blonde's bare buttocks with it. The fierce obsession possessed her completely and though Susie tried to concentrate on the matter in hand the thought of the leather slipper tormented her. She longed to crush the cold leather to her hot nipples and then, when the leather had grown warm with use, kiss the cruel hide and taste its harsh tang.

'Blindfold them,' madame ordered calmly, her cool tone of authority breaking Susie's train of thought. 'The blindfolds are over there, in the drawer beneath the one which held the hairbrush and slipper.'

Like the first drawer, the second slid open and shut easily and silently. Beeswax, Susie surmised, helped the runners glide home so obediently. Susie liked the sticky, waxy feel of polish. Being a virgin still, she was not quite sure but thought that when a man spilled his hot excitement it would probably feel the same between her fingertips. Only beeswax was cold and a man's seed would no doubt be hot.

'The blindfolds, please,' chivvied madame waspishly.

Susie dutifully gathered up the five strips of black velvet and one by one, firmly secured them over the eyes of the first four yoked girls. When binding the eyes of the blonde, she accidently brushed the slipper out of the red lips holding it. Their eyes met fleetingly as the slipper fell with a soft thud at her feet. Gathering it up, Susie crushed the leather sole against her left breast before returning it to the blonde's mouth. Above the red lips, the blonde's blue eyes widened with alarm but Susie bound the blindfold over them, consigning them to the delicious darkness of suspense.

'Leave her,' madame motioned, pointing to the fifth girl. 'A blindfold for her is not necessary.'

As bidden, Susie tossed the spare strip of velvet aside and rejoined madame behind the first of the bare bottoms.

'Hold the paddle while I spank.'

Susie's nipples grazed the buttocks of the first girl as she leaned across the captive to withdraw the wooden paddle. The sharp tang of the yoked girl's wet excitement rose up to Susie's nostrils. The girl was clearly aroused even before her fierce pleasure had commenced. Sheer anticipation alone had juiced the flesh of her hot slit. How right, Susie thought, madame was to prolong these preparatory stages. These young women were already on fire with the heat of lust before even a single stroke had been administered. Madame was right to pace the punishments, deliberately delaying the ultimate moment of painful pleasure.

Smack, smack. The crisp double echo announced that the spanking had commenced. Madame's slender hand cracked down again, reddening the curved cheeks with another harsh double spank. This time firmer notes rang out as the punishing hand swept down to savagely caress the passive flesh. The chastisement, with a deliberate pause between each double spank, progressed with maddeningly slow intimacy. Madame pressed her thigh against the flanks of the captive girl, fusing the flesh of both punisher and punished into one warmth. Susie suddenly understood the raw pleasure of being dominated, of being naked and helpless before this beautiful, stern dominatrix. To offer up one's bare bottom to her relentlessly accurate, merciless spanking hand. To submit oneself absolutely to her ruthless affection, her tender severity, Susie acknowledged, was to surrender to a limitless delight.

The scorched cheeks flushed a deeper and angrier hue as madame's slightly curved palm sought out and scorched their velvety peach-curves. The punished girl moaned throughout the chastisement; it was a low, tuneless song in praise of sorrow.

'Apply the paddle. Six strokes. And be sure to cover every inch of her bottom,' madame instructed Susie in a dispassionate voice, as if instructing her naked assistant on how to ice a cake.

Susie weighed the wooden paddle in her trembling hand and stepped up towards the bare, recently spanked bottom. In her excitement, she moved too quickly, too closely, and accidently crushed her nakedness into the hot cheeks. The rasp of her pubic nest across the swell of the spanked buttocks brought a gasp of delighted response from the lips of the yoked girl. Susie checked the writhing hips of the girl she was about to discipline, holding each cheek briefly between her cupped palms. The girl in the stocks became still, though her legs quivered imperceptibly at Susie's dominant touch. Dropping her left hand down, Susie firmly fingered the seam of the self-support stocking that hugged the shapely left leg. The captive tightened her buttocks and inched her thighs together.

'Legs together, closer,' Susie murmured, thumbing the seam of the stockinged right leg. Immediately, the honey-nyloned legs clamped together tightly.

Susie swung her arm round. The large paddle kissed the naked spheres of flesh vehemently, scalding and reddening them instantly. For the second stroke, Susie brought the paddle against the buttocks at a sharper angle, ensuring that it truly punished their heavy swell. The sufferer pinioned in her utter submission squealed and pawed the carpet frantically with her stockinged feet. Susie sidestepped slightly, positioning herself directly behind her helpless target.

'Open your legs,' she whispered.

The penitent obeyed timidly.

'Wider.'

The stockinged legs inched further apart. Susie levelled the paddle and dipped it down into the shadows beneath the hot cheeks, snuggling the blunt snout of the wood into the glistening flesh of the sticky plum-like slit. Withdrawing it, Susie noted the silvery wetness where the parted lips of the labia had kissed it fleetingly. Closing her eyes momentarily, Susie wiped the tip of the wet wood against her left buttock.

'Legs together, at once,' she barked.

Her brusque command was obeyed and she swung

again. The wooden paddle, stained darkly at the tip, sought out the firmer flesh of the upper thighs, stinging the rump savagely with its double Judas-kiss.

'Take her to the showers and give this to her,' madame instructed, removing the blindfold and reaching up to release the punished nude from her bondage.

Susie took the eleven-inch dildo – a potent, ebony shaft – in her left hand, and escorted the punished girl out to the showers.

Moments later, having peeled off the sheer nylon stockings, Susie guided the red-bottomed girl into the gentle warmth of a tepid shower. The girl sighed with bliss as Susie palmed shower gel across the naked breasts and belly, then nudged the dildo's tip down along the cleft between the punished cheeks. Rejoining madame, Susie was just in time to witness the second bending girl receive her prescribed discipline: six swift strokes of the paddle followed by a slower, more deliberate application of the leather strap. Susie realised that madame had coiled up the short strap and placed it in the girl's panties before commencing with the paddle. During the scorching with the wood, the coiled leather had pressed up against the suffering girl's labia above. The paddle rendered the crowns of the poised cheeks red and shining. Removing the strap, madame unfurled its cruel length and plied it to the hot rump, lashing the soft cheeks eight times.

Susie loved the chastisement with leather, and her wide eyes eagerly devoured every tiny detail: the slender hand grasping the thin strip of leather; the quivering cheeks clenched fearfully; the split-second whistle and loud snap of the loving lash; the faint pink stripe where hide had kissed flesh. Susie missed nothing of the punishment, and judged it superb.

Seraphim Savage. Susie repeated the name softly to herself, marvelling at the strangely appropriate name. Madame did indeed embody the angelic and the demonic, dispensing delicious, dreadful punishment and the dark delights of pain. Madame's bare breasts bounced as she delivered the final strokes, swiping the strap across the girl's helpless cheeks with venemous accuracy. Bending down immediately, madame kissed each scalded buttock. As her lips pressed into the hot flesh twice, Susie repeated madame's name silently: Seraphim Savage.

With her blindfold removed, the whipped girl obediently followed Susie out of the tutorial room and down along the corridor to the showers. Susie soon guided her naked charge into the delicious stream of soothing water, leaving the soundly punished girl to enjoy the dildo madame had prescribed. Glimpsing into the cubicle where Susie had left the first girl, she saw her squatting down upon her up-turned shaft of ebony, arms outstretched against the white tiles to steady herself.

'There is an art in caning,' madame said to Susie upon her return. The words were spoken in a tone Susie associated with lectures at La Bella Figura.

Bending her length of bamboo to judge its flexibility, madame thrummed the air twice and nodded her satisfaction. At the sound of the cane slicing through the air, at the eerie whistle of the thin wood signalling its potent malice, the stocking-clad girl squirming in her stocks whimpered. Madame, stepping back a pace, lowered the length of cane down across the bare bottom instantly calming its quivering. Tamed into silence and absolute stillness, the third pupil surrendered to madame's stern will. Susie felt hot, wet splashes of excitement scald the naked flesh of her inner thighs. Already approaching a seething climax, the mere sight, together with the delicious sound, of the potent cane threatened to spill her over into full, fierce orgasm.

'I will administer eight strokes to this naughty young lady's bare bottom. Watch and learn, Susie. It is an art, and to achieve perfection the punisher who plies the cane must acquire certain skills. Observe.'

Susie took a deep breath, relishing the rise and fall of her swollen breasts. She spread her feet apart, scrunching her toes into the carpet. As if privileged to witness some forbidden rite, some dark, ancient lore, she thrilled at the sight of madame raising the cane up from the naked cheeks to hold it aloft above the buttocks below.

103

'Flex the elbow, and keep your shoulder loose. Do not allow the caning arm to stiffen or grow tense. The stroke should be a graceful, fluent action –' Swish, swipe. The thin wood scored a pink stripe across the creamy cheeks. The caned girl gasped. 'Thus,' madame declared. 'The next stroke should fall a quarter of an inch below the first –' Swish, swipe. Once more the wood whispered its cruel note. Once more, the slicing cane-kiss left a tell-tale pink stripe. 'Thus. Very often,' madame grunted softly in her exertion, 'the caner makes the mistake of rushing the strokes but if I am not mistaken both punisher and punished prefer a lingering chastisement.'

The length of glinting yellow bamboo hovered above the poised peaches below. Susie pressed her palms together and forced them down between her hot thigh-flesh. Do it. Do it now. Please. Stripe her. Stripe her bottom. Please. Susie, tormented and tantalised as voyeur to the caning, silently beseeched madame to continue the disciplining. The maddening pauses between each stroke threatened to drive Susie wild. Stripe her. Do it now: Susie's mind rioted with her mute pleading. Suddenly unable to contain herself any longer, she pleasured her slit with two fingers.

'Pay attention,' madame barked, swishing the cane lightly against Susie's curved thigh.

Susie's belly imploded at the soft bite of the bamboo which had moments before scorched the satin cheeks of the yoked girl's bottom. The climax she had been struggling to deny washed over her unleashing its fury in a pulsing orgasm. Madame saw the tremors rippling through her young assistant's nakedness and addressed the bare bottom before her. As the cane swept down against the buttocks in rapid succession to slice the peach-flesh, Susie stumbled and sank down upon her knees. The haunting sound of the strokes filled her brain; suddenly she ached to be in the place of the girl in bondage, ached to feel madame's loving lash. With her face pressed into the carpet, Susie yearned to feel the dominant touch of madame's foot at the nape of her neck and burned for a taste of the dominatrix's discipline.

'Skill, not strength, is the secret of a successful whipping, Susie. Look. See how this girl is now actually offering up her naked bottom to my cane. She has tasted pleasure-pain and desires more. Of course,' madame remarked, flexing her bamboo rod, 'an understanding of the bottom is essential. Please pay attention and observe where I place the next two strokes. Here, and here.'

Susie looked up – directly up at the poised cheeks of the bare bottom – and watched as the cane tip indented the ravaged flesh at two precise points. Madame pressed the wood into the fleshy curves then inched the cane upward. Swish, slice. The caned girl yelped her ecstasy as the cane scorched her buttocks in precisely the promised places. Susie buckled down into the carpet and started to climax; before madame had shouldered her rod Susie came violently. Indifferent to the sweet suffering of both Susie and the punished girl, madame swished the cane vigorously.

'For the finishing strokes I always recommend rekindling the flames ignited by the first. Observe.'

Madame swung the cane. Had she been able to focus properly, Susie would have seen that madame applied the cane exactly across the faint pink stripes of her opening strokes. The cane swished down across the earlier lines of pain with precision, rocketing the young woman in her harness into paroxysms of sweet sorrow.

'Take her to the showers,' madame murmured, shouldering her cane evidently satisfied with her handiwork.

Susie struggled up to her feet, blushed furiously and took the caned girl – who pressed the dildo madame had presented her with to her left breast – out towards the showers. In silence, broken only by the hiss of sluicing water, Susie stood and watched as the girl offered up her striped buttocks to the balm of the healing shower, working the dildo up inside her at the same time. Susie saw the naked girl's knees pressed together, and knew that the whipped one had climaxed. In the next cubicle, she discovered the first two girls embracing tenderly, their eyes wide with wonder as they examined each other's reddened bottoms.

Back in the tutorial room, the whipping school was reduced to two pupils: the naughty blonde and the excitable girl who had been left unblindfolded. Both trembled in their strict bondage as their moment inexorably neared.

'What did we prescribe for this very, very naughty young lady?' madame asked.

'Hairbrush and slipper, madame,' Susie replied.

The question was superfluous: the cherrywood hairbrush remained wedged beneath the blonde's soft cheeks, caught and held by the tight band of the panties below, while the slipper dangled from the mouth at the other side of the stocks.

'Ah, yes. Hairbrush and slipper, was it not? And correct me if I am mistaken, but did not this young lady arrive late? And not wearing the regulation white panties?'

'She was late,' echoed Susie, answering madame's quizzical look. 'And her panties are blue, not white, as you had instructed.'

'Then we must see to it that her punishment is both severe and memorable. Remove the slipper and her blindfold.'

Susie raised her left eyebrow up a fraction.

'I want you to observe her closely,' madame explained. 'How she reacts to her chastisement. The eyes can be so eloquent in signalling sweet sorrow.'

Susie took up her position at the front of the wooden stocks and removed the blindfold. The blonde looked up at her with undisguised excitement. Susie took the slipper away from the succulent, red lips.

Thwack, thwack, thwack: the red lips formed a perfect rosebud as the blonde responded to madame's deft application of the hairbrush to her bare bottom. She brought the brush down again. Susie gazed down into the widening eyes of the squirming blonde. In their blue depths, the shadow of pain failed to extinguish the spark of delight. Susie stepped back and studied the captive held within the wooden halter. In their strictures, the blonde's fingers splayed out and taloned back into a clench as the polished cherrywood hairbrush blistered her buttocks. Relentlessly, the savage tenderness of madame's disciplining scalded the

106

blonde's soft cheeks. Susie stepped up to the stocks, bent down and fleetingly kissed the blonde's red lips. Then she probed the jerking blonde's wet mouth with her own hot tongue. Immediately, the blonde responded in kind. Another staccato flurry of the ravishing cherrywood brought the blonde up on to her stockinged toes and forced her tongue deep into Susie's mouth. Straining and squirming in her bondage, she squealed her pleasure-pain, her cries muffled by the pressure of Susie's lips. Snatching her head away, Susie smothered the blonde's renewed cries of pleasure with the leather-soled slipper. The blonde's blue eyes gazed up imploringly. Her slit must be on fire, Susie thought: she wants my tongue at her slit. Sovereign of the moment, Susie merely turned the supple leather sole towards her own tongue, and licked it slowly. The punished blonde bucked and writhed in sweet torment.

'Come here and slipper her bottom, Susie,' madame ordered.

Quivering with anticipation, Susie strode around the stocks and addressed the blonde's already reddening buttocks with the slipper. Almost tenderly, she tapped the cheeks which she was about to beat.

'Suffer and learn,' Susie whispered hoarsely, words which earned a brisk nod of approval from madame. Positioning her own naked bottom up into and against the stocks, and facing away from the blonde, Susie slipped her arm around the hips of the bending girl to encircle the captive's waist completely. Settling her left thigh against the flank of the yoked blonde, Susie bent forward slightly and held the slipper aloft.

'Twelve,' pronounced madame, walking away from the stocks to return her cane to its proper resting place on top of the chest of drawers.

'Twelve,' echoed Susie, pausing to crush her right peaked nipple with the supple sole. She tightened her grip and noted how the bending blonde inched her rounded bottom upwards, presenting her trapped cheeks perfectly for the slipper's leather lash.

* * *

107

In her shower, after the pupils had dressed and departed, Susie's toes trod the scented foam that tickled her naked feet. Utterly exhausted, yet exhilarated by her afternoon's experiences in the tutorial room under madame's stern supervision, Susie sank back against the cold, white tiles and surrendered her aching limbs to the reviving waters of her shower. After slippering the blonde's beautiful, bare bottom, Susie had taken her willing victim to join the other three in the showers. Returning, she recalled, she had discovered madame taking the fifth, highly excitable, girl out of the stocks. Tapping the nearly nude pupil between the thighs, madame had indicated that the afternoon had already proved too much for the girl: she had orgasmed twice. Then over madame's naked lap, the girl – who, unblindfolded, had witnessed every searing swipe and stroke in the multiple mirrors – was squeezed and fondled by madame but her bare bottom remained unspanked. After six or seven minutes across madame's knee, having her breasts tormented and the dark cleft between her upturned cheeks thumbed, Susie saw the girl climax again.

In her shower, Susie smiled fondly at the memory and stretched up to adjust the stream of water. As she did so her toes nudged something hard. Stooping, she searched the foaming bubbles and found the dildo. Unlike the ebony specimens given by madame to the first three punished girls, this one was fashioned from sterling silver. It had a thickened knout. Susie's wet fingers thrilled to the slippery weight of the shaft they gripped so tightly. It was, Susie realised, the blonde's dildo abandoned no doubt after she had used it feverishly following her stern discipline.

Susie drew the silver dildo up to her throat and stroked her flesh firmly. Then she dragged the engorged head of the silver phallus down over each nipple, punishing the wet, pink buds until they throbbed with raw pleasure. Connecting the blonde's abandoned dildo to her own warm flesh immediately flooded Susie's brain with vivid memories of the slippering. How madame had returned to observe the chastisement – stopping Susie after the fifth swipe to finger the ravaged cheeks of the blonde and inspect their hot flesh

108

intimately – then stood behind Susie as the remaining strokes of the slipper were administered. Susie recalled how madame had pressed her bosom into Susie's naked back. In response, Susie had dared to arch up her buttocks into madame's pubis.

Susie turned the shower off. A single droplet gathered above her and, after shivering for a moment, spilled down to splash between her eyes. Blinking away the beads, Susie traced the swell of her belly with the dildo's blunt tip. The silver shaft glided over her wet skin like a passionate tongue-tip. Susie closed her eyes, remembering the moment when the slippering had stopped. How madame had patted Susie's bare bottom affectionately, and how Susie had furtively managed to kiss the hot leather sole of the cruel slipper. Unshackled from her stocks, the blonde had dropped down upon her knees and buried her shining face between madame's parted thighs. Sternly indifferent to this display of gushing adoration, madame had merely gripped a fistful of the blonde's tangled curls and subjugated the kneeling nude.

Gripping the silver dildo, Susie fingered her labia apart, splaying the soft flesh to reveal the opening to her fiery slit. Yes. Memories of the gentle violence of the blonde's chastisement swept over her as Susie plied the dildo. Yes. Madame cracking the gleaming cherrywood hairbrush down across the bunched cheeks. Yes. Susie raising the leather-soled slipper up. Yes. That delicious sound as the hot cheeks received stroke after stroke. Yes. The squirming nude unable to evade her sweet pain. The dildo slid up and down more feverishly as the images of discipline fuelled Susie's furious fantasy: soon she was on the brink of an explosive climax. Squeezing her eyes tightly shut she trembled, her knees buckling slightly, as she conjured up the blonde's bare bottom: the creamy, soft cheeks reddening under the unerring strokes.

Suddenly, Susie's hand froze. Two familiar voices broke into her consciousness. Giggling excitedly as they both stripped off and squeezed into a single shower unaware of Susie's hidden presence, the two voices merged into one excited whisper as they melted into the mutual pleasure of intimacy. Susie's face paled and her eyes, normally so clear and wide, clouded and narrowed as the dark light of jealous anger suffused them. Not ten feet away, naked and unashamed, Svetlana was tenderly soaping the breasts, then the belly and buttocks, of Annette. Hot tears of anger stung Susie's eyes. Blinking away her tears, she stole out of the shower room into the cold corridor beyond. A stray bubble of shower gel had left its perfumed taste on her lips, but it could not mask the bitter tang of jealousy that burned so deep within her.

Five

The following morning Susie sat silently at the breakfast table with little appetite and even less conversation. Madame was being bright and brisk, handing out instructions along with fresh rounds of toast to Annette and Svetlana. Susie burned with jealous rage, but was particularly angry with Annette who she felt had betrayed the intimacy their mutual nakedness had known before the arrival of the ash blonde Russian. Madame glanced across at Susie's sullen frown then returned her attention to her plate of bacon and mushrooms.

Susie wearily took up her spoon and pulled the double egg-cup towards her. The boiled eggs held no interest for her and she twiddled her tiny egg spoon impatiently. Svetlana, smearing blackcurrant jam on to a golden finger of buttered toast, giggled as she bantered with Annette. Susie bit her lip and fingered the warm domes of her boiled eggs: suddenly imagining them to be Annette's upturned buttocks, she thrilled to the feel of their smooth, hot shells and grinned despite herself. In her thrall she fingered the imagined cheeks, believing their heat to be the result of a severe spanking she had just administered.

Madame chivvied a stray mushroom with the jabbing action of a heron – successfully cornering the little morsel up against a diamond of fried bread and forking it dispassionately. She noted every gesture Susie made. Susie thumbed the hot dome of the egg just as she would have thumbed Annette's scalded left buttock after smacking it severely. Unaware of madame's scrutiny, Susie gloated on her imagined revenge and sighed with deep contentment.

Oblivious to Susie's dark thoughts of revenge, Annette stole a finger of buttered toast from Svetlana's plate and popped it into her mouth. The edge of the toast was red – not from a stray smear of jam but from the lipstick on Svetlana's lips.

'Sugar, please,' Susie said, generously prepared to give Annette a chance to make amends.

Dazzled by Svetlana's smile, Annette absently passed Susie the salt.

Crack. Crack. Crack. Madame looked up knowingly as Susie brought her little egg spoon down upon the hot, rounded shells.

Madame Seraphim Savage strode into Susie's bedroom without knocking. Susie, brushing her rebellious, dark tangle of hair, shot the intruder a glance of resentment in the mirror and placed the hairbrush, bristle side up, on the dressing table.

'I have a few things to discuss with you.'

She's come here especially to thank me for my successful afternoon in the whipping school, Susie thought to herself smugly. She sat up attentively, preening herself.

'I am very much afraid to have to tell you that your behaviour yesterday was well below the standard I expect here at The Rookery. Well below.'

Susie reddened slowly and bowed her head down in shame.

'Those improvisations of yours yesterday afternoon may have been artistic but were not strictly essential. You were there to serve my clients, girl, not your own desires. Do you understand?'

'Yes, madame.'

'And as we are a small crew down here at The Rookery I like to run a tight ship. No room for jealousy. It causes friction. Do I make myself plain?'

Susie nodded meekly, secretly amazed at madame's omniscience.

'This evening you will be assisting Annette, who is more experienced than you.'

Susie flushed at this irony. She gazed down at her hands, folded together in her lap.

'I am running another Patron's Evening.'

Susie looked up.

'Once in a while,' madame explained, 'I throw a party to say thank you to the men who fund our most valuable clients' expensive tastes. It is, after all, their generosity which keeps the enterprise here thriving. These men believe that their partners merely buy expensive lingerie, a deceit I am perfectly willingly to perpetuate. They have come to regard these parties as a special treat, hoping for some very choice entertainment.'

'Will I have to –'

'No,' intercepted madame quickly. 'I'm not running a bordello here. Well, not exactly. No, these wealthy patrons merely expect to enjoy some sophisticated fun. Besides, their consorts are not that liberally disposed. The women think that the men who attend my little entertainments are treated to a lingerie show.'

Susie frowned.

'Don't be obtuse, girl. You will quickly learn that it is perfectly possible to please a man with the aid of a lace bustier, satin brassière and a pair of nylon stockings. Come along with me. I will select a suitable outfit for you to wear tonight.'

Moments later, Susie found herself stripped naked in front of a full-length mirror.

'Try these,' madame instructed.

Susie took the coffee-coloured silk stockings and eased her feet into each one before palming them up the length of her shapely legs.

'Waspie.'

Susie encircled her slender waist with the silver suspender belt, then carefully snapped her silk stocking tops into place.

'Brassière,' madame murmured, passing a silver satin specimen to Susie.

It was underwired and very sensuous. Susie shuddered as the weight of her warm breasts snuggled into the cool, silken cups. The enhanced cleavage gave her bosom a generous, bulging swell. Susie felt suddenly dizzy with narcissistic delight. Madame stood back to study the overall effect then approached the scantily clad girl and stood directly behind her. Susie shrank back a fraction at first as madame encircled her and fingered the silver suspender belt then placed her hands over her cupped breasts. The touch of madame's hands was sure and professional, but Susie felt the dominant force of Seraphim Savage as the maturer woman adjusted the underwired brassière to her complete satisfaction. Madame's cool hands remained at each heavy breast, then slowly began to squeeze the imprisoned flesh.

'I have selected a leather, pleated mini-skirt for you to wear tonight. You have the height and the legs for it, my girl.'

Such a compliment from so august a fashion expert as madame sent Susie tipsy with delight – that, and the controlling, squeezing hands of madame at her bosom. Susie smiled broadly, instantly restored to her pert, customary self-confidence.

'Can I try it on now?' she enthused.

'Very well,' madame replied, as if giving the matter considerable thought.

Susie clapped her hands with glee as madame gently unwrapped the tissue paper which contained the tiny skirt.

'Treat it with respect. It is from Helsinki. A very up-and-coming country in the haute couture world.'

Susie swathed the leather mini-skirt around her thighs and turned to examine the effect looking over her shoulder into the long mirror. Wiggling her bottom, she vamped in front of the glass. The leather was dyed cream, and the effect with the coffee-coloured silk stockings was, Susie had to admit, absolutely terrific.

'Be sure to throw yourself wholeheartedly into the proceedings tonight, my girl.'

'Yes, madame,' Susie replied.

'No repetition of yesterday's episode with that slippered young blonde.'

'No, madame.'

'And just to make absolutely sure that tonight is a success –'

Susie's heart fluttered: some exquisite jewellery, perhaps? Or was madame going to bestow her with exotic perfume?

'Bend over.'

Disbelief stunned Susie's spinning brain but she was already well disciplined and obeyed madame instantly.

'A short, sharp reminder will do you no harm. No harm at all, young lady. Touch your toes.'

To Susie's horror, madame picked up a cane from its resting place in a corner of the room and strode slowly back towards her bending bottom. Fumbling nervously, Susie stretched her splayed fingertips down to touch her stockinged toes.

'Six. I am not a great believer in the time-honoured six of the best. I believe it is the duty of the chastiser to deliver six of the very worst.'

Susie swallowed. Madame flicked at the leather hem of the mini-skirt with the cane tip, flipping the material up over Susie's hips to reveal the bare buttocks, pantyless and unprotected against the withering strokes to come.

'Legs apart.'

The coffee-coloured silk stockings parted tremulously.

'A fraction more,' stipulated madame, always the perfectionist.

Susie obeyed, and was now able to glimpse her own cheeks through her thighs in the full-length mirror. As madame ran the tip of the bamboo rod up from Susie's stockinged heel to the swell of her left buttock, the bending girl grimly acknowledged the devilish genius of the majestic dominatrix: arranged thus, the whipper had ensured that the one to be whipped would suffer double torments. Susie would not only feel the cut of the cruel cane as it lashed her naked flesh, but she would witness every withering slice in the tell-tale glass into which she was forced to gaze.

Swish, slice: Susie blinked as she saw the first stroke whip down across her exposed cheeks, searing them with a scalding fire. She saw the second bite into her heavy

115

cheeks, licking the creamy flesh with another line of invisible flame. She gasped and arched up on her stockinged toes at the cane-kiss of the third searing cut. Already, both in the mirror and in painful reality, her bare bottom blazed beneath the quivering bamboo.

'Kneel.'

Susie, the threat of salt tears brimming in her large eyes, dropped down upon her knees.

'Bottom up. Higher. Give it to me, girl. I want it up.'

The kneeling girl thrust her scalding cheeks up to their appointment with pain, presenting her buttocks round and tempting to the cane.

'Yesterday afternoon, and indeed this morning at breakfast, you behaved in a selfish and spoiled manner. Let this be a lesson to you, my girl. One I trust will prove memorable.'

Three times the rod rose up and swept down to stripe and sear the defenceless cheeks below. Three times Susie gasped and blinked away her tears of shame. Without uttering another word, madame returned the cane to its resting place. Susie held her breath. Would madame return to soothe and caress the bottom she had just completed punishing? Would she bend down to kiss the hot cheeks she had just lashed? No. Susie was to taste disappointment as well as strict discipline for madame strode out of the room. The caned girl slowly rose and, turning her bottom towards the full-length mirror, inched up the pleated leather mini-skirt over her hips.

Framed by the silver suspender belt above and the darker bands of coffee-coloured stocking tops below the swell of her cheeks, she carefully examined her buttocks in the reflecting glass. Four angry stripes attested to the recent visitation of the blistering bamboo. Four? Susie frowned, expecting to count six cane-kisses. Surely, she thought, she had been given six. Of course: madame always revisited the stripes of her first two lashes with her final strokes. Yes. Susie saw that two of the pink cane cuts were deepening to an angrier red; the scalded flesh of her rump darkening at the effect of being accurately double-lashed.

Tears of self-pity welled up in Susie's eyes. She hated madame, and Annette and The Rookery. She detested them. Forlorn, betrayed, whipped and isolated, Susie fiercely resented her forthcoming role in the entertainments scheduled for madame's clients. After all this how could she strive to be creative, imaginative and indulgent to a hot roomful of elderly, monied, tired men?

'You look great. Gorgeous outfit.'

Susie smiled uncertainly, pleased with but surprised by Annette's ungrudging admiration.

'It's only on loan,' she replied, proudly smoothing the creamy leather of her pleated mini-skirt. 'Madame wants it back, in mint condition, later tonight after the party.'

'Dress you specially, did she?' Annette laughed. 'Like a fairy godmother?'

'Mm. To please the guests.'

'So, Cinders, you shall go for their balls after all.'

Susie grinned.

'They'll be waiting for us. We'd better go down.'

In the oppressive drawing room, full of heavy Victorian furniture, Susie was astonished to find four suave young men sitting in deep armchairs sipping cognac from balloon glasses. She had expected a party of about a dozen aging roués, thinking perhaps that money and maturity formed a natural alliance.

Annette quickly supplied a brief biography of each of the guests. 'That one runs private casinos and clubs throughout the country; madame dresses all his young hostesses. He,' she nodded to a cruel-mouthed Adonis, 'farms about a quarter of Devon and made his maiden speech in the House of Lords last month. His two cousins come here for discipline every weekend. He,' she indicated to the third, a tall, aloof young buck, 'owns and hunts over two thousand acres; madame dresses his aunt and canes his sister and he,' she concluded, gesturing subtly to the fourth man, 'is a player in the bullion markets. A twenty-four carat swine.

Annette, scantily clad in velvet, peach hued basque and

shining black stockings, dimmed the lights and turned up some erotic music. Seconds later she was performing a sensuous strip-tease, keeping her rounded buttocks turned towards the four young men throughout. Susie, standing in the shadows, was utterly captivated by the erotic display. Turning, she frowned angrily as she saw the bullion dealer slowly masturbating into his empty brandy glass, while the others busily discussed off-shore tax loopholes and the fiscal probity of agricultural set aside allowances.

Bored, monied and rude; she fumed, impatient with their casual response. As Annette finished her entertaining bump and grind, Susie gasped as the bullion dealer tossed the sticky contents of his balloon glass on to Annette's bare bottom. Annette peered down over her shoulder at the wet splash on her cheeks. She smiled indulgently but Annette saw the shadow darken the naked girl's eyes. Taking a deep breath, Susie strode into the pool of light that bathed the square of richly patterned carpet before the fireplace. Smiling brightly, she eased the lid up off a large white box and took out several items of exotic lingerie. Annette, pale and nude, approached, planting her feet slightly apart. The evening's entertainment proceeded with Susie slowly and intimately dressing – and then undressing – Annette three times in an array of provocative scanties. The four voyeurs appreciated the two girls' performance but soon turned away to become embroiled in a heated exchange about the UN's role in Bosnia.

'Superior air power. Get some bloody F1-11's up. Win the skies and you've won the war,' the cruel mouthed Adonis insisted, his eyes narrowing into fierce slits as they raked Annette's naked buttocks, revealed once more as Susie peeled down a pair of flimsy panties.

'Chuck a squadron of Harriers at 'em. Our boys'd soon give anyone breaking the ceasefire a good spanking,' the huntsman countered, belligerently flying the flag.

Susie grew close to losing her temper. They were behaving as though they were in their London Club, or on the nineteenth of a private golf course. How rude and arrogant. They should, she resolved, be taught a lesson. She reined her fury in tightly: not to do so would be to render the party for these wealthy patrons a disaster, and incur madame's stinging displeasure. However, she bridled at their rudeness and chose her strategy carefully. Annette, her thighs astride the studded arm of a bottle-green leather Chesterfield, was just about to ride the hide when Susie reached out and flicked on all the lights. The loud banter ceased abruptly. Annette kissed the leather with her labial lips. Susie clapped her hands sharply.

'Stand up, all of you. Stand up and strip. At once,' she scolded them. 'Quickly.'

'What –?' started the nightclub owner, amazed.

'Strip,' barked Susie, pleasantly but firmly.

Have you gone mad? mouthed Annette silently from her leather perch. Trust me, Susie smiled by way of mute reply.

Confused and delighted, three of the four men undressed quickly, tumbling out of trousers and shoes with much horseplay and laughter. The fourth, the bullion-broker, sat stock still and gazed insolently at Susie with amused tolerance. Susie considered him carefully, this man with lizard-like eyes who in the course of his working hours controlled so much, so many – as indeed did all of these young men in the drawing room of The Rookery. With a sudden flash of feminine intuition, she realised why perhaps they were bored and behaving with indifference to the delights offered up to them. They habitually controlled all around them but had never been themselves controlled. Spoiled and monied, they had yet to savour the harsh delights of discipline or the exquisite sorrows of subjugation. Sauntering over to the pale-faced bullion-broker, Susie stood directly in front of where he sat. She waggled her bottom, causing the hem of her leather mini-skirt to graze the tip of his nose. Gently pressing the soft leather into his face, she stroked his thick, dark hair.

'Bullion-broker?'

He inclined his head in assent, probing her pubis briefly with his hawk-like nose.

'Risky?'

His eyes flickered up, a spark of interest kindling their poker-player's darkness.

119

'Fancy a little bet?' Susie smiled.

'I never gamble,' he grunted brusquely.

'Fibber,' she cooed, tugging at a tuft of hair. 'You brokers create risk, assess it, manage it and then exploit it. You gamble on other's greed, every transaction. Don't you?' she teased.

His mouth managed a grimace rather than a smile.

'If you're such a good gambler, what colour panties am I wearing? Strip if you're wrong, do what you will with me if you're right. Is it a bet?'

His eyes widened with lust. He remained impassively silent. Susie could almost hear his mind whirring busily. Calculating the odds. Got you, you bastard, she thought.

'Anything?' he whispered into the leather hoarsely.

'Anything,' she nodded gravely.

'They're –' he blurted.

'Ah, ah,' she tapped his nose gently. 'Don't guess. Let's do this scientifically. You're supposed to be good at calculating the odds. At managing risk. Think. Coffee-coloured stockings, a cream leather mini. Now what would a sweet little whore like me wear stretched tightly across her bottom, hmm?'

'Crimson – no, wait. Chocolate silk – no, cream; I mean white. Tight, white cotton –' he babbled, tipsy with confused lust.

That's a busted flush, sucker, Susie grinned to herself.

'Wrong. I win. Strip,' she commanded.

'What colour?' he grunted in a dazed voice.

'Look,' taunted Susie, inching up her mini-skirt a heartbeat at a time. She twirled, presenting him with her bare, pantyless buttocks. 'If you'd said peach, it'd have been honours even.'

'Bitch,' he hissed, grabbing at her buttocks angrily.

'Naughty,' Susie said with a pout, sweeping his hands away. 'You can kiss but you can't touch.'

'Yes,' he said thickly.

'Yes, what?'

'Please,' he said softly.

'Not my bottom. Not just yet. But you may kiss my

stocking tops.' Susie bared and offered her thighs to his mouth. She shuddered as she felt his tongue flatten against the thin material and rasp against it. He withdrew, leaving a hot, moist patch.

'That's all you get for now. Strip,' she murmured.

He hesitated.

'A gentleman always settles his debts,' she whispered.

Chastened and defeated by her wit and wilfulness, the bullion-broker peeled off his dinner jacket and slowly disrobed. Susie skipped out of the drawing room and returned bearing four velvet blindfolds from the drawer in the tutorial room down the corridor.

'Kneel,' she instructed the naked men. 'This party needs livening up, boys. Tonight,' she announced boldly, attaching a blindfold to the landowning huntsman as Annette wrapped a strip of velvet around the eyes of the nightclub owner, 'I will be your Mistress of Ceremonies and my colleague here will be the Lady of Misrule.'

Soon, all four kneeling men were blindfolded. Fishing out four loose nylons from the white lingerie box, she tossed two to Annette and knelt down in front of the bullion-broker. Carefully threading the gauzy nylon around his gently bobbing balls, then wrapping it around the kneeling man's thickening shaft – and motioning Annette to do the same to the other three – she tamed and tethered him. Moments later, all four young men were naked, blindfolded and deliciously ensnared. The guests were already erect after Annette's earlier strip-tease and Susie's subsequent lingerie games. But submitting to female rule, their blindfolds and tied by the soft nylons, they grew potently engorged.

'Up,' commanded Susie, tugging at two of the nylons. Her captives winced and rose obediently.

'Up,' echoed Annette, successfully disguising the glee in her voice. Her tethered slaves obeyed.

'Follow me,' Susie instructed, leading her naked prisoners towards the door. They shuffled behind her. Annette flashed her pal a grin of naughty delight. Susie returned the grin, but touched her finger to her lips,

121

bidding Annette to remain silent. Susie's slaves trod the cool flagstones in the corridor carefully. Blindfolded and exquisitely bound, they could not but obey. Out in the deep Devon night, a fox barked twice. The huntsman paused and strained to listen.

'No hunting for you tonight,' Susie whispered softly. 'Tonight, I'm in the saddle and you are my quarry and –' Susie jerked the nylon stocking tied to his shaft '– tonight I shall have your brush.'

In the tutorial room where madame had conducted the whipping school the previous afternoon, the four naked men were soon yoked and helpless in the wooden stocks. Pinioned in their halters, they quivered with anticipation.

'We will deal with this one first,' Susie instructed Annette as she undid the blindfold from the nightclub owner's eyes. 'Take this and pleasure yourself,' she added, passing Annette a dildo from the drawer.

Annette, now stripped down to a white cotton sports bra, stood directly in front of the yoked man and deliberately, intimately plied the dildo, stroking her nipples beneath the bra's white cotton cups. Her captive audience struggled within his firm bondage, stretching out his fingers and tongue. Mere inches away, so tantalisingly near, so frustratingly far, Annette lost herself in an ecstasy of narcissistic pleasure. Grunting thickly, the nightclub owner swore and cursed as Annette guided the blunt tip of the dildo down towards her pubic nest.

'Witch,' he hissed in frustration, thrashing in his torment.

Susie joined Annette and slowly unthreaded her silver suspender belt.

'I am going to whip you. Whip your bottom slowly with my silky suspender belt. When, and only when, I deem it fitting to do so, I will untie the nylon stocking that binds you and allow you the relief you will crave.'

Susie unclasped her suspender belt and slipped it down over her thighs beneath the cream mini-skirt. Addressing the bare buttocks of her captive, she dangled it lengthways down along his cleft, then forcing the silk between his cheeks, ravaged the flesh between. He cried out in pure delight, squeezing his cheeks to trap and contain the delicious torment but Susie was adept with her strip of stretchy silk and continued to work on his sensitive flesh.

Annette, still inches away from the nightclub owner's face, turned her naked buttocks to his gaze and inserted the dildo's tip between her heavy cheeks. He roared in frustration, rattling the wooden harness that trapped him. Swish, swish, swish: Susie lashed his bottom with her suspender belt, scoring the cheeks with sharp, reddening stripes. The silk suspender – heaven to wear as lingerie but hell to bear as a lash – rocketed the naked man into paroxysms of sweet agony. Annette grunted as her dildo did its devilish work inches from his parted lips causing his erection to grow hot and huge. Again Susie swept the suspender belt across the crown of the scarlet rump. Between his thick lustful grunts, he began to beg for mercy. Stepping around the stocks to face him, she gently pushed Annette aside and held the warm silk with which she had just whipped him to his lips.

'Kiss,' she commanded.

Obediently, he submitted to the suspender.

'Open wide.'

His lips parted a fraction.

'Wider.'

He obeyed her stern injunction. Susie crammed the hot silk into his wet mouth taking up the nylon stocking which tethered his twitching shaft as she did so. Tugging at it gently, she stared down dominantly into his pleading eyes.

'Now,' he begged, arching his stiffened body up in his bondage. 'Please. Now.'

She slipped her left hand down between his thighs and released his engorged shaft from the strictures of the tight nylon stocking: he shuddered and instantly shot his load, the arc of hot silver squirting straight on to Susie's leather mini. Susie sensed the hot splash against her, then felt the slow drip of his release against the top of her thigh. Fingering the sticky wetness that stained the cream of her skirt, she closed her eyes. It was just as she expected between her inquisitive fingertips: warm beeswax. The man's liquid joy was like warm beeswax as she rubbed it playfully between her fingertips.

'Now look what you've done,' she chided him sternly. 'All over my nice, new leather mini. I must punish you most severely. Give me a bamboo cane, Annette.'

Annette supplied the required cane in silence.

'No, please. I'm sorry –'

'Silence,' Susie commanded. 'Blindfold him once more,' she instructed, tapping the open palm of her left hand with the tip of the yellow wood as she strode back towards his naked buttocks.

Annette obeyed, crushing her rounded breasts into the yoked victim's face as she tightly applied the band of black velvet to his eyes. Standing directly behind the already punished bottom, Susie stroked the cleft with downward strokes of the cane tip. He tightened his cheeks, in a futile attempt to resist the dominant touch of bamboo, but Susie lowered the cane tip between his thighs and tapped his balls.

'Open your cheeks,' she instructed.

His silence signalled his refusal to obey. Susie tapped more firmly: immediately, she saw the punished cheeks unclench. Placing her pincered finger and thumb above his sphincter, she prised his flesh apart and introduced the tip of the bamboo cane. Rotating it gently, she drove him into renewed ecstasies of frenzied thrashing. Intent on mastering him completely, she slipped her free hand to cup his balls and squeezed. Bucking and writhing in his bondage, he cursed her with a sweet savagery, his words became mere carnal grunts as Susie slid the first inch of the whippy cane in between his cheeks.

'Silence, or you will be whipped without mercy. Do you understand me?'

Abjectly, he nodded his submission to her will.

'I am going to see to our other guests, but I shall return.' With this dark promise, Susie placed the length of cane in between his buttocks, and, wrapping her suspender belt around him, bound the instrument of exquisite suffering securely.

'This one?' Annette asked, nodding to the landowning huntsman. 'Shall we entertain him next?'

'Yes,' Susie replied. 'But keep the blindfold on.'

Their next victim stiffened in his wooden halter. Already, his thickening, veined shaft threatened to explode and soak the shining stocking that swathed its erect length.

'Give him your bottom. Panties on,' Susie instructed.

Annette took a small footstool and arranged it so that, when standing up on it, she was able to crush her cotton-pantied cheeks into the man's face. Moaning, he buried himself into the soft, sensuous warmth between her heavy, rounded cheeks. Susie untied the nylon stocking from his erection and slipped the warm cup of her brassière over the swollen bulb-tip. Sinuously threading the bra between his thighs, she jerked it up behind him and pulled. He screamed softly. Susie yanked the brassière, taking care to torment his balls as she dragged the silken cup that crowned the throbbing shaft. Buried deeply into Annette's generous buttocks, the naked man scrabbled his feet on the floor below. Susie pulled at the brassière with increasing vigour, bewitching her victim to the imminent point of climax – which she ruthlessly denied to him.

'Tonight, I will teach you to kneel before the sweet sovereignty of lingerie. I will make you bend your knee to the potent mystery of women's second skin. Repeat after me,' she whispered. 'Bra, panties, bra, panties.'

Muffled by Annette's swollen bottom, the huntsman uttered the mantra as Susie had commanded. Bra, panties. Bra, panties. Susie jerked the silken torment faster, in time to his cries. Bra, panties, bra, panties. His feverish words spilled from his lips urgently. Annette thrust her cheeks back into his face, smothering his excitement. Bra, panties, bra, panties; he did not cease his incantation even as, after a furious jerk of the brassière, he came in a pulsing stream. Susie returned to his perspiring face, slipped off the blind-fold and forced him to gaze down upon the soaking bra cup.

'Just look at what you've done,' she scolded, holding it close to his face.

125

He closed his eyes, his face pale and drained.

'I will be all sticky now.' She pouted playfully, easing her breasts into the soiled brassière. 'See?' she whispered, slipping her left breast out of the wet cup and holding her shining, dripping nipple up to him.

'Naughty boy,' she said sternly, palming the sticky release of his orgasm into her soft, rubbery flesh. 'I am going to cane you. Cane you very hard, across the bare bottom,' she chided, reaching up with her wet fingers to slip his blindfold back on, binding the velvet tightly. 'But not just yet. In a little while. Until then, I want you to think carefully about the silk cup of the brassière, my wet breast and your hot stripes to come.'

Susie took a pace sideways, positioning herself in front of the third guest – the farmer.

'Deal with him,' she said with a nod to Annette, jerking her left wrist up and down rhythmically – the oldest gesture in the world.

'Yes,' replied Annette enthusiastically, slipping around to the rear of the trapped man and leaning closely against his nakedness, crushing her bosom into him. Reaching down around his thigh, she closed her fingers around his stockinged shaft.

Susie peeled away the blindfold from the cruel-mouthed Adonis and slipped the velvet band down around his sensual lips. His eyes bulged up at her severe gaze as she tightly gagged him.

'Stain my cream leather mini with your wetness and you shall suffer. Suffer severely,' she warned, slipping her fingers down to scratch at his exposed nipples.

Annette worked his straining erection slowly and skilfully, pumping the nyloned shaft and pausing, from time to time, to gently squeeze. Already on the boil from the unseen but understood pleasuring and disciplining of his yoked colleagues, the farmer tensed and stiffened quickly, coming only seconds later with a soft scream of delight. Susie felt the liquid jet of his hot release patter against the soft leather of her pleated mini. Gazing down at the blotching stain, she shook her head slowly in mock sorrow.

'I warned you, you silly boy. Now I'm going to have to whip you. Aren't I?'

Closing his eyes, he lowered his head. Gagged, he could not reply. Silence reigned supremely over his cruel mouth.

'What? No snivelling pleas for mercy?' Susie taunted.

He opened his eyes and pleaded for forgiveness with them. Susie merely smiled and lifted up her leather skirt, catching it coquettishly by the hem. Displaying his sticky splashes, she counted them aloud.

'Eleven,' she concluded. 'I count eleven spots. Am I right?'

He stared at them as if hypnotised, then nodded slowly.

'Shall we say eleven strokes of the cane, then? Good.'

Annette rejoined Susie as the blindfold was returned across the farmer's eyes.

'Ah, our bullion-broker. It is time for his pain. Unlucky with panties, aren't you?' Susie teased.

Remembering how she had tricked him earlier, the sullen broker grunted his contempt.

'Don't sulk, or I'll give you something you will have true cause to regret. Do you hear me?'

He nodded slightly. She removed his blindfold, meeting his defiant gaze with an amused smile.

'Let's see if we can change your run of luck. Untie the stocking, my dear, and replace it with your panties.'

Annette peeled off her white, cotton briefs, her breasts bulging deliciously as she did so. Seconds later, having unwound the clinging nylon stocking, she wrapped her panties tightly around his swollen rod.

'I seem to recollect your somewhat insulting response to my colleague's earlier offering,' Susie murmured.

He frowned, uncomprehending.

'I shall now entertain you and we shall see how you applaud this time. I'm sorry I have no brandy to offer you.'

Suddenly remembering, he blushed deeply.

Annette, as bidden, flexed a length of bamboo and tapped the broker's buttocks smartly. Looking up, she awaited Susie's signal. Susie started to strip-tease slowly, then paused semi-naked, and nodded. Swish, swipe. Swish, swipe: the thin cane swept down across his naked cheeks, slicing them with cruel accuracy and leaving the yoked sufferer with two reddening stripes. Gently increasing her tempo, Susie continued her powerfully erotic strip, spilling out of her silk and satin scanties. Again, Annette whipped the cane down, searingly lashing the defenceless flesh. Swish, swipe. Swish, swipe. Another double agony as the bamboo licked his bare skin. Susie worked feverishly now, stripping off the final vestiges of wispy nothingness to reveal her ripe nakedness. Annette echoed the increasing excitement, applying the bamboo more rapidly across the reddening bottom. Exultant, Susie stood perspiring and naked before him. Swish: Annette's single swipe launched him into orgasmic climax. He came furiously, rattling the wooden halter that imprisoned him like a penned bull. Susie's eyes widened as she watched his engorged shaft pump and squirt into the white, cotton panties, and shivered as he groaned his loud joy.

'Hot bottom?' she whispered, moments later.

He tried to avert his bleary eyes from her cool, penetrating gaze.

'I think we should have something for that, haven't we?' she said to Annette.

Annette, remembering her own shame after her earlier strip-tease, gleefully unwrapped the sticky panties from his still engorged muscle and pressed them against his scalded buttocks. The bullion-broker shuddered in his bondage.

'There,' murmured Susie. 'I told you I'd teach you some manners, and I have, haven't I? The next time a beautiful girl performs for you, you will applaud her properly, won't you?'

He looked away, his face a sour mask of resentment.

'Won't you?'

Annette, obeying Susie's gesture of command, whipped away the wet panties and lashed the bare buttocks twice with her cane.

'Yes,' he groaned through clenched teeth. 'Yes.'

Satisfied with his response, Susie patted her broker captive's face gently. 'Good,' she crooned. 'My colleague shall withdraw for a little while. You will remain here. In silence. Understand?'

He nodded.

Absolute silence,' she instructed, reblindfolding the bullion merchant she had just tamed into submission. 'But I will be back.'

Showered, powdered and refreshed, the two young women returned to their four bound party guests less than twenty minutes later. Between them, they carried two glasses, a bottle of chilled Chardonnay, napkins and a plateful of delicious ham sandwiches. Annette bore a little silver pot of freshly made mustard. Their light repast vanished quickly, the fruity wine a superb companion to the moist Devizes ham.

'Lingerie,' Susie resumed, dabbing at her lips with a napkin, 'is often seen by men as a frippery, a symbol of female vanity. How wrong they are. It is my duty, and indeed my pleasure, to educate you four young men this evening, demonstrating how important and how potent those wisps of silk and snatches of satin actually are. Remove their blindfolds, please.'

Annette was prompt in doing so, asking if she should gag the naked captives.

'An excellent suggestion. Please do. I have no wish to hear their foolish views. They are here to listen, and to learn. Gag them firmly.'

As Annette completed the preparations for the schooling, Susie produced a long, leather strap and snapped it twice. Over their gags of black velvet, four pairs of eyes widened fearfully.

'We will commence with the brassière,' Susie snarled softly. 'Observe.'

Annette knelt down before them, cupping her naked breasts and offering them up to their collective gaze.

'For the bosom, or breasts, there are four fundamental designs of brassière which will now be modelled. Later, you will be introduced to the bustier and basque.'

Crack. Crack. As Annette, nude and kneeling, filled the

empty cups of a selection of brassières, Susie strapped the naked buttocks of the spellbound voyeurs. Indifferent to both their yearning eyes and their suffering, Annette became lost in the sensual, feminine pleasures of adorning, enhancing and defining her beautiful bosom. The powerful mix of her naked intimacy with her cool aloofness fired the men who devoured her with fiercely focused eyes. Again the strap snapped down across the row of scalded buttocks in between Susie's running commentary, punctuating her intimate descriptions with flashes of scalding pain. Susie, fingering the hot leather she had just plied so expertly, explained the art of the corsetière to the men, sharing the secrets of how the brassière could bewitch by moulding, uplifting and pronouncing the charms of the ultimate feminine attribute: the breasts.

Crack, snap: four more searing lashes crimsoned the bound men's bottoms as Annette, now standing with her back turned to the captives in their stocks, posed and displayed five different designs of panty; from the clinging silk of cami-knickers to an immodest suede thong. Devoting their eyes to her pert rump, the men suffered the torments of her tantalising beauty before them while simultaneously enjoying the sharp taste of harsh discipline behind.

'Feminine beauty stands supreme –' the leather lashed '– when naked and unadorned,' Susie declared. 'But the ingenuity of the corsetière can add a certain piquancy, a relish with her satin, silk and lace.'

Annette, stripped naked once more, tempted her audience with a coquettish display of opaque tights, mesh stockings, seamed nylons and exquisitely provocative self-support nylons. The men delighted in her lithe legs and heavy, swollen cheeks. The nightclub owner came once more, pumping the empty space before him with his spurting erection.

'Just as the dressing of mustard added zest to our light supper of ham sandwiches, so lingerie perks up the female form. It is designed to flatter the female, as well as provoke the male.'

Kneeling down, Susie picked up the tiny silver mustard

pot from the supper tray Annette had deposited on the floor. Gazing up at the array of punished cheeks lined up before her and at the tight clefts which divided each set of buttocks, Susie smiled a dark, devilish smile. Instantly, the buttocks tensed as the four men heard Susie flip off the top of the mustard pot and stir the thick paste within. Rising softly, she approached the first bottom, slowly stirring all the time. The nightclub owner – as did his three bare-bottomed colleagues as their moment of pain came – hissed his tormented delight as Susie daubed the cleft between his cheeks with the dripping mustard spoon. The smear of yellow paste stung his sensitive flesh. Moments later, all four were jerking in severe ecstasy.

'Piquant,' whispered Susie, snapping her leather strap once more in readiness for the administration of pain. 'Like mustard is to ham, so satin cups are to the female bosom and lace or leather are to her waist and bottom. Please note,' Susie said matter-of-factly, 'how my colleague always ensures that her seams are perfectly straight. There is an art to dressing in stockings and suspenders. Strict rules have to be observed in order to achieve perfection. Very strict rules.'

Snap, crack. Again the harsh leather spoke, announcing that the illustrated lecture was to continue, as was the scalding pain of the captive audience.

'You were a remarkable success, Susie. Remarkable. Our guests were most profuse in their gratitude. Your imagin-ation and flair left a deep and lasting impression on them. One might almost say indelible. All begged, simply begged, for more. They were insisting that these occasional soirées became a regular feature – weekly, if possible. I said that I would review the current arrangements, but made no firm promises. Congratulations, my dear.'

'Thank you, madame.'

'You have instilled in them an admiration, more, a deep respect, for the art of the corsetière. They are all devoted to lingerie now. Why, two of them insisted upon settling outstanding accounts there and then. And,' madame concluded, 'I believe they left a substantial tip with Annette. Half of which is yours, of course.'

Susie looked up and beamed, basking in madame's approval.

'There is, alas, a matter which I cannot overlook. The state of the mini-skirt.'

Susie blushed, suddenly remembering all the stains. Madame added that it would cost at least two hundred to make good. Susie frowned.

'Fortunately, Annette received a tip of five hundred. Your share should cover the damage.'

Pulling a face of disappointment, Susie nodded silently and turned to leave.

'Sulking, girl? I simply cannot have that. Come here at once.'

'But madame –'

'At once.'

Fearfully, Susie stepped forward. Madame, sitting on a high-backed chair at her tapestry frame, pointed to the cream leather mini-skirt.

'That is one of a limited production from Helsinki's leading houses. You will pay for its restoration.'

'Yes, madame.'

'I had expected you to treat it more carefully. For that, and for sulking, I am going to spank you. Bend over my knee. Now, girl.'

Susie stumbled forward. Having removed the mini for madame to inspect, she was already stripped down to her coffee-coloured stockings and suspender belt.

'Bare-bottomed. How very convenient,' madame murmured as Susie crushed her bosom into the firm thighs and offered upturned cheeks for spanking. Madame pinned the unhappy girl by the nape of her neck and rested her free hand across Susie's bottom.

'You have a beautiful bottom, Susie,' madame said.

Susie squeezed her cheeks together, anticipating the hot pain to come.

'Very beautiful,' madame said again gently, palming the cusp of each cheek.

Susie squirmed beneath the delicious touch of the dominant hand and at the threat of impending punishment.

'How exquisitely soft, and rounded, your little bottom is upon close inspection. Stay perfectly still,' madame ordered, causing Susie to shiver at the thought of pain, 'while I sketch its outline into my tapestry.'

Susie relaxed as the threat passed for the moment. Her softened cheeks wobbled. Looking up over her shoulder, she tried to glimpse at the incompleted tapestry. Madame pinned her back firmly across her lap.

'Be still, girl. I want your bottom,' madame chided, busily sketching with a stick of charcoal on to the soft canvas.

'What will the picture be?' Susie asked, her words muffled by the warm thigh-flesh into which her lips were pressed.

'It is from a copy of an old Etruscan wall painting. Sappho guarding her fig tree. There is Sappho, and these will be her chosen maidens. The Etruscans believed that this Thracian fig had magical properties, fruiting only once a decade. My composition depicts Sappho and her naked beauties guarding the fig at its hour of fruiting. All eyes are drawn intently at the ripe, succulent bud. It is about to split wide open, revealing its sweet, secret flesh.'

Susie swallowed, her mouth suddenly dry.

'Excellent,' madame said with a smile, tossing aside the stick of charcoal. 'Now, where were we? Ah, yes. I was about to spank your naughty little bottom. Am I not correct?'

'Yes,' whispered Susie, dreading yet desiring the hot chastisement.

'But you have tried so hard and done so well, Susie, that I am loathe to punish you. This time.'

Please, oh please spank me, Susie thought silently, thrusting her bare bottom up as if to tempt and seduce the hovering hand.

'No, girl, not tonight. I shall not spank you, but you will pay the full cost of the damage done to the skirt.'

Madame cupped and squeezed each cheek gently then

firmly fingered Susie's sticky cleft, pausing to rest her fingertip at the tight rosebud of the anal whorl.

'The fruit of the Thracian fig must have been extraordinarily luscious,' madame purred, teasing the sphincter in her thrall as she spoke. 'It exercised such a great fascination over Sappho and her lovers. Extraordinarily luscious, hmm?'

Susie gasped as madame's straightened index finger slid into her tight warmth.

'My tapestry is a poor imitation, of course. The original is lost. It was last seen in Prague before the Nazis swept in. It was catalogued as *In Servitude*, and forbidden to the common gaze – only the privileged were permitted to see the painting. The title refers to Sappho's bondmaidens, hand picked to serve the sometime queen of Lesbos. I rather like to think that the Thracian fig fruited more frequently,' madame said, dropping her voice to a velvet whisper. 'Much more frequently.' She sighed, gently pumping between Susie's cheeks with her probing finger.

Susie clamped her thighs tightly together, thrusting her bare bottom upward.

'Must I sit and watch, like my figures frozen in their tapestry? Sit and watch to see if the fig will ripen?'

Slowly, imperceptibly, Susie responded, inching her thighs apart. Slowly, rhythmically, madame stroked the labial flesh-lips revealed within.

'Goodness,' madame said and chuckled in a tone of mock surprise. 'I think the fig is almost ripe. Why, yes. It is quite sticky with nectar, oozing with the sweet promise of juicy delight.'

Susie groaned into madame's firm thigh as a second finger slid swiftly and surely inside her innermost flesh.

'Can I have my share?' Susie said, standing at the doorway, but not entering Annette's bedroom. The room was in darkness.

'What?' Annette replied in a sleepy voice.

'The tip they left. For the party. I want my share. I have to pay for the mini-skirt.'

'I haven't got any money,' she said simply, adding in a hasty lie, 'There was no tip.'

'Yes, there was. Where is it?' Susie demanded.

'Go away,' came the sullen response. 'There's nothing for you here.'

Stung by the barbed irony of these words, Susie grew hot and angry. 'I want –'

'You heard what she said. Now go away,' the voice of Svetlana rang out in the darkness. 'There's nothing for you here.'

Susie clicked on the light and stepped inside the bedroom. Five-hundred pounds lay folded up tightly on Svetlana's side of the bed. On the sheets, the two naked girls lay entwined.

'Get out,' the ash blonde Russian hissed.

'When I get my share.'

'There is no share for you,' Svetlana rasped, reaching out to place her hand over the wad of notes. She sprang out of bed and, brushing Susie aside, firmly closed the door.

'I'm taking charge of that money. There are riches to be made here at The Rookery. Riches, and I don't want any trouble from you, bitch.'

'Stay out of this,' Susie warned. 'This is between Annette and me.'

'There is nothing between Annette and you, fool,' Svetlana snarled. 'She is mine, and so is all the money. I'm going to leave here rich, and you are not going to stop me.'

They sprang like cats, grappling their nakedness to each other and toppling down across the bed; Susie gained the upper hand.

'Get her off me!' Svetlana commanded hoarsely.

Annette hesitated for a fraction of a second, hovering over the wrestling nudes indecisively.

'Get her!' the Russian hissed.

Susie yelped as she felt Annette tugging at her hair with one hand and squeezing her left breast with the other. Releasing her grip on Svetlana, she squirmed beneath the onslaught from above. Seconds later, Svetlana struggled free and easily overpowered her foe, straddling Susie's bottom and pinning her face down into the warm, rumpled sheets.

'Tie her hands to the bedposts, then get her feet.'

Susie bucked beneath the warm weight of the nude Russian but was soon tied securely by Annette. Spread-eagled and restricted in corded bondage, she lay entirely at Svetlana's mercy.

'Gag her. We'll do this as quietly as we can. No need to disturb madame.'

Do what as quietly as they could? The question burned in Susie's brain as she wriggled and writhed. What was the ash blonde Russian going to do that required her victim to be naked, bound to the bedposts and firmly gagged?

'Watch the door,' Svetlana ordered crisply.

'But –' Annette faltered.

'Do as I say.'

Susie heard Annette scamper across to the door.

'Now, Susie, I think it's time I made things plain,' the Russian whispered. 'Annette is mine, understand? Keep your eyes and hands off.'

Susie felt the slim fingers of her tormentress slipping between her squashed breasts and the sheets beneath. She felt them scrabbling for her nipples, then felt the flash of burning pain as Svetlana pinched and tweaked them savagely.

'I've seen your jealous eyes, watching and hating our friendship. I do not wish to see it anymore. Understand?'

Susie buried her face in the pillow as the cruel fingers at her nipples punished them anew, ruthlessly ravaging their tender pink peaks.

'And as for your so-called share, forget it.'

The tormenting fingers slid down to the base of Susie's belly and tugged at her pubic curls. Susie's squeal was drowned by her gag.

'There are rich opportunities for me here, and I want no trouble from you, bitch.'

Again, the Russian's fingers tormented the girl who lay bound and helpless beneath her.

136

'Madame's coming,' Annette whispered urgently from the door. Switching off the light, she bounded silently across to the bed and slid her nakedness alongside Susie, crushing her breasts and thighs into the captive's passive flesh.

'Untie her hands,' Svetlana whispered.

Susie felt her hands being unleashed, only to be dragged down and held by each naked girl lying alongside her. Annette pulled a sheet up to cover the three nudes just as madame entered the bedroom.

Straining into her gag, her face squashed into the pillow, Susie lay helpless in her bed of bondage. Madame, leaving the light switch alone, tiptoed into the darkened room. Bending down, she sighed contentedly at what she took to be a cameo of loving friendship: three sleeping girls entwining their naked warmth.

'*The Three Graces*,' she murmured, gently stroking and then patting the cheeks of the upturned bottoms below.

Svetlana, feigning sleep but in reality pinning Susie's arm in a vice-like grip, sighed blissfully – giving madame what she knew she wanted. Nodding her satisfaction, madame stole out of the bedroom, delighted that peace had broken out between her girls.

'She's gone,' Annette said in the darkness after the door had clicked shut. 'Shall I turn the light on?'

'No. I can do what must be done in the dark,' Svetlana replied.

Susie shivered at the ominous words. Then shivered again at Annette's treacherous request.

'Can I help?'

'Tie her hands back to the bedposts,' Svetlana said.

Annette obeyed the order promptly, lashing Susie's wrists to each wooden post with fiercely tied nylon stockings.

'Excellent. Now we will teach this bitch to leave us well alone. Come,' the Russian said silkily.

Tremors of fear fluttered in Susie's tightening belly. Would it be the cruel cut of the cane? Or the scalding lash of a leather belt? What would the Russian use to punish her bare, defenceless bottom? Or had the maid from Moscow more terrible pleasures in mind?

'Make the gag secure,' Svetlana urged. 'She may squeal.'

Susie felt the Judas-touch of Annette's betraying fingers checking the tightness of the gag.

'It is secure.'

'Good. Now come to me. Let us use this bitch as our pillows, as our bed of delight.'

Susie groaned as her bare body bore the full weight of the embracing nudes above. She could feel Annette's squirming rump crushing down into her own upturned, splayed cheeks as her one-time lover took the full force of the dominant Russian on top. Wet, licking sounds rapidly degenerated into a hungry lapping and sucking. Was Svetlana mouthing Annette's throat and breasts, or were her cruel lips at the belly and pubis of the girl beneath? Jealous torments stabbed Susie's heart. Stung by the uncertainty of not knowing for certain, Susie burned with angry rage; rage which spilled over into fury at the ignominy of being used as a bed for the amorous sport above. Writhing in her spreadeagled nakedness, she struggled to dislodge the lovers.

'Stay still or I shall whip you,' Svetlana admonished.

Annette gasped aloud, then pounded Susie's rump with her own tightened buttocks as she climaxed violently. Susie felt the slick of hot wetness from above scald her bottom, and bucked and writhed to rid herself of the burden of flesh that pinned, humiliated and dominated her helpless body.

'Move over,' Svetland growled.

Annette rolled over, belly down, grinding her slit into the mattress.

'I will ride her,' the Russian snarled, 'but first, a taste of the pain she must learn to fear. And through fear, she will learn to obey.'

Spank. Spank. Spank. With her thighs tightly scissoring Susie's trapped cheeks, Svetlana administered an explosive burst of spanking. She scorched the wobbling buttocks a scarlet shade of pain. Susie grunted her anguish into the gag that sealed her mouth. Her bottom burned beneath the frenzied flurry of spanks. Then, to her horror, she felt her cruel Russian tormentress mount her; Svetlana eased her shaven pubis and sticky labia down on to the punished bottom. Dominantly supreme, Svetlana dragged her labia down against the hot swell of Susie's spanked cheeks repeatedly. Susie froze, hating the arrogant intimacy of the Russian girl who rode her so brutally, so ruthlessly. Atop and triumphant, Svetlana reached down and grasped her victim's breasts, squeezing and ravishing them painfully as she ground her wet plum into the scalded cheeks of her victim. Susie's gasp was silenced by her gag: she jerked her hips in a futile attempt to rid herself of the Russian, but Svetlana held on hard, taming and subduing the naked English girl between her hot, wet thighs.

'The hours of night are long,' Svetlana hissed. 'I will break and train this bitch and bend her to my will before dawn.'

Six

The late April sun warmed the backs of her legs as Susie, in a plain white vest and severely cut shorts, lay face down in the Devon meadow. High above in the cloudless sky, a lark sang sweetly. A strong scent of peppermint rose up from the grass. Frowning, Susie eased herself up on to her elbows. Where her breasts had crushed the grass, they had pressed down into a small patch of pennyroyal, releasing the pungent aroma. She sank down slowly once more, a clump of buttercups tickling her swollen thigh. The day was bright but Susie's thoughts brooded darkly on revenge. Annette had betrayed her utterly last night with Svetlana: Susie burned with angry shame as she recalled the dominant spanking she had suffered at the hands of the cruel Russian. She quivered with rage at the memory of how Annette had played with herself openly, stretched out alongside the spreadeagled nakedness of the spanked girl clearly enjoying Susie's suffering. Annette had, when Svetlana slept and Susie was still gagged and bound, taken further furtive pleasures with the helpless nude.

Rolling over on to her back, Susie gazed directly up into the azure ceiling of sky. She could hear, but not yet see, the lark. She sensed the slight trace of ozone in the air, bracing and invigorating. The Rookery must be close to the sea, she calculated. On her short walk after an early breakfast, she had seen no sign of gulls in the air or of sea pink at her feet, both sure signs of a nearby coastline. She was straining slightly as she lay in the sunshine, not to catch the sweet larksong, but to catch the harsh crackle of a Vespa. Vespa: the Italian for wasp. The dominant brunette, the whipping poetess, was due to arrive at The Rookery at eleven, booked in for a session with Annette. Susie had formulated a delicious revenge. How appropriate that her avenging angel would arrive on a Vespa, buzzing along like an angry wasp. And how much more appropriate, Susie reflected, that the striped wasp was speeding towards Annette: to deliver its terrible sting.

Susie shaded her eyes and scanned the undulating horizon but saw no sign of the poetess – dubbed the Sultan's Favourite – who swished bare bottoms while reciting erotic verse. Susie's thoughts turned to Svetlana's strange words. Being punished for lusting after Annette, that much Susie could understand. But what were the Russian's other boastful words all about? Svetlana had pocketed the entire tip the young men attending the party had left, but there was something else, something Svetlana had let slip in her moment of exultant triumph over Susie's subjugation. Money was to be made at The Rookery: Susie was not sure how or when Svetlana intended to strike, but she resolved to watch the Russian very carefully.

The staccato crackle of a Vespa drowned the trill of the lark. Susie sprang up and trotted down towards the flint sheep track. The approaching snarl increased to an angry buzzing as the Vespa rounded the corner, then spluttered and died as the brunette brought the machine to a spluttering stop alongside Susie, dipping her arched foot into the flint to steady herself. Easing off her white helmet and tossing her hair free, she smiled up at Susie warmly.

'Sunbathing?' she asked, eying Susie's tight shorts hungrily.

'Not really,' Susie replied. 'Just out for a little stroll. I didn't know you were coming this morning,' she lied carefully.

'Mmm. I'm seeing Annette.'

'Oh,' Susie replied, putting as much calculated disappointment into her voice as she dared. Then, judging the moment to be right, added: 'I do love your poems.'

'Really? Why, thank you.'

Susie flashed the poetess a shy smile, fuelling the other's vanity.

141

'Give you a lift back?'

Nodding happily, Susie slipped on to the warm leather saddle and snuggled up closely against the brunette, jamming her pubis into the soft bottom in front. Susie grinned as she felt the brunette thrust her cheeks back, pressing herself into Susie's warmth.

'Better hang on tight,' she shouted over her shoulder above the crackle of the Vespa as she kicked it into life. 'I haven't a spare,' she added, tapping her white helmet.

Susie encircled the poetess with her arms, hugging the firm bosom tightly and squeezing hard as the scooter tore along the flint track. The brunette waggled her bottom in response, grinding it into Susie's splayed thighs and the pubic mound between. By the time the Vespa had scrunched to a stop in front of The Rookery, Susie was wet. Dismounting, she saw the sunshine sparkling on the two damp patches that dulled the glistening leather seat.

'Nice ride,' Susie said softly, fingering the hot saddle.

'Mmm,' agreed the poetess.

The moment for Susie's planned revenge had come: she had to be very careful, though. One slip and all would be lost.

'You've dropped something. It fell out of your back pocket,' the brunette remarked, her breasts bouncing beneath her blouse as she yanked up the Vespa on to its stand.

Susie feigned surprise at the piece of paper she had just deliberately let slip from her fingers. Stooping, she picked it up.

'These are not my shorts.' She grinned, tugging at the tight fabric wedged into her cleft. Palming her cheeks coquettishly, she waggled her hips. 'Too tight. I've got Annette's by mistake. This,' she said casually, the pulse in her throat quickening with excitement, 'must be hers. Oh it looks like poetry. I knew she wrote. Would you give it to her when you see her?'

Susie followed the pair down through the kitchen garden through the wooden gate and along the moss-covered path towards the spinney. On madame's advice, it being such a fine day, the Sultan's Favourite was taking Annette outside into the sunshine for an al fresco whipping. Annette strolled blithely along through the sun-dappled greenery, pausing only to behead sowthistles and dandelions, frothy white parsley and docks with the whippy cane she carried. A few paces behind her, with brunette hair cascading down as she bowed her head in concentration, the poetess scanned for the third time the piece of paper Susie had given her, and read:

> I know a bitch who is fat and dumb
> Whose dreadful verse will leave you numb;
> And when the recitation's done –
> She'll spank and cane your naked bum.

Susie hugged herself with glee as her planned revenge unfolded before her in the sunlight. Annette strode confidently on towards the clearing in the glade, shouldering the length of yellow bamboo which she hoped would soon be playfully striping her bare bottom. Behind her, the poetess paused, her face a mask of gathering fury. Shaking her head in angry disbelief, she read:

> She spends a wasteful age of time
> To find one word to end a line
> So that her stupid verse will rhyme:
> Such writing really is a crime.

Susie hid behind a larch tree and watched as the poetess, her face quite pale with anger, slowly looked up from the page and gazed at Annette's swaying bottom. The two satirical verses, penned in a few minutes by Susie after breakfast, disappeared in a crumpled ball as the hand that held the page quivered and clenched into a fist. Tossing aside the screwed up paper the poetess rubbed her palms together slowly.

'This will do,' she barked crisply. 'Give me the cane.'

Annette turned and passed the wood back to the

brunette. 'Where do you want me? Against this tree? Or over that log?'

Susie had to contain herself as she drank in every moment of Annette's approaching doom. The sunbeams dancing in the glade, their golden light sculpting with shade the ripe breasts straining beneath Annette's tight vest. The luscious curves of her bottom, sheathed within the tiny shorts. Her happy voice, playful and unsuspecting. The glint of the cane as it arrowed down in a straight line along the length of the brunette's left leg. The touch of white at the knuckle which gripped the cane so hard.

'Strip,' commanded the poetess, stung by the mocking lines which she believed Annette had penned.

Annette obeyed promptly, eager for a touch of light discipline from this stern beauty. Reading no more than the expected touch of severity in the order to undress, she sensually peeled off her vest. Her heavy breasts bounced free, only to swell and bulge as she bent to wiggle out of her tiny shorts. Naked, she turned and presented her soft nakedness for inspection. Susie saw the cane flicker up in a salute to pain.

'I think this branch will serve my purpose,' the brunette remarked, dropping her cane down on to the mossy earth and stretching up to pull down a supple spur of hornbeam. 'Come. And bring your shorts.'

Annette, still unaware of her fate, scampered across the sun-filled glade, shorts in hand.

'Hands up,' the poetess ordered.

Annette thrust her hands upward, passing them over the branch. Threading and binding the passive hands through the shorts, the poetess stepped back, releasing the branch. Her naked victim rose up in the air, dangling helplessly her feet scrabbling several inches above the ground. Annette squealed as she spun a quarter turn in the sun beams. Her wrists burned as they took the weight of he suspended nakedness. She slowly spindled back to face he chastiser. Susie crouched down, spied out the land for closer, more intimate vantage point, then crawled silentl towards a thick clump of ferns directly behind Annette.

'Head up. Legs together,' snapped the brunette.

Annette shivered with delicious anticipation at the crisp command.

'I am going to cane you very slowly, very severely, young lady, until you repent. Repent, and make a full apology.'

Still unaware of the seriousness of her plight, and taking these stern warnings merely as a delicious threat, Annette giggled and hugged her thighs together tightly. Gazing down at the woman who was about to whip her buttocks, she tilted her head to one side and asked if there were to be no poems that morning.

'What?' snapped the brunette, twitching the rod.

'No lovely poems?' repeated Annette, laughing.

Perfect, thought Susie, drinking it all in. A fatal thing to say, of course, but perfect: Susie herself could not have hoped to have scripted a better line for this unfolding drama.

'I think there has been enough poetry written recently,' barked the brunette, stooping to untie her white trainers. Kicking them off, she slipped out of her jeans and jumper and stretched herself luxuriously in the sunshine. 'Sufficient lines have been written, but there are many more yet to be produced. Red ones, across your bare bottom.'

Annette, catching for the first time the waspish tone of anger, turned pale. Bound by the wrists and suspended from the branch of hornbeam, she twisted her face and peered over her shoulder anxiously. She saw the brunette, braless and now stepping out of her tight, white panties, standing nude and glistening in the shafts of sunlight. Utterly naked except for a pair of red cotton ankle-socks, she flexed the cane. Susie glimpsed the spasm of concern that flashed across Annette's face, noting with satisfaction the fear that clouded the dangling girl's eyes.

'Anything to say to me, girl?' the poetess enquired.

Susie licked her lips as she saw Annette twist and turn feverishly as she dangled in her naked bondage. Satisfied with her plan, the watching girl gazed up at Annette's bare bottom, and waited for the cane to bring its pain.

Swish. Up on tiptoes in her red ankle-socks, the poetess swept the cane across Annette's plump cheeks. Swish:

145

again, the thin rod sliced into the helpless buttocks. Again, and yet again, the wood sang in the sunlight, searing the curved cheeks relentlessly. Susie fisted the soft moss beneath her in an ecstasy of revenge. Suffer, my beautiful Annette. Suffer. Susie mouthed her rejoicing in silence. Let the cruel cane kiss you and may your bottom burn.

'I am waiting,' the supple nude snapped, thrumming the sunbeams with her bamboo cane. 'Still silent? Very well. I have given you another chance to apologise but still you refuse. So be it. This half-dozen should loosen your tongue, girl.'

The stinging six certainly did loosen Annette's mute tongue: she squealed in anguish as the thin rod whipped across her softly rounded cheeks, biting her bare bottom with fierce affection. The cane loved her flesh, and burned it with unbridled passion. Her quivering globes blazed as they darkened from pink to scarlet. The punishing lashes left reddening stripes where the wood whipped the flesh. Susie counted, then re-counted, each line of pain.

'I'm sorry! I'm sorry!' Annette yelped.

'For?'

'I'm sorry, so sorry,' Annette whimpered, writhing in her painful bondage.

'And what, may I ask, are you apologising for exactly?' the chastiser demanded, planting her feet wide apart in the soft moss and tapping the palm of her left hand with the tip of the cane.

Susie squirmed with delight. Annette was all too willing to repent, to say anything to avoid the scalding strokes. But how delicious, Susie grinned: Annette's suffering was doomed to continue as the required apology would not be forthcoming. How could it? Annette did not even know why she was being whipped.

'Still stubborn, hmm? It is entirely your choice, girl.'

'Please –' Annette whined.

'Yes?'

'I don't –'

'Lost for words?' taunted her tormentress.

Susie hugged her breasts with delight. Lost for words

146

There was a double irony in the cruel phrase. Annette's fate was sealed when Susie had successfully dropped and lost the words on that page of mocking verse earlier on.

Swish, slice. Annette's bottom was indeed a beautiful specimen, Susie thought. Heavily fleshed and ripely rounded, the cheeks were fully pronounced, superbly curved and deeply divided at the dark cleft. Normally a shade of creamy gold, they now trembled in a blaze of scarlet pain. Hot tears scalded the punished girl's face as she hung from the hornbeam, miserable in her suffering and sorrow.

'I am putting down my cane, here, where you can see it. I am going to leave you to contemplate. Gaze upon this cane and fear for future pain. I will return,' the poetess whispered, 'and expect you to make a full and frank confession.' Approaching the buttocks she had just ruthlessly whipped she reached up and placed the splayed fingers of both hands upon the scorched cheeks. Taloning her fingers, she squeezed the punished flesh.

Annette bucked and thrashed in exquisite torment but there was no escaping the intimate attentions of her chastiser. Turning, supremely indifferent to her victim's distress, the poetess walked away. Susie ducked down low as the whipper walked away from the whipped one and disappeared into a leafy thicket. Silence returned to the glade, broken only by Annette's sniffling sobs. A wood pigeon alighted in the upper branches of a nearby oak, cooing its warm, throaty notes. Susie rose up and crept softly up to a spot a few feet behind the suspended nude.

'Painful?' she murmured.

Annette started in surprise, then twisted her face to turn her sorrowful eyes down over her aching shoulder.

'What are you doing here?' Annette whispered.

'Enjoying watching you get a taste of what you deserve. Just as you enjoyed my suffering last night.'

Annette gulped. 'Sorry,' she mumbled. 'Svetlana's very –'

'You had a choice. Your choice was for me to suffer.'

'I didn't –'

147

'Do much to help me.' Susie let the words hang heavily in the warm air between them. Annette acknowledged the accusation in silence, sinking her chin into the burning flesh of her shoulder.

'She's gone a bit mad.'

'Who? Svetlana?' Susie enquired, relishing Annette's suffering.

'No, no. The poetess. The one you call the Sultan's Favourite. She's given me over a dozen and there's plenty more to come.'

'I watched. You deserved them, every one. But I think you've had enough. Trust me. Do not be alarmed by anything I say or do. Just trust me.'

'I do,' Annette said simply, and immediately Susie forgave and forgot the girl's betrayals.

'Just pretend I'm not here. You'll understand in a few minutes. I think I know what to say.'

'I'm sorry about Svetlana. And everything,' Annette whispered huskily.

'Shush. Not now. Later.'

Susie gently tiptoed towards the spot where the poetess had been swallowed by the shubbery. Peering carefully into the thicket at the edge of the glade, she spied the brunette spreadeagled on a patch of warm moss furiously fingering her hot slit which glistened between her splayed thighs. Excited by the recent administering of punishment, the poetess was soon grinding her buttocks into the moss earth as she came.

Susie watched, fascinated. She was indeed the Sultan's Favourite: thick, brunette hair tossed across the green moss; an arched, white neck straining in the paroxysms of passion. Susie saw the superb breasts quivering, the nipples stiff and almost purplish pink. Below, the sweep of the taut belly, then the sensual curves of the ripe thighs. Susie focused on the face of the woman in orgasm: the features slack and drained by the climax ravaging her nakedness. The dark, unseeing eyes and at the wanton mouth, thick red lips parted in a silent scream of ecstasy.

Retreating back to the glade, and positioning herself

next to Annette, Susie took a deep breath. Easily mimicking Annette's estuary vowels – all expensively schooled girls acquired the twang once free from the strictures of the upper sixth – she intoned sorrowfully:

> 'I bow down naked and repent
> For foolish moments I have spent
> Penning verse I never meant
> To merit such strict punishment.
>
> I beg you to be harsh with me
> And cane me with severity;
> Punish my cheeks 'til you can see
> My sorrow sobs flow tearfully.'

'What the hell –?' Annette hissed.

'Shut up. It'll be OK. Trust me,' Susie whispered, scampering back to crouch down in her hiding place.

Out of the bushes on the opposite side of the glade the poetess, her pale face still slack from orgasm, emerged crawling on hands and knees. Stealthily, like a leopard, she prowled towards the suspended nude. Looking up, she raised her head and uttered:

> 'Your words of sorrow please me much
> So now I'll use a healing touch;
> No more I'll whip you with my cane
> But soothe your bottom's burning pain.'

Rising to her feet, the poetess clasped Annette's hips and drew the caned bottom to her parted lips kissing, then licking and lapping the scorched cheeks with her flattened tongue. Annette relaxed in response as the searching velvet of the punisher's tongue pleasured the flesh which had, only moments before, been sliced with the harsh cane. Gasping her pleasure out loud, Annette screamed softly as the wet tongue rasped the curves of her punished cheeks. Up in the nearby oak tree, the wood pigeon ceased its burbling notes. Susie, rising to leave in silence, froze as she heard the muffled voice of the poetess – her lips crushed against the creamy swell of Annette's buttocks – declaim:

> 'Then, my mouth between your thighs,
> I'll suck – and listen to your sighs –
> As, tonguing your sweet hot sticky plum,
> I'll pleasure you until you come.'

Tennyson was never quite up to that, Susie thought as she melted into the shadows of the spinney, heading back towards The Rookery. As she reached the edge of the spinney, a second carnal scream split the air. The poetess was certainly delivering her promise Susie smiled, watching the startled wood pigeon launch up into the warmth of the April morning.

'Sticky plum,' Susie echoed in a whisper, wondering what was for pudding today. At least Annette got her just desserts.

Susie brought a huge appetite to the lunch table and relished the cottage pie. Eagerly, she closed her lips over the warm mouthful hovering on her fork. Would the poetess be enjoying her warm mouthful of Annette's wet slit still, she wondered, or would both punisher and punished be embracing on a grassy patch in the secluded glade. Susie glanced at Annette's empty place at the lunch table and smiled. Justice had been done, and had been both seen and heard by Susie to be done: Susie remembered the swishing strokes of the cane, and the resulting thin red stripes of pain across Annette's bare bottom. Ignoring Svetlana, who crept in slyly, Susie left the table to seek out madame in her boudoir, where she was greeted by an imperiously raised hand which kept her at the door. A soprano was filling the room with crystal-clear notes. After a few minutes, the voice and music died.

'Handel's *Alessandra*. The Roxanne aria. A most moving piece, though I am almost certain that soprano is still a virgin. A certain lack of lubrication, I thought.'

Susie's eyes strayed to the tapestry. *In Servitude*. Spotting her buttocks, she noticed that they looked a little over-ripe, like a pippin in late September. Madame had deepened the flesh tones with a hint of scarlet silk.

'Maritta telephoned,' madame said, finishing off a dark pubic patch between a pair of creamy thighs; she bit the inky silk between her white teeth. 'Not her usual day but never mind. Seemed quite anxious to have an appointment with you. This afternoon.'

Susie beamed proudly.

'I do not as a rule reschedule our appointments but in her case I deemed that an exception could be made. I do like regularity. Regularity and, of course, punctuality. Svetlana still keeps Moscow time, I see. Late for breakfast and late again for lunch. How very remiss of her. I must have a little word with that girl before things get beyond repair.' Driving her needle home with unerring precision, madame signalled that the interview was over.

Susie left, exulting in Svetlana's doom. Remembering the hot-bottomed fate of the blonde who had been late for the whipping school, Susie rejoiced to learn that Svetlana was to be brought to task for similar transgressions. But why was Maritta coming this afternoon? And why, particularly, to see Susie?

The kingfisher-blue Kensington sped up the flint track towards The Rookery at breakneck speed. Susie watched it swerve to a halt and saw Maritta, tightly gloved and forced to mince provocatively in her tight Chanel skirt, slam the car door shut. In an oppressive silence, the Finn joined Susie in a small, tastefully furnished room. To Susie's surprise and slight regret, Maritta peeled off her tight leather gloves.

'I've brought it,' the Finn rasped angrily, avoiding Susie's smiling eyes and throwing down a Knightsbridge carrier bag. 'But never again and I do not wish to speak of it.'

Susie frowned, her fingers stroking the soft carrier bag absently. What could it be? A mistake in the size or was it the wrong colour? Susie took her work as a corsetière very seriously. Mistakes annoyed her.

'What's the problem? Has there been some mistake?'

Maritta narrowed her eyes and pointed to the bag. 'Just take it, but never try a thing like that again. Never.'

Susie blushed and placed the bag on a nearby table. Whatever the mistake – too deep a shade of blue silk, or, worse still, a mistake in the cup size of an underwired brassière – it caused Maritta too much distress to speak about it. Susie decided to humour the Finn, make it up perhaps this afternoon with a special session of stern domination followed by a slow, luxurious spanking. Susie fingered her blouse and began to unbutton. Turning, she saw that Maritta was already stripped down to her sports bra and dark navy tights. Lithe, supple and superb, she would be a pleasure to spank and dominate. Yes, Susie reflected. The Finn would melt like butter beneath her hot hands. She would make the girl kneel on a polished wooden chair for her bare-bottomed discipline, and perhaps introduce those perfect peaches to a taste of the hairbrush. But Susie was to be disappointed.

'Today, I am the punisher,' the Finn snapped angrily. 'Give me your bare bottom.'

Susie's frown deepened. The afternoon certainly wasn't going the way she had expected. First, the return of some unsatisfactory lingerie. Now, a reversal of roles. And, she realised, her services as a corsetière, in which she could both measure and pleasure her client, were not required. Nor did the Finn want Susie as a stern disciplinarian. This afternoon, Maritta wanted to punish, and Susie was to suffer.

'Come. Across my knee.'

Susie sensed the fury of Maritta as she was pinned down across the warm, tight-enmeshed thighs of her chastiser, a strong hand at the nape of her neck. Susie's unruly hair tumbled down to curtain her eyes. Naked, with her breasts squashed into the shining fabric of the warm tights, Susie wriggled but the Finn's grip was firm.

With startling venom and stinging accuracy, Maritta began to chastise her bare-bottomed victim. Susie squealed her astonishment at the unleashed fury. Writhing across

152

the dominant Finn's lap, her pubic curls scratching the sheen of the tights, Susie desperately tried to swerve her bottom away from the stinging rain of pain but Maritta's cruelly curved palm sought out every inch of Susie's upturned cheeks. With controlled fury, the spanking hand cracked down, scalding the swell of Susie's suffering peaches. She squealed aloud but the Finn was implacable. A sudden flurry of five loud spanks launched Susie into a paroxysm of squirming. Maritta dropped her hot hand to steady her victim, pressing her strict palm against the upper thighs just below the sweep of the buttocks above. Susie bowed down her head and lay obediently still. Docile and disciplined, she was anxious not to enrage her punisher any more. Maritta slid her palm up across Susie's hot buttocks, resting it across the crimson globes. Pressing her hand even more firmly, the Finn flattened the blazing bottom dominantly, then slipped her fingertips down into the cleft, dragging the buttocks apart. Refining the discipline, she squeezed the captive cheek nearest to her bosom, grazing it with her stiffened nipples. Susie screamed softly but the Finn was deaf to her pleading.

'Never do that to me again. Understand? Do not take me for the fool you think me. I have done what was required, but only this once. But never again, I warn you.'

Bewildered, Susie twisted her head around and gazed up at her furious punisher.

'What is it that you –' she began, but got no further.

Spank. Sank. Spank. Again, Maritta slapped the naked buttocks harshly, each crisp spank ringing out loud. Hot tears misted Susie's eyes as she tried to remove her bottom from the rain of pain. Suddenly, as if contemptuous of her victim, Maritta tossed Susie from her lap. Susie rolled on the carpet, her hot cheeks grazing the material painfully. The Finn rose and straddled the naked girl beneath. Placing an arched foot on Susie's upturned bottom, she pressed down hard spreading the hot cheeks savagely apart.

'Never again.'

Maritta gathered up her clothes and stormed out

angrily. Sore-bottomed, mystified and confused, Susie knelt up slowly. She trembled slightly after the recent onslaught and gazed around in bewilderment. Spotting the bag on the table, she stretched out and pulled it towards her. Opening it, she did not find the expected piece of lingerie but almost a thousand pounds in tens and twenties. Frightened by her discovery, she folded the bag up quickly and tossed it away into a far corner. Outside, she heard the nippy little Kensington spitting gravel as Maritta raced away, departing as angrily as she had arrived.

'Did Maritta bring anything?' Svetlana enquired, standing in the doorway.

Susie's mind pounced on the question. Svetlana had said bring, not return: the Russian was clearly expecting something.

'No,' Susie lied, her brain working frantically.

'Are you sure?'

'I don't think so,' Susie said slowly, playing for time.

She had to be sure, she had to be absolutely certain. She laid the bait down carefully. 'Oh, you mean that item of lingerie? It might be a brassière she took last time, I don't know. She left it over there.' She nodded to the bag.

Svetlana strode over to the table in the far corner and picked it up, opened it and smiled.

'Is it that brassière?' Susie asked nonchalantly. 'I wasn't sure that ivory suited her flesh tones.'

The Russian nodded and clutched the bag tightly.

Snap: the trap was sprung. Susie guessed the truth in a flash. Svetlana had boasted about the opportunities to make money down here at The Rookery, and this was one of them. Blackmail: the extortion of money from madame's clients under the threat of exposure. But how had it been achieved? And why had Susie been given the money, together with the outraged Finn's retribution?'

'I'll see to this little matter,' the Russian said. 'No need for you to trouble madame.'

Susie was left alone. She knew she needed proof before exposing Svetlana, and the evidence had just left the room. Going to madame now would be quite useless. Svetlana

154

had blackmailed the Finn using Susie as a go-between, a stooge. How, Susie was intrigued to discover, had the Russian schemer pulled it off?

'Oh, your poor bottom,' Annette remarked, peering in.

'A client with a bit of a temper,' Susie replied ruefully, turning her reddened buttocks around and examining them over her shoulder in a mirror.

'Not our day, is it? Thank you for rescuing me earlier on.'

'I bet your bottom's still sore.' Susie grinned.

'Very.'

'I've got some cold cream in my room. We could –'

'Oh yes, please. Let's go,' Annette replied eagerly.

Upstairs, with a cool breeze from the open window playing across the bed, the two naked girls lay belly down, palming cold cream into each other's buttocks. Susie sighed blissfully as Annette's fingertips glided across her hot globes. Annette moaned sweetly at Susie's healing balm as it swept across her stinging cheeks. The late afternoon sun's rays stole through the rippling lace curtains, fingering their ivory nakedness with blushing gold. Susie felt Annette's circular sweeps decrease slowly until her hand paused, gently resting across the passive cheeks. A finger drummed the soft curve of her left buttock, then spidered inward finally hovering over the cleft. Seconds later, the fingertips stroked the entire length of the cleft with a timorous caress. Susie grunted softly and inched her bottom up. The finger dipped down, this time stroking more boldly. Susie parted her thighs slightly, and settled down with a squirm into the bed. Once more, Annette's questing finger caressed the buried ribbon of flesh more firmly, coming to a pause before tapping the rosebud sphincter. Susie sighed deeply into the pillow as she felt the fingertip against her anal whorl; she immediately repaid the gesture in the same coinage, probing Annette's tight button with her slippery finger.

As if responding to an unseen but understood signal, they both pushed their fingers in deeply, sliding swiftly and surely into the tight warmth between their passive cheeks.

155

Pumping gently and rhythmically, they synchronised their mutual pleasuring; both girls eagerly accepting the devilish delight that burned within them. Susie felt Annette tense and stiffen just as her own trembling thighs and belly tightened: moments later, both were pumping harder and faster. They inched their faces closer together. Lips found lips and tongues flicked from wet mouth to wet mouth.

'Am I forgiven?' Annette whispered huskily, burying her words into the flesh of Susie's soft, white throat.

'Mmm,' Susie murmured, spearing her finger into the other girl's bottom savagely. 'Forgiven.'

'Be careful of Svetlana. She's got it all sorted –'

But Annette did not complete her warning. Gasping as her violent climax broke out within, she twisted on the bed and slammed her naked body into Susie's. Turning to meet the breasts and belly with her own, Susie started to come too. They smothered their cries of pleasure with each other's mouths and grinding their sweating hips, united the wetness of their pulsating, hot slits.

Be careful of Svetlana. Annette's words of warning floated back into Susie's brain as she lay in her bath, remembering the crowded hours of an eventful day. Something teasingly eluded her memory as she soaped her breasts slowly creaming each tremulous, shining flesh-mound with suds of scented soap. Be careful of Svetlana. Those were Annette's words, but there were more. She's got it all sorted. Nothing of significance there, Susie sighed, guiding the soap down to pleasure her belly.

Suddenly, Annette's words made sense: she's got it all sorted. Not 'it', Susie's brain realised, but I. T. Eureka! Susie stood up in the bath, bubbles of creamy soap slithering down her thighs. Lessons at Wyevenhoe Hall came flooding back, and changes to her timetable in the upper sixth. Susie remembered the big fuss about a new subject all the girls had to do, and remembered having to scratch out double geography on Thursday mornings and write I.T. in its place. Information Technology – computing. Now Susie understood Annette's whispered warning

The Russian was raiding madame's computer to run her blackmail operation.

Grabbing a towel, Susie briskly dried her breasts, crushing them savagely in her mounting excitement. Later, she resolved, when The Rookery slept, she would keep wakeful watch.

It was still early, a little after nine. In London, Susie's friends would be preparing for the night ahead. Perfume would be annointing nipples and thick, waxy lipsticks would be rising up, proudly erect, to smear pursed lips. Eager hands would be pulling fresh panties up tightly into the deep cleft between soft cheeks. Down in deepest Devon, where the night air was free from the noise and neon of the King's Road, Susie undressed and slipped naked between her sheets.

Beside her, Annette rose up on one elbow and gazed into Susie's eyes. In them she saw a fierce tenderness. Annette reached out and pushed Susie's naked body down and swiftly mounted her, straddling her with open thighs. Kneeling up, she ground her rump into the flesh beneath, then inched back so that she could spread Susie's legs apart. Shuffling further back down the bed, and still in absolute silence, she lowered her face down towards Susie's wet slit. The naked girl on the bed responded, inching her soft bottom up a fraction; as Annette's flickering tongue licked at Susie's labia she inched a fraction more. Slipping her cupped hands under the raised buttocks, Annette sank her face into the exposed pubis. Sucking at the sticky, wet flesh-lips, she drew them into her mouth, gently nipping their rubbery delight with her tiny teeth. Susie whimpered her pleasure, urging her hot wetness firmly into the face between her thighs. Annette's grip on the captive buttocks hardened; she squeezed and spread the cushions of firm satin flesh savagely, tonguing the peeping clitoris until it rose like a sweet thorn. Susie gasped aloud and reached back over the pillows to grasp the bedposts. The flickering tongue-tip teased its quarry. Around the wooden bedposts, the knuckles whitened.

157

Soon the ravished nude felt the hot muscle of the dominant tongue enter her, probing gently before sliding its swollen length deeply. A finger from the clasping hand that squeezed her right buttock strayed into her sticky cleft, prodding at her sphincter. The fingertip grew bolder, no longer scratching at her tight anal whorl but exploring the warmth within. Susie started to writhe and squirm but Annette's dominance was supreme. Glimpsing into her innermost desires, Susie trembled at the very edge of self-knowledge. She could, she reasoned with that fraction of her brain that still functioned, buck and bounce in order to unseat her sweet tormentress from her throne of flesh. Even as she half-understood this, the small light in her brain died, leaving Susie overwhelmed with animal desires. This, she recognised, was true surrender. This was utter submission. She groaned as both finger and tongue worked within her.

To obey a harsh command thrilled; to suffer the sharp spanking hand delighted; to offer up a hot, bare bottom for further cane-kisses was sublime. All these, and more, fruits of submission and surrender had been tasted by Susie, and she had found the flesh of these strange fruits sweet. But this was absolute: to let another dictate the terms of climax. To be held in thrall by the one who orchestrated the impending orgasm. That fruit still shivered on the branch inches from Susie's lips, untasted. Minutes later, the violent storm that shook her naked body spilled the fruit down to her lips where it burst, spreading its sticky juices. It had the sweetest, haunting taste, and soon had Susie begging for more.

Midnight came and passed. Soon it was close to one in the morning. Susie, barefooted, stole out of her bedroom and stood listening intently in the darkness of the corridor. Dressed in jeans and jumper only, she felt her naked body beneath prickle with expectation. Her nipples peaked against the fabric of her jumper as her heavy bosom thrilled to the hammer of her heart within. Stealthily, she tiptoed down the unlit staircase and edged softly toward the door to madame's office. It was firmly closed. Leaning carefully against the wood, Susie strained to hear. In the darkness, silence was supreme. But wait – what was that? A soft beeping. Yes, there it was again. Someone was at the computer. A slight squeak told Susie that the chair at the desk had just been vacated. She skipped back into the shadows just in time to avoid Svetlana, who closed the door behind her and crept upstairs to her room. Susie waited in the darkness then entered madame's office.

In the gloom, she felt her way across to the desk. The seat of the chair was still warm from Svetlana's bottom. Sitting down, Susie searched the desk in front of her but found nothing. Dare she risk a light? She turned the small lamp with the green shade on, flooding the leather surface of the desk with a pool of yellow light. Reaching down, she scrabbled in the waste paper basket, but all she found there were innocent scraps. So far, nothing to incriminate the wily Russian. She turned her attention to the computer. Svetlana had been using it; Susie had heard the tell-tale beeping. With a trembling finger, she reached across and turned it on, lighting up the screen immediately. Somewhere in this electronic memory bank, Svetlana was burrowing for gold. Blackmail: was Maritta's payment to be the first of many? The Russian would have to hack into the innermost secrets of the data-base to pull off such a scam. Not the information held in the files behind the little Eve logo, where Eve nurtured an apple to her bosom. No, Susie realised. Svetlana would have to penetrate the files guarded by the little black-stockinged Eve who flexed a whippy crop.

Just as Susie clicked the mouse, the door creaked softly behind her. Susie turned and froze. Madame loomed large in the doorway, her features distorted by the yellow lamp-light from the desk.

'Who is there?' she demanded, peering at Susie's silhou-ette.

'I'm sure that it is Susie,' the sly voice of Svetlana whispered. 'I saw her creeping into your office when I came down for a hot drink.'

The Russian had done it again, outsmarting Susie completely.

Madame turned on the main light. 'What exactly do you think you are doing, girl?' she thundered.

'I —' Susie faltered.

Beep. At precisely that moment, the computer clicked into life, throwing up the naked Eve logo on to the screen. Madame glimpsed the black-stockinged nymph brandishing the short crop and paled angrily.

'You seem to be very interested in my data, girl. Why? What is your purpose for this trespass?'

'Nothing,' Susie stammered, blushing. 'I was just looking.'

'I think that you had better come upstairs with me. This instant.'

'But I never —'

'Upstairs.'

Susie's palms felt hot and clammy as she mounted the stairs, her mind in a whirl. What should she tell madame? What could she tell madame? Svetlana had placed her neatly in the frame — a frame clearly labelled guilty. It was Susie who had been discovered at the forbidden files, not Svetlana. But Susie trusted madame's judgement: whatever happened tonight, Susie would remain quiet about her suspicions. The Russian was a slippery fish, but Susie resolved to catch her. Net her and catch her, then enjoy the punishment madame would most certainly dispense.

Inside the bedroom, madame ordered both girls to strip naked. Sitting on her soft bed, madame remained in the crisp white satin basque that hugged her breasts and hips. Susie glanced at the superb buttocks dimpling the silken duvet. Stepping out of her jeans and kicking them free, she looked across at Svetlana, slim and athletic, who was running her fingers through her cropped, blonde hair. The impatient gesture thrust the Russian's pert breasts outward — the nipples were already erect.

'As part of your training in the arts of discipline Svetlana, I want you to punish this girl. I shall ask the questions, you shall apply the lash.'

160

Susie shuddered at the words, then burned with fierce resentment at the idea of Svetlana whipping her bottom.

'Over that stool, girl,' madame ordered.

'No,' Susie shouted, her face hot and red.

'Bend over that stool this instant,' barked madame.

Susie stubbornly refused, hating to disobey the woman she adored, but hating even more the cruel command to submit to the girl the despised.

'I am perfectly happy that your presence in my office tonight was nothing more than curiosity. Inquisitiveness and idle curiosity. I am prepared to accept that there was no malice in your behaviour. However,' madame continued, instantly extinguishing the light of hope in Susie's eyes, 'you present me with an ideal opportunity to develop Svetlana's skills in discipline and chastisement. Punished you must be, Susie. Svetlana is new to The Rookery. She knows little of what we do, and understands less. She needs to develop a wide range of skills to satisfy our clients. Her lessons begin tonight. Bend over.'

Bowing her head down, Susie reluctantly obeyed.

'Bondage is an essential part of your training, Svetlana. Take Susie here. Naked and bending. How would you bind her?' madame enquired.

'I'd tie her hands together,' the Russian said with a shrug.

'Show me.'

Svetlana spread her hands out and asked for some rope.

'Rope? Oh, dear me, no. You really are a novice. Rope, waxed cords, they really are so crude. I can see that you are in urgent need of tuition, girl. Let us begin with the basics. We will consider the punishment positions, they are so important. After that, suitable methods of bondage. Come.'

Susie was instructed to stand, arms by her side, legs and feet together.

'Observe the nude in repose. The buttocks are relaxed, the cheeks soft. The head, you will note, is held up proudly,' Madame remarked, approaching Susie and patting her bottom to illustrate her point. 'But see how pleasing it is for the punisher to bow down the head of the penitent, thus.' Madame forced Susie's head down slowly, gripping her by the nape of her neck. 'Already, the balance of erotic power has been shifted and the authority of the chastiser has been asserted. A bowed head is a potent symbol of submission.'

Svetlana nodded her understanding.

'For caning,' madame continued, 'the caner must arrange the subject to be striped in a bending posture. The bottom must be round, the cheeks tight. Touch your toes, girl.'

Burning with resentment, Susie obeyed. Her breasts felt heavy as they swung down, bunching slightly as she stretched to touch her toes.

'Now, do you see how this makes the buttocks much more vulnerable, more poignantly passive? A much more tempting target. Why, softly swollen cheeks such as these simply beg for bamboo,' madame whispered, palming Susie's rump. 'Bending, the subject presents her buttocks perfectly poised for the cane.'

Svetlana took a step closer to Susie's naked bottom and caressed the taut curves briefly. 'Yes, I see,' she said softly. 'The tightened flesh will suffer more when whipped.'

'A small detail to observe. The feet,' madame pointed out.

'Together, or apart?' the Russian enquired.

'Together for the first six strokes, then slightly apart. Yes, I recommend that the legs are parted,' madame replied, 'as the punishment progresses. It is of course a matter of personal choice, but with the cheeks spread slightly, the pain is more evenly distributed.'

'And what position for the strap and paddle, madame?' Svetlana murmured, cupping and squeezing Susie's naked cheeks.

'Kneeling,' came the reply. Madame's slender hand pushed Susie down on to her knees. 'The important thing to remember though is to ensure that the forehead touches the ground.' Madame dominantly forced Susie down into the carpet. 'This makes the bare bottom rise up most satisfactorily, see? Up it comes, big and round.'

'Excellent,' Svetlana hissed excitedly. 'So helpless.'

'Yes. Perfect for the lash. The arms,' madame added. 'We must not forget the hands and the arms. Most important.'

'The arms, madame?'

'They must be placed out in front. Palms down, fingers splayed. And the head should go between, on one side gazing at the feet of the discipliner, for extra pathos.'

Susie was forced to demonstrate. She knelt, her tummy dipped, her bare bottom thrust up.

'Knees together, girl,' madame commanded.

Susie's cleft widened a fraction as she obeyed. She shivered as Svetlana's fingertips firmly stroked the length of sensitive flesh between her exposed cheeks.

'When applying the strap or paddle, be sure to strike the upper surfaces here,' madame advised, tapping the swell of Susie's bottom immediately beneath the narrow waist, 'and there.' This time, madame knuckled the fleshy curves where the cheeks became the upper thighs. 'And it is essential to pause when using the strap or paddle across a naked bottom. Reddening occurs so quickly, and one wants to make sure that every inch of the entire bottom has been thoroughly chastised.'

'Bending over, for the cane, and kneeling for the strap and paddle. Are these the only two punishment positions you recommend?' the Russian asked.

'Not at all.' Madame laughed gently. 'There are at least twenty positions. Thirty, if one includes Arab and Chinese methods of disciplining the female. But tonight, I propose to guide you through the beginner's stages only. Watch.'

Svetlana stood and gazed at Susie's nakedness, raking her cruel eyes over every shadowed curve, every supple swell, as madame forced Susie to squat, hands upon her head; to spreadeagle, face down; to curl up in a ball, buttocks uppermost; to assume a variety of humiliating punishment positions which all demanded that her bare bottom was presented for hot pain. Susie was rendered passive and utterly exposed time after time, repeatedly forced to offer her naked cheeks up in total submission to her skilful dominatrix.

163

'My preferred punishment is spanking,' madame murmured, ordering Susie to get up and approach the bed. 'Hand spanking a bare bottom is my favourite method of disciplining. Too many make the mistake, I find, of simply bending the girl across their knees and letting rip. But see how the bottom changes as I modify the girl's posture. Simply across my knees, thus,' madame remarked as she eased Susie across her lap, 'means that the cheeks are not tight enough. See?'

Approaching the bed and kneeling down, her eager face only inches from Susie's bare bottom, the Russian nodded.

'But watch this.'

Susie felt madame's satin basque rasp her flesh as both her legs were trapped and tamed beneath the dominant woman's firm thigh. In this position, jack-knifed across the knees, Susie's bottom loomed large and round, the creamy globes spread deliciously for the imminent spanking hand.

'Pinning the neck down is optional, but I do like to see a spanked girl twist and squirm. You may prefer to tame the neck thus, with your leg –' madame illustrated her point, trapping Susie's neck beneath her right thigh '– or concentrate on controlling the wrists, drawn together and held thus.'

Susie submitted to the imprisoning, pinioning positions.

'Do not over restrain the subject. It is very pleasing to observe the punished girl tossing her hair and wriggling in a futile effort to escape. Always give the illusion of the possibility of escape, by the way. The punished girl will always make a bid for it. It heightens the sense of absolute control for the chastiser. But if the subject in hand is wilful, and refuses to submit, the remedy is simple. Observe.'

Madame gathered Susie's hands together at the wrists and pinioned them just beneath her shoulders, at the same time inserting her right leg between Susie's thighs, trapping the flesh within. As Susie squirmed, the fierce grip tightened: Susie found it impossible to move or twitch, so absolute was madame's dominance of her nakedness. In this posture, with madame's upper thigh inserted between her legs, her bottom was pinned down ruthlessly, the cheeks spread painfully apart. The flesh at her yawning cleft burned fiercely.

'The breasts remain free and exposed, note. Perfect for an extra measure of dominant control, should it be required.'

Madame slipped her left hand down to cup and squeeze Susie's soft breast, rocketing the bending nude into a jerking frenzy. Madame squeezed harder: Susie gasped and lay rigid, perfectly prone and passive. Satisfied, madame stroked the bare buttocks.

'This girl is now completely immobile. I have asserted my supreme sovereignty over her, and she has surrendered her bottom up to me. It is mine to pleasure with pain entirely as I choose. The spanker, Svetlana,' madame explained, 'must establish total control then maintain it. Once achieved, you may do to the buttocks what you will.'

'Yes,' Svetlana hissed. 'Yes, I see.'

'Which brings us to bondage. Bondage, the requirement of submission and the application of humiliating strictures, is a form of punishment itself. I frequently whip those I pleasure while they are in bondage,' madame continued, 'but for some bondage in itself is sufficient. It renders those in its thrall entirely helpless and subjugated. They surrender their nakedness up to the cords and knots that bind them. They are eager for the moment when the last knot is tied, leaving them totally unable to resist, totally unable to escape.'

Madame released Susie from her lap with a playfully sharp spank across her bare bottom. The soft cheeks wobbled and reddened under the stinging crack of the palm. Ordered to kneel before the bed, her hands behind her back, she awaited futher indignities and torments. Madame stood up and stripped off her basque, peeling the second skin of satin from her voluptuous breasts and hips. Susie peeped at the superb bosom as it bobbed gently in its freedom from the satin's restraint.

If only Svetlana was not here, Susie thought. She would lift her face up to the heavy breasts and bury herself in the warm flesh, licking the white belly slavishly and then beg to be permitted to tongue between the thighs. To be naked, kneeling and subject to madame's will – that would be sublime. But Svetlana's presence spoiled everything. Susie hated it. She burned beneath the cruel gaze of the Russian, despising Svetlana for having a criminal mind that poisoned the pleasures of The Rookery. Alone with madame, Susie suddenly realised, she would not only be able to unburden her mind of its worries and concerns but succumb to the sensuality of submission. With Svetlana present, Susie must stay silent and suffer.

As she knelt before the bed, madame began to discuss straps, belts, nylon stockings and handcuffs with the Russian. They considered the merits of supple leather, the versatility of stretchy nylon, weighing them against the strictures of rigid handcuffs and ankle shackles. An array of bondage equipment was produced and each item was carefully examined. Susie felt her labia growing slightly sticky despite her growing alarm at the sight of the cruel strictures spread across the bed and on the floor around her. Before long, Svetlana was kneeling alongside her, a pair of glossy nylons draped across the open palm of her right hand.

'Let me see you bind her tightly,' madame ordered, reclining on to the silk duvet beneath her naked body. 'I want to know if you have a natural flair for this.'

Svetlana arranged Susie's hands and, having bound them severely at the wrists, lowered them down into the kneeling nude's naked lap. Shuffling behind Susie, she bound her ankles with fierce knots, using the second nylon stocking. Susie flinched a little at the burn of the bondage as it bit into her helpless flesh.

'Not bad, for a beginner,' madame remarked. 'But not very effective. See, the girl is still just about able to stand up, and she can still move her arms a little. Far too much freedom, my dear. In bondage, there must be no slack whatsoever. It may be necessary to let the victim hobble, pleasurable even, but you have not captured the essence of bondage. Look.'

Madame rose from the bed and stood next to Susie. In

166

a few seconds, the knots were loosened and Susie's limbs were free.

'Stand up,' madame instructed.

The nude obeyed. Madame worked quickly, threading the length of sheer nylon stocking between her captive's thighs, down around her ankles and about the naked soles of Susie's feet. The second nylon stocking was woven tightly around Susie's bulging breasts then back to where Susie's wrists were tied securely, leaving her helpless hands resting upon the naked cheeks of her bottom.

'There,' madame said, stepping back a pace to admire her efforts.

'That is marvellous,' the Russian gasped in genuine admiration.

Susie found that she could not move a single muscle, so effective were the restrictive knots. Her labia, sticky after the brush of madame's bosom against her own, grew quite wet. Despite her circumstances, and the shame of being used this way before Svetlana's scornful eyes, Susie thrilled to the strictures that rendered her helpless and immobile – helpless and immobile before Seraphim Savage, her beautiful, naked dominatrix.

'Suspension, and for the more advanced, inversion are very important aspects of bondage. Tied, gagged and dangling upside down, the naked subject becomes a mere plaything to the whim of the controlling chastiser. Both enter into realms of indescribable pleasure,' madame continued, bending over Susie and loosening her bonds. 'But that must wait 'til later. Tonight, I want to demonstrate two simpler examples of how the basic pleasures of bondage may be achieved.'

Forcing Susie down on to the carpet, she arranged the naked girl on to her side, then gathered her hands together and dragged them down to her feet. Susie had to draw her knees up to squash her breasts in order to achieve this crab-like posture, spreading her thighs apart to reveal her seething slit. Firmly binding Susie's hands to each ankle, madame stood up and reached out to gather up a bamboo cane. Flexing the cane, she slashed it through the air, twice.

'The girl cannot move, but she can be moved by the discipliner. That is a very important distinction. Watch. I can move her over by rolling her on to her face and knees, see?'

Susie felt madame's soft foot flip her naked, bound body over into the required position. Curled up and motionless, Susie kissed the carpet, her arms thrust down and wedged between her splayed thighs.

'Her bottom is poised for whatever punishment I wish to administer. The cheeks are fully rounded, perfect for both strap and cane.'

Madame tapped Susie's bunched cheeks with the tip of her quivering cane.

'Perfect,' whispered Svetlana. 'Absolutely perfect.'

'The subject can be positioned so that each cheek can be separately whipped. This is a very effective form of bondage. My control over the girl is absolute, her submission to me complete. Her bottom,' madame whispered softly, dragging the tip of her cane down along the length of Susie's opened cleft, 'is utterly mine.'

Susie shivered with excitement and shame as her hot wetness oozed, silvering the flesh between her thighs and flooding the bedroom with the pungent odour of her arousal.

'Always check to test for tightness. Maximum discipline may only be achieved by making sure that the bonds bite,' madame added in a clinical tone as she fingered the stretched nylon at Susie's wrists and ankles. 'Yes, perfectly secure.' Madame smiled with satisfaction as she stood up and swished her cane softly above the bound nude below.

'One important point, Svetlana. The subject must be made to face her chastiser at some stage during discipline.'

Matching her words with actions, madame tipped Susie over on to her back. Susie lay helpless, bound and trussed at madame's mercy. Naked and supreme, madame straddled her victim, stroking the nipple of the squashed left breast with the cane.

'Holding your subject in a sustained, dominant gaze is essential. A blindfold may be added at a later stage for the more esoteric disciplines, but I do recommend that eye contact is established.'

'Is it really that important?' murmured the Russian.

'It subdues and quells even the most disobedient subject,' madame replied in a low, clear voice. Staring down directly into Susie's wide eyes, madame gazed steadily and unblinkingly, as if her eyes were penetrating into Susie's mind. Sensing that the girl aching in her bondage was almost ripe for orgasm, madame bent down and loosened the knots that bound each wrist to her victim's ankles. 'On to the bed. Face down,' she barked.

Susie stretched herself belly and breasts down on to the silken duvet. Madame sat down alongside her, squashing the mattress with her heavy buttocks.

'Come closer, Svetlana, and bring me four leather belts.'

Susie's bottom quivered apprehensively. Madame palmed the creamy cheeks of the supine girl, flattening her hand into the upturned bottom with tender dominance. Svetlana approached the bed, bearing four brown leather belts.

'This one will bind the breasts,' madame whispered, leaning forward and crushing her bosom into Susie as she threaded the supple band of leather around the girl's breasts and then snapped it tightly together at her back. 'And this one is for the ankles, thus.'

Susie gulped into the pillow as the burning sensation at her bunched breasts was surpassed by the fiercer bite of leather around her feet. 'And this one, for the upper thighs, just below the bottom.'

Susie felt her thighs being almost welded together such was the severity of the third belt around her soft flesh. She knew that her welling climax was about to spill over into full orgasm any moment, and began to dread the impending shame when she came.

'The fourth belt, madame. Around the bottom?' Svetlana asked eagerly.

'Not exactly, no. Always leave the bottom bare. I find it more convenient if the subject requires continuing discipline and correction. The bare bottom remains a delicious threat to the victim, as well as an instant target for the cane.'

'There?' Svetlana hissed, pointing to Susie's glistening slit.

'Again, I prefer to leave the labia unfettered and exposed. It may be essential to finger, tongue or indeed dildo the subject during the bondage session. After all,' madame explained, 'bondage must be a bitter-sweet experience, with as much pleasure as there is pain. The Persian poets of the fifteenth century allude to it as a sugared sorrow. No,' madame said, deftly rolling Susie over on to her back, 'the fourth belt goes here. Observe.'

Arranging Susie's hands so that her fingertips rested a mere half an inch away from her clitoris, she used the fourth leather strap to pinion the wrists firmly against her thighs. Susie flexed her splayed fingers but could not move her hands.

'That is known as the Tantalus. Study it carefully. See? The subject is extremely close to climax and the urge to touch and pleasure herself is overwhelming. She must, she simply must, touch – but the dominatrix denies her that ultimate urge. See how this girl strains in her bondage to finger herself there,' madame murmured. Seraphim Savage fingered Susie's wet labia with a firm, downward stroke as she spoke. Susie's bottom jerked and bounced, hammering into the duvet below. 'But because of my strict bondage she cannot do that which she yearns to. I am in supreme control. Watch.'

Svetlana sat down on the bed, brushing Susie's face slightly with the soft cheek of her left buttock. Gazing down across the swell of the bound breasts of the helpless girl, the Russian drank in every nuance of the exquisite bondage the tight sheen of the stretched leather; the straightened legs, pinned at the ankles; the scrabbling fingers searching for relief, failing to achieve it because of the restrictive belt that bound the victim's wrists to her hips.

'I believe it is time to finish our lessons for tonight Svetlana. You have learned much, and you have learned well.'

'You have taught me much, and taught me well, madame,' the Russian fawned.

'As for this girl,' madame remarked, thumbing Susie's slit lightly, 'I'd better roll her over and finish her off.'

'May I?' Svetlana whispered, her voice thickened with lust.

'Of course. She is yours.' Madame smiled.

Susie shrank from Svetlana's touch as the Russian girl flipped her back over on to her belly, leaving her bound body face down. She shrank again as Svetlana wiped a gleaming dildo on the silken duvet and teasingly introduced the blunt nose against the wet flesh of Susie's pulsing plum. Tightening her buttocks and clamping her thighs together, she tried to resist the brutal supremacy of the dildo. It probed, slipping into her hot slit easily. No, Susie grunted into the pillow. Not Svetlana. Not that, there. Anything would be better than to be mastered by the Russian bitch. She bucked and writhed, her fingers dabbling helplessly at her thighs.

'Madame?' Svetlana asked silkily.

'Mm?'

'Did you want me to whip this girl for being in your office tonight?'

'Why, goodness me, I quite forgot. Take a crop to her bottom and give her a dozen.'

Better to be whipped than ravaged, Susie consoled herself, sighing into the pillow. She shuddered as the dildo was snatched away from her hot flesh and groaned as the ivory shaft dragged against her wetness. But to her great relief, Svetlana was going to punish – not pleasure – her.

Swish, crack. Planting her bare feet wide apart on the carpet alongside Susie's bed of suffering, Svetlana whipped the crop down across the upturned buttocks of the girl in her tight bondage. Susie's tears flowed freely as her bottom was kissed viciously by each successive stroke of the crop. They were not the bitter sobs of sorrow, but tears of joy. Susie had been spared that which she most feared: having to acknowledge Svetlana as her sovereign, and crumbling into climax at the cruel Russian's command.

Seven

Susie was woken by a tiny wren fluttering in the ivy at her bedroom window. It promised to be a gloriously hot day, the first of a long, hot summer. In Chelsea, Susie thought as she gazed up at the clear blue sky, VW Passats and restored Austin Healeys would be cruising with their hoods off today. She crumbled a biscuit for the wren and decided upon a bath. Would she still be here in The Rookery when the late-summer thunder storms arrived? Risking a naked scamper down along the corridor, Susie made it to the bathroom and slipped inside unseen. Closing the door gently, she sensed warm, moist air on her shoulders and breasts. Someone had had the same idea and was already having a bath.

'Who is there?' madame enquired, splashing as she turned towards the door.

Susie tapped on the cubicle door and stepped inside. Madame was thigh deep in scented foam, her glistening bosom heaving gently as she lay back in her bath. She was sipping from a large breakfast cup and lazily scanning a copy of *Society Spy*. Susie spotted last week's edition of the *London Gazette* strewn on the cork-tiled floor. Madame was clearly keeping an eye on her clients' movements from this remote spot in Devon.

'Another early riser. What is that tune? I seem to recognise it but the title quite escapes me.'

Madame, to Susie's delight, was listening to 'Shut Up And Dance', a choice club mix on the little-known Green Man indie label.

172

'It's a sample,' she explained. 'Taken from *The Chocolate Soldier*. They mix it in –'

'Of course, *The Chocolate Soldier*. How very curious.' Madame's wet finger stabbed at the off-switch, and silence settled down upon them both.

'Take my cup, I am ready to be dried.'

Susie placed the large cup and saucer carefully on to the cork-tiled floor. It rattled slightly, betraying her nervous excitement. Gathering up a white towel, she greeted madame's shining nakedness as it rose up out of the bath. Head bowed slightly in submissive servitude, Susie covered the scented, shining skin with the towel, shuddering as her hands sensed the warmth within.

'Dry me, girl,' madame instructed, her tone firm and dominant.

Susie thrilled to the command and completely swathed the naked woman with the fluffy material, patting the neck and shoulders timidly. Peeling off the towel, she cupped a generous handful and returned to the slightly swollen breasts, palming the ripe flesh slowly and intimately. She dabbed at the sparkling droplets nestling in the deep cleavage and on the white belly below. Madame turned, presenting her bottom and legs to the towel. Kneeling, Susie dried the shapely legs and svelte thighs tenderly, but her attentiveness to the buttocks above lapsed as excitement overtook her and caused her to grasp the towel and rub the bouncing globes vigorously.

'Carefully, girl, carefully. If I were a client, I would be dismayed – and have good cause to whip you. You must learn that *la dame à toilette* is a most intimate experience and you must conduct yourself with delicacy and restraint. I see that you need to be taught properly, girl,' madame sighed as she spread her legs apart. 'Cup the towel loosely, that's better. Now dry each cheek slowly. Mm. Better, that's much better,' madame remarked as the kneeling girl applied the towelling to each creamy globe.

'Like this?' whispered Susie, tremulously guiding her fingertips beneath the soft towel across the sweep of each satin cheek.

'Exactly,' hissed madame, her voice thickening. She rose up on her toes in response to Susie's brief caress at the cleft.

Susie swallowed down her mounting excitement and concentrated hard on her task. She was, she acknowledged, very privileged to learn. Madame was generous enough to teach her these precious skills and so Susie struggled to set aside her overwhelming delight at madame's nakedness. She lingered, luxuriously, as she dried the swell of each cheek just above the thighs, fingering the towel into each invisible crease.

'And finally,' madame murmured, as she turned to present her glistening pubic mound to the face of the kneeling girl, 'the handmaiden must dry her mistress here.'

Susie's heart hammered as she gazed spellbound into the glorious fig before her. Madame inched her thighs apart and placed her fingertips at either side of her pubic nest. Pulling slightly, the fingertips revealed the sweet flesh of the pouting labia.

'Place a fistful of towel below and gently, very gently, wipe it upward. Repeat this gesture at least four times.'

Trembling as she did so, Susie obeyed madame's instructions. On the third sweep upward, madame grunted thickly.

'Gently, girl. Inflame me and I shall punish you.'

Susie introduced the handful of towel back between the parted thighs, but caught the tip of the clitoris just as she dragged the cloth away from the splayed labia. Susie knew she had erred as she saw madame's toes scrunching into the cork-tiled floor, responding to the slip up in a controlled spasm of ecstasy.

'I shall spank you, girl. Be warned.'

The final sweep of the towelling betrayed Susie completely, for she accidently allowed a creased fold to enter in between the labial lips causing madame to moan. Panicking, Susie made the fatal mistake of rasping the length of the towel against the clitoris as she hastily retrieved it. Madame screamed softly, her left leg buckling at the knee.

'Bend over, girl. You will have to learn the hard way,' Seraphim Savage commanded, recovering her composure a little.

Susie bent over the side of the bath, spreading her arms apart and drawing her thighs, legs and naked feet together tightly. She shivered with pleasure – suppressing a sigh of expectation – as madame stepped forward, wedging her warm thigh against Susie's and placing her left hand down on the nape of Susie's neck.

'Serving the client, or mistress, must at all times be a selfless, not a selfish, experience.' Madame's curved palm swept down twice to sharply slap the bending girl's bottom. 'The delight must be hers and hers alone. Not yours. You must deny your own.' Madame dominated the soft cheeks with her spanking hand, searing their curved flesh mercilessly and reddening them rapidly. Susie inched her bottom upward despite the hand that pinned and positioned her so fiercely for the painful chastisement. 'It is a bad maid,' madame declaimed, scalding the upturned cheeks severely, 'that steals forbidden pleasure from the nakedness of the mistress she must serve. And bad maids,' madame grunted softly as she spanked the bare bottom harshly, 'have to be disciplined into devoted obedience.' The sharp staccato of palm ringing out against cheek echoed loudly in the tiled bathroom, adding to the thrill – the dreadful delight – of the punishment. Susie squirmed but could not evade the ruthless, unerring smacks: her sweet sorrow soon made her slit hot and juicy.

The hot hand paused and came to rest, alighting on the punished buttocks to soothe the hotter flesh with slow, circular sweeps.

'You are not a bad maid, Susie. Just a little green and perhaps a little wilful. Nothing that strict training cannot improve. Yes,' madame whispered, flattening the curved cheeks beneath her hand, 'you are green. I must see to it that you ripen quickly.'

The five fingers caressing the spanked bottom became one, which found Susie's cleft and stroked it firmly. In response, Susie tensed and spread her legs apart, revealing

herself and submitting herself utterly to the nude dominatrix above.

'Perhaps if you were given permission to shave me –'
madame nodded at her own wisdom '– that might develop
the self-control you so obviously require. It is still early.
The house is sleeping. Come,' madame ordered, giving
Susie's bottom an admonishing slap, 'you will shave me
and serve me.'

Susie felt her hot slit prickle with arousal, curiosity and
the excitement of alarm. Her spanked bottom tingled as
she eased herself up from the bending position over the
side of the bath.

'Kneel,' madame instructed.

Susie's knees kissed the cork-tiled floor.

'Over here.'

Seraphim Savage sat down on a stool next to the hand
basin. Susie approached, head bowed, shuffling on her
knees. Arranging a towel across the seat of the stool,
madame knelt down, her knees and thighs apart. She
reached out to steady herself, her left hand gripping the
edge of the hand basin.

'Wet me, foam me and shave me, girl,' she ordered
crisply. 'If it is not to my satisfaction, mind, you shall be
caned severely.'

Susie gazed at the tight pubic coils nestling in the
shadowed delta. Inching her face closer – then closer still
– she flickered out her tongue and lapped at them, licking
them into neat array. Moments later, she pressed her lips
into their crisp softness, kissing her spittle into them.
Madame gasped, and was just on the point of clutching
Susie's hair with an outstretched hand when she felt the
kneeling girl's teeth gently nipping and tugging at her coils,
teasing them away from the ultra-sensitive flesh in readiness for shaving.

'Good. That is good,' madame observed, withdrawing
her taloned fingers from above Susie's bowed head. 'Continue.'

The order was ambiguous: should Susie continue to kiss
and tongue the pubic nest or prepare them with foam for

the blade? What would an obedient maid do? A maid in servitude? The answer was simple and came to Susie in a single word: pleasure. A maid must serve and pleasure her mistress, of that much she was sure and certain.

Susie lowered her face down between the warm thighs and kissed the matted coils softly, working her lips cunningly to worry the flesh beneath. Madame took a sharp intake of breath as the kneeling girl's tongue darted down, its pink tip trimming and taming the wet wisps into shape. Almost drowning in her own delight, Susie felt with alarm her own self-control slipping away: she was within seconds of piercing madame's warmth with her tongue, eager to probe the pungent flesh she lapped at. Withdrawing a fraction from the velvet flesh of the labia – and just out of reach of temptation – Susie closed her eyes and shuddered. To kneel, naked, down before madame was a giddy delight. Susie was approaching intoxication, but glimpsed through her tipsy ecstasy that should she fail, the whip awaited her. If she displeased, the cruel bamboo beckoned. Susie knew the risk but dared to defy. She closed her lips down upon the pubis, mouthing her mistress in order to shave her but slipping through the strict bounds of servitude to kiss the innermost flesh of the woman she had come to adore. Madame, sensing the fervour that trespassed into the forbidden territory with increasing boldness, returned her taloned fingers to Susie's hair. Grasping a dominant handful of dark hair, she wrenched Susie's head away from her lap and pulled the face upward. Gazing down into Susie's wide eyes, she turned the captive head slowly from side to side.

'I told you to proceed. Do so, and remember my cane.'

Blushing at Seraphim Savage's knowledge of her naughty wilfulness, Susie lowered her eyes and humbly nodded her obedience. The glass shelf above the nearby sink held all that was necessary for her to shave her mistress. In silence, she reached up and took down the foam. Released from the can, it wriggled out on to her fingertips like a living thing and when applied to the pubis, spread like melting snow into the coiled nest. The matted

177

curls felt like velvet beneath the creamy foam and Susie had to fight the temptation to stroke and tease them up into wisps. She was tempted but remembered the delicious threat of madame's cane. Denying her own appetite for such delights, Susie resolved to play the part of maid properly, and returning her hand up to the shelf above, took down an elegant gold razor.

'Good. Now do your duty,' madame instructed, steadying herself by placing her hands on Susie's shoulders and thrusting her foamed pubis forward.

'Yes, madame,' Susie whispered hoarsely. Lowering the blade down to the flesh at the base of the white belly, she swept it down with a delicate stroke. With a soft rasping sound, the foam curled away before the blade, leaving a glistening band of shaved flesh. The pulse at Susie's slit quickened to a burning throb. Never before had she been so close, so intimately close, to another's secret flesh. The experience was thrilling: she was in powerful control of the naked woman to whom she had submitted. It was a delicious paradox, a sublime sensation. To briefly master one's mistress. Susie quivered as the thought burned deep in her brain. Madame's splayed delta lay at her mercy inches away – yet Susie lay under the constant shadow of the cane's pain, utterly in madame's thrall. Confused by these delicious, conflicting thoughts, Susie froze. Madame gripped the naked girl's shoulders and squeezed them, ordering Susie to continue. The dominant touch to her flesh brought Susie out of her reverie and back to the business in hand: the golden razor and the foaming pubis. Dedicating herself to her duties, Susie plied the razor once more. The blade dealt with the matted curls easily, and Susie warmed to her work. A few moments later, she placed her fingertips on to the pubic mound and stretched the skin, applying the razor deftly to trim the creased fleshfolds with surgical precision. Relieved with her success, Susie sank back, her hot, spanked cheeks bulging as they squashed down on to her ankles. Seraphim Savage examined herself intimately and then gazed steadily into Susie's blue eyes.

'Not at all bad, girl. Now lick me.'

Susie's tongue returned to the shaven skin, thrilling to the sharp tang where it met traces of the foam. Closing her eyes, she lapped eagerly at the warm flesh, forgetting to withdraw as the flattened tongue found the clitoris. Madame gasped aloud.

'You are a wicked, wilful girl. Why do you not obey me? Do you not fear the lash?'

Susie drew back her head and gazed up sorrowfully at her stern mistress. Madame studied the large pools of cornflower blue, determined to glimpse the devilish sparkle in their depths.

'You have done well, girl, except for –'

'It was an accident –'

'But last night was not,' madame countered. 'You were in my office. For what purpose?'

Susie pressed her face down into madame's lap. Her hurried explanation was muffled by the labia which kissed her lips. Safe and secure in the warmth of madame, Susie unburdened herself of the tormenting knowledge which was haunting her. Her words spilled out unchecked and unguarded. Madame's enterprise at The Rookery was under threat. The blackmailing of Maritta and Svetlana's boast of riches were revealed. Susie promised proof of all these allegations.

Silence cloaked the two naked figures as they remained motionless in the early morning sunbeams. At length, Seraphim Savage guided her finger down and placed it under Susie's chin.

'Are you absolutely sure of this?' madame demanded, tilting Susie's head back.

'She's hacking into your computer and sweeping the files and Maritta came and paid up – a big bag of money – and Svetlana said that –'

'Because if you are telling me a lie,' madame purred, placing her finger upon Susie's lips to stem the outburst, 'your bottom will never forgive you.'

Anxious to avoid Svetlana, Susie passed the morning in the kitchen garden. The heat promised at dawn became a blaze

179

of golden sunshine well before noon. Madame had withdrawn to her office immediately after Susie's tearful revelations. She was, Susie presumed, busy on the telephone to all her special clients. Scuffing along the narrow cinder path, Susie felt forlorn and depressed. She was sorry she had made her suspicions plain, and hated the idea of being a sneak. If only she had tried to solve the situation herself, presenting madame with solutions rather than problems. She would have liked more time, more proof – but the sudden intimacy with madame had slightly overwhelmed her. Before she knew it, she had told her stern mistress all. Scrunching her toes into the gritty cinder, she relaxed a little. Maritta would confirm everything Susie had said. There would be a painful interview for Svetlana, no doubt with a very painful outcome. Then what? Would the Russian be sent away into exile, leaving Annette for Susie's nocturnal pleasures? Svetlana would most certainly be punished. Susie relished the idea of the beautiful bottom being striped as it received the punishing cane. Susie looked up from the raised earth bed she had knelt on to study a crow up in a withered elm. It glistened in the sunlight, despite its dark plumage. Susie bowed her head to commence the task she intended to complete before lunch. Crumbling a tablet of borax into the zinc watering can, she watched it dissolve. It was to be sprinkled over the tender celery shoots peeping up from the earth bed. Borax, she had learned from her auntie's gardener, prevented heart rot.

A tinkling from the open kitchen window attracted Susie's attention. Standing up, she wiped the dry earth from her shorts where her plump buttocks had grazed the soil, and stole softly across to the window. Annette would be preparing lunch, Susie grinned to herself. On a chilly day, like the day before yesterday, she had served up a cheese salad. Madame had spanked her soundly after lunch. Today, with the mercury rising steadily, Annette would be doing a fish pie, mixed grill or something equally inappropriate. Susie imagined the devilled kidneys seething under the fiery grill; plump sizzling sausages splitting their sides in the furnace of the pan; curled rashers shrivelling as they crisped and chips spitting in the bubbling hot fat.

At the window, she peeped into the kitchen and spied Annette – hot and flustered – standing at the sink. A haze of pale blue smoke confirmed that a mixed grill was well under way. Annette wore a short, pleated gym slip and a tight, sleeveless vest – her kitchen fatigues. The vest was already damp with perspiration and moulded to her full breasts superbly. Susie eyed the peaked nipples straining up beneath the stretch of tight cotton. The cold tap was running and Annette was gazing down into the sparkling cascade longingly. Suddenly, as if unable to resist the temptation a second longer, she swiftly removed the bowl of chipped potatoes being sluiced beneath the cold tap in readiness for the pan, cupped her hands and scooped the water up to her hot face. Susie shivered with envious delight as the cold water splashed Annette's face and neck, soaking the vest to reveal even more of the bosom it vainly attempted to conceal. Dabbing at her face with a towel, Susie's friend swiftly peeled off the clinging vest, pausing when it was half way over her head to struggle. Her naked breasts bounced as she struggled with the tight band of cotton.

Susie could not help herself: she reached in over the window ledge and, cupping her hand under the cold tap, dashed its sparkling contents up into Annette's beautiful bosom. Annette squealed, instantly dropping her hands from her head to protect her naked, shining breasts.

'It's only me,' Susie said and giggled.

'Where are you? I can't see,' Annette, still blinded by the vest, shrieked as she floundered against the sink. A sudden crash announced that the chipped potatoes had been swept down on to the flagstone floor.

'Stay still,' Susie cautioned. 'Mind your feet on the broken bowl.'

Annette obeyed, inching up against the deep stone sink and presenting her breasts to the warm sunshine. Susie mischievously snatched up a long-handled washing-up brush and thumbed the stiff bristles firmly.

'Come closer,' she whispered huskily.

Annette obeyed, straining towards the source of the sweet command and offered her bare bosom to Susie.

'Stand perfectly still,' Susie insisted.

Annette whimpered, sensing an imminent pleasuring. Cupping her breasts with both hands, she willingly surrendered their moist, rounded weight up to whatever delicious fate awaited them. Susie stroked the nipple of the left breast with the stiff nylon bristles, making Annette arch up on tiptoe and gasp aloud. A second firm stroke raised Annette up once more, and the nipple to a painful peak of pleasure. Susie applied the brush to the other nipple with equal tenderness reducing Annette into a quivering, jerking frenzy.

'Closer,' teased Susie's voice from the window, her tone softly seductive.

Despite her blindfolding vest, Annette climbed up on to the sink and, thrusting her bottom out into the kitchen behind her, knelt out into the window frame. Her heavy breasts swung down inches from Susie's waiting lips, the nipples already peaking with anticipation.

'And in here we have the kitchen where –' Madame's voice stopped abruptly, as did the speaker herself, in the doorway. 'What on earth? Annette,' she barked, 'get down from there at once.'

Smothering her giggles, Susie grabbed up at Annette's arm and took it firmly at the wrist, holding her captive as she knelt – still blindfolded by her vest – at the open window.

'That girl is utterly impossible,' madame said to the unseen visitor behind her. 'Annette, I am showing my client here the appurtenances of The Rookery and what do we discover? Well, wretched girl? A mixed grill spoiled while you idle in the sunshine. If it is heat you seek, my girl, heat you shall most certainly have. A very hot bottom. Take that wooden spoon, my dear. No, the larger of the two, that's right,' madame said to her client. 'Give that naughty girl a thorough scolding. At least a dozen. Bare-bottomed, if you will.'

Madame left the kitchen. Susie heard the door close

behind her, and then the footsteps of the new client approaching Annette's bottom. Annette wriggled in Susie's grip as the hem of her pleated gym slip was flipped up and her white panties expertly thumbed down. She grunted thickly into the vest that almost gagged her as she felt the unseen, unknown hand palm her rounded cheeks. Then she squealed softly into her restricting vest as the wooden spoon swept down across her exposed bottom. Up in the withered elm, the crow fluttered in alarm, splaying its ragged feathers. Unseen and unsuspected by the spoon-swiping chastiser, Susie inched up cautiously and closed her mouth over the left breast of the chastised, thrilling to the spasmodic jerks of the stiffened nipple against her tongue with each fierce crack of spoon to buttocks. Madame, stepping back into the kitchen briefly, called out in a laconic voice for Susie to join her immediately in her office. Susie, believing herself invisible even to madame's eagle eye, rose up from her concealment and startled the young woman chastising Annette. Pausing between strokes, she gasped as Susie stood upright and turned away from the window. Susie's feet crunched down along the cinder path skirting the east wing of The Rookery, but her footsteps were not loud enough to drown out the renewed sounds of curved wood across exposed cheeks as Annette's punishment resumed.

'Sit down at the desk. Take your shorts off, girl. I don't want my nice Venetian chair soiled,' madame said pleasantly.

Susie peeled off her shorts, still grubby from her excursion into the kitchen garden, and plumped her bare bottom down on the silk-cushioned chair. The computer sat before her on madame's desk, flickering and beeping.

'I'd like you to write a three-hundred word piece on why I should consider sending you to Madrid for the fashion extravaganza there next month. Would you do that for me, Susie?'

Susie turned her adoring eyes on madame. 'Oh, madame. I would be so –'

'Just write it all down for me, my girl,' came the swift response.

Susie's fingers flew across the keyboard, quickly using up her allowance of words. Madame padded softly over to where Susie sat and, reading over her young assistant's shoulder, scanned the statement on the flickering screen.

'Jolly impressive – and very persuasive work. You are already helping me to make up my mind,' madame opined in a strictly neutral voice. 'Can you turn this into a document? Print it out, say?' madame enquired casually.

Eternally grateful for her switch from double geography to computers at Wyevenhoe Hall, Susie tapped the keys. Instead of just reading about Madrid, Susie would soon be going there thanks to her knowledge of information technology.

'So, you can operate this machine?' madame asked, seemingly more interested in Susie's actual skills rather than in what they had produced.

'Oh, yes. Computers are easy once you know how.'

'Mmm,' countered madame. 'Now let us suppose that I was not here to read your statement, but in London. Back at La Bella Figura. Could you get that message to me?'

'By post?' Susie queried; no post, to her knowledge, ever seemed to come to or to go from The Rookery.

'Perhaps,' said madame.

'There's always e-mail.'

'Is there?'

'Yes, I could send it to you from this desk. It's easy.'

'Show me.'

Susie fingered the mouse, clicking it rapidly, proud and excited to be able to demonstrate her hidden talents to madame. Susie completed the necessary functions and turned to madame, her finger paused above the send button.

'No,' madame said softly. 'Do not send the document. You have shown me enough.'

Susie frowned. Madame appeared to be satisfied – but curiously not exactly pleased – with the successful demonstration.

'Thank you, Miss Pelham-Heys. Go and sit over by the window, please.'

Somewhat dismayed by the cool tone, and the formal use of her full name, Susie rose up from the Venetian chair. Peeling her bare bottom away from the silk cushion, she vacated the desk and walked across in silence to a seat by the window. A polite tap at the door was greeted with the crisp command to enter. Svetlana did so, closing the door behind her. Susie's heart thumped wildly at the sight of the ash blonde who returned her glance with dismissive scorn.

'Are you familiar with computers, Svetlana?'

Yes, you are. You bitch. You can use them perfectly well, Susie thought.

'A little, madame. I think that they have an important –'

'Just sit down and show me exactly what you can do,' madame suggested smoothly, nodding to the chair at the desk.

Svetlana sat down and drew the mouse towards her.

'Please tap in the names of three designers you think we should be studying at La Bella Figura next term.'

Svetlana concentrated, then obliged.

'Excellent. Now,' madame continued, 'could you send your suggestion to my secretary in London.'

'Madame?' Svetlana looked up blankly.

'Why not e-mail it, now?'

'I do not understand,' Svetlana lied carefully. 'Is that a local courier you use?'

'Have you never used e-mail, my dear?'

'No, madame. I'm sorry to disappoint you.'

Liar, Susie fumed. Why was the bitch lying? Susie knew that the Russian could operate the entire system.

'Thank you, Svetlana. You have told me all I need to know,' madame said softly.

'Then you like my suggestions for next term's designers?'

'Among other things. As I say, Svetlana, you have told me all I need to know.'

Svetlana. Madame had used the Russian's first name, yet she herself had been coldly addresssed by her full name. What was happening? Susie felt uneasy, but didn't quite know why. What, she wondered, was going on.

The door opened silently, admitting Maritta. Madame greeted the Finn with a warm welcome and drew her across to the fireplace.

'My dear, how very good of you to come.'

Susie's heart fluttered excitedly. Maritta was here; now Svetlana was for the high jump.

'Before we retire for a little sherry, there is a somewhat unpleasant matter with which I believe you are acquainted and which I feel you may be able to help me clear up.'

'Unpleasant matter?' Maritta echoed indistinctly as she tugged at the fingertips of her tightly gloved left hand with her teeth.

'Blackmail,' madame said crisply.

The glove dropped from Maritta's teeth to the floor. Madame stooped down, retrieved it gracefully and returned it to the Finn.

'Blackmail, my dear. Do not be alarmed. I am close to the truth behind the whole sorry business. All that remains to be done is return your money to you and punish the wicked perpetrator. So do not be afraid, just tell me all you know, and all that happened to you. Take your time.'

At first, Maritta hesitated, but at madame's gentle insistence, narrated events as she had experienced them.

'I received a message –'

'Post or telephone?'

'No. On my computer. By e-mail. It told me to bring money, a lot of money –'

'Was it signed?'

'Not signed, no. But Susie –'

Susie, following every word intently, looked up in alarm. 'I never –'

'Silence, girl,' snapped madame fiercely. 'Continue, Maritta.'

'I was to book a session with Susie. Those were my instructions. And bring her the money in a bag.'

'And did you?'

'Yes. I did. I booked an earlier appointment and gave the bag of money to Susie but I told her,' Maritta added quickly, 'I would only pay once. She –'

'Is this true, Miss Pelham-Heys?'

'No. Yes. It was not like that.'

'Answer the question directly, girl,' madame commanded.

'I did see her and she did give me a bag but I didn't –'

'Did you take money from Maritta?'

Panic began to choke Susie. It was all going horribly wrong. The appointment with Maritta. The bag of money. And madame had tricked the two girls into demonstrating their ability to use the computer: Svetlana had cunningly pretended to be ignorant of e-mail. It was all conspiring against her and Susie was afraid.

'Did Maritta give you a bag of money?' madame insisted.

'No. I mean, yes, but not to me. She gave it to me but you must understand, I didn't –' Susie wailed.

'You are making very little sense, girl. Explain yourself.'

'I took a bag from Maritta but Svetlana came and took it.'

'Did you see Svetlana, Maritta?'

'No,' the Finn replied.

'But that was later. She –'

'I saw the bag, madame,' the Russian whispered, 'Susie told me it contained lingerie Maritta had returned.'

'Yes, but only to see if you knew –' Susie shouted.

'Miss Pelham-Heys,' madame interrupted angrily. 'I am very much afraid I have been nurturing a viper in my bosom in extending to you the hospitality of The Rookery. You have clearly shown your ability to use both the computer and e-mail facilities. Svetlana, may I remind you, cannot. Maritta has just confirmed bringing a payment in response to a threat of blackmail. You have just admitted taking that bag from her. Svetlana did not. Not half an hour ago I took the liberty of searching all the bedrooms. I found this bag containing a lot of money in your room, girl. Not in Svetlana's. Furthermore –'

'No,' Susie cried, leaping up and pointing at Svetlana. 'She took it. You must believe me, madame. I wouldn't lie –'

'Except to blacken Svetlana's name and character. I do

not believe for one moment, Miss Pelham-Heys, that you were going to blackmail all of my special clients but I do believe that you engineered this whole wretched business to damn Svetlana and have her banished.'

'Why?' Maritta asked, puzzled.

'Jealousy. Miss Pelham-Heys is jealous of Svetlana,' madame explained.

Maritta shrugged and flexed her gloved hand slowly. 'I still do not understand.'

Madame smiled. 'Annette,' she said softly.

'Ah,' the Finn nodded, returning madame's smile.

'No, you are wrong,' Susie protested. 'You fool –'

'You are the foolish one, Miss Pelham-Heys. In a moment, I shall see to it that you are punished most severely. Both Maritta and Svetlana will witness your chastisement as you have abused them both so monstrously. Then,' madame's voice rose imperiously, 'you will be consigned to your room until I can make the necessary arrangements for your return to London. You will be dismissed from La Bella Figura, of course, and I shall see to it personally that the world of fashion is closed to you henceforth.'

The room spun around Susie and she staggered backward, slumping down in her chair. How could she prove her innocence when her adversary was so cunning? It was like a deadly game of chess, and Svetlana was playing a mastergame. All her moves were perfect. Susie had been outwitted and was in checkmate. She was to be whipped then sent into exile, not only from madame's realm but from the entire world of fashion.

'None of it is true,' Susie wailed. 'You are wrong.'

'Gag her. I have no wish to hear any more from Miss Pelham-Heys, not even her pleas for mercy when I take my cane to her bare bottom,' madame said emphatically.

Maritta and Svetlana had Susie gagged in seconds, binding her hands behind her back for good measure.

'Shall we take our sherry here?' madame enquired pleasantly. 'The day is far too warm for a full lunch. Yes, sherry and sandwiches, I think, before we punish the girl.'

Susie squirmed in her chair, bitterly resenting her plight. To be outsmarted by Svetlana rankled, but much worse was to be in disgrace with madame. And there was her future exclusion from the career she adored. Madame pressed the bell-push and Annette entered in response, her eyes widening at the sight of Susie tied and gagged.

'Bring sherry and sandwiches. Do you think you could manage that simple task without any nonsense, girl?'

Blushing at the punishment she had just received after madame had discovered her in horseplay at the window, Annette turned to the door, head bowed.

'And invite our new client to join us. You too may stay and lunch with us, Annette. Miss Pelham-Heys will not be taking sherry. A glass for her is not necessary, thank you.'

Annette departed, rejoining madame, Svetlana and Maritta with a bottle of chilled amontillado and a delicious selection of sandwiches. The new client, a slender brunette with magnificent legs, was welcomed warmly.

'Tongue?' madame asked, offering her guest the plate. 'An eventful visit for you my dear,' madame enthused, raising her glass to her lips. She sipped and approved the amontillado. 'We are lunching lightly as there is sterling work to be tackled and completed shortly. A little local difficulty which I hope to resolve within the hour. Discipline is required. Will you stay for the punishment? It might amuse you.'

'Delighted,' the brunette replied, her white teeth biting into the wholemeal bread of her sandwich.

'You may wish to assist. A capital opportunity for you to get to know us and our methods here at The Rookery,' madame observed. 'Did you have any problems with Annette?'

Annette reddened at the memory of the spoon across her naked buttocks.

'A most instructive experience,' the brunette replied. 'For us both.'

'Then you will find this afternoon's whipping equally instructive,' madame countered, returning the glass to her lips.

189

The calm air of the impromptu lunch gathering – the polite exchanges and the chink of glasses – added to the apprehension welling up inside Susie. To be dealt with immediately would have been terrible enough, but to have to sit bare-bottomed, bound and gagged, in front of her punishers was unbearable. The cane madame was going to stripe her with was on view for all to see. Susie gazed at its cruel yellow length as if hypnotised. Soon the wood would be striping her naked buttocks. Shivering at the thought, she turned away, only to glimpse Svetlana licking her fingertips delicately. Susie burned angrily at the thought of the Russian witnessing and relishing every painful swish and every searing stripe across her bare bottom. The new client, who had chastised Annette so severely, would be in attendance too, appraising and appreciating madame's capabilities with the cane. The tension inside Susie was soon knotting her more tightly than the cords that bound her wrists. She sat ashamed and seething in her disgrace.

'Fruit?' madame enquired, offering her guests a silver dish of nectarines.

All assembled declined, anxious for other delights. Madame smiled knowingly and stood up. Pacing leisurely across to the corner of the room by the window, she picked up the cane and swished it twice through the empty air. Susie shivered at the eerie note.

'Stand up, Miss Pelham-Heys,' she ordered.

Falteringly, Susie obeyed.

'Svetlana, Maritta. Untie her hands and arrange her for her punishment. I will administer the first four strokes. Bend her across my desk and hold her down.'

Susie shrank back from the touch of Svetlana's fingers as they gripped her arm, then shuddered as Maritta's gloved hand grazed her flesh. Her hands were unbound but her freedom from the bonds was brief. They pinned her arms firmly to her side as she was marched across to the desk. With the gag still tightly in place, she could not make a last-ditch protest. Justice was to be denied to her as she stumbled to her doom.

'Across the desk, legs together,' madame ordered.

Susie could not but obey, so absolute was the combined power of Svetlana and the tightly gloved Finn. She managed a token resistance, but was easily spread across the large desk, her breasts squashing down into the polished surface. The gloved hand of Maritta pinned her face sideways into the gleaming wood. Susie was breathing hard, her tongue working furiously against the gag.

'Secure her.'

Madame's command was promptly carried out. Maritta and the Russian each took an arm and pinioned it ruthlessly, then trapped Susie's ankles with strategically planted feet. She stretched across the desk, utterly helpless and immobile.

'I will not burden our new client with the details of your wrong-doing, Miss Pelham-Heys. Suffice to say that they merit strict chastisement. I cannot say that I am not disappointed,' madame continued as she flexed the cane, 'but I set aside my dismay and focus strictly on my duty. And my duty is to discipline you. Discipline you most severely.'

Susie, naked and defenceless, felt a stab of raw fear at these cold, calculated words. She struggled in vain, twisting and wriggling but her bare bottom remained before the hovering cane, the upturned cheeks waiting for their pain.

'Four strokes,' madame whispered, tapping the curved domes lightly with the cane tip. 'Then each of those present will take the cane and administer four apiece. They may select the position you must adopt to receive your strokes. The decision is theirs entirely.'

Swish. The first of madame's four sliced down, striping both cheeks severely. Susie's hips jerked into the desk as the wood kissed her buttocks, leaving the rounded cheeks seething beneath a single thin red line. The second, a cruel cut, left a reddening lash-line exactly an inch below the fierce memento of the first. Susie's left leg spasmed as her soft cheeks accepted the bamboo's caress. The third swipe brought the supple wood crisply down across the upper curves of her bare bottom. Susie, her face forced down into the polished desk beneath Maritta's controlling glove, gasped audibly despite her gag. Madame's fourth stroke scorched her upturned domes, spreading a flame of pain across the curved globes.

'Take the cane, Maritta, and give her four strokes.'

Maritta accepted the wood, clasping it tightly within her gloved fingers. She motioned to Svetlana to arrange Susie face down across the desk. Madame assisted, dragging Susie's belly across the sheen of polished wood. Svetlana stepped around to the top of the desk to hold the captive's arms down as madame remained at Susie's feet, clamping them together.

Swish. Swish. The punished girl's pubis pounded into the desk as her buttocks suffered the double swipe of blazing bamboo. Two more reddening stripes joined the four bequeathed by madame. Susie grunted as her belly and breasts pressed into the wooden surface, her cheeks on fire after Maritta's fierce lashes.

'Excellent,' murmured madame, relaxing her grip a fraction on Susie's pinioned feet. 'Annette.'

Annette took the cane and lowered it down across Susie's buttocks. The cheeks clenched anxiously beneath the dominant wood.

'Kneeling?' madame asked briskly.

Annette nodded slowly, having little appetite for the punishment of her friend.

'Come along, girl. Miss Pelham-Heys has been very wicked. The details do not concern you but the discipline does. Four strokes.'

They arranged Susie so that she knelt for her stripes. Face down into the carpet, with Svetlana triumphantly astride her, her hot, striped bottom rose up to greet the imminent strokes. Svetlana signalled her victory by squeezing Susie between her glistening thighs. Annette raised the cane up and paused, allowing it to quiver for a moment above the upturned buttocks before swishing it down. Susie bucked and jerked between Svetlana's warm thighs as the whippy wood bit into her peaches. The Russian suddenly squatted down, pinning Susie beneath her oozing plum, the weight of Svetlana's splayed cheeks heavy or

Susie's trapped head below. Annette sliced the cane down twice in rapid succession. Svetlana's eyes sparkled with malice as she felt Susie squirming beneath her. The gag at Susie's lips silenced the squeal as the fourth stroke left yet another crimson stripe.

'Svetlana,' madame said curtly, taking the cane from Annette's trembling fingers and passing it across to the Russian's eagerly outstretched hand.

'I will have her in the schoolgirl position.'

'Capital. Four strokes.'

Svetlana needed little prompting. Ordering Susie to stand up, she placed the tip of the cane against Susie's nape and bent her forward, down to touch her toes. Under madame's approving gaze, she ensured that Susie's fingers were splayed out around the tips of her toes, taking pains to draw the legs tightly together. Susie loathed the Russian's casual intimacy but feared her cruel attentions even more. Svetlana did not hurry or rush the punishment, lingering on the preparations and savouring every moment. Positioning herself alongside Susie's buttocks, she fingered the swell of the cheeks gently. Susie groaned into her gag as she felt Svetlana sweep her flattened palm down across the tight curves of her bottom. Seemingly dissatisifed with Susie's posture, the Russian shouldered the cane and inserted her thumb into Susie's hot cleft. Dragging it down firmly, she forced the bending girl to inch her cheeks apart a fraction thus softening the flesh for its stripes. Judging the result to be an improvement, Svetlana swished the cane in a practice stroke as she took two paces back from the bending nude.

Swish. The glittering yellow cane sliced down, scalding the cheeks with clinical precision. Susie's toes curled, then dug into the carpet in an exquisite wave of torment. Swish. Susie's legs trembled and threatened to buckle beneath her. Svetlana tapped the outer curve of the punished girl's thigh dominantly, steadying her victim for the third. The stripe was planted directly across an earlier red line, rekindling the fire that scorched Susie's flesh. Svetlana deliberately delayed, then savagely delivered the fourth. The bamboo

193

kissed the upturned buttocks with vicious tenderness, leaving them scalded.

'Perfect.' Madame applauded, breaking the spellbound silence. 'An excellent chastising.'

Svetlana acknowledged the tribute.

'An outstanding example of sound discipline. You placed each stripe carefully, judging them well. You distributed the pain across the bottom. Yes. A superb display. Well done, my girl. And now, my dear,' madame said, turning to the new client, 'would you care to complete this wicked girl's punishment? How would you like her, hmm?'

The brunette smiled and took the cane in her left hand.

'Ah, left handed. This should be interesting,' madame observed.

'Up,' the brunette ordered Susie in a soft whispering tone.

Susie blinked back the tears of shame and pain brimming in her blue eyes and stumbled to her feet. Her bottom, blistered by the bamboo, burned fiercely.

'Across this chair,' the brunette commanded, swinging a chair down in front of Susie. 'Head and shoulders right through the frame, belly across the seat.'

The instructions were terse, delivered in a tone that denied disobedience. Susie was soon trapped beneath the wooden frame of the chair's back, her nakedness crushing the silk cushion of the seat. Madame watched with growing appreciation as the brunette placed her right foot down on to Susie's dimpled spine and grasped the chair with her right hand. Susie's red cheeks lay utterly exposed beneath the cane in the brunette's left hand. They tightened as the cane was carefully lowered down upon them to judge the distance of the strokes, then writhed as the bamboo pressed down into their smooth, hot domes.

'Goodness,' madame whispered thickly, her voice unable to conceal her excitement, 'I believe you are going to be a great asset to The Rookery. Your dominance is superb, my dear, quite superb.'

Annette, gazing in awe at the brunette's stern display of absolute authority over the bare bottom, plucked her wet panties away from the pubic mound beneath. The punisher raised the bamboo cane up, repositioning the foot that pinned the punished girl to her chair, and gripped the frame of the chair with her right hand. With a sudden thrust, she jerked the chair forward, raising the front legs clear from the carpet. Susie's bottom rose up to receive the swish of the withering lash. The slicing cane bit into the defenceless cheeks, sending Susie's trapped nakedness into a renewed spasm of delicious anguish.

The brunette eased the chair back down on to the carpet, immediately placing her left foot down upon the ravished buttocks. As the cruel toes scrunched into the reddened cheeks, madame gasped audibly, her hand flying up to flutter at her throat. Once more, the brunette positioned her left foot, then savagely jerked the chair forward. Susie's suffering buttocks loomed up round and large, perfectly poised for the cane. Swish. It whispered down, searing the flesh below. Madame's eyes grew wide with wonder as she watched the dominant brunette tap Susie's thrashing feet imperiously with the cane. The whipping proceeded, the concluding two strokes delivered in exactly the same manner. As her bottom was savagely striped, Susie wriggled and writhed, but her confinement under the frame of the chair rendered her utterly helpless.

Surrendering the cane to madame, the brunette knelt down to kiss the cheeks she had just caned, planting her warm lips slowly and lingeringly against the warmer flesh of Susie's scalded buttocks. In spellbound silence, the others looked on; only the sound of the brunette's soft kisses broke the stillness of the afternoon. As the punisher rose up from the upturned buttocks of the punished, madame crossed over to the table and snatched up her glass draining the sherry in one gulp. Her dry mouth moistened, she composed herself before speaking.

'I really must congratulate you, my dear. That was simply exquisite. The wretched girl deserved the most severe discipline but I never expected – you quite exceeded – that is to say –'

The brunette accepted madame's praise and glass of amontillado with cool aplomb.

'Maritta,' madame called across to the wide-eyed Finn. 'As you suffered the most by her behaviour, it is only right and fitting for you to have some time alone with her now. We –' madame included the others in the room in her all embracing gesture '– will withdraw. When you have finished with her, Miss Pelham-Heys is to go to her room.'

Madame escorted Svetlana, Annette and the new client who had proved to be such a superb dominatrix out of the room. Maritta knelt down next to Susie, who was still bent over and trapped within the chair. Susie flinched from the perfumed breath of the Finn who pressed her face close to Susie's to whisper sweet words of revenge, intimating that Susie's bare, striped buttocks were now helplessly at the mercy of the tightly gloved hands.

'You are now mine, all mine, bitch. I am going to inspect your bottom. I want to see the effects of the cane, to make sure you have suffered. If,' the sweet breath whispered, 'I am not perfectly satisfied with what I discover, then I will make sure that you suffer more punishment.'

Susie squirmed as Maritta rose up and sat down, using the chair normally but having Susie's nakedness as a cushion. Easing her buttocks down upon Susie, Maritta straddled her victim. Drawing her firm thighs slowly together, she captured and contained the body beneath her. Bending forward, Maritta lowered her face into Susie's ravished bottom, framing the outer curve of each cheek with cupped, gloved hands. Susie squealed into her gag as the leathered fingers sank into her flesh, squeezing and splaying the hot crimson globes. She squealed again as Maritta pinched a finger and thumbful of captive flesh from each cheek and tugged. Susie's groans melted into moans as the taloned fingers released their fierce grip and returned to the whipped cheeks to drum the satin flesh.

Imperceptibly, each thumb inched towards her cleft. Susie held her breath. The thumbs dipped down inquisitively, rasping the velvet of her shadowed flesh within. More absolute than the kiss of the cane, the gloved hands controlled and owned Susie's bottom entirely. Her submission and surrender was complete. Her bottom belonged to Maritta.

The door opened softly, then closed with a click.

'May I join you?' Svetlana whispered hoarsely, her throat tightening with cruel lust.

'Of course, my dear,' the Finn replied, dismounting to kneel in front of Susie's upturned buttocks. 'I was just about to complete my examination of this girl's punished bottom. Bring me a strap, or a leather belt will do.'

'At once,' Svetlana hissed. 'I will get –'

'Do not rush away, I do not need it immediately. I like to be thorough. I will need at least thirty minutes to complete my inspection.'

Svetlana knelt, bringing her eyes a mere six inches from Susie's which blinked above her gag. The Russian grinned – and Susie whimpered – as the probing, gloved fingers began their intimate, humiliating examination of Susie's whipped rump.

Back in her bedroom, one hand tied to the bedpost by Svetlana as a precaution against escape, Susie pulled her lips inward just as she would after applying lipstick. They were so sore after the harsh gag – but not as sore as her bottom after the harsher cane. She lay on her tummy, her face resting upon a single, white pillow. Shuddering at the memory of Maritta, she attempted to roll over but the restriction of her bound hand prevented her. The strap Svetlana had promised to supply had not been used: the Finn had passed a full hour palming and pinching, cupping and squeezing Susie's punished cheeks. The helpless buttocks had provided the Finn's gloved hands – and the Russian's avid gaze – with an endless source of delight. The examination ended with Maritta straddling Susie's trapped nakedness to pleasure her pubis against the upturned buttocks.

Susie, stretched out on her bed, burned at the memory of this final ignominy. She shook her head as if trying to rid her mind of the image of Maritta dominating flesh with flesh. But the image burned brightly behind her eyes. Susie shrank back from the flood of sensations: the increasingly firm touch of the wet labia dragging down across the curve of her upthrust cheeks. Again and again, Maritta had ridden the captive bottom and Susie had moaned softly as the erect clitoris had scored her hot skin. Susie's muffled groans, and Svetlana's gasp of lust, had both been drowned as Maritta cried out in sheer ecstasy as she pounded her hips into Susie, crushing her sticky fig into the satin cheeks. Then, Susie recalled with a shudder, the Finn's gloves had gripped her breasts. The leather cupped the heavy breasts fiercely; sensing Maritta's renewed fervour, Susie had felt the downward strokes of wet labia against her hot buttocks. Maritta rode Susie more violently this time, quickly approaching a savage climax. Susie had felt the Finn spasm then orgasm, once more slamming her slit into the buttocks beneath. And all the time, not six inches away, Svetlana's glinting eyes. The mocking, cruel gaze and the triumphant smile – Svetlana savouring victory.

A single hot tear welled up in her eye. Susie blinked, squeezing the teardrop on to the pillow. She burned at the injustice she had suffered, and at the shame and pain of her punishment. Remembering her impending exile, fresh tears threatened to spill down to her pillow.

A sound at the door made her freeze with fear. What fresh torment was about to visit her, to cause more humiliation and pain? As Susie twisted on her bed to see the door, Annette opened it, slipped into the bedroom and stole across to the bed.

'They say you did something dreadful,' she whispered, tenderly stroking the unruly dark fringe of hair from Susie's large, blue eyes. 'It must have been Maritta. Did you disobey her? Madame gets very cross if the clients are upset. That was a terrible punishment and I'm sorry if I hurt you.'

Susie gazed up, managing a smile through her tears.

'Thank you for –' she began.

'I can't stay long,' Annette gushed. 'Svetlana's watching me like a hawk, and I have to be careful now. She's shot up in madame's esteem; acts like her deputy. They went for a long walk in the garden before tea. I let my cake burn and they spanked me but I heard them talking about you.'

Svetlana was now madame's favourite: these words, confirming Susie's darkest fears, stung her as sharply as a slice of the cane.

'They were talking about sending you back to London. The day after tomorrow, I think. What did you do?'

Annette's question was answered from the doorway.

'She was foolish enough to tangle with me,' Svetlana hissed, creeping into the bedroom as silently as she had arrived.

Annette withdrew her hand from Susie's head and stood up awkwardly. 'I only came to see if –' she blurted.

'You have no business here. I, and I alone, am to look after her until she goes. Madame has given me my clear instructions. I am in charge around here now. You knew that this room was forbidden to you. Why did you come?'

'I only wanted to see if –' Annette started to reply, her fear evident in her timorous tone.

'You disobeyed a direct order. This girl is poison to madame and all at The Rookery. Have you any idea what she did?'

'No,' Annette mumbled, staring down at her feet.

'Are you sure? You were not by any chance involved in her wickedness? Assist her in any way?'

Susie's eyes blazed up at the Russian as Annette, subconsciously distancing herself from the bed and its occupant, inched towards the door.

'Wait,' snarled Svetlana, calling over her shoulder to Annette as she retied the gag around Susie's mouth. 'I will teach you to disobey a direct order,' the Russian said, panting slightly from her exertion. 'Kneel.'

Annette fluttered her hands uncertainly, her eyes widening with anxious dread.

'Kneel,' Svetlana whispered, her finger arrowing down to the floor.

Annette sank down before the figure of the stern, ash blonde. Svetlana strode towards the kneeling girl. Annette looked up, shivering at the sight of the blaze of cruel light in the Russian's eyes. Svetlana reached down to the hem of her pleated skirt, fingered it briefly then dragged it up around her ripe hips. Inching forward, she pressed her thighs into Annette's startled face.

'Take my panties down. No, with your teeth, bitch.'

Obediently, Annette nipped at the tight cotton, then tugged at it, straining as she peeled the panties down.

'Now lick me. Thoroughly,' Svetlana ordered, inching her thighs apart as far as the restricting panties above her knees would allow.

Susie wriggled and thrashed but remained helpless on the bed to which she was bound as her loyal friend was subjected to the cruel domination of the Russian. Susie tried to block out the sucking, lapping sounds of her friend's subjugation and humiliation, but the sound of Annette's searching lips and tongue at Svetlana's open flesh haunted the room. Try as she might, Susie could not drown the sounds made by the kneeling girl, or deny the increasingly pungent odour of the Russian's wet response.

'Wait,' Svetlana cried, her voice shrill with arousal.

Annette's sorrowful eyes flickered up. The Russian turned and thrust her bare bottom into the kneeling girl's upturned face.

'Pleasure me, bitch.'

Annette probed the cleft between the heavy cheeks with her quivering tongue, closing her eyes and wincing slightly as she found the hot flesh of the acrid sphincter.

'Harder, faster, deeper.'

Annette, anxious not to cause Susie any more torment at Svetlana's cruel hands, responded instantly and feverishly, bringing the Russian up on her toes with a squeal of delight. The thick tongue rasped the sticky velvet flesh between the clenched buttocks then forced its way into the tight warmth within. Svetlana twitched and her knees buckled slightly. Pressed close to Annette's face, the sleek thighs trembled. Spinning around suddenly, she clasped Annette's hair in her left hand and forced the captive face back into her glistening pubis. Inching backward, dragging Annette with her, Svetlana reached Susie's bed. Snapping her fingers harshly, she ordered Susie to position herself so that her face was directly beneath her. Susie had to stretch in her partial bondage to obey. Inch by tantalising inch, the Russian sat down, guiding her buttocks directly towards Susie's face. Annette, still held captive to the Russian's hot slit, licked and sucked furiously.

'Now we shall see who is in control here,' Svetlana gasped, jogging gently up and down as she rode her buttocks across Susie's face. The heavy cheeks splayed, burying Susie's face entirely. 'I am in charge and you will do exactly what I say and what I want. So, bitches. Pleasure me,' she snarled, grinding her soft flesh down into Susie and clutching Annette's hair savagely. 'Faster, harder, deeper.'

Annette's misery was complete: humiliated and forced to serve the girl she had grown to hate, her heart ached for Susie who was now utterly dominated beneath Svetlana's bottom.

Susie, despite her subjugation, sobbed dry tears for Annette. What would happen to Annette when she was left to the mercy of the pitiless Svetlana when Susie was in exile? Crushed beneath the rubbery buttocks, Susie still thought only of her friend, over whom Svetlana now had supreme control.

Bouncing violently as she approached her climax, the Russian cried out aloud as her hot juice stung the faces of the two girls in her absolute thrall.

'I am in charge,' she grunted, squeezing her thighs and buttocks together tightly in orgasm – suffering sweetly as her two subjugated slaves sweetly suffered – and gasping her fierce lust. 'Now I am in control.'

Eight

Susie stretched and yawned, still sleepy despite her early evening nap. Outside, the warm day had retreated into a cloudless sky of deepening violet seared with pink. She could already count five – no, six – tiny silver stars. Tired and weary, she rolled over on to her belly, sighing with relief as she remembered that her wrist had been untied from the bedpost and her gag roughly peeled away from her mouth by Svetlana during her earlier domination.

Lonely and confined to her bedroom, she closed her eyes and remembered her eventful days – and even more eventful nights – at The Rookery. Soon she would be exiled from this strange, erotic house and return to a bland existence in London. Back in the capital, there would be no afternoon tea parties where beautiful, bored women took cake and discipline in the afternoon. Spritzers at Harvey Nic's could never match tea at four at The Rookery, she mused. Then Susie recalled her moments of fearful shame followed by delicious pain, at the hands, lips and canes of madame's clients that afternoon. After the date and walnut cake there was discipline. How tongues, which had lapped at honey-glazed crumpets, had probed her own sweet hive, licking her labia fiercely. She imagined the knives glinting as they sliced into moist cheesecake and firmer cherry Genoa – just as the glinting canes had later sliced down across perfectly presented pink bottoms. Susie rolled over on her bed, shuddering slightly at the vision of the blonde's teeth closing down over a buttered scone only minutes before closing down over her own spanked bottom.

Outside, an early owl hooted mournfully, adding to Susie's deepening melancholy. She crushed her face into the pillow and squashed her breasts into the bed. Shortly after the bizarre tea party, Susie remembered attending the whipping school where she assisted madame in the induction and assessment of willing, bare-bottomed novices trembling deliciously in their wooden yokes of bondage. What delicious memories she had of The Rookery, its unusual clients with unusual needs and of serving Seraphim Savage. Susie had grown bold, then even bolder, during that long afternoon. She had tasted the pleasures of punishing and controlling the beautiful young women's naked bodies. The naked and the beautiful: the words haunted the troubled girl as she lay spreadeagled, face down on her bed.

Suddenly, the harsh tang of the leather slipper – the supple hide still hot from scorching the buttocks of the girl bending in her bondage – tormented Susie. She ground her hips into the bed beneath her. Slipping her hands down to cup each softly rounded breast, she held their warm weight firmly as she willed herself back to the tutorial room where the whipping school had been held.

Yes: she pictured the fourth girl along, bare-bottomed and yoked into submission and surrender. Susie weighing the slipper in her hand. Yes. The girl being scolded by madame. Vivid snapshots flickered before her mind's eye: the girl's sorrowful eyes, upturned and pleading; the eyes had widened with fear as Susie had crushed the leather sole of the slipper against her own bosom. Moments later, the soft swish and harsh crack of punishment being administered: the swift, sure strokes of the slipper down across the helpless, reddening cheeks. And, Susie remembered as she turned her cupping hands against her trapped breasts and squeezed, the proudly naked body of madame. Regal and superb as she orchestrated the punishment of the five naked girls. A capable chastiser, she was more than competent with the cane: she bewitched the buttocks bending before her as she pleasured their creamy cheeks with angry stripes of pain. Susie fingered her hardening nipples, tugging and tweaking the berries in delightful torment as she pondered the magnificence of madame, lingering over every nuance of the beautiful dominatrix: her heavy buttocks; lithe thighs; swollen bosom and unblinking, all-seeing eyes. Susie had witnessed, that afternoon in the whipping school, a superb example of female discipline being administered and accepted.

Rolling over on to her back once more, she opened her eyes and let her left hand slide slowly down over the swell of her belly. Her bedroom was growing dark as the encroaching night engulfed The Rookery. Somewhere in the distance, beyond the ragged line of elms, an owl hooted sombrely. The soft sorrow of the sound reminded Susie of the night she and Annette had entertained madame's four male revellers. She recalled how that evening had begun with the men, fully dressed and eager for pleasure, ravaging the two naked girls with lustful eyes. She aso remembered how the evening had ended with her whipping the naked men, their hot stripes dispensed entirely at her whim. The four monied studs had at first owned Susie's bare bottom with their eyes; by midnight, she ruled their naked cheeks with her cane.

The severity of her pleasure at these memories of her time at The Rookery made her pubis pulse; behind the velvet curtains of her labia, her tingling slit juiced. Susie's fingers inched down. She spread her thighs apart, squashing her buttocks into the bed beneath her. Her fingertips paused for a brief moment then drew the velvet curtains apart. The sticky flesh lips peeled back obediently at the touch of her dominant fingers. With a riot of memories and rampant images flooding her brain, she dipped her fingertips down into her hot, wet flesh. Her hips jerked in response, pounding her tightened cheeks into the bed. With the remembered sights and sounds of harsh pleasure and sweet pain – the delights of discipline – whirling inside her mind, she teased out her clitoris and subjected it to the ruthless tenderness of her stroking thumb. A spasm rippled across the milky skin of her smooth belly and coursed along the sheen of her moon-bathed thighs.

Susie's thumb quickened, stroking more firmly, more punishingly: the spasms intensified, the fires within her blazed. Suddenly, she missed the gag at her lips; the tight gag which had bruised her lips and smothered her whimpering during her earlier chastisement. She yearned for the bite of restraining bondage at her ankles and wrists, wishing them to be tightly bound and immobile. Above all, she longed for the naked presence of madame. As her thumb flayed her glistening clitoris with eager precision, Susie ached for the dominatrix she feared and adored. To be bound and gagged, and bare-bottomed before madame's severe beauty. To have madame's hot cane across her buttocks and then madame's cruel touch at her clitoris. These alone were the burning desires that melted her mind as she climaxed, coming with a ferocity that almost frightened her as she shuddered in repeated orgasm.

It was hard to focus as she counted the stars, giving up after seventy-three. Her eyes were still bleary with lust. The moon was riding the dark clouds, its pale light cold and clear. Shivering slightly, she snuggled down under her duvet and surrendered herself to approaching sleep. The sadness of her impending exile grew larger in her tired brain, and instead of sleeping gently, her thoughts turned to Svetlana. Susie grew hot and angry as she considered the enormity of the Russian's deception and guile. What was the blackmailer really up to? Had she extorted the money out of Maritta just to see if it could be done? Were there plans to blackmail all of madame's special clients? Surely madame would be alert from now on; nobody would be able to hack into the data-base for such purposes. Susie sighed sadly; her innocence would never be proved as Svetlana would be cautious and avoid madame's vigilant eye. The special clients would all be safe, Susie realised. The Russian was greedy but not stupid. Stupid, perhaps, to try it once, but clever enough to get Susie the blame.

Susie sat up in her bed, her face burning in the darkness. She fumed at the sheer injustice of it all. She had been framed, punished and now faced certain exile from The Rookery – and madame. All accomplished by a greedy little schemer like Svetlana. Then, with a sudden flash of complete understanding, Susie guessed the truth. Svetlana had only blackmailed the Finn to see if Maritta would pay up, but it had been merely a trial run. Svetlana had no intention, Susie saw, of picking off madame's special clients one by one. That would be too slow, and too risky. No, Susie nodded slowly in the darkness of the night, Svetlana was sweeping the files to build up a complete profile of all madame's special clients: she was going to blackmail madame herself. In one clean strike, Svetlana would demand a single, huge pay-off, or ruin the enterprise at The Rookery completely.

A soft footstep approached the door. In the darkness, Susie heard but did not see the handle turn.

'Asleep?' whispered Annette's voice.

'Not yet,' replied Susie, relieved to discover that it was Annette – and not Svetlana – paying her this nocturnal visit.

'Got you some things,' Annette explained, approaching the bed. 'Put the lamp on.'

A small pool of yellow light bathed Susie's head and naked shoulders, shadowing the cleavage between her bare breasts deliciously. Annette spilled her assorted gifts down on to the bed and fingered the unruly fringe away from Susie's blue eyes.

'Biscuits, an apple, a piece of cheese. And a couple of books.' Annette smiled, her eyes devouring the heavy satin breasts as Susie reached out for her unexpected treats. 'Don't know if you'll like 'em, I pinched them earlier on. You OK?'

'Mmm,' Susie replied indistinctly, nibbling at her wedge of Stilton, her red lips shrinking slightly from the lactic sharpness. Annette inched her bottom closer to Susie's thigh and stroked her friend's dark hair tenderly. Susie punctuated her mouthfuls of cheese with bites from the sweet apple – the combination was divine. Looking into Annette's eyes, she smiled her gratitude.

'Better not stay. Madame would –'

'I know,' Susie said and nodded. 'Have they told you why I was punished? And why I have to leave?'

Annette glanced down at the duvet, avoiding Susie's gaze.

'So they did,' Susie said sadly.

'Svetlana told me. Is it true?'

'No. It is not true. Svetlana blackmailed Maritta.'

'She lost the money though, and won't try again.'

'She doesn't have to, don't you see?'

'Why?' Annette frowned.

'She's got all the information she needs. She'll go for the jackpot next time.'

'You mean madame?'

'Exactly.'

A noise from somewhere within the house silenced the fierce whispering. They crouched together in fear, but there was no more cause for alarm and they resumed their intense exchange.

'What can we do? Madame will never believe either of us. Especially you,' Annette said and shrugged, adding, 'and I've no proof.'

'You must get it.'

'How? What proof?'

'She'll have a disc, I'm sure. She'd have copied all the files on to her own disc.'

'But madame would have found it,' Annette reasoned, 'when she was searching for Maritta's bag.'

'You're right. OK, let's think. That means she's stashed it away securely somewhere. Somewhere inside The Rookery.'

'But where do I start looking –?'

Annette's question was abruptly interrupted by another slight but definite sound. A door clicking shut, or a stair creaking. She sprang up from the bed. 'I have to go. I'll be whipped if I'm found with you.'

'Go to madame, now. Please. Go and ask her to come and see me,' Susie pleaded.

Annette slipped out of the bedroom in silence, closing the door behind her. Susie nibbled at the apple core and picked up a book. It was a French paperback, published by Hachette in Les Grands Ecrivains series. The foxed

207

condition attested to its age. Susie examined her apple core. It had turned brown, so she placed it on her bedside cabinet and returned to the unpromising book. It was a novel by Colette, completely intact and unread; the pages, yet to be cut, remained sealed and virginal. Tossing it aside, she picked up the other book, silently hoping that Annette's second choice had been more fortunate. It was a cloth-bound pre-war Sherlock Holmes omnibus. Hell, Susie thought, surely Annette could have done better than this.

'She said no,' Annette whispered through the door. 'Madame said she never wanted to see you or speak to you again. I'm sorry, Susie, but she was very cross. I couldn't persuade her.'

'Did you say anything about Svetlana?' Susie asked eagerly.

Annette remained silent.

'Well? Did you?'

'I couldn't,' came the whispered reply. 'She was in bed with madame.' Annette locked the bedroom door. 'Madame's orders.'

In bed with madame. The words seared through Susie's brain like fire. Not only did they seal her fate but they ignited her jealousy. She picked up the Sherlock Holmes and angrily flicked through it resenting the locked door, but resenting even more the thought of the Russian bitch pleasuring, and being pleasured by, Seraphim Savage. Susie's anger subsided as her eye fell on a familiar chapter, then ebbed as she read another. Soon she was engrossed in old favourites, known by heart since late childhood. She could almost hear the clip-clop of the horse's hooves on wet cobblestones as the celebrated sleuth bowled through the London fogs, dogged by the faithful if bumbling Watson. Finishing her fourth chapter, Susie nodded over the book and drifted off to sleep.

Thump: the book slipped from her fingers down on to the floor. The soft thud stirred Susie in her shallow sleep. She opened her eyes, blinked, then sat bolt upright in her bed. She was wide awake and excited. The door, she remembered angrily, was locked. There was nothing for it but to risk the window, and then the ivy clinging to the outer wall. Only the slightest of squeaks betrayed the opening of her sash window. Seconds later, Susie was lowering herself down against the brickwork, feeling frantically for a firmer handful of thick ivy. Inching along sideways slowly and carefully, she reached another first-floor window. It was dark, the room within deserted. Calculating rapidly as she shivered in the chill of the night, her breasts crushed into the waxy leaves, she knew that Annette's bedroom was either the next window – or the next but one.

Don't look down. Whatever you do, don't look down, she thought. Susie's knuckles whitened as she made her precarious way towards the next window ledge. She had forgotten how terrified of heights she was, and pressed closely to the wall, grazing her soft bosom against the mellow brickwork. Nearing the window, she saw the haze of pale light from within. Good. Annette was probably still awake, she thought. But peering over the window ledge cautiously, Susie's heart skipped a beat as she saw Svetlana lowering her splayed thighs down on to madame's upturned buttocks. Snarling softly, Susie blinked the image away from her tear-filled eyes – tears of jealousy, tears of frustration – and continued her high-level quest for Annette. Her friend was sleeping lightly, and gamely bounded across to the window in response to Susie's sharp tap. Annette pressed her nose against the cold glass, her eyes wide with surprise. She opened the window quietly.

'What are you –?'

'Shush,' Susie hissed. 'Listen. Tomorrow, very first thing, I want you to start a fire.'

'You're mad.'

'Not a real one. Just burn the toast – you usually do. Or the bacon. Just do it early and make lots of smoke. But make it seem real.'

'I don't understand,' Annette murmured doubtfully, shivering after the warmth of her bed.

'Please,' Susie urged. 'It's important.'

'OK,' Annette replied with a shrug.

209

'Sure? You won't get cold feet?'

'Probably get a hot bottom from madame.' Annette grinned.

'Thanks. I'll explain later.'

'Better get back. Be careful, we're high up. You can come in if you want.'

'No,' Susie replied, sparing her loyal friend the risk of discovery and a subsequent whipping. 'I'll be OK. Just promise me there'll be lots of smoke before daybreak.'

The pale grey sky told Susie that it was dawn. She had slept fitfully after inching her way back in the cold, dark night from Annette's window ledge to her own. Clad only in the flimsy protection of her satin scanties, her breasts and thighs had suffered in the nocturnal excursion. Waking up to the shout of 'Fire!' she remembered her plan. Footsteps scampered outside in the corridor. Already, a whiff of acrid smoke was tainting the bright morning air.

'Fire!' Annette's alarmed voice rose to a thrill cry.

More footsteps – firmer this time – paced the corridor purposefully. A hand rattled the key in Susie's door.

'It's all right. False alarm,' Annette's voice rose up from the kitchen downstairs.

Susie heard the hand at her door drop from the handle and turn the key. Madame's voice rasped out her anger with Annette. Whatever it was madame had hissed under her breath about the foolish domestic, Susie did not quite catch it: she was leaning out of her window peering down at the gravel below. Yes. Her plan had worked. Svetlana skipped down the steps and stood outside the front entrance, madame's tapestry tucked securely under her left arm. Susie withdrew, hiding from sight, but strained to listen as a murmured exchange floated up a minute later.

'Stupid girl. A tea towel caught fire. She always cooks over a high flame. Terrible smoke, though,' madame's voice said. 'Come back inside, my dear girl, you'll catch your death out here. What have you there?'

'Your tapestry,' Svetlana replied. 'Of all the things worth saving,' the Russian fawned, 'I thought of you. And this.'

'You are a perfect darling,' madame, delighted and flattered, gushed warmly. 'Now do come inside. After a warming breakfast of bacon and mushrooms we'll spank the bare bottom of that careless girl, hmm?'

Up at her window, Susie hugged herself with delight. She had caught Svetlana in a trap worthy of the Master of Baker Street himself.

'Yes?' she said, turning at the knock on her door.

The door was unlocked and Annette was pushed into the room. Svetlana followed, cane in hand. It was only a few minutes since The Rookery had woken up abruptly to the cry of alarm and a cloud of pungent smoke, and already Svetlana was skipping breakfast in order to administer harsh discipline. Annette looked anxious, her large eyes downcast and sorrowful. Svetlana closed the door and stepped arrogantly into the room.

'Come away from that window and kneel,' she snapped.

Susie, who had peeled off her bra and panties – spoiled by the scratching ivy – and replaced them with a white shirt, obeyed.

'This is your last day here so I thought we might have a little farewell party. Madame has given me permission to punish Annette for her clumsiness a little while ago. Then I am going to punish you, bitch. Your bottom is mine to do with what I please. Let us think of it as a little going-away present.' Svetlana laughed softly. 'Some stripes to remember me by.'

Susie flushed angrily but choked down her anger. To resist or rebel now would have very painful consequences, both for herself and for dear, loyal Annette. She would have to bide her time and watch carefully for the right moment. The right moment for her revenge.

'Didn't get much sleep last night in madame's bed,' boasted the Russian, taunting Susie. 'And was woken early,' she flashed angrily at Annette. 'So,' she sighed, with mocking regret, 'I am too tired to punish you. What am I to do? For punished you must, and most certainly will be. I wonder,' she mused aloud, evidently relishing every moment of her teasing and tormenting preamble. 'It is a bit of a problem, isn't it? Two girls to be whipped and the whipper is too tired to carry out the punishment. Why,' she said as if suddenly solving her problem, 'they can stripe each other.'

Susie and Annette exchanged fearful glances as they understood their fate. The Rusian was going to take cruel delight in humiliating them by ordaining that they would each stripe and be striped.

'Up. Bend over, across your bed, bitch,' Svetlana whispered, passing the cane to Annette. 'Give her five strokes.'

Five? Susie frowned, perplexed by the odd number of lashes she was about to receive across her bare bottom.

'On each cheek,' the Russian continued gleefully, knowing that she had seduced Susie into a false sense of relief, only to dash her fragile hopes away replacing them with dread.

Annette swished the cane and approached the bed across which Susie was now bending, her long legs stretching down to the carpet where her feet were pressed together. Svetlana knelt against the bed, her breasts squashed into the mattress, alongside Susie's naked thigh. Delicately fingering the tail of Susie's shirt, the Russian teasingly inched the flap of crisp cotton up slowly over the swell of the cheeks, revealing the ripely rounded flesh.

'Five,' mumbled Svetlana, her warm lips pressed into Susie's thigh. 'On each cheek.'

Annette raised her cane and lowered it carefully, adjusting her stance so that the tip of the whippy bamboo wood came to rest a quarter of an inch from the cleft dividing the peach-cheeks. The length of cane across the sphere of the left buttock slowly depressed the swell of satin flesh.

'Wait,' commanded Svetlana. 'I want to enjoy this.' She encircled Susie's lower thighs with both her arms, hugging them tightly and causing the trapped buttocks to bulge. Lowering her face down, she crushed it against Susie's right cheek.

'Commence,' she ordered, her voice drowning in the warm flesh. 'Cane her severely.'

Trembling slightly, Annette took a deep breath, flexed

her wrist and swept the cane down. With a soft hiss, it kissed the rounded left buttock with a thin, reddening line of pain. Susie suppressed her squeak of surprise as she jerked in response to the bamboo's bite. Svetlana tightened her grasp of the punished girl's naked thighs, absorbing Susie's spasm of suffering.

Eager to be rid of this unpleasant burden, Annette brought the cane down across Susie's left cheek twice in rapid succession, scalding and striping the exposed buttock with the searching strokes. Susie's wriggling thrust her right cheek into Svetlana's open mouth – the lips, teeth and tongue busy and brutal.

'Harder,' Svetlana ordered in a lust-thickened voice. 'Stripe the bitch harder.'

Annette's eyes brimmed with tears as she whipped the soft creamy buttock twice more, adding two more angry lines to the three weals of fire.

'Continue,' Svetlana whispered, her words muffled by the buttocks she was slowly mouthing. 'Five more, on the same spot, but backhanders this time and make sure they sting.'

Backhanders: the dreaded cut of the wood delivered by the more powerful, more venomous, backhand stroke. And, Annette gulped, on the same scalded cheek which had just been lashed. Both punisher and punished shivered at the command. Reluctantly, but obediently, Annette continued the punishment, slicing the reddening cheek with five sharp strokes. Susie's buttock throbbed as, free from the Russian's encircling arms, she rolled over, hugging her knees to her warm bosom. Svetlana rose up and took the cane from Annette.

'Touch your toes. Legs apart,' she instructed.

Hesitantly, Annette adopted the required position, her naked cheeks thrust up and perfectly poised for pain. Svetlana placed the length of the glittering bamboo along the cleft dividing each cheek. It was a dominant gesture, one which seemed to tame and subjugate the naked buttocks. Annette shuddered beneath the supple cane, flinching at its cruel proximity and fearful of its impending bite.

'You. Take the cane and give a swift dozen,' Svetlana said to Susie in a excited whisper. It was a cruel command, calculated carefully to torment. Svetlana knew that Susie would suffer as much as the girl she was about to beat.

'Wait,' Svetlana hissed, half-kneeling, half-squatting to position herself beneath Annette. The Russian then pressed her face into the quivering girl's pubis. Comfortably wedged between Annette's thighs, with her lips and tongue exploring the sticky slit, she grunted the command to commence the caning.

Susie paced the dozen, delivering the first four strokes slowly, almost leisurely. The bare bottom rippled with each searching swipe of wood against flesh, the pale globes quickly displaying each pink line of pain. Svetlana feasted at the pubis below as the cane cracked down across the buttocks above. Relentlessly, her hot mouth worked busily at the base of the punished nude's belly; remorselessly, the hotter cane worked busily across the punished nude's bottom. Eight, nine, ten. Two strokes remained to be administered. Susie wiped her moist palm down across the swell of her left buttock, her momentary forgetfulness causing her to wince as she touched her own scalded flesh.

'Stripe her, bitch,' thundered the Russian, impatient at the delay.

Susie glimpsed Svetlana's thighs through Annette's parted legs. She saw the thumb of their tormentress strumming at her own wet slit; the thumb had paused, pressing down against the tiny pink clitoris, waiting for the concluding strokes. Raising the cane up slowly, she closed her eyes unable to bear the sight of her friend's suffering or of her foe's pleasure.

Behind her self-imposed darkness, two haunting images blazed brightly: the caned cheeks and the thumbed clitoris. Almost as if trying to dispel the vision, Susie swept the cane down, slicing the bamboo twice across the hot buttocks and bringing the punishment to a painful conclusion. Annette shivered beneath the double lash, and shuddered as Svetlana's hungry mouth devoured her wet flesh. The Russian clasped the whipped cheeks with both hands, burying herself into Annette as she came, her climax punctuated by low, carnal grunts of satisfaction.

'Here she is,' Svetlana announced, pushing Susie naked and hot-bottomed into madame's office. 'I have punished her, madame. A souvenir to remember us by.'

Madame merely nodded and remained seated at her desk. Susie shielded her breasts with her right arm and placed her left hand down between her thighs. Blushing in her shame, she gazed down at her feet.

'Turn around,' madame ordered the naked girl. 'Ah, I see that only one cheek was whipped. How interesting. Why?'

'I left the other for you, madame,' Svetlana murmured deferentially.

'Why, Svetlana, how extraordinarily unselfish of you. I do believe we are going to become close frends. Very close. As it happens, a taxi is at this very moment on its way to collect this wretched girl. Turn around and face me, girl,' madame barked. 'Arms by your side. Stand up straight.'

Susie complied with madame's crisp instructions, revealing as she did so her utter nakedness.

'I am bitterly disappointed in you, Miss Pelham-Heys. I had great hopes for you. Very great hopes. You showed great flair for my little enterprise but proved untrustworthy, jealous and of criminal propensity.'

Susie suffered the tongue-lashing in silence, fighting back her tears of sorrow.

'Have you nothing to say, wretched girl?'

Susie knew that the next few words she uttered could alter the entire shape of her future: choosing the right words would secure her happiness here at The Rookery, but choosing the wrong ones would ensure her exile from it. She must, she suddenly realised, not mention Svetlana at all. Denying her urge to denounce the treacherous Russian girl for the scheming blackmailer Susie knew her to be, she raised her eyes up to meet madame's and spoke in soft, submissive tones.

'I beg your forgiveness, madame, and humbly thank you

for all your kindness to me. I am truly sorry I have disappointed you and beg to ask of you only one thing.'

'Pretty words, Miss Pelham-Heys, but I cannot grant you a pardon or a reprieve. Into exile you must and will go.'

'Yes, madame. I submit to your ruling completely,' Susie whispered in response. 'But may I take –' Susie paused, counting her words carefully '– a small souvenir of my happiness here with you?'

Madame's steely gaze softened and she rose up from her chair. Pacing gently around the desk and approaching Susie, she embraced the bare-bottomed penitent tenderly and whispered into Susie's dark hair.

'You naughty, naughty girl. Despite everything, I am going to miss you sorely. Well? What is it that you want? A piece of wicked lingerie? An illustrated catalogue of our delicious wares?'

'Oh no, madame. Something much more special. I would treasure most the beautiful tapestry you made; the one you call –'

'*In Servitude.*' Madame smiled as she finished Susie's sentence. 'Why?'

'Because I was most happy when serving you.'

'No,' snarled Svetlana. 'No, you can't. She must not have –'

'Must not?' challenged Seraphim Savage, bridling at the brusque outburst. 'I think that it is for me and for me alone to decide whether Su– Miss Pelham-Heys is to have her wish granted. And a most touching request –'

'No,' Svetlana shouted angrily. 'You mustn't give that bitch –'

'Mustn't?' came the cool reply.

'She deserves nothing. She –'

'Made a single, stupid mistake,' madame intervened, her tone icily controlled. Her arm encircled Susie protectively, almost forgivingly. The gesture threw the Russian into a blaze of fury. Madame bridled, Svetlana's tantrum confirming a decision she was struggling to make. 'This girl has disappointed me, and disappointed me most gravely.

She must leave The Rookery as a punishment, but it is for me to decide whether or not she takes with her a souvenir of happier moments.'

'Not the tapestry,' Svetlana hissed viciously.

'Really, my dear girl,' madame said sternly. 'I simply will not be spoken to like that –'

The Russian skipped across the room and snatched up the tapestry.

'Svetlana? What on earth?' madame cried angrily.

Panicking, Svetlana turned and ran towards the door, colliding with Annette who was just entering. They swayed and toppled, the tapestry cartwheeling across the floor.

'Hold her,' Susie cried to Annette.

Annette gamely overcame the Russian, straddling her quarry and pinning her face down into the carpet.

'Madame,' Susie panted, retrieving the tapestry and returning it to its stand, 'inside the canvas you will find, I am almost certain, a disc. If I am right, that disc will contain copied details of all your special clients. It is Svetlana's disc.'

'What?' thundered Seraphim Savage, pouncing upon the canvas and fingering its softness frantically. A few seconds of searching brought the disc to light.

'Bitch,' hissed Svetlana, struggling and squirming violently.

In a few brief moments, Susie explained her suspicions, what Svetlana's true intentions were and what she suspected the disc contained. In total silence, madame slotted it into her computer: the screen lit up and Svetlana's crime was laid bare for all to see. Turning to the girl on the floor, she asked a single question.

'Can you send e-mail?'

'No,' spat the Russian.

'I am going to whip you, whip you mercilessly, until you send an e-mail message, which I fully believe you can.'

'But that's not fair –'

'Bring me my cane, Susie,' madame said coolly.

'No, wait,' the pale-faced Russian wailed. 'I can, I will. I can send e-mail.'

'Just as I thought.' Madame nodded, returning her face impassively to the glowing screen. She clicked the mouse button twice. 'What have we here? Well, well. The actual blackmail note to Maritta, or at least a copy. You really should learn to edit and not save such incriminating evidence, my girl. And what is this? A letter to me?'

Madame read the blackmail note in silence. Susie joined her at the desk, reading over madame's shoulder.

'Her plan was to rip you off, madame. Maritta was only a practice run – and a way of getting rid of me.'

Madame clicked the mouse; together they read the contents of the entire disc quickly.

'To be paid into her own named account in Rome, by which time she would be back in Moscow,' madame muttered, still white with shock and anger. 'But how did you now about this disc?'

'It was guesswork, then logic – then a little bit of help from Sherlock Holmes.'

'Sherlock Holmes?' madame echoed faintly.

'There was a classic case for him to solve. A crowned European prince desperately wanted some indiscreet letters retrieved. Holmes created the illusion of a fire in the house of the adventuress. As he predicted, she went straight to her hiding place, betraying their whereabouts.'

'So Annette's little charade before breakfast?'

'Well worth the pain.' Annette grinned.

'I set it all up and watched Svetlana. When she ran out with the tapestry –'

'Of course. Smoked out,' madame said and smiled grimly.

'Yes, madame. Smoked out.'

'Bring her here,' Seraphim Savage ordered.

Susie helped Annette to drag the squealing Russian before madame.

'Kneel,' thundered the mistress of The Rookery.

Svetlana dropped to her knees.

'Twenty-five thousand, wasn't it? And if I refused, you would destroy my entire enterprise and resort to frightening my clients into making payments. That was your plan?'

Svetlana remained silent, but her quivering confirmed her guilt – and her dread of the dire consequences to come.

'Answer me, girl. Susie was correct, wasn't she?'

At the mention of her hated rival's name, the Russian tossed her ash blonde hair and laughed scornfully.

'You stupid bitch, I could have cleaned you out. Like a fat hen, waiting to be plucked and put in the pot. I fooled you completely and would have –'

'Twenty-five thousand. Twenty-five seems a perfectly reasonable figure,' madame purred. 'A perfectly reasonable, and most fitting, number of strokes for you to receive. For your first taste of punishment. There will of course be much more to come, much more,' madame promised warmly.

'No,' shouted the kneeling Russian.

'Gag her, then take her away and administer the prescribed chastisement. Cane her hard,' madame's voice rose imperiously. 'I will not whip the girl myself. Today. Nor will you, for the moment, Susie.'

Susie. Not the coldly formal Miss Pelham-Heys of recent hours, Susie thrilled secretly, but Susie. Susie.

'No, madame. I think that Annette, who has suffered Svetlana's cruelty, should dispense the discipline.'

'Wise, and generous, words, my dear girl. Annette, you must be the first to chastise her. Take her to the tutorial room where I conduct the whipping school. Susie may assist and then observe. Arrange this wretched girl in the stocks and then beat her bare bottom with my cane. Susie, you may witness but you may not, for the moment, whip.'

'Very well, madame,' Susie said.

Svetlana struggled all the way along the corridor but her smothered cries and futile writhing were easily managed by her resolute captors. Gripping her soft flesh in several sensitive places, they propelled the Russian to her doom. Inside the tutorial room where the whipping school was held, Svetlana was bent down into her restricting yoke. There, helpless to resist, she was slowly stripped bare, her silken bra and panties held like trophies in Susie's hands. Annette's eyes sparkled with lustful excitement as she examined the cane.

'Do not be tempted to rush the punishment,' Susie counselled. 'Take it slowly. And use the leather for the first fifteen, and then the cane for the remaining ten,' Susie added. 'She must suffer. Learn, and suffer. So punish her slowly. We have all the time we need.'

Svetlana groaned as she heard these words, straining in her harsh wooden yoke as Susie's cool voice outlined the suffering to come.

'After all,' Susie reasoned, 'this stupid girl will be here at The Rookery for many days, many weeks, perhaps. We can punish her at our pleasure whenever we want. For now, a severe taste will suffice. Let it be a piquant appetiser for the banquet before us.'

Svetlana's eyes grew wide with fear as she listened to Susie's reflections. Suddenly glimpsing the enormity of her impending misery, the naked Russian shivered with fearful apprehension, causing the smooth flesh of her naked buttocks to ripple with a frisson of dread.

'The leather,' whispered Annette hoarsely, replacing the yellow wood with a supple strip of dark hide. She snapped it twice: Svetlana's toes curled. 'I will commence with the leather across her buttocks.'

'Excellent,' Susie replied, sinking down on to her knees, her thighs wide apart. 'But remember, slowly.'

Crack. Susie dragged the tip of her tongue across the roof of her mouth as the curved lash kissed Svetlana's defenceless buttocks. Gazing directly at the bare bottom she had craved for so long, Susie watched the swollen cheeks redden where the strap had stung. The second stroke whistled down and echoed loudly as supple hide punished satin skin. Susie slipped her finger into her mouth, sucking hard on it as she probed her sensitive flesh. Her eyes devoured the suffering cheeks unblinkingly.

As the red badge of shame and pain spread across the softly rounded buttocks, the heat in Susie's tingling slit increased to a burning torment. The invisible flames of fire flared as she saw Annette slowly raise the length of shining leather up once more. Dropping her hands down, fingertips touching, to frame her pubic delta, Susie gently strummed the velvet hood of her clitoris with her thumb. This time it was Susie herself who spasmed violently, so fierce was the next crisp lash. She saw Svetlana's cleft disappear into an invisible crease as the Russian tightened her cheeks in scalded anguish.

'Slow down,' Susie admonished. 'You're going too fast.'

Annette, pausing to finger the elastic waistband of her panties and pluck the moistening cotton away from her pubic mound, nodded. Retreating two paces, she let the leather strap drop down limply along her right thigh. Susie shuffled on her knees across to Svetlana's bending buttocks and pressed her face closely against them. Brushing her lips against their hot curves, she felt the punished Russian wriggle in her yoked bondage. After planting a dominant kiss on the shining crown of each whipped cheek, she shuffled back to a spot from where she could gaze serenely upon the bare bottom as it burned.

'Proceed,' she whispered.

Again, the leather strap scorched down across the vulnerable domes. Again, the wooden frame restricting the naked Russian rattled in response to her writhing. Susie's thumbtip returned to strum at the hot wet pulse at the base of her belly, teasing and tormenting her clitoris. Svetlana grunted into her gag as Annette whipped her bottom searchingly and accurately. Susie echoed the grunt with a carnal moan as her clitoris stiffened and rebelled beneath her dominant thumb. The slow, deliberate and controlled punishment continued until eleven strokes had been administered. Annette paused, withdrew to lean back against the wall, and crushed the warm leather against her painfully peaked nipples.

Susie rose up from her knees and approached the seething cheeks. Lowering her breasts down over their hot curves, she dragged her heavy bosom across Svetlana's bottom slowly, allowing her stiff nipples to graze the suffering flesh. Thrilling to the touch of her cool satin breasts against the hot cheeks, Susie closed her eyes and relished the moment. It was the moment she had yearned for: to own, possess and utterly dominate Svetlana's delicious buttocks.

Framing the Russian's sleek hips with her hands to steady and control the captive cheeks within, Susie ground her breasts savagely into the bare bottom. Svetlana's struggles ceased as she became passive and docile, surrendering her whipped cheeks to Susie's absolute domination. Susie lingered, savouring her moment of supreme triumph. Soon, she would relinquish the buttocks, returning them to the lash. But for now, they were hers. She hugged her hot prize to her bosom and sighed.

'Shall I continue with the whipping?' Annette murmured, drying the wet leather where it had been rubbed against her weeping slit.

Annette's question broke the delicious silence. Susie opened her eyes and blinked as if emerging from a dream. She turned and smiled at Annette over her shoulder. Nodding her agreement, she peeled her breasts away from the hot cheeks and strode around the wooden stocks to face the girl they constrained. Svetlana flickered her sorrowful eyes upward and met Susie's stern gaze.

'It could have been different. So very different,' Susie said sadly, tracing the Russian's cheekbone with her fingertip. 'But you were greedy and had to spoil it all.'

Annette positioned herself behind the naked bottom and snapped the leather belt twice, patiently awaiting Susie's signal. Susie raised her left hand up and, lifting Svetlana's face up sternly in her right hand, gave the expected sign. Crack. For a timeless moment, Susie and Svetlana explored each other through the intimacy of their eyes. Susie raised – then swiftly dropped – her left hand once more. Annette responded instantly, whipping the length of hide down smartly to scald the bare bottom below. The Russian's eyes widened with pain, but continued to gaze up directly into Susie's. The right hand that controlled the punished girl's captive face squeezed tightly ·as the left hand swept down to give a double signal. The leather snapped twice in response; Svetlana jerked twice as her naked buttocks suffered the double swipe across her upturned cheeks.

Susie almost swooned as her slit began to seethe. Teetering tipsily, she released her hold on Svetlana and supported herself against the wooden stocks. Recovering her poise, she clutched a handful of the Russian's hair and spoke softly.

'I will remove your gag for the final strokes of the leather. Keep still,' she admonished. With a touch of brutal tenderness, she tore off the gag. Svetlana licked her lips and snarled. Susie stroked the pale face firmly with her straightened index finger then quickly slipped it into the Russian's mouth. Svetlana's eyes widened in surprise.

'Give her the final stripes.'

As the leather came down Susie felt Svetlana's teeth bite gently into her finger but she did not withdraw it from the wet warmth. Annette raised the supple belt aloft as Susie probed the mouth once more, forcing her fingertip up against the roof of Svetlana's sensitive flesh. A curt nod brought the strap whistling down. The hide hissed against the scalded cheeks. The probing finger muffled the squeal of anguish, and soon the room was echoing eerily to a fierce sucking sound as Svetlana devoured Susie's rigid flesh.

'And again,' commanded Susie.

Svetlana grunted as the lash blazed her bottom with fresh fire, but dragged Susie's finger deeper into her mouth, sucking feverishly in her frenzied torment.

'And now?' Annette enquired as she rolled up the length of leather into a tight coil between her fingers.

'The cane. Ten strokes, to complete her punishment,' Susie replied, pumping her finger into Svetlana's mouth.

'At once,' Annette whispered, stooping to scoop up the pliant cane.

Swish. Susie felt the hot mouth tighten around her finger as the first of the ten strokes sliced down across the Russian's naked buttocks. Swish. Again, the bamboo sliced; again, the naked girl spasmed beneath the searing stroke. Susie retrieved her finger and lowered her face, brushing her warm lips against those of the caned nude. Swish. Svetlana's lips opened to form a surprised circle in response; they met Susie's pursed lips with even greater

223

surprise and lingered submissively against their sweet velvety flesh.

More double cane cuts forced Svetlana to thrust her face out in an ecstasy of anguish. Susie greeted the Russian's mouth with her tongue, spearing the sweet flesh deeply. Svetlana gasped as she accepted the dominant length of muscle obediently. Again Annette plied the supple bamboo unerringly, searchingly and remorselessly across the bare bottom; it had once been a pale shade of ivory, but was now scalded, striped and reddened. Susie gazed down into Svetlana's eyes for the concluding strokes.

'Four more,' Annette announced quietly, pausing briefly to rub the length of glittering yellow cane down between her closely clamped thighs. It emerged sparkling with her juice.

'Suffer, my darling Svetlana,' Susie mumbled, her lips pressed firmly against the startled Russian's mouth. 'Suffer, and know sorrow. Accept your fitting punishment. You deserve every burning stroke.'

Swish, slice. Svetlana squealed as she thrashed in her bondage, but Susie merely kissed the anguished girl's eyes. Swish, swipe. Jerking in her hot torment, Svetlana gasped aloud as she felt Susie reach down to cup and squeeze her loose and lovely breasts, pinching the nipples just as the bamboo bit her bottom. Yoked in her wooden harness, the helpless girl began to climax. Susie sensed the approaching – but denied – orgasm, and relished the Russian's fresh suffering. The merest touch of her fingers to the hot slit below would suffice, rocketing the Russian into ecstasy. But Svetlana was to be punished, not pleasured: her climax was forbidden.

'Two more, my dear Svetlana. And a dozen more if you come.'

'Please,' moaned Svetlana, begging for release and relief.

'One for discipline –' Susie whispered.

Swish: Svetlana screamed softly, her buttocks ablaze.

'And one for desire –'

Swish: Susie smothered the Russian's cry of response with her hungry lips and tongue.

'Ten,' announced Annette. 'She has received her pre-scribed chastisement.'

'Excellent,' Susie's lips murmured into Svetlana's. 'You may leave us now.'

'Leave? But –' Annette's voice rose.

'You may leave us now,' Susie repeated, raising her face up and resting her chin down on the blonde hair of her captive.

'Madame said you weren't to punish –'

'I said go.'

Annette tossed the cane down. It rattled on the floor. Stamping her foot crossly, she stormed out of the tutorial room angrily, slamming the door behind her.

'No –' hissed Svetlana.

'Be silent,' Susie warned.

'No more, please. I have been punished enough.'

'For now, perhaps. That is strictly for me to decide, not for you to dictate. Do you understand?'

'Yes,' whispered the Russian submissively.

'Good. We are alone and you are completely mine. I own and control every naked inch of you.'

'You can't –' Svetlana protested, her words instantly silenced by the gag Susie replaced around her mouth.

'Silence. You have been whipped. By Annette. I too have the inclination to deal with you, Svetlana. And deal with you I most certainly will,' Susie whispered, threading a blindfold around the Russian's eyes.

Gagged and blindfolded, Svetlana shivered in total sub-jugation. Susie paced around the yoked nude and stood directly behind the hot, bare bottom which attested to the sweet severity of the recent chastisement. Svetlana strained in her bondage, writhing within the wooden harness but froze as she felt not the expected flash of pain but Susie's gentle fingertips playing across her hot rump's curves.

'You betrayed me. Betrayed me and smashed into pieces my desire and affection for you. I will not be so cruel. I forgive you, you foolish, stupid girl. I forgive you, and still want you.'

Svetlana tensed, uncertain of what was to come.

'Though you are wicked, you are still beautiful to me.'

Susie, despite her knowledge of Svetlana's sinfulness, bowed down before a greater knowledge: desire. Her quivering tongue found the cleft between the reddened cheeks and lapped at the deliciously soft ribbon of flesh within. As the tongue licked her secret velvet, Svetlana shuddered with delight and thrust her buttocks back into Susie's face.

'You have caused me so much sweet pain. Now the time has come for me to repay you. In the drawer over there, by the wall, there is a ten-inch golden dildo. In a few moments, I am going to take that shaft of beaten gold and pleasure you, dear Svetlana, there.'

The Russian groaned drunkenly as Susie tapped the wet labia between her splayed thighs with a dominant fingertip.

'And there.'

Again, the yoked nude buckled in her bondage beneath a surge of raw pleasure as Susie's finger alighted and remained against the tight sphincter.

'Madame was very strict in her orders. She forbade me to punish you. That pleasurable task was Annette's duty. But I do not recall madame saying anything,' Susie whispered as she caressed the outer curve of the punished left cheek, 'about pleasure.'

Susie padded softly across to the drawer. It opened with a soft squeak. In her severe bondage, the Russian groaned once more as she heard Susie's footfalls return. The wooden harness rattled violently as the naked girl felt the cool tip of the golden shaft nuzzle her labial fleshfolds.

'Not unlike a La Perla brassière but notice how these cups hug the breasts so fiercely. Yes. A perfect fit.'

'Thank you,' Susie's client whispered. 'It is superb.'

Susie adjusted the left shoulder strap a fraction and stood back. Apart from the black bra, her client was utterly naked.

'Anything else?' murmured Susie, absently brushing her hand against the soft, bare buttocks, then cupping the cheeks and squeezing them. 'Any special requirements?'

She dragged her fingertip across the warm peach-cheeks slowly, imitating the tip of the cane before the bamboo's bite.

'N–no,' her client stammered, blushing. 'Just the bra.'

Strange, Susie frowned. This one usually has a crisp six strokes – a straightforward caning across the bare bottom – after selecting a few items of lingerie.

'As you wish,' Susie said. As she added the brassière to the four pairs of panties and a little underwired bustier, and wreathed the purchases in whispering tissue, she made a mental note: she must speak with madame. Immediately. Something was not quite right. Not quite right at all.

'Stand still. Legs apart, no – bend over a little more. Capital. No. I should not be too concerned,' madame continued, stroking Susie's parted labia with the pliant rubber dildo. 'That client is a friend of Maritta's.'

'Perhaps Maritta told her. Warned her of the threat of blackmail.'

'Possibly.' Madame nodded. 'Keep still, girl. No, I have reassured Maritta that the problem has been nipped in the bud. My special clients have absolutely nothing to fear. Discretion is assured. I said stand still,' madame chided. 'All the same, I had better make a few phone calls. Allay any fears.'

Susie squealed with delight as the length of rubber slid inside her.

Spank. Madame slapped the softly curved left buttock of the bending girl.

'Be silent, minx. I saw you at work on Svetlana not an hour since. You may demonstrate enthusiasm but clearly have little idea of how to use one of these. Your technique is sadly lacking so be quiet and learn.'

Susie gasped aloud as madame sank the rubber shaft home swiftly and surely.

'This is how to pleasure a client. And like this –'

Madame suddenly twisted the pliable phallus around, rotating it twice inside Susie. The bending nude moaned deeply and felt her belly implode and collapse inside.

'I much prefer to pleasure my clients, and indeed myself, with this rubber version, my dear. The ivory and the gold versions may be hard but that is a superficial delight. Notice how this wicked little chappie hugs the muscles, hmm?'

'Aaahhh,' was all Susie could manage by way of a coherent response.

'Yes, I thought you would agree,' madame said and laughed softly. 'You say,' madame stated in a businesslike tone, 'that your client refused her customary special services this evening. She usually enjoys the cane, does she not?'

'Yes,' gasped Susie as the dildo was driven deeper inside her. 'I think her reluctance was due to her being scared. Frightened, perhaps, of any future risk of exposure or blackmail.'

'I'm rather afraid I can only agree. Something must clearly be done. Not too tight, my dear?'

'Nnnngghh,' Susie grunted, choking down the orgasm that already threatened to drown her.

'Jolly good. Now let us analyse our problem in a scientific manner,' madame announced, easing out the glistening shaft.

Reluctant to lose the pliant length of sheer delight, Susie whimpered and gripped at it with her inner muscles. Madame felt the resistance, smiled, and let the rubber dildo rest with half of its cruelly curved length within the bending girl.

'Consider the following: we have avoided a crisis but still have a problem. One of our special clients was blackmailed. The solution: Svetlana was unmasked, punished and is now safely under lock and key in an upstairs attic. Result?'

'Possible loss of confidence,' Susie murmured, feeling a reply was expected. 'Maritta and her friend – friends, perhaps – need greater reassurances. And friends have friends. Women network, after all, that is how you recruit.'

'An excellent observation. You think rumour and doubt could spread? Has already begun to do so?'

'Friends tell friends. Whispers spread.'

'Mmm.' Madame rested her curved palm against Susie's left cheek, caressing the upturned flesh-globe meditatively with slow, circular sweeps. 'Loss of confidence, the worst plague to strike any business, and as you so rightly observe, my dear, friends have friends. How shrewd you are. Who knows how far the whispers might spread.'

'To restore confidence, you need to make a big gesture. A splash,' Susie said suddenly, her words tumbling forth excitedly. 'Don't rely on discreet persuasion. Be bold, madame. Throw the doors of The Rookery wide open –'

'Wide open?' echoed Seraphim Savage, utterly aghast.

'Mm. Why not invite all your clients to a fashion show. And get some high-profile publicity –'

'Publicity?' madame screeched.

'Yes, listen. I could get *Society Spy* down. They could do a shoot for a spread in next month's issue. Great publicity for the lingerie side of business and –' Susie gasped as madame absently rammed the entire length of the rubber dildo deep inside her '– it would recruit more customers and reassure the special clients. Show them you are in complete control.'

'I've never heard anything quite so –' madame snapped. Then, in a softer tone, she changed tack. 'Quite so brilliant. How splendid. Bluff our way out of these recent difficulties and scotch any lingering rumours or doubts about our probity. We'll do it. Why, my dear Susie, I really must reward you for coming up with such a capital strategy. There is no time to lose,' madame decided, pulling out the dildo.

Susie groaned.

'No, I am wrong. There is always time for pleasure. Give me your bottom.'

'Madame?'

'You failed to deal with Svetlana to my complete satisfaction. I was observing your efforts from the door. I am going to teach you how. Come along, dear girl. Open your cheeks wide.'

Still bending, Susie inched her thighs apart. She thrilled

229

instantly to the touch of the rubber snout at her anus. Her delight was intense, compounded by her submissive posture and total vulnerability. Pleasure, raw and savage, threatened to suffocate her, so intense was her delight. But most delicious of all was that it was Seraphim Savage – strict, stern and beautiful – who was pleasuring her with such fierce intimacy. The only experience that surpassed being soundly punished by the dominatrix was to be pleasured by the woman she adored. Madame pretended to be teaching Susie an instructive lesson in the rites and arts of the phallus – so that Susie could serve the special clients more effectively – but Susie knew that madame was rewarding her for loyalty, devotion to duty and the brilliant strategy which would restore confidence in The Rookery.

'Wait,' madame commanded, a note of severity in her tone. The crisp note of authority juiced Susie's slit with excitement. 'I have something special to share with you. Let me demonstrate. Although, Susie, like a rare wine of elusive vintage, this must be sampled on very, very special occasions.'

Guiding the rubber shaft deep into the moist warmth beyond Susie's rosebud sphincter, madame withdrew her right hand and placed it on Susie's neck, gripping the nape lightly but firmly. Susie's hot wet response caused her inner thighs to glisten and shine. With her left hand, madame reached down and picked up a dimpled rubber thimble which she attached deftly to the tip of her straightened index finger.

'Now,' she whispered, bending closer to her quivering captive. 'Now you will learn what true pleasure is. Thighs a little wider.'

Susie, trembling with delight, obeyed. She smothered her grunts as madame teased the dildo lodged up in between her buttocks; she began sliding it with increasing ferocity back and forth. Susie scrabbled up on her toes in response. Spank. The stern touch of her dominatrix steadied and quelled her. Susie moaned softly as the rubber-thimbled finger slid between her thighs, stroked her labia firmly then tapped against her tiny pink gland of joy. After brushing the clitoris lightly, the dimpled rubber bud returned to the sticky, splayed labia, to punish-pleasure the fleshfolds ruthlessly. Susie squealed. Spank. Another brisk touch of gentle dominance silenced her loud delight. Susie squeezed her smacked bottom, then convulsed at the effect on the rubber dildo within. With a shrill cry, she came: the rippling pulses arrowed down from her belly, bathing her epicentre in golden fire. The very moment of orgasm was celebrated by a double spank across her tightened cheeks, which rocketed Susie into delirious spasms. Madame held the bending nude down firmly by the nape of her neck and returned the finger annointed with the dimpled rubber cone to the erect clitoris. The thimble raked the clitoris up and down. Susie moaned and collapsed into another immediate orgasm.

Blinking through lust-bleary eyes, she saw the carpet at her feet erupt into a blaze of molten gold. Smashed by the velvet fist of a third climax, she buckled, swayed and collapsed down, down down into a deep abyss where all sensations fused. Down on her knees, she crushed her belly, breasts and face into the carpet, bucking and jerking her hips as she felt madame's dominant foot crush down on her upturned rump. Pinned helplessly in her ecstasy, Susie hovered on the very edge of consciousness.

'There's more,' whispered madame, kissing Susie's hair softly as she stooped to pluck the rubber phallus from the tightly clenched buttocks that imprisoned it. 'More.'

Susie's knuckles whitened as she tried to claw the carpet. Sweet profanities spilled from her slackened lips. Confused, wild words beseeching madame to cease – and continue.

Straddling Susie masterfully, madame inserted the tip of the dildo between the pink, wet labia resting the thicker base of the rubber shaft against her own pubic mound. Crushing herself closer against the kneeling nude, she thrust her hips forward plunging the shaft deep into Susie. The ravished girl's squeal of delight was smothered as she buried her perspiring face into the carpet. Madame drove in the length of slightly curved rubber with a final punishing thrust then rasped her pubis down against Susie's upturned buttocks. Again, again and again – with the cruel contempt of the victor over the vanquished – the beautiful dominatrix rode her helpless victim, grinding herself harshly into Susie's swollen cheeks. The smouldering embers of previous orgasms flared up, immediately igniting Susie into another. Squirming and writhing in madame's absolute thrall, Susie broke free and turned to bury her face submissively between the thighs of her sweet tormentress. With the dildo still delighting her, Susie's lips sought out madame's slit. In complete surrender, she kissed the pungent flesh of her dominatrix fiercely, lovingly and in total obedience.

'Susie in servitude,' madame murmured, gazing down affectionately at her happy victim. 'Have you learned? Have I taught you well?'

Susie mumbled something dreamily, nodding into madame's warm lap.

'Hmm?' madame insisted.

'Yes, madame,' Susie mouthed into the flesh she adored.

'Good. In a little while, when we have taken some wine, you may show me. Show me what you have learned.'

Susie inched her face up a fraction. Had she heard correctly? Was she being asked – no, instructed – to pleasure madame? As fully and as frankly as madame had just pleasured her? Her heart pounded wildly as madame tilted her face up and planted a lingering kiss on Susie's trembling lips.

'Let the wine wait. There are darker, sweeter juices to be sampled.'

With these words, madame knelt down and bowed her face into the carpet, presenting Susie with the perfection of her naked hips, buttocks and thighs. Between the splayed thighs, the dark fig glistened. Susie licked her dry lips.

'Show me,' the maturer mistress whispered to her avid young slave. 'Show me what you have learned.'

Nine

Exactly one week later, the warm May evening air was filled with the subdued chattering and laughter of over forty female guests. In the lower paddock, Range Rovers, Bentleys and Saab Turbos thronged the pasture, glinting expensively in the setting sun. At the rear of The Rookery, on a rolling lawn which had been mercilessly manicured, two long tables groaned under a delicious array of tempting delicacies. Delivered from Knightsbridge in a familiar large, green van, the buffet-supper – together with a small lighting rig and music system – had arrived at noon. The female guests were clustered in small groups, refreshing themselves with salmon mousse, chicken Kiev and chilled Hock.

'Everything seems to be perfect,' madame observed as she surveyed the scene. 'All the guests have arrived. None declined, which is promising.'

'The models are in the pantry. They've commandeered it for the evening,' Susie rejoined. 'They'll be ready in four minutes.'

It had been madame's idea to employ professional girls. Not known names, admittedly, but young beauties whose faces would be worth a fortune in a year or two. The agency had delivered them just before teatime in a white helicopter from which they had descended, sun-glasses jilted on their cropped hair like radar discs, with ill-concealed disdain for the rural setting. Creatures of the city, and the night, they found sunny Devon somewhat beneath their aspirations. Susie had been given the delicious duty of overseeing them. Initial preparations for the evening show had commenced briskly under her stern management with a visit to the bathroom for a hot shower. Afterwards came the process of body make-up, in which Susie had been intimately involved.

'Are you sure they will not be cold. Young girls like that are more expensive than two-year-old colts. And more delicate. The pantry is quite a walk from the lawn. In their scanties.'

'They will wear furs right up to the shell.'

Susie and Annette, inspired by the Botticelli Venus, had designed and constructed a huge silver shell as a backdrop. Households in the vicinity had generously donated all their stocks of silver kitchen foil for the project. The plan was for each model to walk across the lawn, squired by one of the four young men Susie had recently pleasured at their private party. The men would be immaculately attired in full evening wear and the models would be draped in furs. Reaching the small stage at the end of the lawn, they would mount the dais in front of the silver shell: the escort would remove the furs leaving the girls to model the lingerie beneath. Crimson spotlights had been rigged up to bathe the silver backdrop, adding a warmth and sensuality to the event.

'I think it's time,' madame said, 'I joined my guests. Mingle a little. Things seem pretty tame. I do hope the evening livens up a little.'

'We're ready to go soon,' Susie replied. 'I'll give Annette the signal.'

Annette nodded in response to Susie's wave and turned to her small bank of switches. An expectant hush greeted the soft crimson lights that flooded the small stage. A crisp drum roll scattered some sleepy rooks from the elms as Rossini's rousing overture to *The Thieving Magpie* filled the evening air. It had been Susie's choice to play Rossini. She knew that its pert, decorous vigour would set an erotic tone.

Susie scampered into the pantry and snatched up a stopwatch and clipboard. Stage managing the lingerie show would be thrilling, but success depended upon split second timing and a strict schedule. She frowned as she saw a girl still bare-bottomed, and not in the scarlet basque she should already be zipped into. Striding towards the proud nude, she tapped her clipboard.

'Why aren't you ready?'

'It's only a village bop,' the Sloane vowels drawled.

Spank. Susie slapped the girl's soft buttock sharply, just as she had seen the matrons in Milan scold their sullen beauties. 'Get into that basque, quickly. This is an important gig. They're shooting it for *Society Spy* so don't foul up.'

Spurred by the crisp spank and the presence of *Society Spy* the Sloane and her colleagues sprang into action. Breasts bounced and thighs quivered as they scurried around the pantry, bumping and colliding as they struggled feverishly into the stern constraints of satin, leather and lace.

'You're first,' Susie warned a brown-eyed blonde who was palming her ripe breasts into a silver basque. 'Quickly, give her a coat. Black sable.'

The four young men – madame's bankrolling bucks – had turned out to escort the models. They stood at the pantry door, feasting on the naked beauties within. They had donned black ties and were impeccably groomed, except for the huge bulges straining their trousers.

'You,' Susie nodded to the bullion-broker.

He turned his inane grin towards her.

'Black sable fur for the blonde. Go.'

Turning his adoring eyes from Susie to the petite brown-eyed blonde who burgeoned in her tight basque, he quickly threw the heavy fur around her naked shoulders and steered her out on to the lawn.

To the polite applause of the seated guests and the sensual strains of Rossini, the perfectly poised couple trutted down the aisle between the audience and gracefully mounted the dias. Gallantly, the bullion-broker whipped away the dark fur and withdrew, revealing the brown-eyed blonde in her silver basque. It was front-stitched, in the German manner, giving her bosom a superb cleavage.

Silver stiletto shoes, gleaming stockings and an arrogant expression completed her ensemble. Madame, off-stage and using the PA system, described the outfit in crisp, professional tones, referring to the catalogue the audience had been supplied with at Susie's suggestion. The silver basque met with the female audience's approval and gentle applause. Twisting her hips, posing provocatively yet remaining cool and aloof, the brown-eyed blonde displayed her lingerie to full effect. The triple flash of pure white light froze her instantaneously as the young camerawoman from *Society Spy* snapped her.

Back in the pantry, Susie chivvied the bustling beauties into their black stockings, underwired brassières, waspie suspender belts and micro-panties. Outwardly cool, calm and in complete control, she was in fact trembling with both anxiety and excitement. The week had been hectic, whirling with decisions, alterations, cancellations and frantic telephoning. Now, she realised, it was too late to change anything. Everything had to work; there was only one chance.

'Yes, it's you,' she said, checking her clipboard, to a brunette who was swathing her sports bra and tight white panties in a mink fur coat. 'And when you come back, the opaque tights. What? No, I want you topless. Just cup them with your hands.'

The models entered into the spirit of the occasion gamely, and the audience grew warm in its response. With the ever flashing presence of the *Society Spy* camera, the agency girls grew competitive, adding a little extra to each display. Bosoms and buttocks were increasingly glimpsed much to the onlookers' delight.

A return before the silver shell by the brown-eyed blonde saw her offering her bottom to the audience as she palmed down the black satin cami-knickers she was supposed to be demonstrating. Lust-thickened voices shrilled their approval. Next, the brunette lingered, slowly removing her brassière to thumb the cups. Madame improvised on the microphone, commenting on the elasticity of the fabric. Nipples were now frankly on show – if briefly – before coy teasing hands smothered their creamy breasts, squashing them provocatively. The audience cheered as loudly as they would have done as sixth-formers at a hockey cup-tie. After her, the lithe, leggy beauty in the opaque tights minced slowly back towards the pantry, her fur draped over one shoulder. She paused only to let inquisitive fingers stroke the spangled fabric that sheathed her buttocks and thighs.

The four young men behaved impeccably and Susie promised them a very special reward. Half way through the show, it was suggested that they remain on stage with each model, to assist. Susie was doubtful but the audience yelled their approval and so it was agreed.

Somehow, Susie mislaid her stopwatch and the meticulously prepared schedule on the clipboard ended up forgotten in a puddle of champagne. Rossini died and the Rolling Stones bruised the twilight with their raw funk. The *Society Spy* camera snapped the brown-eyed blonde as she mounted the stage, tossed aside her contrasting sable and ported her minimal scanties. The camera was lowered and lay dormant as the landowner knelt down before his escort, accepting in trembling hands the brassière she unclasped and removed slowly, and then the panties she tantalisingly thumbed down. Swathing the nude in her sable, she romped back to the pantry to thunderous applause.

The mood had swerved violently from polite interest to the riot of carnival. Susie's vision of an evening of upper crust elegance rapidly evaporated as the throng of female guests clapped and bayed for more. The models scampered back and forth, their initial coldness melting into provocative posing and sensual posturing.

Neither Susie nor madame had calculated for this but managed, just, to adapt to the events as they spiralled out of control. The *Society Spy* girl was cautious with her camera, snapping only what could make it into her magazine's glossy pages. Off-camera, the presentations of stockings, suspenders, basques, bustiers and bras became a thrilling mix of taunting strip-tease and erotic pleasure. The onlookers had abandoned their carefully arranged

237

chairs and pressed around the tiny, floodlit stage. Squeals of delight replaced the decorous applause of the show's opening moments and Hendrix, Blur and 'jungle' provided the vital pulse.

Madame, bemused and somewhat overwhelmed, watched helplessly as she saw ladies who rode with the hounds swigging Hock directly from the bottle, and members of the county set wrestling for a black leather thong tossed from the dais into their midst.

'Great, isn't it?' Susie whispered breathlessly as she passed madame a reviving glass of wine.

'Janet Reger goes to St Trinian's. What have we done? I can see the headlines now,' madame groaned, passing her hand feverishly over her worried brow. 'If *Society Spy* print even a tenth of this, I'm ruined.'

'Oh, I'll fix all that. Chloe's a poppet. Nothing to worry about there.'

'I remain to be convinced,' madame sighed, draining her glass. 'What, pray, is that?'

Annette had decided to play the Brazilian biu-bumb tape. The assembled throng shuffled, samba-like, to the commanding beat.

'Oh, that's a party number. They love it.'

'I had rather hoped for Elgar,' madame replied faintly.

'I'll go and have a word with Chloe.'

'Chloe?'

'The *Society Spy* girl. Make sure she prints what's fit to print. Then I'll go and organise a finale.'

'Now be careful –'

But Susie had already gone, swallowed up by the Latin-driven crowd.

The finale was a riot. All the models skipped down the grass cat-walk and jumped up on to the stage. Their four young squires – perspiring freely, their black ties long since abandoned – lined up behind them and in a perfectly synchronised movement, snatched away the fur coats. The girls were superbly nude, each posing with one hand above her head, the other hand placed on her hips. A carnal cheer rang out to greet them.

'Camille is wearing Chanel,' Susie announced, taking command of madame's microphone. The young landowner bit the stopper from a phial and splashed the fragrance down over the naked model, glistening the ripe swell of her breasts. 'While Paulette prefers Orange Water.'

One by one, the naked models knelt down, allowing their four attendant escorts to drench their breasts, thighs and buttocks with scandalously liberal amounts of perfume. The night air was permeated with the scent of opulence and decadence; as Susie had predicted, it drove the audience into a frenzy.

'Kill the lights,' Susie hissed into Annette's ear. 'I'd better clear the stage.'

Coffee was served to soothe and calm, but the guests remained volatile and excitable almost an hour after the blackout. Gentle Vivaldi was played and eventually the buzzing throng broke up into small, chattering groups. Hair was patted and lipstick was applied as the women returned to their seats, eager to be snapped and interviewed for *Society Spy*.

'They'd stay 'til dawn to get their names and pictures in,' Susie said and laughed.

'A triumph.' Madame beamed happily. 'Simply a triumph. I've filled more order forms than ever before and my circulation list has almost doubled. Certainly no loss of confidence there. Your plan has worked perfectly, my dear Susie. Perfectly.'

Down in the paddock, the first of the departing Range Rovers purred into life, its strong quartz beams stabbing the darkness of the Devon night.

'Our guests are beginning to leave. I'll go and have a quick word with Chloe.'

'Chloe?'

'In here,' the girl replied. 'Just having a bite to eat. I'm starving.'

Susie entered the kitchen to find the young photographer sitting on the table, swinging her legs happily as she gnawed at a well-fleshed chicken leg.

239

'You're surely not going back tonight?'

'Not to London, no. I've got a shoot at ten tomorrow morning at Ascot. Trainers' wives. That sort of thing.'

'Busy little beaver. Thanks for coming down.'

'No problem. It was worth it. You should go pro. Pack 'em in at Leeds Castle or Houghton Hall. Sort of Harvey Goldsmith to the aristos. Great show – can't use most of it,' she said and pulled a face, 'but there's plenty of footage. And big names. The guest list was dripping with Right Honourables.'

'They pack 'em in to the acre hereabouts. Can't throw a stone without clocking a titled nob.'

'Speaking of which, who are those hunks?'

'Never mind. I've got plans for them later on.'

'Bet you have. I've got good copy. Our readers love that mix of money and fashion. Great shoot, great story.'

'Can't you stay? I could fix you a lift in the models' chopper. They're flying out in the morning.'

'OK. I rang my partner. We've a flat in Earls Court. She was in a bitch of a mood. Complains she never sees me anymore.'

'That's tough for both of you.'

'Beautiful girls tonight. That little brown-eyed blonde will go far.'

'All the way,' Susie replied softly.

Chloe licked her chicken bone for the last vestiges of sweet flesh.

'Glad you enjoyed yourself,' Susie said with a smile.

'Mm. Camerawork is great. Creative. You lose yourself.'

'Ever been snapped yourself?'

Chloe looked up and shrugged. 'Nope. Never.'

'Give me your Pentax,' Susie said, a plan already formed in her mind. 'Quick.'

'What for?'

'Let's do a shoot – of you. Snaps for your partner back in Earls Court. Something for her to have when you have to be away.'

'But I've never –'

'Then now's the time. Come on. Trust me.'

Chloe produced the Pentax from the leather satchel and twiddled with the flash gun. 'Be careful. That's my living.'

'I will be,' Susie promised. 'Now get rid of that chicken bone, wash your hands and follow me.'

Dipping into the pantry, where Susie discovered the models being most assiduously attended to by their male escorts, she snatched up a box of exotic lingerie and skipped back into the kitchen. 'This way.'

They climbed the stairs and entered the bathroom at the end of the cool, darkened corridor. A beam of light swept through the window as a Bentley floundered in the paddock outside. They entered the end cubicle, which had been converted into a shower.

'That's better,' Susie said, returning to click on the light. 'Get undressed and take a shower. Give me a chance to do some action shots. Then, in my bedroom, we'll do a couple of serious studio stills. You can pose in these.' Susie nodded down to the box frothing over with satin and lace. 'Strip off and under the hot shower.'

Chloe was a little reluctant at first, but soon had her jeans and cashmere jumper around her feet.

'Here,' Susie murmured as she approached the shivering girl, 'let me help you with those.' Her expert fingers had the brassière and cotton panties peeled off in seconds.

Spank. Giving the bare-bottomed girl a playful slap, Susie sent her scuttling into the shower.

'Ahh, this shower's so good,' Chloe sighed, rubbing shower gel into her naked breasts.

'Don't be alarmed,' Susie called out above the noise of the steaming jet of water. 'I'm going to turn the light off and use the flash.'

'Bit dramatic,' Chloe said.

'Exactly. Sharp contrasts. Great for the female nude.'

'Who is the photographer round here?' Chloe warbled.

'I am,' Susie whispered softly to herself. 'I am.' Then loudly enough to be heard, she said, 'And I'll catch you unawares every time. Nothing too posey. What's her name?'

'Who? My partner? Isolde. Would have been Tristan if she'd been a boy. I call her Issie.'

'Then think of Issie as you enjoy your shower, Chloe. Pretend she is watching, watching and waiting with a big, soft white towel.'

'You mean just like it is back in Earls Court?'

'Just like bath time in Earls Court,' Susie agreed.

Susie switched off the light and traced her way in total darkness towards the sound of the shower.

'OK?' Susie asked.

'Mmm.'

'Relax, just think of Issie.'

Susie aimed the lens into the sound of cascading water and clicked the auto. The flash exploded three times, freeze-framing Chloe starkly: cupping her breasts; squeezing them, eyes closed; then squeezing them, eyes and mouth open.

'Nice shot.' Susie chuckled. 'Just carry on, enjoy your shower.'

Kneeling down, then revising her posture and steadying herself on one knee, she aimed the lens up into the darkness. Still on auto, she took three shots, almost dazzling herself as the flash exploded, its sudden light spangling the cascade of streaming water sluicing Chloe's pale nudity. Susie had captured Chloe soaping her left buttock; soaping her cleft; then palming the cusp of both fleshy cheeks, the soap frozen on film as it fell to the floor of the shower.

'Turn,' Susie ordered excitedly.

'You mean –'

'Do it now,' came the curt command.

Again, the triple explosion of blue-white light, the up-turned lens capturing Chloe's wet pubic nest: the labial lips sealed, her thighs pressed together; the pink flesh parted slightly as the legs splayed; then the labia greeting the lens with a widening smile.

'Against the shower wall. Spread your thighs,' Susie cried, the intense excitement and erotic charge of the moment electrifying her.

Snap. Snap. Snap. The gorgeous breasts of the naked girl in her shower were caught pressed and squashed against the wet, white tiles; Chloe's face, her streaming wet hair across her eyes; and then the shining curved flesh-cheeks of her rump. They were all captured by the eager lens.

'Great. Again,' Susie shouted. 'Against the wall, feet wide apart – wider.'

Chloe squealed as her breasts grazed the hard tiles. The eerie explosion of silent light illuminated her round but-tocks. Susie, raking the wet nude from an acute angle, filled her lens with bottom shots, catching for eternity images of the heavy, glistening orbs of swollen flesh.

'OK,' Susie called out, retreating to the light switch and flooding the bathroom once more with yellow light. 'Rinse and get dried. We'll do some formal shots in my room.'

Bouncing her breasts within the white towel. Chloe was eager to obey.

Naked, powdered and beautiful, Chloe stood in front of the long looking-glass. A single nylon stocking dripped sinuously down from her left hand, its honey-bronze hue in stark and delicious contrast to the white flesh of her thigh.

'Put the stocking on. And remember, Issie is standing where that looking-glass is, OK? Look directly into the glass, and then look down at your foot. Do it several times. And when I say hold, you freeze absolutely. Get it?'

'Got it.' Chloe smiled, dragging the nylon briefly up between her thighs, taking surreptitious pains to snag her clitoris as she pretended to absently recapture it.

Susie saw the movement in the reflecting glass – saw the soft band of honey-bronze gauze slide up between the clamped thighs below the heavy buttock cheeks – emerging in front to rasp the labial fleshfolds. She knew it had been a deliberate gesture, not the careful negligence Chloe had pretended.

'Less of that. These are family snaps.' Susie grinned. 'Do anything like that again and I'll spank your bottom hard.'

Chloe blushed but her tightening buttocks betrayed to Susie the eloquent truth: a spanking would be welcomed by the soft-bottomed nude. Susie bent over the Pentax, adjusting the speed. Glancing up quickly into the mirror she saw Chloe drag the scrunched up nylon stocking against her sticky labia, leaving a small moist spot on the bronze material.

'Chloe,' she purred.

The buttocks of the nude tensed once more as the crisp warning promised the possibility of a spanking.

'Just put the stocking on.'

Chloe obediently raised her left leg, prinking her foot.

'Bend over a little more. Give me a rounder bottom. That's better. Hold it.'

The shutter snapped; the Pentax captured the superb image.

'Go on, pull the stocking up. No, elbows out. I want to get your breasts in. Let them fall forward more. Great. Hold it.'

Again the shutter snapped; the spilling breasts, caught and bunched softly by the girl's left forearm, the entire image reflected by the looking-glass, fell prey to the avid lens. Susie felt the sticky juices at her slit as she gazed up to arrange the bending nude for another stockinged shot.

For just under an hour, Susie captured Chloe on film, taking her from every angle, missing no aspect of her naked glory. Easing her ripe breasts into the empty cups of a brassière; then peeling off the brassière to allow the soft bosom to burgeon. Punishing the dark nipples with the taut bra strap; then binding the bulging breasts with a single, punishing nylon stocking. But for the most part, the camera – and Susie, who guided it – lingered on the lithe legs and gorgeous bottom. Panties on; panties off; panties teasingly half way down. The most erotic shot, Susie considered, was of Chloe, stockinged legs apart, thumbing the panties down her thighs; there was a sliver of silk left between her labia.

It had, of course, ended in a spanking. The Pentax recorded nothing of the sudden, lustful display of dominant affection; Issie was spared Chloe's momentary lapse. Susie had caught Chloe using the nylon stocking against her labia once too often and had wrestled her subject down across the duvet, then arranged the bare-bottomed girl across her lap for punishment. Palming the soft, satin flesh-mounds – quite outside madame's category of female buttock types – Susie had gazed down upon the upturned cheeks in wonder. Too large and swollen for apple-buttocks; too ripe and heavily fleshed to be peach-cheeks. What were they? How should they be classified?

'Issie calls them her Pillows of Venus,' Chloe whispered thickly into the duvet. 'She adores my bottom.'

'Pillows of Venus,' Susie whispered, flattening her palm down across their swollen, creamy warmth. 'How beautiful.'

Then the spanking had commenced; almost two dozen slow, deliberate applications of flesh to flesh, turning the Pillows of Venus from a blushing pink to a deeper shade of punished scarlet. Just as the final spank rang out, Chloe's hips bucked and bounced as she pounded her pubis against Susie's. Stiffening, she tensed then collapsed, coming uncontrollably as she lay across Susie's warmth. The dominatrix fingered the cleft of the climaxing girl, probing the hot sphincter and launching Chloe into renewed spasms of delight.

Susie found the four young studs down in the pantry sipping champagne. The bulges in their trousers had gone; in the case of the nightclub owner, so had his trousers. Susie took the champagne glass out of his hand and sipped from it. He looked up expectantly.

'Have you been naughty while I was busy upstairs?' she asked. 'Were you naughty with the pretty little model girls?'

'Yes,' he answered, his voice tight with excitement. 'Are you going to punish me?'

'I was naughty too,' chorused the other three in unison, anxious not to be overlooked by the beautiful, stern young woman.

'But how do I know that you've been wicked. Let me examine you.'

Placing the champagne glass down, Susie fingered the

nightclub owner's tumescent shaft. The end of the warm spear was still sticky from his evening's sport with the brown-eyed blonde.

'So, you have been a bad boy. And what do bad boys get?'

'Punished,' he replied promptly, his manhood twitching expectantly.

'And yet you were all very, very good boys for me earlier this evening. And what do very, very good boys deserve?'

'Punishment, please,' they replied.

'Exactly. Follow me. I have arranged something quite special, as I promised. Did you study poetry at Eton and Harrow?'

'Economics, actually,' replied the bullion-broker.

'I think you'll wish you had,' Susie rejoined enigmatically as she led them to the tutorial room. 'In here,' she commanded.

They filed in obediently.

'Strip, then into your wooden harnesses. I will be back, and will be very severe with anyone not in position for punishment on my return. Understand?'

Their scrabbling at socks and shirt buttons was answer enough for Susie, who nodded curtly and departed, a dark smile playing on her lips. In their eagerness to obey, the young men had overlooked the obvious. Only three of them could possibly be harnessed on her return, assisted by the fourth who would not be able to place himself in the wooden yoke unaided. Susie was a cruel dominatrix, a point on which she took great pride. Set your victim impossible targets and punish failure. That was the rule she had learned from Seraphim Savage, a rule she had learned extremely well.

When she returned, three of the men were arranged in their yokes of bondage, bending in bare-bottomed eagerness for the licking stripe of Susie's cane. The landowning farmer, naked and trembling, remained standing at the stocks.

'I can't manage it alone. I helped the others —' he bleated.

'I want neither explanations nor excuses. You heard my warning. You shall suffer sweetly for this.'

'But –'

'Silence. You failed; a failure for which I shall reward you,' Susie whispered, forcing the naked man down into the wooden halter. 'Or rather, see to it that you are rewarded. I, personally, will not be whipping you tonight.'

Cries of dismay rose up to greet this announcement.

'Be quiet,' she retorted. 'A promise is a promise. You will be whipped – and more – tonight. Allow me to introduce Sappho, who is our poetess in residence here at The Rookery. And this is Maritta. Sappho was, as you know, the first recorded female poet. Her namesake is here tonight to polish up your pentameters and tighten your couplets. Maritta has other skills, which you will each discover when she takes you in her gloved hands.'

Maritta, naked except for a pair of snow-white leather gloves, strode in front of the four bowed, naked men. Looking up at her in wonder, their eyes feasted greedily on her heavy breasts, her supple thighs and the white gloves folded across her pubis. Teasingly, Maritta revealed her shadowed delta as she flexed her gloved fingers and let them stray up to her pink nipples. Susie noted with satisfaction the yoked men's response: their twitching erections flickered up to salute the naked Finn as her leathered fingers tweaked her hardening pink buds.

'Once whipped, you will kneel down in turn for the touch of Maritta's gloves. But first, a few lines from Sappho.'

Susie smiled grimly. They were no doubt expecting poetry. Poetry, they would get, along with pain from the cane of the eccentric bard.

'Good evening, gentlemen. How is your Homer? Is your grasp of Chaucer firm? Do you know your Donne?'

Remaining tantalisingly out of their line of vision, the husky poetess tapped each bare bottom lined up before her with the tip of her cane. 'Goodness, what a feast of pleasure awaits us tonight. It promises to be as exciting as a sonnet from the master himself. The master being?'

'Shakespeare,' the bullion-broker replied in response to a tap of the bamboo.

'Correct, my little philistine. Shakespeare. And how many lines make up a sonnet?'

The bullion-broker was stumped.

'Well? Come along, young man. How many?'

'Ten?' he hazarded.

'Wrong. There are fourteen. I propose to give you fourteen strokes of my cane. A lesson you shall never forget, I trust.'

Susie stole out of the room as the first of the slicing cane strokes whipped down across the naked buttocks of the suffering student of poetry.

'The boys are being entertained. A little reward for their efforts tonight,' Susie explained.

'Capital. Everything went swimmingly. All our little problems have been solved. All except Svetlana. She remains a question to which I have no answer. What are we going to do with her?'

'Keep her for a little while, madame. With a little strict training and a lot of stern guidance we may be able to make something of her yet. The girl is not entirely without promise.'

'Hmm, you may be right. We'll speak to her together tomorrow, after lunch. And *Society Spy*? Have you seen the cameragirl?'

'Oh, yes, madame,' Susie said. 'I have seen Chloe. And everything is going to be fine. She will do a wonderful spread for us. Some very good shots, and great copy. She's up in the bathroom now. We converted it into a temporary darkroom and she's developing the prints overnight. She's very versatile and a slave to that Pentax of hers.'

Madame shot Susie an appraising glance but decided against pursuing the matter too closely.

'Now we have all had a little warm up, I am expecting great things of you, class,' the poetess threatened.

Susie rejoined the four young studs in the tutorial room

just in time to hear the poetess admonish her caned boys. Maritta stood in front of them, still squeezing and fondling her breasts within her white-gloved hands. All that had changed was that her slit was juicy after witnessing the young men being severely caned. Susie glanced at the four bare bottoms: each had already been thoroughly caned, with at least twenty cruel stripes apiece. A little warm up, Sappho had said. What would it be like when things got really hot, Susie wondered. When the dark leather belt the poetess was unfurling was relentlessly plied. Why, their buttocks would be ablaze. She decided to stay and savour the impending discipline.

'This is how our little poetry lesson will proceed,' Sappho said brightly. 'And there is absolutely no need to rush. We have all night. That is to say, I have you all night. I will give you each a line which you must match – in length, metre and end-rhyme. Understand?'

Two of the four men grunted, the other two remained aloof.

Crack. Crack. Crack. Crack. The leather belt snapped down rapidly across each bare bottom, bringing the men in bondage up on to their toes.

'Answer me properly, class. Do you understand?'

'Yes, miss,' they sang out dutifully.

'Excellent. Bottom number one. Complete this couplet: When crisp bamboo stripes creamy skin –'

Bottom number one – the nightclub owner – was nonplussed. He had a game attempt, but failed in his efforts, trying to rhyme 'skin' with 'sting'.

'No, no, no,' Sappho declaimed loudly, landing the leather belt just as loudly across his scorched rump.

'Try again, and do not try to rhyme "skin" imperfectly. No half-rhymes allowed.'

She repeated the first line again. His response was a poor, stuttering disappointment.

Crack, crack. Sappho lashed the nightclub owner's bare cheeks twice, leaving them seething and ablaze.

'I will return to you, bottom number one, in a little while. Be sure to have a conclusion ready for me. Heaven help your bottom if you fail to complete your couplet.'

Maritta walked around the wooden stocks and placed her hands down over the nightclub owner's buttocks. Slowly, she squeezed the ravaged flesh between her leather-gloved fingers, spinning the naked man into an ecstasy of anguish. Susie stood back against the wall and watched as the gloved hands spread the punished flesh apart. The Finn, supreme and dominant in her control of the hot bottom, deliberately grazed her pubis against his left cheek.

'Bottom number two,' Sappho said, fingering the exposed rump. 'Your line to complete is: When buttocks are bared to receive their pain –'

'The penitent prays for the strap not the cane,' replied bottom number two quickly.

'Why, that is excellent. What a very clever young man you are, bottom number two. Not gifted, nor indeed talented, but clever.'

Susie, herself impressed by the smart response, saw bottom number two's – the bullion-broker's – shaft thicken and twitch as Sappho dangled the leather strap down and brushed his defenceless buttocks with it teasingly. The reddened cheeks feared the leather, and tightened as they felt its cruel presence.

'So the penitent prays for the strap not the cane,' Sappho intoned. 'How fortunate it is that your prayers are to be answered. I do in fact have a strap in my hand, and I note, fortuitously, that your buttocks are indeed bare, young man. Yes, feel the leather.'

Susie's belly tightened as she watched Sappho drag the harsh hide against the hot cheeks.

'In a few moments, you will receive it across your bare bottom. But well done, bottom number two. When I have whipped you to my complete and utter satisfaction, Maritta will take you in hand for your reward.'

Susie's sticky labia parted instantaneously at the touch of her fingertips. Watching Sappho at work, utterly dominating the naked young men, was exhilarating. The poetess was in complete control of them, Susie conceded, owning them body and mind. And whatever they came up with, Susie knew that Sappho would out-wit them, trumping

their hopeful kings with her supreme ace every time. Yes.
Sappho would counter every response and then mercilessly
ply the lash.

Sappho began the punishment with her customary zeal.
Susie lost count after the seventh stroke of searing leather
against hot flesh. Bottom number two burned redder and
brighter.

'Take him now, Maritta. Bind his hands with my nylon
stocking. Take him and pleasure him.'

Maritta gently removed the naked, whipped man from
his wooden harness and bound his hands firmly behind his
back with the black nylon stocking Sappho delicately
peeled off. The bullion-broker was forced down on to his
knees; Susie saw him straining in an attempt to catch a
glimpse of Sappho, but Maritta twisted his head down then
knelt closely behind him, squashing her breasts into his
back and her sticky slit into the swell of his hot rump.

Insinuating her gloved hand beneath his balls, she
gathered up his throbbing erection in her leathered right
hand. Pumping slowly, and squeezing his captive balls
firmly, she milked him expertly. Grunting thickly, he
arched back, his jet of hot release splashing Sappho's thigh
then dripping down along the length of her remaining
black stocking.

'You may, I repeat may, have the makings of a passable
poet, bottom number two, but you most certainly lack
etiquette and even a modicum of manners. Back in the
stocks with him, Maritta. I will attempt to teach him some.'

Susie shuddered as she watched the bullion-broker stag-
ger almost drunkenly back into his bondage, his shaft still
thick and pulsing.

'But first, bottom number three, here is your line to
complete: After harsh punishment, pleasures sweet –'

'Visit on tiny, velvet feet?' suggested bottom number
three tentatively.

Susie smiled at the landowning farmer's attempt.

'Velvet feet? We are not of the rural school, I trust,
bottom number three. We do not wish to compose poems
about moles, voles or fieldmice.'

She plied the lash. The strap scorched the bare buttocks of the bending man. He lurched in exquisite anguish within the strictures of his yoke.

Sappho fingered the hot leather. 'Try again,' she urged, then repeated his line for him. 'After harsh punishment, pleasures sweet –'

'Come to complete the perfect treat,' came the mumbled reply.

No, he's not quite there yet, Susie thought: which probably meant that his bottom was about to get it.

Again, the bare buttocks were clinically whipped with the unerring lash.

'Almost there, bottom number three, but not quite. Do keep trying, though. After all, workaday verse is more perspiration than inspiration. I will leave you but be assured, I will return.'

Susie thrilled to the way Sappho managed these men, and grudgingly realised that the bizarre poetess had already enslaved them completely. Gazing at their scalded cheeks, Susie knew they would never serve another.

'Bottom number one. Have you prepared a response? Let me refresh your memory. Your line was: When crisp bamboo stripes creamy skin –'

'It leaves a stripe as red as sin,' gasped the nightclub owner, quivering at the threat of the lash.

'Excellent, bottom number one, but –' the leather blazed down across his naked buttocks '– you spoke too quickly, spoiling the rhythm of the line and quite frankly, I am a stickler for strict rhythm. Understand?'

'Yes, Sappho,' grunted the nightclub owner devotedly.

'Notwithstanding your metrical lapse, you did passably well. Maritta. Take bottom number one out of his bondage and use your gloves on him with all your skills. Pleasure him as a princess serves her prince.'

This time, Susie noticed keenly, the nightclub owner was quivering with anticipation. Maritta guided him out of his harness and tied his hands firmly behind his back, but kept him standing. Kneeling down to press her face into his left buttock, she reached out with her gloved hand to palm the tip of his bulbous shaft. He screamed softly as he came, almost instantly: the leather glove cupped and enclosed the glistening knout of his pumping erection to capture and contain his spurt of release.

'And this must be bottom number four.'

Crack, crack. Sappho announced her presence with both words and leather.

'Here is your line: When naked woman wields the strap –'

Immediately bottom number four recited faultlessly:

> 'The lucky chap across her lap
> Waits for the hide to come to rest
> And have his rump kissed by her breast.'

Susie was amazed. Sappho stood astounded, the length of leather hanging limply from her right hand. 'We have a ghost among us. The ghost of Betjeman, no less. Maritta, please release bottom number four from his wooden yoke.'

Susie stirred from her wall and stood upright, her interest kindled by the curious change in Sappho's tone. Maritta steered her captive from his harness of wood and presented him, naked and erect, before Sappho.

'An almost perfect quatrain,' the poetess whispered, kneeling down in homage before the unsuspected versifier. 'I must teach you to perfect your iambics, dear boy, but all in all, a sterling efort. Maritta, take the cane to the buttocks of our reluctant poet over there.'

Bottom number three, the landowning farmer, thrashed in his bondage as the cruel Finn fingered the cane. She had, Susie observed, peeled off the soiled leather glove from her left hand; only her right hand remained sheathed in the tight, white second skin. With the straightened, dominant finger of this gloved hand she dimpled each bare buttock with a touch that was almost tender. Stepping back, she transferred the cane into her right hand and enclosed it with a fierce grip of hide.

Swish, swipe. The bending bottom suffered beneath the searching strokes. When Susie had feasted her eyes to their fill upon the caned man's sorrow, she returned her gaze to Sappho. The poetess was now straddling the successful rhymester and, pinning him down by his shoulders, was lowering her splayed thighs down upon his throbbing erection. Sinking her wet warmth on to his hot shaft, she completely absorbed every pulsing inch of him. Susie watched, amazed, as this supreme display of female domination unfolded.

'Sprung-rhythm is an obsolete, much neglected technique, dear boy. Let us reconsider its merits,' Sappho hissed, riding her mount with increasing vigour. Susie saw her breasts dancing inches above his adoring eyes while behind, her sumptuous buttocks tightened in ecstasy.

'Sprung-rhythm comes to us in our earliest years,' she gasped, approaching her climax as she pounded down on the erect muscle inside her. 'One immediately recalls the nursery rhyme, "Ride a Cock-horse to –" aaahh.'

Susie slipped out of the tutorial room, her ears filled by the loud celebration of orgasm. She was satisfied that the four young men had indeed been expertly rewarded for their efforts earlier that evening.

Susie tiptoed into Annette's bedroom. The light was out, the curtains drawn together denying the moonbeams access to the darkness.

'Asleep?' Susie whispered softly.

'Of course not. I hoped you'd come.'

'Thought you'd be asleep. Or with that leggy brunette.'

Annette poked her tongue out at Susie under the protection of darkness, just as Susie switched on the light.

'Gotcha,' Susie said and grinned, pointing at Annette accusingly.

Giggling happily, Annette dived under the duvet.

'I saw you watching her struggling into – and out of – those opaque tights. Lovely bottom.'

'Didn't notice,' Annette lied.

'And such long, slender legs – oooh,' Susie teased, tugging at a corner of the duvet and uncovering the naked flesh of her friend.

Bared and displayed, Annette curled up into a tight ball.

'She's only three doors away if you really want to slip along and see just how far those endless legs of hers go,' Susie whispered.

'Cat. Anyway, who says I want to?' Annette pouted primly. 'I like to pick and choose. I'm very choosy.'

'And so who do you choose?' Susie purred, snuggling into Annette's soft warmth.

'You, of course.'

'Little liar. I bet you've got an assignation with that leggy brunette. I bet she'll be at the door before midnight.'

'Haven't,' Annette retorted hotly.

'I think she will.'

'No,' protested the naked girl unconvincingly. 'I want you in my bed –'

A soft tap at the door silenced their whispering. They huddled down under the duvet, smothering their excited giggles. The door squeaked a little as it eased open a fraction. Then it opened wide as the lithe brunette from the model agency slipped into the bedroom.

'Annette? I'm here –'

'Sorry, wrong room,' Susie replied as she emerged from the duvet, feigning sleepiness. 'She's the fifth door down along the corridor,' she lied, directing the unsuspecting brunette towards Maritta's room. Madame was sportingly putting up a few of her clients for the night. 'Just go right in. Keep the light off and be sure to talk to her about leather gloves. Tell her how much you love the rasp of supple hide between your thighs.'

Under the duvet, Annette – silenced and stilled by Susie's controlling hands – threatened to explode with laughter.

'Got it,' the brunette gushed gratefully. 'Fifth door down. Light out. Gloves. Touch of leather. I'll remember that. Goodnight.'

'Goodnight,' Susie replied drily. The door closed. 'Maritta will give her a night to remember all right,' Susie said playfully. 'But what was she doing here, eh?'

Annette emerged, rubbing her eyes, pretending that sleep

was imminent. 'Shush. Talk about it tomorrow,' she murmured. 'Sleepy now.'

Spank.

'Ow.'

Spank. Spank.

'No – I didn't – She wasn't –' Annette wailed.

Spank. Spank. Spank.

'I'm sorry –'

Pinning the wriggling nude down into the pillows by the nape of her neck, Susie slapped her bare bottom briskly. The pillow smothered Annette's squeals as she struggled to protect her peach-cheeks.

'Take your hands away. You deserve a spanking, and a spanking you shall have. Hands up on the pillow.'

'No. S'not fair. Bully.'

'I can wait all night if I have to,' Susie warned.

'I'm sorry,' Annette mewed, obeying the more dominant girl. 'Don't punish me – too hard.'

Susie thrilled to the touch of Annette's velvety flesh as her curved palm swept down to smack each upturned cheek. The punished buttocks wobbled deliciously at every gently stinging swipe. Then Susie rested her hand palm down across the warm domes, pressing them down slightly to flatten their rubbery flesh. Annette, gripping her pillow with both hands, moaned softly and wriggled beneath the tender dominance of the spanking hand. Susie smiled as she felt Annette's buttocks inch upward in a mute appeal for more.

'Naughty girl. Making secret trysts with long-legged brunettes. Beautiful, lissome brunettes.' Susie emphasised each reproachful word by stroking Annette's cleft firmly with her thumbtip.

'We're not all saints like you,' Annette retorted. 'Can't all be perfect.'

'Perfect? Me?' Susie laughed, immediately claiming to have conquered the brown-eyed blonde in the potting shed after tea.

'Bitch,' Annette hissed, her voice seared with raw jealousy. Struggling free from Susie's grip and scrambling up to kneel on the duvet precariously, she continued crossly. 'And you dare to spank me. Anyway, I had two clients behind the laurels and a model girl in her shower. So there,' she boasted defiantly.

'Did you really?' Susie whispered, unperturbed.

'Well,' Annette hissed, 'you had all those –'

'No I didn't. I was only teasing. I remained true to you.'

Silence settled between them. Only Annette's bosom-heaving panting could be heard.

'I – I was only boasting, too, you know.'

'To make me suffer?'

'Yes.'

'Are you sorry?'

Annette remained silent.

'Sorry enough to be spanked?'

'Suppose so,' Annette whispered softly, touching Susie's nipples fleetingly with her fingertips.

Susie pinned Annette down into the pillows again, face upward this time, and bent down to kiss her eyes, nose and lips. As Annette responded, the tips of their tongues flickered and probed. Susie's mouth grew more dominant, more possessive, as she tasted the supine girl's sweet wet warmth. The sucking lips, nibbling teeth and wickedly delightful tongue strayed down slowly along the pale white skin of Annette's throat, coming to rest upon the swell of the left breast. Susie feverishly sucked the hillock of flesh up into her mouth as Annette moaned. Placing her hands on Susie's naked shoulders, she made a token gesture of resistance. But the mouth at her bare breast was persuasive, and slowly the hands at the shoulders pulled Susie down.

Burying her face completely in the soft cleavage, Susie nuzzled hungrily, her hand sweeping down across the firm belly beneath until the fingertips traced the fringe of Annette's pubic fuzz. The thighs inched apart to receive Susie's hand, but Susie paced their pleasure, choosing instead to drum her fingers against the firm pubic mound.

Maddened by this deliberate delight, Annette thrust her hips and buttocks upward, offering her labia and the tingling slit within submissively. Susie's mouth remained to pleasure the naked bosom but her firm forefinger slid up and down between the velvet labia. The sticky fleshfolds parted slightly at the dominant touch: Susie's finger accepted the invitation, and soon glistened wetly with Annette's hot juice.

Passive in her pleasure, Annette suddenly broke free and knelt up once more on the soft duvet, breast to breast, nipple to nipple, with Susie. It was not rebellion that kindled the dancing flame flickering in her eyes. It was affectionate desire. The urgent desire to return the delights she was receiving, the desire to share her exquisite joy with Susie. It was a moment of psychological impasse: the erotic equation between the two glistening nudes had yet to be balanced. Such was the intensity of their unfulfilled desires, it remained unresolved.

'Perhaps,' Seraphim Savage whispered softly, 'I can help.'

Susie and Annette turned swiftly to the door.

'Let me help you solve your little difficulty. It is a question, after all,' madame whispered, closing the door behind her and entering the bedroom, 'lovers must face and answer. Who is the lover? And who will be loved? In every collision of burning hearts and flesh, there is the kisser, and the kissed.'

She strode over to the bed and towered over them, a slipper in her right hand.

'There is a way, of course. There always is. Down on the bed both of you. No, not face to face. Annette, change position. Place your head down by Susie's feet.'

The naked girls complied, arranging themselves as instructed.

'Excellent. Now, Susie, curl down and place your head between Annette's thighs. That's right,' madame soothed, flexing the rubber slipper absently at the sight of Susie's bunched buttocks. 'Clasp her bottom, cup it firmly and draw her to your mouth. Annette, yes, that's right. Do as Susie does. Good. Clasp her bottom tighter. Now kiss.'

Locked into their soixante-neuf, the two young naked women sucked at each other furiously.

Madame then paced around the bed, liberally spanking both bottoms with her slipper as she urged the young lovers on.

'So important to have a happy staff. Now things are improved at The Rookery, there will be plenty of work for you both in the coming months. And a happy staff –' the slipper interrupted her words briefly '– is a busy staff.'

Up in the attic, the language lesson was progressing smoothly. Madame, in her office after lunch, had suggested that Susie should spend an hour each day for the next few weeks helping Svetlana improve her English.

'Her syntax is sound, but she needs to acquire a little idiom, more colloquial colouring.'

Stretched across Susie's lap, the bare-bottomed Russian thumbed her dictionary frantically.

'What was the word?' she whined.

'Quarenden,' Susie replied patiently for the third time, squeezing the delicious buttocks below with her spanking hand.

'Quarenden,' Svetlana mumbled, squashing her bosom into Susie's thigh as she flicked through the pages.

'Q.U.A.R.E.N.D.E.N.' Susie spelt it out, a sharp slap ringing out nine times as her curved palm swept down across the Russian's bare bottom.

'I have it,' Svetlana whimpered, fearful that the firm palm would revisit her scalded cheeks. 'A deep red apple, found in Devon. Yes?'

'Yes,' murmured Susie, palming the rump she proposed to punish severely. 'A deep red apple, found in Devon.'

NEXUS NEW BOOKS

To be published in October

VAMP
Wendy Swanscombe

A beautiful dark-haired lesbian lawyer from central Europe travels across the sea to the legend-haunted realm of Transmarynia, where she is to help a mysterious blonde stranger prepare for residence in Bucharest. What she discovers is beyond her most erotic nightmares and may mean the end of the world as she and her sisters know it. Bram Stoker's tale of obsession and desire is turned on its head and comes up dripping with something quite other than blood. Read it and stiffen with much more than fright.

£6.99   ISBN 0 352 33848 2

GIRL GOVERNESS
Yolanda Celbridge

Sloaney blonde ice maiden Tamara Rhydden, nineteeen, thrills to her own exhibitionism and teasing. Working for a London escort agency, her aptitudes fit the job description, but Tamara doesn't 'go with' clients; she finds that some men – and women too – prefer to be spanked for their insolence. A rich slave gets her appointed as governess of Swinburne's, a bizarre academy for grown-up schoolgirls in the earthy West Country, where maids come to study 'etiquette'. The etiquette, she uneasily discovers, is that of discipline. The maids practise a role-playing, spanking cult of Arthurian chivalry ... Tamara tries to put her past behind her, but the cheeky minxes compel her to exercise her caning arm, despite the governess's new-found tastes for being governed. How will Tamara make sure her *real* needs are taken care of?

£6.99   ISBN 0 352 33849 0

THE MISTRESS OF STERNWOOD GRANGE
Arabella Knight

Amanda Silk suspects that she is being cheated out of her late aunt's legacy. Determined to discover the true value of Sternwood Grange, she enters its private world disguised as a maid. Menial tasks are soon replaced by more delicious duties – drawing Amanda deep into the dark delights of dominance and discipline.

£6.99   ISBN 0 352 33850 4

To be published in November

JULIA C
Laura Bowen

When Julia Dixon marries her boyfriend Andrew she knows nothing of his association with 'The Syndicate', a secretive organisation devoted to the exploration of sex. Unwittingly becoming an apprentice to this clandestine corporation – where all new recruits are given a name beginning with C – Julia, now known as Caroline, is made to re-examine her clear-cut feminist principles as she confronts her innermost desires through a series of strange erotic challenges.

£6.99   ISBN 0 352 33852 0

WHEN SHE WAS BAD
Penny Birch

Penny's friend Natasha Linnett is a minx, and when she's bad she's very, very good. When a dominant, wealthy American wine buyer takes an interest in Natasha, she realises she can pretend to secure for him some bottles of real Napoleon-era brandy. She doesn't realise, however, just how many are the bizarre and lewd sex acts in which she must collude to maintain deception. Will Natasha manage to line her pockets as she wishes, or will she be caught out ignominiously like the bad girl she really is?

£6.99   ISBN 0 352 33859 8

THE SUBMISSION OF STELLA
Yolanda Celbridge

Stella Shawn, dominant Headmistress of Kernece College, crabes to rediscover the joys of submission. Her friend Morag suggests an instructive leave of absence, and enrols her at High Towers, a finishing school in Devon, whose regime is the total submission of women to women. The strict rules and stern discipline at High Towers ensures that even Stella can learn once more how to submit to the lash.

£6.99   ISBN 0 352 33854 7

If you would like more information about Nexus titles, please visit our website at www.nexus-books.co.uk, or send a stamped addressed envelope to:

Nexus, Thames Wharf Studios,
Rainville Road, London W6 9HA

NEXUS BACKLIST

This information is correct at time of printing. For up-to-date information, please visit our website at www.nexus-books.co.uk

All books are priced at £5.99 unless another price is given.

Nexus books with a contemporary setting

ACCIDENTS WILL HAPPEN	Lucy Golden ISBN 0 352 33596 3	☐
ANGEL	Lindsay Gordon ISBN 0 352 33590 4	☐
BARE BEHIND £6.99	Penny Birch ISBN 0 352 33721 4	☐
BEAST	Wendy Swanscombe ISBN 0 352 33649 8	☐
THE BLACK FLAME	Lisette Ashton ISBN 0 352 33668 4	☐
BROUGHT TO HEEL	Arabella Knight ISBN 0 352 33508 4	☐
CAGED!	Yolanda Celbridge ISBN 0 352 33650 1	☐
CANDY IN CAPTIVITY	Arabella Knight ISBN 0 352 33495 9	☐
CAPTIVES OF THE PRIVATE HOUSE	Esme Ombreux ISBN 0 352 33619 6	☐
CHERI CHASTISED £6.99	Yolanda Celbridge ISBN 0 352 33707 9	☐
DANCE OF SUBMISSION	Lisette Ashton ISBN 0 352 33450 9	☐
DIRTY LAUNDRY £6.99	Penny Birch ISBN 0 352 33680 3	☐
DISCIPLINED SKIN	Wendy Swanscombe ISBN 0 352 33541 6	☐

THE TORTURE CHAMBER	Lisette Ashton	☐
	ISBN 0 352 33530 0	
UNIFORM DOLL	Penny Birch	☐
£6.99	ISBN 0 352 33698 6	
WHIP HAND	G. C. Scott	☐
£6.99	ISBN 0 352 33694 3	
THE YOUNG WIFE	Stephanie Calvin	☐
	ISBN 0 352 33502 5	

Nexus books with Ancient and Fantasy settings

CAPTIVE	Aishling Morgan	☐
	ISBN 0 352 33585 8	
DEEP BLUE	Aishling Morgan	☐
	ISBN 0 352 33600 5	
DUNGEONS OF LIDIR	Aran Ashe	☐
	ISBN 0 352 33506 8	
INNOCENT	Aishling Morgan	☐
£6.99	ISBN 0 352 33699 4	
MAIDEN	Aishling Morgan	☐
	ISBN 0 352 33466 5	
NYMPHS OF DIONYSUS	Susan Tinoff	☐
£4.99	ISBN 0 352 33150 X	
PLEASURE TOY	Aishling Morgan	☐
	ISBN 0 352 33634 X	
SLAVE MINES OF TORMUNIL	Aran Ashe	☐
£6.99	ISBN 0 352 33695 1	
THE SLAVE OF LIDIR	Aran Ashe	☐
	ISBN 0 352 33504 1	
TIGER, TIGER	Aishling Morgan	☐
	ISBN 0 352 33455 X	

Period

CONFESSION OF AN ENGLISH SLAVE	Yolanda Celbridge	☐
	ISBN 0 352 33433 9	
THE MASTER OF CASTLELEIGH	Jacqueline Bellevois	☐
	ISBN 0 352 32644 7	
PURITY	Aishling Morgan	☐
	ISBN 0 352 33510 6	
VELVET SKIN	Aishling Morgan	☐
	ISBN 0 352 33660 9	

Samplers and collections

NEW EROTICA 5	Various	☐
	ISBN 0 352 33540 8	
EROTICON 1	Various	☐
	ISBN 0 352 33593 9	
EROTICON 2	Various	☐
	ISBN 0 352 33594 7	
EROTICON 3	Various	☐
	ISBN 0 352 33597 1	
EROTICON 4	Various	☐
	ISBN 0 352 33602 1	
THE NEXUS LETTERS	Various	☐
	ISBN 0 352 33621 8	
SATURNALIA	ed. Paul Scott	☐
£7.99	ISBN 0 352 33717 6	
MY SECRET GARDEN SHED	ed. Paul Scott	☐
£7.99	ISBN 0 352 33725 7	

Nexus Classics

A new imprint dedicated to putting the finest works of erotic fiction back in print.

AMANDA IN THE PRIVATE HOUSE	Esme Ombreux	☐
£6.99	ISBN 0 352 33705 2	
BAD PENNY	Penny Birch	☐
	ISBN 0 352 33661 7	
BRAT	Penny Birch	☐
£6.99	ISBN 0 352 33674 9	
DARK DELIGHTS	Maria del Rey	☐
£6.99	ISBN 0 352 33667 6	
DARK DESIRES	Maria del Rey	☐
	ISBN 0 352 33648 X	
DISPLAYS OF INNOCENTS	Lucy Golden	☐
£6.99	ISBN 0 352 33679 X	
DISCIPLINE OF THE PRIVATE HOUSE	Esme Ombreux	☐
£6.99	ISBN 0 352 33459 2	
EDEN UNVEILED	Maria del Rey	☐
	ISBN 0 352 33542 4	

- - - - - - ✂ -

Please send me the books I have ticked above.

Name   ....

Address   ....

                 ....

                 ....

                 .... Post code....................

Send to: Cash Sales, Nexus Books, Thames Wharf Studios, Rainville Road, London W6 9HA

US customers: for prices and details of how to order books for delivery by mail, call 1-800-343-4499.

Please enclose a cheque or postal order, made payable to **Nexus Books Ltd**, to the value of the books you have ordered plus postage and packing costs as follows:
  UK and BFPO – £1.00 for the first book, 50p for each subsequent book.
  Overseas (including Republic of Ireland) – £2.00 for the first book, £1.00 for each subsequent book.

If you would prefer to pay by VISA, ACCESS/MASTERCARD, AMEX, DINERS CLUB or SWITCH, please write your card number and expiry date here:

....

Please allow up to 28 days for delivery.

Signature ....

Our privacy policy

We will not disclose information you supply us to any other parties. We will not disclose any information which identifies you personally to any person without your express consent.

From time to time we may send out information about Nexus books and special offers. Please tick here if you do *not* wish to receive Nexus information.   ☐

- - - - - - ✂ -